The sounds of the organ swelled.

The maid of honor came down the aisle. Rich swirls of rose, fuchsia, blue and green covered her from neckline to embroidered shoes.

Next came half a dozen little girls in pale pink, mincing down the long aisle, distributing rose petals, in tulip-shaped organdy skirts.

At last it was time for the bride to come. She was a vision in a gown of silk taffeta, scooped at the neck, gently padded at the shoulders, fitting close against her slender arms and coming to a point below her waist. A simple A-line skirt of taffeta broke as she walked, so that panels of lace could be seen. Her train, also, was made of this lace, which was the finest in all the world.

The bridal veil was held by a massive diamond tiara which did not obscure the brilliance of her necklace. One hundred diamonds, each weighing a carat, and one hundred pearls, were set in a lacy net of white gold, the diamonds flashing fire, the pearls shimmering with soft light. The bridal bouquet was an overflowing cascade. Easter lilies, white hyacinths, and giant gardenias protruded from among languid white lilacs and wisteria.

The bride glowed with a luminescence that welled from her very soul. As she gazed up to her beloved, her eyes shone, so bright, so pure, that there wasn't a man or woman present who did not believe her a virgin. . . .

"Fantasies like Gila Berkowitz' should always come true."
— Vera Wang, fashion designer and president,
Vera Wang Bridal House, Ltd., New York City

"Amazing!"—Sydney Biddle Barrows

The

BRIDES

Gila Berkowitz

ST. MARTIN'S PAPERBACKS

THE BRIDES

Copyright © 1991 by Gila Berkowitz.

Bridal gown on front cover: Illissa by Demetrios.

Library of Congress Catalog Card Number: 90-26942

ISBN: 0-312-92827-0

Printed in the United States of America

St. Martin's Press hardcover edition/June 1991
St. Martin's Paperbacks edition/June 1992

10 9 8 7 6 5 4 3 2 1

For Arvin

And I shall remember you; the kindness of your youth and the love of your bridal days, when you followed me into the wilderness, in an unsown land.

Jeremiah 2:2

Chapter One

⦿

T HE LACY BODICE dripped beads of blood.

Erica squinted. No, they were pearl beads, the kind they always had on wedding gowns. It was just that pain made her see everything through a red haze.

The pain was excruciating. She concentrated on staying conscious.

"*Ach*, Erica, isn't that the most beautiful dress you ever saw?" said her mother, clasping her hands to her chest, her face radiant.

Erica looked down at her mother and realized for the first time that the woman's hair was entirely white. Not snowy, like the dress they were admiring, but somehow, sadly lacking any strands of color. The hands she clasped had cracked skin and smelled permanently of chlorine bleach.

For a minute Erica forgot her fresh, sharp pain and remembered a duller, older one. Her mother was old and worn out with work. Erica fought back tears of defiance. Maria Valenta was a good woman, a fiercely loving wife and mother, a hard worker, an intelligent human being. What did she have to show for any of it?

Erica walked the few steps to another of Goldsmith Bridal Salon's windows. It was like walking on razors. The clean, physical pain cleared her mind, let her talk in a normal tone of voice.

"I kind of like this one better, Mama."

The skirt on the second dress was thigh-high. The mannequin wore a futuristic cape, a white astronaut's helmet, and a huge op art breastplate. Erica gazed with lust at the dummy's flat cloth slippers. Her own feet felt as if they were being tortured by the Gestapo. But even the Gestapo couldn't make her talk. Even if it killed her, she would maintain that her shoes were pillows of comfort.

Her mother sniffed. "That is a dress for a bride? I think even if you were getting married on the moon, my darling, we would want a *real* wedding gown. But you are right. This lace one is pretty, but not as pretty as the one they had last time we came. Remember that one, Erica? The one with the silk roses and the tulle train?

"When you get married, we'll buy one like that. Only with a longer train. And in white, not ivory. A respectable bride should wear white."

"Mama! I don't even have a date for the Senior Prom, and you're making plans for a wedding? Besides, we couldn't buy a dress at Goldsmith's. This is the most expensive bridal salon in the city. The cheapest thing they have costs a thousand dollars."

Her mother frowned. "Why you always worry about money, Erica? Don't you have everything you need? That is why we come to America, Papa and me, to work hard and buy whatever you need. We have some time, sure. You are not even seventeen. Time enough to think about marriage in at least two years. But Papa and me, we save up money and we buy you the most beautiful dress in the world. Here, in the fancy store on Fifth Avenue.

"And you go to the Senior Prom. Stupid boys don't see how beautiful is my Erica! Papa will be your escort. He is still one handsome man! You will look like a princess on his arm. The boys will bite their lips they don't ask you first."

"I'd *die* if he took me. Besides, I'm glad no one asked me to go. The really cool kids think proms are bourgeois."

That wasn't entirely true, Erica admitted to herself. The fact was that there were only four boys in the entire class who were taller than she was, and all had chosen more popular—shorter—dates.

Of course Buzzy Alpert could have asked her. Buzzy, her lab partner, really liked her, she knew. Buzzy was terribly bright, a sure bet for valedictorian and a brilliant scientific career after that (if his draft lottery number was high enough and he didn't end up in 'Nam, instead). And he was not intimidated by her reputation for being smart.

It was Buzzy who had snorted that proms were "bourgeois." She wondered if that was the reason he wasn't going, or whether he was ashamed to dance with a girl whose corsage would be level with his nose.

Anyway, what with the outfit and all, the prom would be expensive. Despite her mother's protests, money *was* an issue. After all, her father and mother worked as a handyman and a chambermaid in a cut-rate motel. They got part of their pay as a rent-free apartment in the motel, but the rest didn't amount to much.

Erica wished she could get a part-time job. After all, she was sixteen now, it was legal. Lots of other kids in her class worked after school. But her parents had flatly refused to allow it. They had a point, she had to admit. If she didn't bust her butt her grades would definitely fall. She wished she were like Buzzy. All he had to do was crack the books a day or so before a test and he'd fly in like Superman. She, on the other hand, had to grind for every single A, even in Art and Health Ed. There were some courses—this year it was French—where she could never get past a B, no matter how hard she studied.

If only she had some claim to fame, if only she had been born rich or beautiful or with a special talent, how much easier life would be. But she was ordinary. She had no choice but to scratch her way uphill, inch by inch, with her fingernails.

It wasn't that she was ungrateful for her blessings. For starters, she had the best parents in the world. Maybe their English wasn't the greatest, but, after all, they left Czechoslovakia when they were over forty years old, and she didn't have much of a knack for foreign languages, either. The important thing was that they loved her so much, that they cared only for her. She was truly their whole life. She'd taken this for granted until she had met her best friend, Tangee. No adult gave a damn about Tangee.

Erica was glad for Tangee's friendship, too. Erica was the first white person, Tangee said, that she had ever trusted. Probably the first person, period. Erica was positive that Tangee would one day be *great*. A leader of Afro-Americans. Erica could just see herself, arm in arm with Tangee, marching like Martin Luther King and Bobby Kennedy—come back to life as women.

Another unexpected blessing: teachers liked her. Even the French teacher. They liked her despite the fact that she was seldom really outstanding in class.

Even physically she had good points. Her hair was thick and a nice shade of dark red. It was grown down to her waist and, if she ironed it after washing and wrapped it tightly around her head when she went to sleep, it hung almost perfectly straight. She had pretty green eyes, true, but then, almost everyone has pretty eyes.

And when she sucked in her cheeks, she had a model's high cheekbones. Trouble was, few people could get up high enough to see them. She was five-eleven now, and she had become positively religious in an effort to bribe God out of making her any taller. Kind people said she looked like a model. "Willowy," they said, "like Twiggy." Skinny, flat-chested beanpole, she knew, was what the boys in her class called her.

And what good was it to have a fashion model's body when all she could afford were bargain-basement clothes? They looked just as cheap on her as on a shorter girl. There was just more cheap stuff to look at.

It hurt Erica to wear cheap things. That, more than her offensive height, was what made her hunch over, fold her arms around her chest, try to disappear.

It made her feel poor inside. Her parents would object if she said that, and she had no intention of spoiling their illusions about making it in their beloved new homeland. But she did feel poor, really and truly. Oh, not welfare poor, like Tangee, but *needy*. Poor in a way that even money couldn't fix. The shoes that were now crippling her were a case in point.

The Friday after Thanksgiving—there wasn't any school—her mother had apologized.

"I'm sorry, darling, I can't come shopping today. Mr. Singh says today will be very busy, he wants me to be available in case all the rooms get used up early."

"Shopping" was what they did whenever Erica had a free day. She and Mama would get dressed in their finest, take the subway to Columbus Circle, walk down Fifty-seventh Street looking in all the windows. They would stop for a long while in front of Lillie Rubin, and comment on the appropriateness of the evening wear for the resort season—always other than the season in New York. The little, brown-uniformed doorman at Henri Bendel would nod at them, and they would blush. Then it was across the street to Bergdorf Goodman. There they would be amazed, as always, by the corner window, where Van Cleef & Arpels showed their collection of Empress Josephine's crown jewels. Over to Tiffany's with its simpler, yet somehow even more snobbish jewels, to Bonwit's, and so on, down Fifth Avenue until Saks, then south two more blocks where they reached the *pièce de résistance*, the frosting, as her mother called it, on the bonbon.

Goldsmith's was the oldest, largest, most elegant—in fact, the only—bridal salon on Fifth Avenue. It took up an entire square block on the east side of Fifth, although the Madison Avenue side was leased to several expensive shops. A golden canopy extended from its ornate bronze doors, and huge windows, rimmed with polished brass, flanked the shaded doorway. In the right window there was always a traditional bridal dress, an ethereal creation from the collective fantasy of little girls' dreams. In the left window, always, a designer gown, the very newest and most avant-garde confection, something from the cutting edge of fashion. In the other, lesser windows, simpler gowns for simpler weddings, costumes for other members of the wedding, supportive finery.

After Goldsmith's windows, any other store's would have been a letdown, so Erica and her mother went to a coffee shop for lunch, ordered tuna fish salad on white bread, with a chocolate malted to share. It was an exotic meal to them; Mrs. Valenta bought dark, heavy bread from a European bakery, and always served hearty meats for lunch.

Then they would walk down to Thirty-fourth Street and west to Herald Square. On that one block they would sometimes make a small purchase at a discount store. Afterwards, it was down into the subway and home to Brooklyn. Mrs. Valenta began work at four, and Erica usually had studying to do, but the glitter and tulle drifted before their eyes well into the night.

Erica knew her mother was disappointed that their plans were ruined.

"Never mind, Mama, we'll go some other time."

"No, no. *You* go. I don't want to spoil your fun."

"You know what," her father interjected, "today, you buy something."

"Do we need anything from Thirty-fourth Street?"

"No, no, from *Fifth Avenue*. You are a big girl now, you need nice things. You buy from one of the stores with the nice windows."

"Papa, that's crazy . . ."

"No, Papa is right," her mother said. "Is time you had some nice things."

Over Erica's protests, her father extracted a wad of bills from behind the silverware drawer. Mr. Singh paid the Valentas in cash, for he was wary of the tax man, and they stored much of their wages behind the rarely used dessert forks. "Take money from the drawer," they always urged Erica. But Erica rarely took more than her weekly carfare. Her parents would be needing that money, one day soon, when they were too old to be working as hard as they were now.

Her mother took the bills and folded them into a small square. This she wrapped in a tiny handkerchief, whose knot she secured with a safety pin.

"Put this in your bra," she whispered, "for safekeeping on the subway. Lots of pickpockets, too, in Manhattan."

Erica pinned it securely to her underwear. She had no intention of spending the money. The five dollars in her purse would be plenty for the subway fare, the tuna sandwich and the Coke, which she would have instead of her half of the traditional malted.

The outing went as usual, except for the absence of her mother's cheerful, optimistic, enthusiastic commentary on the finery of Fifty-seventh Street. That day, the riches of New York were just a sadistic joke on Erica. How could she ever become one of the women she saw around her, shopping as if these stores were their natural, God-given habitat?

Many of the shoppers wore "peasant dresses." What a joke! Her parents had had occasion to work the land, and her mother had even had an embroidered apron when she was young, but the word "peasant" made Mama's cheeks burn. "We are not peasants, we are *bourgeois*," she said with pride. Thirty years of communist occupation couldn't change that attitude, and neither could the Age of Aquarius.

Besides, Erica wasn't fooled by magazine puffery. She knew what *real* peasants wore in the brave new world of the 1970s. The real peasants wore patterned skirts that didn't fall just so; they wore bonded polyester, not wool challis. The salt of the earth was shod in patent leather boots that cracked, not buttery suede that laced up smoothly to the knee. The honest proletariat wore eyeliner that was a little too thick, lipstick that was just a shade too chalky, fake lashes that failed to look Jean Shrimpton–saucy.

It was as easy to distinguish the ladies of Fifty-seventh Street from the peasants of Brooklyn as it had been ten years before, when the former wore neatly tailored Oleg Cassinis and the latter wore the Klein's Basement knockoffs with glued-together seams.

Erica stopped at a poster shop. "Frame included," said a price tag, "$100—." The poster itself asked plaintively, "They shoot students, don't they?"

Erica did enjoy Josephine's jewels. At least *they* were fantasy objects to everyone. Nobody really wore diamond tiaras anymore, so they were just a fantasy, not a tease.

Next to the regal display, the door into Bergdorf's was wide open. Many customers were milling around and the store didn't seem as intimidating as usual.

Erica saw that there was a shoe sale, with the shoes on

display at half price. Before she realized it, she had wandered into the store. Never before, shopping with her mother, had they dared to cross the threshold into a shop.

She picked up a white shoe. Its insole was stamped with the arms of the Queen of England. Could it be that Queen Elizabeth herself had tried on this very shoe and its mate? Was this her size?

"May I help you?" roared a deep, angry voice.

Erica jumped. She felt as if she had been caught shoplifting. "I, I was just looking at this shoe . . . I . . ."

"What size are you?" the salesman demanded brusquely.

"A, um, nine, I think?"

"Sit here," said the salesman, as if she were a dog who was likely to disobey. He disappeared into some hidden sanctum.

Erica looked at the other shoppers. They all seemed to be dressed in shades of beige and gray. Their hair was smooth, also in shades of beige and gray. Only she was wearing a red coat, bought two years ago, on sale, in Brooklyn. She had mostly outgrown it, and an embarrassing amount of wrist stuck out of the sleeves.

She wished she could disappear, but the carpet, while plush, wasn't nearly deep enough for that.

The salesman returned. "All I had was a nine quadruple A," he spat.

"My feet are really pretty narrow." Erica felt as if she had to reassure him. She hadn't known they *made* quadruple A's.

He scooped her heels into the shoes with a shoehorn. Erica stood up, feeling dizzy. The shoes felt magical. She had never worn anything like them. She took the few steps to the mirror. The shoes were as snug as what she imagined to be a lover's embrace. The mirror reflected two regal feet, as removed from her body as the feet of Queen Elizabeth. Even though the shoes were white, a color reputed to make feet look big, her feet actually looked, if not quite petite, definitely trim.

"Oh, they're precious on you," gushed a woman in fawn-colored hair and cocoa-colored mink.

"I . . . I'll have to think about them."

"Sale ends tomorrow," snapped the salesman.

"Do you have those in an eight and a half?" the woman asked.

"If you'll be kind enough to take a seat, I'll be happy to check," said the salesman. It was as if another man's spirit spoke from his body.

"Why don't *you* sit awhile and *think*," said the salesman with his original voice, as he went off in search of the size 8½.

Erica was frozen with mortification.

"How much are they?" the woman asked.

"I don't know," gasped Erica.

The woman leaned over and raised the shoe box. A woodsy perfume curled up from her furs. "Heavens. Fifty-five. Well, you can't do much better than that, can you?"

Erica shook her head, wide-eyed, mute.

"Of course you can't wear white shoes except between Memorial and Labor days. Even your generation must follow *that* rule, mustn't it?"

Erica nodded, mute.

"Well?" growled the salesman.

"I'll take them," Erica heard herself say. Was there a ventriloquist in the room?

The salesman didn't change his attitude at the promise of a sale. "Cash or charge," he threatened.

"Cash," mouthed Erica silently. But wait! How could she get at the money? It was pinned into her bra, safer than her virginity.

"C-can you hold it for me for a few minutes? I need to go to the ladies' room."

The salesman rolled his eyes heavenward. "Unless you pay for it now I'll have to give it to the next customer."

Erica could only blush. Everyone was staring at her.

When she reached the ladies' room she pushed down a wave of nausea. She was shaking and a dew had formed on her upper lip. She took her time washing her face with cold water. She found she really had to use the bathroom.

With infinite care she removed the knotted handkerchief from her bosom. She counted the money in the privacy of the stall. Eighty dollars, much more than she had expected. She clutched the little bundle tightly. What should she do?

Perhaps fate would decide for her. Maybe someone else had bought the shoes. Maybe the size 8½ lady found her pair too small.

She went back to the shoe department as if to a firing squad. Wordlessly, she bought the shoes. The salesman stamped the receipt "Final Sale." On her way out, she tripped over the size 8½'s that the beige woman had left strewn on the floor.

When she got out on Fifth Avenue, her spirits suddenly lifted. It was just as her mother said, in America your money was as good as anybody else's.

In Tiffany's dark windows she caught a reflection of herself. There was a beautiful mane of red hair and below it the subtle mauve shopping bag of Bergdorf Goodman. Her shoulders straightened and a bounce came into her walk. Outside of St. Patrick's some guys eating lunch whistled at her. The world was a wonderful place, and, any day now, the Beatles would be back together again.

Her parents were thrilled by the purchase.

"Ach, you can always tell quality," her father said, sniffing the leather like a fine wine.

"Oh, it will be beautiful. You wear to Christmas at Cousin Jiri's," her mother bubbled.

"Oh no, Mama. No white shoes between Labor Day and Memorial Day. Classy people wouldn't."

So the shoes had been lovingly wrapped in tissue paper and nestled in their box for the winter. She had unwrapped them only to show Tangee.

"Shee-it," said Tangee, "amputate at the knees! She's turning into Tricia Nixon."

What did Tangee know about class, anyway. Where Tangee lived they would steal shoes like that while you were walking in them.

At long last, it was Memorial Day. She'd been up since dawn. Erica couldn't have been more excited if she were going to the prom. Today she'd be walking across Fifty-seventh Street and down Fifth Avenue, and she'd be just like the other people walking there! And she'd be walking proudly with her mother, who could say, better than most of the women there, I have earned every stitch we are wearing.

But the minute she put on the first shoe, she knew that something was horribly wrong. The shoes were too small. Much, much too small. Her feet had grown at least one full size during the winter and spring. She had to grit her teeth even before she stood up.

No matter. She would walk with her mother in Manhattan, no matter what.

She smiled broadly at breakfast as Mama and Papa oohed and ahed.

"Oh, it makes the whole outfit look expensive."

"Ach, now aren't you glad you spent the money? Doesn't it look better on you than on the dessert forks?"

Thank God they had gotten seats on the subway. When they came out on Fifty-seventh Street the avenue blocks loomed before her like the Long March of China. By the time they got to the corner of Fifth Avenue, it felt like she had the Empress's jewels crushed in among her toes, facet side in.

By the time they left Goldsmith's she was daydreaming longingly of emergency rooms.

Sitting in the coffee shop relieved her a little, but the memory of pain made paste of the white bread in her mouth and Maalox of the malted.

"Ah, Erica," her mother sighed. "You always saying how Papa and me work too hard. You know, is *fun* to work when we can buy things like your new shoes. It's the best feeling in the world."

That was just too much. Erica started to cry.

"What is it? What is, Erica?" Her mother was alarmed. Erica rarely cried, and certainly not in a place as public as a coffee shop.

Erica thought, confession would be good for the *sole*, and her crying turned into a manic laugh.

Mrs. Valenta's face went white. She reached across the table and clutched Erica's shoulder, half bracing, half clinging.

"Erica, you must tell me what is going on. You are my whole life. I will love you and help you, no matter what."

Erica struggled to think of something, anything. She would die rather than tell her mother about the shoes.

"It's . . . it's Tangee."

"Oh," said her mother, the corners of her lips turning down.

Erica tried to gain time by blowing her nose into one of the starched linen handkerchiefs her mother considered essential to ladyhood.

Now that she thought of it, she *was* worried about Tangee.

"She hasn't been in school for two weeks. They don't have a phone in her house, so there's no way to reach her. Mr. Birnbaum—the assistant principal?—he even sent a telegram, but nobody answered. They can't get a truant officer to go to the apartment because Tangee is too old. The law says she doesn't have to go to school if she doesn't want to. But she *does* want to. I *know*, Mama. She's doing great now. I bet she'll get the English prize. The only reason she would stay home this close to graduation is because something awful has happened. I just know it.

"Mama, if Tangee doesn't come back to school soon, she's going to miss out on the chance of going to college. She'd never risk that. Something terrible has happened!"

"You are being too dramatic. Those people always drop out of school."

"Mama! That's horrible, it's racist . . ."

Her mother's back snapped straight. "We are not racist. In wartime your papa's family hid Jews on their farm. You know what that meant? If the Germans found out, they shoot all of us.

"And we never saw a Negro till we came to this country. So far, they haven't impressed us. Not even your friend Tangee."

Erica sputtered without answering. Race was a touchy issue in their household. For her parents, America was perfect. The United States was a table set with opportunity to those who wanted to work hard. If the blacks had failed to rise from poverty and degradation, it had to be their own fault.

But Erica saw civil rights differently. For her the movement was like America itself had been to her parents. She knew it was an impossible dream, but still, if only people could be themselves, treated fairly no matter who they were, or where they came from, or what they wanted to do with their lives . . .

• • •

Second grade . . . Mama in school, picking her up an hour early! Her heart skipped quickly under the dress that had been washed thin.

"We are going to the bank, little one. They make a mistake on the letter, and I no can explain good in English. I tell you in Czech, and you explain to the bank man in English."

At the bank Maria explained slowly and patiently what the problem was. Erica translated faithfully. She wished desperately that she could figure out what the numbers meant! It had something to do with *money*, money they needed to survive.

The bank officer sat and smirked through the recitation. After Maria was done, he chucked Erica under the chin. "Little girl, you know this is a big bank. We have hundreds of thousands of dollars in here."

Erica's eyes opened wide.

"An institution such as ours," he continued, "seldom makes mistakes. Now you take the statement home, sweetie, and you tell Grandma to take her shoes and socks off and reckon the numbers again."

Erica's face blazed. How dare he! Her parents were not ignorant! They hadn't always worked in a cheap motel. In Europe her mother had taught in high school, had had poetry published in a newspaper. And her father was the chief foreman of a factory where they made the most beautiful crystal in the world.

He had called her mother "Grandma." Erica wanted to cry. Her mother *was* old. The other children in her class had mothers who were young and pretty. Her mother was already in her late forties. Old. Someday she would die. Perhaps it would be soon. Certainly sooner, much sooner, than all the pretty young mothers.

She felt weak with fear. How could this happen? The money was *theirs*. Her parents had worked for it. How could the bank just take it away? She stared at the paper with all the numbers. The figures swam before her eyes. What did they mean? What secret was locked in them that gave them the power to control people's lives?

She swore she would find out.

Her mother started to lead her out of the bank. Erica

wrested her hand free. She turned and looked back at the bank officer. She saw him clearly. The frames of his glasses were taped together and there were loose threads hanging from his tie. He didn't own the bank; he had no claim to the polished brass and the marble floor. He was just some lowly employee, and he was trying to prove he wasn't nothing by lording it over an immigrant and a child.

Sophomore year, when black students began to be bussed to her high school, Erica was among the first to volunteer for the Each One Teach One program. Superior students—Erica certainly qualified—helped tutor the stragglers.

Erica was assigned to Tangee White, and the two hit it off immediately. Tangee had been living in a shell all of her life. When Erica started teaching her, Tangee picked up skills and knowledge like a sponge. She hadn't Erica's dogged patience for learning by rote, but she had a vivid originality and a wicked humor. Soon she was in Erica's accelerated classes in English and history.

Their rapport was instant. For one thing, Tangee was the only girl in the whole grade who was taller than Erica. And their other point in common was their ludicrous names.

There were always pedantic teachers who insisted on calling students by their official names. This was annoying enough to the Bartholomews who preferred "Bart," the Sals who cringed at "Salvatore." But the class inevitably burst into raucous laughter when the roll call monitor intoned, "America Valenta; Tangerine White."

By the time they had reached the United States, Erica's parents had long given up the hope of having a child. When Maria found herself pregnant, the couple was ecstatic. All of their dreams realized at once! They expressed their gratitude and hope, and honored their new country by naming their daughter after it.

In Tangee's case the naming was considerably less sentimental. Her mother had bided her time in the hospital, a kind of vacation she tried every trick to extend. Each day the lady from the birth registry came to ask her what name she had chosen. Each day she said she hadn't thought of one yet. At last Tangee's mother was ready to go, and the registrar insisted that she give her baby a name.

Tangee's mother looked around. The lunch tray was still at the bedside. She was trying to get her shape back and she hadn't eaten the dessert. It was a tangerine.

Together they could laugh at the humiliation of having odd names.

"Good thing your folks didn't move to Byelorussia!"

"Lucky they weren't serving pudding that day!"

Erica had had other friends, but none as close as Tangee. One reason was that they could spend a lot of time together. The Crest Motor Lodge was not the sort of place that most girls' parents approved of their visiting. Who would go to a motel in Brooklyn? No businessmen, and certainly not family. What sort of self-respecting family would let their kin stay at a *hotel*?

The Crest, conveniently located off the Belt Parkway, entertained a different sort of guest. Gentlemen registered while the ladies stayed shadowed in the cars.

The men would rent rooms for the night, but stay only an hour or two. Or they would stay only for the lunch hour. Either way the room could be rented for the night again and again, with only a quick cleaning by Maria after each set of visitors. Guests paid cash and Mr. Singh made a lot of money.

The Valentas blithely ignored the goings-on at the Crest. They were respectable people, and they did honest work. But the mothers of young girls didn't quite see it that way.

Tangee's mother didn't care. In fact Tangee hadn't seen her mother since she was three. That was the time, during one of her mother's infrequent visits, that the rent money had disappeared. Tangee's grandmother told her not to come around anymore.

Tangee's grandmother also didn't care. She was ten years younger than *Maria*. The grandmother was very beautiful but always seemed to attract the wrong kind of man. She worked as a nurse's aide and wore a uniform that exposed virtually all of her thighs. Her private life was scandalous, or at least

Tangee made it sound that way in the long, long conversations she and Erica had about sex.

They talked about sex, and clothes, and music, like other girls. But the special thread that ran between them, that bound them close, was never expressed in words.

Erica and Tangee had to be *somebody*. They had to do something special with their lives. Whether they loved them or despised them, they could not be like their mothers and their grandmothers before them.

What to be wasn't clear for Erica. She knew only that she would have to do something to bring her family security and to pull them up the social ladder. She'd have to make money too, a lot of money. You couldn't kid yourself about that. But how? How could a *girl* do that, an ordinary girl? It would come to her in college. She would work very, very hard and then it would come to her.

It was different for Tangee. She didn't really have a family, much less one that depended on her future. But Tangee's people needed her. She would serve them well, if only she could break out of the urban nightmare of East New York in time.

Chapter Two

THE SUBWAY taking Maria and Erica home lumbered underground until it was well into their home borough. Then it reared up into the sunlight, rising on elevated tracks.

There is a certain Victorian beauty to Brooklyn, even though its ideal is the treadmill modernity of "Noo Yawk." In its private, urban way, Brooklyn is as responsive to nature as a country meadow, and the changes of the seasons are lovely and satisfying to observe. Erica and her mother could see the solidly built brick houses, the neatly maintained frame ones, all shadowed by mature and luxuriant street trees. Early roses were curling over iron gratings and the last of the azaleas blazed around statues of Saint Anthony.

Mrs. Valenta chirped on about the lovely weather, while Erica gritted her teeth for the two blocks from the subway station. She had never been so glad to see the aqua-and-mustard-painted facade of the Crest Motor Lodge. Inside, she flew over the mustard carpet, past the two aqua couches that were overripe with latex stuffing. Mother and daughter nodded at Mr. Singh.

Mr. Singh had come from India twenty-five years before with his wife, five sons, and five daughters. He owned not only the Crest, but a long chain of motels, all in unexpected locations such as Staten Island and Union City, New Jersey. For twenty-four hours every day, 365 days a year, the desk at the Crest—and at each of the other motels—was manned by Mr. Singh, one of his sons, or one of his five sons-in-law (each of whom was called "Mr. Singh"). Despite the fact that his English was even worse than the Valentas', Mr. Singh had become a very wealthy man. Curiously, Erica's parents did not resent him for this. And even though he was a demanding and none-too-generous employer, Maria and Jaroslav Valenta respected and admired him.

"I would like to have Mr. Singh's money, sure," Mr. Valenta would say, "but his big, loyal family I envy much more. If a family pulls together, it can do anything. At least in America."

Mrs. Valenta waited until the guest at the desk checked in. A fat man in a leather jacket and cap, he was startled when he saw the two women. Clutching his key, he hurried out, pretending a fascination with the fading Peter Max posters on the wall.

"A beautiful day!" said Maria.

"Mmm," said Mr. Singh. He was indoors from dawn to dusk, and wouldn't have noticed a snowstorm. Mr. Singh looked pointedly at his watch. Although Maria wasn't supposed to go on duty for another hour, the gesture made her feel guilty.

"Where is my husband now?" she asked.

"Upstair, lyin' down," said Singh, insinuating that his handyman habitually spent working hours eating petits fours and watching soap operas.

"Oh, my God!" said Maria. She knew only illness would take him from his tasks.

Maria and Erica rushed up the steps to their apartment.

"Jaroslav, what has happened? Speak to us, Papa," Maria cried out, her key still in the door.

Erica's father was stretched out on the aqua sofa, rigid as a corpse. Hot water bottles were wedged under his lower back and neck.

"Hello, my beauties. Is nothing, is nothing . . ." he protested, but under the words was a moan.

"Papa," said Erica sternly, "this is not nothing. What happened?"

"Oh, it is the new mattresses came today. I strain my back taking them up to the rooms."

"But, Papa, why didn't the men from the mattress company haul them up?"

"Oh, is holiday. Today is hauling against the union rules. But I'll be all right, now you here . . ."

Poor Papa, thought Erica, it must hurt so bad. Even his English is disintegrating. The old rage rose inside her. How could they do this to him? He was an old man, only years away from retirement, and they made him drag mattresses. Where was the union to protect him? Where were the laws to shield their future? And her parents thought it a dream economy! It was *their* fault too. They'd be old and broken soon—and still singing the "Star-Spangled Banner."

She slammed the door to her room and pried the shoes off her feet.

In the living room, Maria and Jaroslav gave each other puzzled looks. What had they done now? Was Erica upset? Or angry? Perhaps she was just tired? Sometimes it was impossible to understand her actions. Sometimes it was impossible to communicate. If only English were an easier language! There seemed to be such a distance between them and their daughter, and they could not figure out how to cross it.

The phone rang. Jaroslav tried to answer it, but hurt his back in the attempt. Maria got it.

For once the Valentas were glad it was Tangee. At least Erica would come out of her room now.

Erica dashed for the telephone. "Tangee! Hey, are you okay? Why weren't you in school? . . ."

"Yeah, I'm fine. I need to talk to you."

"Sounds serious."

There was a pause on Tangee's end. In the background Erica could hear the sound of sneakers crushing glass, of angry conversations where "fuck" was used as noun, verb, adjective, and adverb.

"Where are you, Tangee?"

"I'm on Pitkin Avenue. The phones on my block are all busted."

"Better get out of there."

"Right. Can you meet me at the Honey Bowl?"

"Sure thing. I'll race you there."

As soon as Erica replaced the receiver, her father announced breathlessly that there had been another call that afternoon.

"It was your teacher, Mr. Birnbaum."

"Mr. Birnbaum? But today isn't even a school day. What was that about?"

"Oh, Erica! The most wonderful news in the world. He says Radcliffe, they are giving you a full scholarship."

"Oh my God, I don't believe it! But, oh, Papa, even with a scholarship it's so expensive . . ."

"No, no, do not think of that. You will go *only* to Radcliffe."

"Radcliffe!" Her mother's eyes went up as if to heaven. "Radcliffe is Harvard for girls. This will be wonderful for you! Think of the kind of people you will meet there, refined girls from elite families. They will be your friends, they will invite you to their homes, they will introduce you to their brothers."

"And intelligentsia, Erica," her father said. "Real intellectuals, like in Europe. Professors who know about life, not just what is in books!"

Erica swallowed. "Well, I hope you're right. But let's talk about it later. I have to go now. I'm meeting Tangee at the Honey Bowl."

"Tangee," her mother said. "You'd rather meet this Tangee than a Radcliffe girl. A Kennedy girl, maybe."

"Yes. As a matter of fact I would. See you later."

She couldn't tell them, but her heart felt heavy. Inside, she knew that Radcliffe would mean the end to the first chapter of her life. Brooklyn, in all its coarse, earthy sweetness, would be a thing of the past. Even if she didn't change, her friends would see her as different. She was going away, and there was no coming back. Without the feelings forming into words, Erica understood that there was an inevitable price to be paid for moving up. She set her jaw tightly.

The Honey Bowl was a hangout near school. Erica and Tangee met there every day after classes, and they always sat in the same booth and ordered the same thing. Of course Tangee wasn't there yet. Bus service from her neighborhood was extremely erratic.

Every day they were served by the same waitress, a girl about their age. She was married to the short-order cook, a man much older than she, who squashed down rows of hamburgers with the unfocused anger of a born bully.

"What a depressing life that waitress leads," Erica had whispered once. "Hard work, that creepy husband, no future. And she can barely write out the orders."

"Can't be that bad," said Tangee, "and probably beats the old country. Back in Greece they'd probably hitch her up to the plow. The guys who own the joint are all relatives. She's probably got a piece of the action. At least her old man does."

The waitress shuffled over. "Yeah?" she said, pencil poised over her order pad.

"I'm waiting for my friend," Erica answered. *As if I've ever eaten here alone.*

The waitress shuffled away. The truth is, she doesn't look unhappy, thought Erica, just numb.

The waitress had a perfect profile and skin as pale and smooth as marble. Like a statue's, her eyes held no expression. Her body was stolid and unpretty. It was as if Phidias had carved the face and left it on its hunk of unworked rock.

She's not unhappy, thought Erica, because she knows her place. I'm ambitious, that's why I feel sorry for her. But maybe she should feel sorry for me. Ambition isn't exactly the key to happiness.

But when you are an only child and your parents are elderly immigrants, you can't afford not to be ambitious. Maybe you can't afford to be happy.

Tangee entered the diner. She made an *entrance*. Tall as a professional basketball player, she was crowned by an Afro with a five-inch radius. She wore an ankle-length dashiki of green, gold, and black. Silver-tone snake bracelets spanned the great distance between her wrist and her elbow.

Erica was so glad to see her that she ran up and gave her a kiss. Tangee didn't react as usual, with a wisecrack that would hide her pleasure. She just wore her all-purpose expression, unreadable as a Cameroon idol's.

"Anything new?" said Tangee, as if her own recent history was a matter of indifference.

"Yes, some. But first let's hear about you. What's going *on*?"

The waitress shuffled over. "Yeah?"

"I'll have a black-and-white ice cream soda," said Erica. "And I'll have a Broadway," said Tangee.

They ordered the same thing every day, but the waitress never seemed to notice or care.

As the waitress lumbered off, Erica leaned impatiently over the table. "Talk, woman!"

Tangee did not settle her shoulders the way she usually did when getting down to a good narrative.

She folded her hands primly on the table. She looked Erica straight in the eye, as if daring her to look away from her gaze.

"I'm pregnant."

Erica's mouth formed a doughnut. She was more than shocked. Despite Tangee's risqué stories, Erica knew that she had been a virgin. It was one of the many threads that bound them together. And she knew that the last time they'd seen each other there had been no romantic interest in Tangee's life. Tangee scorned romance as a roadblock on the path out of East New York.

"Wha . . . wha . . . how?" stuttered Erica.

"The usual way," said Tangee, the familiar sardonic smile returning to her lips. "No Annunciation, or anything like that."

"But who on earth . . ."

"No one you know," snapped Tangee, with that dismissive finality, that tone that said: There is a different world, a black world, and you can never know it, no matter what you do.

"What are we going to do, Tangee?"

"What you mean 'we,' white woman?"

"*Tangee*. You know damn well what I mean. Do you know like, well, a doctor? Let's see, we could ask Darlene Kiefer, she screws around like a bunny . . ."

"Turn up the volume, Erica. I'm keeping the baby."

"Tangee, you're nuts. You'll never get to college. And what about all our plans . . ."

"Exactly, babe. I did it on purpose."

"I don't understand. I don't understand you, Tangee." Erica had started crying. The tears just poured down her face, splattering the chipped Formica. This was the second time in one day that she was crying in a restaurant. Her world was melting like the ice cream, untouched, in her soda.

"Well, it's a long story."

"Well, I'll have my secretary cancel the rest of this afternoon's appointments."

"Okay then." Now Tangee leaned forward eagerly. Her face, with the riveting homeliness of a newborn baby's, took on a bright animation. Tangee lived for the telling of the tale. She could have narrated the story of her own impending execution with relish and style.

"It all started four months ago. My grandmother had a patient who went and croaked on her. The stiff was lately of Georgia, and his people wanted him back for decent burial. Us colored may live like dogs, but Jesus, do we ever die respectable.

"Anyway, Granma is wrapping up the body, nice and neat, when in comes the undertaker, fresh up from Atlanta, Georgia. One look at Granma and he drops in the net. Lord, she's so pretty it's a wonder the morgue cabinets don't slide open and the dead come to life.

"Now the mortician, he's a well-to-do bachelor. No child, him, he's in smart shape for a man of a certain age—no offense to Pan and Pani Valenta.

"Anyway, he takes the cadaver down South and comes right back up here, like a rubber ball. He's taken his first vacation in years, and he's set on courtin' Granma.

"For once she acts with her brains, 'stead of her well-waxed gonads. It's 'Oh honey, watch your hands!' and 'I want to, darlin', but since my late husband died, I haven't . . .' and more of the same. Romeo goes down on knee one and offers two carats, paid-in-full. Juliet accepts."

"Oh, Tangee, that's wonderful. Congratulations."

"Yeah. Granma would have been a fool to have acted otherwise, and I would have been a heartless bitch to suggest it. It's a Shakespearean comedy as far as Granma and her honey are concerned. There was just one little problem, if you can call six feet two 'little.'

"See, Intended has a fine neo-Colonial in the toniest black suburb of the Southland. He pictures setting his love up in it, cooking, shopping, and cuddling in front of the color TV. Trouble is, the picture doesn't include me.

"Granma's got a heart of gold, but she doesn't want to have to choose. This undertaker's her piece of luck in this world; there won't be another. I can't make her choose between us. So I gave her my blessings, told her to go.

"Like the algebra teacher says, state the problem in nonreducible terms. I've got nowhere to live. Granma left me rent for the rest of the year. That's all her savings. She can't ask the guy for money for me, not now, she can't. I can't go to a children's shelter, I'm too old. And I'm not exactly the ideal candidate for adoption for that childless couple up in Larchmont."

"So what are . . ."

"So I got pregnant. Because if I have a baby, Welfare will spring for an apartment for the two of us."

"But, Tangee, that's hell for you! And heartless for the baby. There must be another way."

"Oh yeah? Name it. Are your folks ready to put me up at the Crest? Are they? If so, I'll go have an abortion this afternoon.

"But they aren't, are they?"

Erica looked down with shame. She could not hide from Tangee how her parents felt about their friendship.

"Cheer up, Erica. This isn't the end of the world. Welcome to the college of real life. Introduction to Pragmatism 1.1."

"But the baby . . ."

"Well, it's not exactly unplanned. And it probably won't be unloved. You know, not every kid comes into this world like the Second Coming of Christopher Columbus. That doesn't mean that their lives aren't worth living."

But Tangee's brave pose did not hold out for long. She broke down and wept. The two girls fell on each other's necks. Their long bodies shook with sobs.

What the hell kind of world is this, Erica wondered, where neither brains nor goodness are worth a damn.

"Okay," said Tangee, wiping her nose viciously with a napkin, "and what's new with you?"

"Well, it's nothing really. Just old Birny calling my father, telling him I got a scholarship to Radcliffe. God, it's so scary."

"You're one unnatural girl, America Valenta. You've got a stab at *Harvard*. You're taking it, aren't you?"

"Sure I'm taking it, but who's to say I can make it there, with all those rich, smart kids? I bet I only got in by the skin of my teeth, or more likely, someone made a mistake."

"What the hell does that matter? You better learn to grab opportunity at the first knock, girl. It doesn't usually stick around to woo you with flowers and chocolates.

"Listen to me!" Tangee had grabbed Erica by the shoulders. There was a wild look in her eyes.

"You've got to stop putting yourself down with all this nice-little-girl shit. There will be enough people out there telling you how much better the others are, better than you. How you ought to know your place, and that place is Brooklyn. Don't *you* be the one to suggest it!

"You've got to go to Radcliffe, and positively *rule* it, girl. Go to the fucking White House, if you can. This here is America, like your daddy done told you. Grab the sucker and ride it.

"You owe it to us. Don't you remember everything we swore we'd do? You owe it to us!"

Chapter Three

FIRST THING in the morning Melissa could not wait to get out of the apartment. However, it was close to eleven by the time she actually left it.

The reason she was anxious to leave was the smell of frying fish (for breakfast!) seeping in from the hallway, the screaming of children (the neighbor's boyfriend beat the little ones mercilessly), and the evidence that an expensive visit from the exterminator had failed to drive back the hordes of roaches who claimed tenants' rights.

The reason it took so long to leave? Well, first she had to shower. She had to turn the water on hot; it steamed her perfect complexion to incandescence. She washed with a special soap from Caswell-Massey, taking care to keep the bar out of water so that it would last longer. After patting herself dry, she smoothed on a lotion that was obtainable only at Boyd's.

Next, makeup. A thin layer of Nivea, which, thank heavens, was cheap. Foundation that had been a gift-with-purchase. No blusher, but artful work with contouring cream to make her cheekbones even more striking. As soon as she got her first job, Melissa promised herself, she'd get herself some Erno Laszlo.

The eyes were important. The eyes were her best feature, unique, and she had to do them just right. Deep teal shadow from a theatrical supply store. Black cake mascara from France based on soap (it doubled the length of her lashes, but she had to avoid tears, or even a humid blast from a subway grate, or she'd look like a raccoon). Her eyes stared back in the mirror: enormous, blue as the bottom of a deluxe swimming pool.

Not to forget the lips. Lip pencil, a brush she had to be careful with because they didn't make that kind anymore. Everyone else wore no lipstick or very pale shades, but Melissa knew what flattered her most, Jungle Peach, a shade that had been popular before she was born.

The hair was easy. She just needed to run a brush through it and get the knots out. She used a brush with boar's bristles, carefully, so as not to break the ends. Her hair was almost oriental in its straightness and its blackness. She worked methodically until it resembled a yard of the heaviest, darkest satin. She could thank her Mohican ancestors for that. She was grateful, too, to the refined Europeans who had bequeathed her the delicacy of her nose, the polished oval of her face, the tiny shells of her ears.

Now clothes. She owned only four daytime outfits so it should have been simple to choose. But it wasn't that easy. She wanted to wear something stunning. She felt in her bones that luck would strike today, and she intended to be ready for it. On the other hand, she had an acting class that afternoon and didn't want to look too ostentatious. The other students distracted her by gawking. She was paying good money to learn how to act, for heaven's sake.

Okay, that was settled, on to breakfast. She put water up to boil. For the fourth day in a row, she reminded herself to buy more instant coffee. Today, for sure.

There were no clean cups in the cupboard. The sink was overflowing with dirty dishes. She'd just rinse out one of the mugs. Unfortunately, the mug had previously been used for hot milk. The dried milk skin did not rinse out. Melissa considered scrubbing it out.

"Oh the hell with it, nobody's watching."

Now for some food. There was a little cheese in the fridge,

that seemed inviting. On closer inspection, though, the cheese wore a thick green fur. She was about to throw it out, only to notice that the trash was almost full. One more item and she'd have to take out the garbage. She put the cheese back in the fridge.

Aha! A box of Cheerios. Had she really left the inner bag open last time? She prayed the roaches hadn't gotten into it. Alas, there were no clean bowls left, either. She grabbed a fistful of cereal, slammed the door behind her and escaped the house.

Melissa's apartment was just off Broadway. The great avenue bisected the upper West Side, separating the dismal tenements of the east—Melissa's side—from the youthful, energetic, upward-bound hum of West End Avenue and Riverside Drive. She walked briskly downtown, with a look like a scythe to mow down the men who inevitably stopped to annoy her.

Melissa tried to concentrate while dodging traffic and deliberately ignoring the stares and gasps with which strangers, male and female, greeted her constantly. She pushed through the crowd vehemently. She needed training and she needed luck and she needed to work hard, but above all, she needed to concentrate on her goal. She was twenty years old and she had an uncomfortable feeling about having lost valuable time although she hardly felt that she had missed the boat.

Her mother did. Ever since she could remember, Mom had repeated, ad nauseam, her conviction that "at seventeen, the bloom starts fading off the rose." You had to give Mom credit. She did not drag Melissa off and try to marry her to some decrepit millionaire, as did the mothers of many outstandingly beautiful daughters. Mom had just let nature take its course.

In Akela, New York, a town whose fortunes rose and fell with the Erie Canal, Melissa John was the most beautiful girl. Her marrying the best-looking, most athletic, most popular boy, with the brightest future, was a given. They started going steady in their freshman year in high school, got pinned as juniors. Senior year he gave her his grandmother's marcasite ring. The August after graduation, after a summer dizzy with bridal showers and the purchase of housewares, they were married in the backyard of her parents' house in the semi-rural outskirts of Akela.

Her young husband had it all planned out: college, law school, a tidy office, a gracious home. But what was Melissa supposed to do? Entertain prettily while he realized his modest ambition? Preside over clients' drinks at the country club? All this could be done—done better—by a wife much less beautiful.

And, oh, she was beautiful! A fireball, a nuclear explosion that seared retinas. It wasn't that she was vain. Melissa was a realist and her gorgeousness was a fact, a fact that had to be acknowledged and used.

Her looks were just too much for Akela, for a middle-class marriage. It was an energy that needed an enormous outlet. Her husband could do without the great gifts she had to give. He didn't need her, and she hated that.

But there was a mass out there, a public. Its need was insatiable, it hungered for beauty, the beauty *she* could give them.

Her husband shrugged when she told him quietly that she was leaving. That hurt, that he needed her so little.

"Whatever for?" he asked indifferently.

"To go to New York. To study acting. I want to be an actress."

He didn't even assume there was another man!

"You'll never get anywhere with that," he snorted.

"Why not? I was in all the school plays. I was good."

He smirked. "Maybe. But let's face it, Melissa. You're a lousy lay."

It was true. Just because she had a great body didn't mean she was good in bed. But a smart girl could learn.

Waiting for the divorce to come through, she got a job as a cashier. Men came into the Grand Union, and she smiled at them. They forgot what it was they had come in to buy. They dropped soda bottles. They reached absentmindedly into bags of dog food and popped some in their mouths. It didn't take engraved invitations to get them into her bed.

Melissa was a quick study. She gained experience and, with

it, confidence. She honed her skill and soon it became a talent. Having accomplished that, she left town.

It was funny, people talked about the filthy air in New York City, but she breathed a lot easier downstate. New York was not the ideal place for her; Los Angeles would have been better. But at least she knew people in New York. Every kid in Akela with enough energy to throw his father's lunch pail eventually migrated downstate. They'd helped her find an apartment, told her what lock to buy, mapped out areas not to get lost in. What would she do in Hollywood, hang out on Sunset Strip with every dumb whore in America?

She'd get to the West Coast eventually. Meanwhile she was doing okay. She was learning to act. She actually had real talent, which took everyone by surprise, considering her looks. She had gotten an agent, a pretty good one, people said. And she doggedly pursued the Big Break.

Okay, today she would head across town, to Bloomingdale's, the hottest department store in town. Melissa did not have the money to buy anything new, nor did she shop impulsively. But fashionable places attracted fashionable people, and fashionable people could lead her . . . could lead her . . . to her future.

Well, Bloomingdale's turned out to be a disappointment. The merchandise was nice enough, but the customers were little better than a cross section from Grand Central Station. God, there were a lot of rubes born and bred in this city. In the men's department three men tried to pick her up. "Do you think this tie is okay?" each had asked. Melissa sighed. They were all just variations of her ex—men who felt they deserved a beautiful girl of their very own but didn't have any real use for *her*.

Sometimes she got the feeling there was only one man in New York who kept reappearing everywhere she went. He was a successful, balding pocketbook manufacturer, divorced, and he was so *positive* he could make her happy.

She had gotten a headache at Bloomingdale's and the dirty hustle of Lexington Avenue made it worse. For relief, she walked over to the relative quiet of Park Avenue.

Park was one overrated street, Melissa thought. Cold and

boring, it had none of the elegance of upper Fifth Avenue or Central Park South. Maybe you had to get into some of those apartments to appreciate them. One of these days.

Just before Park Avenue turned into one long row of banks and colorless business offices, she saw the glitter of a few fancy stores. One of these was Martha's. Suddenly Melissa's headache vanished. This was what she expected from a store in New York!

Martha's windows were filled with the most magnificent evening dresses she had ever seen. Accessories had been tossed over beautiful pieces of furniture like dice on a crap table, mannequins were posed petting thin porcelain dogs. The whole window display breathed indolent wealth.

Melissa caught her reflection in the window. Why, her eyes matched perfectly the ball gown of turquoise silk. She wondered what it cost. She wondered, with cool detachment, when she would be getting her first dress from Martha's.

She tried to glimpse the inside of the store. A dress or two was hung on little hooks; the rest of the place looked like someone's living room. Where were the racks? Did they get by by selling just one or two dresses at a time? What if a customer wore a different size? She was impatient to solve these mysteries.

Something slid into the reflection in the window. A limousine. Melissa felt her heart stop, then continue calmly, strongly. Destiny, destiny. She was not afraid.

A chauffeur came to the curbside door and, in the reflection, out came Paul Tremain. Tremain with the naughty cleft chin, Tremain with the boyish smile, the man who made her grandmother squeeze her dried old thighs together whenever his image came on the screen. God! He was almost as handsome in real life.

He remained standing on one side of the car, while the chauffeur helped Diana Tremain to alight. The two men were like an honor guard, as Diana walked between them.

Melissa had to get closer to see more, a crowd was gathering. Smartly coifed Park Avenue matrons were acting like teenagers at a Monkees concert. "Mr. Tremain! O-o-oh,

Mr. Tremain!" They called for Diana, too. In New York, people still remembered Diana from her stage days.

Diana ignored them, walking into Martha's like a woman eager to get in before the shop closed. Her hair was done up like a butter sculpture, her eyes, pieces of Steuben glass.

Paul Tremain lingered for a moment, though. He turned to the little crowd, smiled his heart-stopping, inimitable smile, and waved to the women with pleasure. A collective moan ascended to the spires of Park Avenue. And then he looked at her. Melissa was sure of it. She held his eye confidently for a second or two. He clearly found it hard to break contact. Oh God, she thought, there's a perfect man for me. An equal—or we will be someday. A man like him *needs* a woman like me.

Instead of crowding around the door to Martha's, like the herds, Melissa went to the limousine and tapped on the driver's window. The window whooshed down and the chauffeur got a look at Melissa's face. He reacted just like the guys at the Grand Union.

"Gee," she asked, "are you the Tremains' chauffeur?"

"N-no. I just work for the Stanhope."

"What's that?"

"A hotel."

"Gosh, it must be expensive."

"Yes ma'am, it is. It's a beauty though."

"Where is it? I'm just a tourist. Down from upstate. You must think I'm terribly naive."

"Nah, I been living here all my life and I never heard of the place till I got this job. It's small and real exclusive, way up on Fifth Avenue, across from the Metropolitan Museum."

"The Metropolitan? You must be kidding. That's exactly where I was going. Are you heading back now? Could you give me a lift?"

"Ah, well . . ." but before he could really respond, she had run around the front of the limousine and hopped into the seat next to him. She began to chatter nonstop, and he decided it would be best to go back to the hotel.

He drove up to the Stanhope.

"Sorry, I can't drive you up to the museum. I'm really not supposed to give rides. But, see, it's right there."

"Gee, I'm sorry. I wouldn't have asked if I knew it would get you in trouble. Thanks a million. By the way, my name is Melissa John." She extended her hand regally.

He shook it and shivered involuntarily. Nothing like this girl had ever touched him before.

When she got out of the car, instead of crossing the street to the Metropolitan, darned if she didn't go right into the hotel.

As Melissa entered she smelled something delicious. An enormous arrangement of flowers in a Chinese urn faced the doorway, and some tiny purple blossoms were greeting each arrival with their marvelous perfume. It bothered Melissa that she did not know the name of the flowers. She had so much to learn.

Toward the end of the entrance hall there was a small, exquisitely tasteful onyx-top table with the house phone on it. There was also a silver bowl filled with pink roses and more of the aromatic purple flowers. The fragrant bouquet, the perfection of detail made her want to shrink and become yet another ornament on the table. But fantasy was a waste of time, she had to get to work.

The lounge was the prettiest room Melissa had ever been in. Comfortable sofas and armchairs were upholstered in jade green fabric, and the soothing color was picked up in the wallpaper, the carpets, the enormous vases that held still more of the delightful bouquets. Even the floor was made of what looked like malachite, though surely that would have been impossible.

Melissa waited for two hours. She didn't mind. She could learn to live in a place like this. Then she saw them.

The Stanhope was one of the few places in the world where people were too well bred to show an obvious interest in the Tremains. Paul and Diana reached the elevator undisturbed, with the driver behind them, carrying a stack of Martha bandboxes.

Melissa was suddenly before them.

"Nice to see you again, Mr. Tremain." Her eyes locked into his: battle of the blues. "Mrs. Tremain." Slight nod to Diana, but her eyes did not leave his.

"Who *are* you," demanded Diana Tremain. A Hollywood wag had once said Diana Tremain would make a great bartender. She could frost and salt a row of Margarita glasses with a single look.

"I'm Melissa John. I'm an actress. And I think I should be in your next movie, Mr. Tremain."

Diana stared at her as if a mutt had wandered in from Fifth Avenue and deposited Melissa in a steaming pile on the Stanhope's magnificent rug.

"You're mistaken, Miss John," said Diana, her crystalline eyes scraping Melissa from top to bottom. "My husband does not make porno films."

With that she marched into the elevator, dragging her husband behind her on an invisible leash. As they got on the elevator, Diana looked through Melissa, as if the younger woman was invisible.

Paul Tremain shrugged his handsome shoulders, smiled brilliantly and beamed her the kind of wink that earned him a million dollars a picture.

That afternoon in acting class, Melissa did some "Laura" from *The Glass Menagerie*. She was great. Her teacher could hardly believe how convincing she was as a loser whose every hope is crushed. Now *that's* acting, he thought.

Melissa flopped down on her bed, which hadn't been made in weeks. She had the headache that ate Chicago. At least the kids next door weren't screaming. Ohhh, the boyfriend had probably beaten them to death.

This was the most miserable day of her life.

Just who do you think you are, little jerk. Paul Tremain, one of the top five box office draws for twelve years straight. Diana Tremain, one of the greatest stage actresses in the history of Broadway. Oh Jesus, why did you do it, why, why, why?

The phone rang.

That must be my ex, we need to sign some more papers. I'm too beat to talk to him now.

The phone rang again.

Probably Mom. If she finds me in this state she'll whine at me for hours.

Again.

My buddies from Akela. I won't repay their kindness by slobbering on their shoulders.

And again.

Hey! What if it's Paul Tremain?

She snatched the phone off its hook.

"Hey baby, it's about time. Where have you been? I've been trying to get you for hours."

"Who is this?"

"It's me, your agent. Most of my clients greet me a little more cheerfully, you know."

"Oh. OH! Right. I'm sorry, I just dashed in the door . . ."

"Hey, you should sign up with an answering service. Opportunities can slip by, you know."

"Are you kidding. I can't even afford the phone."

"Well, worry no more. I've got a job for you."

"You do? Hey, that's great. Wow, that's fast. You really are a terrific agent."

"Thank you, thank you. But don't get carried away, this isn't exactly the lead in 'The Fantasticks.'"

"That's okay, I'm just a beginner."

"Now that's the right attitude. Okay, here's the scoop. You know Goldsmith's, the bridal shop?"

"Sure, on Fifth Avenue, near Saks."

"Right. Well, every year they have this show at the Pierre. All the classiest engaged girls in the city come to see the new fashions. So, anyway—you're a lucky gal, you know—their main girl got sick, and I thought you'd be great for the part."

"Christ, you idiot! It's a *fashion show*. Modeling is for lollipops who are looking to get married. The last model to become a major star was, who? Lauren Bacall? That's like twenty-five years ago. I'd rather starve than get into that rut.

"I've got my standards. No porno, no modeling. Besides, I'm only five feet six, that's too short for big-bucks modeling.

And they're supposed to be flat-chested, which I'm definitely not."

"Yeah, I noticed. But hold on, Melissa. This show, see, isn't like a regular fashion show. The top lady at Goldsmith's, Mrs. Marshall, she makes it like a real wedding, y'know. It's like a play, right, with actors. That's why they want you, an actress. Hell, they could have gotten any number of models, but they want an actress. They want you to act, see?"

"No, I don't see. Just what is it I'm supposed to act as?"

"As a virgin bride. Hey, that should take some skill. Ha, ha."

Melissa made a mental note to get a new agent just as soon as she had a few credits.

"When is this thing, and where?"

"Okay, it's at the Pierre. Just about the fanciest hotel in town. And, uh, it's tomorrow morning."

"What time?"

"Does that mean you'll take it?"

Melissa figured that as long as it wasn't at the store, she could always embroider the facts and use it as an acting credit. Besides, she wasn't doing anything tomorrow. Her bright ideas for making it in the city by sheer gumption were fizzling out.

"Yeah. What time?"

"All right! You've gotta be there at nine, 'cause it's a brunch. Will you really, really be there? Should I give you a wake-up call? You gotta be there on time, babe, or my ass is in a sling with this Marshall dame."

"Of course I'll be there on time!" That was the most insulting remark yet. This guy was a jerk. Imagine, doing something so unprofessional as being late.

"That's my girl. It's in the Cotillion Room. Melissy, with that attitude and those boobs, we can go far."

"That's terrific." *Far as the first real job. After that just call yourself my ex-agent.*

Okay, this dumb job was not exactly the U.S. Cavalry coming in to save the day, but neither was it a continuation of the hopeless mess before it.

Melissa realized she was hungry. She did an inventory of the kitchen and groaned out loud. She washed her face, freshened her makeup, and went out.

There was a place over on Columbus Avenue she had gotten to know, a new but comfortable place called Aunt Toni O's. Fortunately, it had yet to be discovered by the trend-lemmings, so if the pickings of men were slim, at least the percentage of married creeps on the make was small.

The bar was not very busy when she walked in; still, a hush seemed to come over it. Men and women stopped what they were doing to look at her. That element, or talent, or whatever-it-is, the promise of which sells every issue of *Cosmo* and *Playboy* on the newsstand, was undeniably hers. It wasn't just beauty, although her beauty was overwhelming. It wasn't just sex appeal, although no man could look at her without imagining himself in her bed.

There was an aura about her. It was impossible but very real. It was universally and instantly recognizable, and there was a breath of the tragic to it, too. Marilyn Monroe had had it, and so had Jean Harlow. So did the little terra-cotta figures that archaeologists insist were once worshipped for their powers of fertility.

She had long ago learned to ignore the stares. Melissa cased the joint expertly, and her eye fell upon a cute guy standing alone at the end of the bar. He was nursing a beer, when all about him were sippers of wine and fancy drinks. She liked that. He was not a guy who pretended to be here for the drinks, for the friendship—or for true love. She also liked the way he was dressed. He wore a soft denim shirt tucked neatly into corduroys that were tight enough to show off his slim hips but not so tight as to outline anything obscenely.

She shook her head a little, letting the hair swing in front of her shoulder. Any gesture more flirtatious would have been openly provocative, not her style. She looked him square in the eye and smiled just a little.

He fell as if clubbed. He and his beer were at her side in a second. She told him her name and he told her his. But just at that moment the music welled up and all she caught was his mouthing two short syllables.

He offered to buy her a drink. She said she really couldn't

drink on an empty stomach. (Actually, she didn't care for liquor at all.) They moved to a small table and she ordered jumbo shrimp salad, steak with home fries and green beans, and apple pie with a scoop of vanilla.

She ate with gusto. He watched her, approving. Melissa realized that most men rarely got to see a girl enjoying her food. Especially a beautiful girl. Most girls ate, whining the whole time about blowing their diets, or sat picking at lettuce, acting as if they should get a prize for being skinny. She looked into his eyes: *He thinks all my appetites must be just as healthy.*

After she finished, they stayed a while longer. The bar had gotten busier, and the music louder, so their conversation didn't amount to that much.

When Melissa figured a decent interval had passed, she gestured to the guy that they leave. She didn't have to ask twice. Outside the bar she invited him over to her place, without feeling, or appearing, the least bit forward. His car was in a pay lot, but he redeemed it. Miraculously, he found a parking spot right in front of her building.

When she opened the door to her apartment, he couldn't help but gasp. It *was* a rat hole, but it was her place and she was damned if she'd apologize for it.

"So," Melissa smiled, "would you like anything to drink?"

"Thanks. A beer would be great."

"Do you mind helping yourself? I thought I'd change into something comfortable." The guy rose shakily to his feet.

He opened the refrigerator door. There was no beer in it, nor any other beverage.

"Uh, you seem to be out, Melissa."

"Oh gee, I'm sorry. Say, would you mind going down to the market to get some? This place around the corner is open all night."

"No problem."

"Thanks a million."

"My pleasure."

"Oh, and could you get me some instant coffee?"

"Sure. Anything else? How about some breakfast stuff? Eggs? Bagels? Fruit?"

"If you want to. Sure, it would be nice."

He ended up buying two big bags of groceries filled with Jamaican Blue Mountain coffee, tropical fruits, and imported cheeses.

When he returned to the apartment, he looked mildly disappointed to find that she was still fully dressed. And obviously she hadn't spent the time cleaning up the place.

Her makeup was off, her hair brushed back, and her skin was lightly coated with lotion. She was still gorgeous, but in a different way.

He asked her what she did. She said she was an actress, and the sides of his mouth went down a drop. She was performing in a small production tomorrow at the Hotel Pierre. Now his lips smiled with proprietary pride.

"An artist," he said, looking at the decrepit surroundings with understanding.

"That's right. Acting is an art. Um, something wrong with my apartment?"

"Oh, no! At least you don't have a lot of that decorator junk."

She asked him what he did. Sure, that was the logical thing to say. He said he was "with IBM."

She had no idea what to say to that, so she said nothing.

"Actually, I'm an engineer. I don't usually say that, because, you know, the princesses think engineers are meal tickets, and the snobs think engineers are boring. You don't think that way, do you, Melissa?"

"No, I don't."

She didn't think about it at all.

After a period of cozy quiet, Melissa led the way to the bedroom. She had turned off one lamp, and was about to extinguish the other.

"Don't do that," he pleaded.

"I was going to light some candles," she laughed.

"Oh. I think I still prefer more light. I want to look at you some more. Has anyone ever told you that you're extremely beautiful? I mean that seriously."

"Gee, that's really sweet of you." She put her arms around his neck and kissed him fully on the mouth.

The first kiss produced a Niagara of sensation.

"Yummy," she said, "I got lucky tonight."

"You're lucky? How about me? Finding you, the most beautiful girl I've met in ages—maybe ever. You know what I like about you, Melissa? You're no prude, but you're not cheap, either."

Melissa was satisfied with him. Sort of like biting into a plain doughnut and finding a pocket of her favorite filling. The guy had decent manners, he wasn't ejaculating all over her within ten seconds of closing the door. But the confident way he held her showed that he was no wimp, either.

As she undressed, she studied his reactions.

"Wow," he breathed, at the sight of her naked body. Not an ounce of fat on her and a stomach as flat as Kansas. But breasts like jumbo globe artichokes and womanly hips.

She looked thoughtful as she surveyed his body. Incredibly broad shoulders—practically real estate in Manhattan. Good looks were important. She didn't think these sessions should be unpleasant. His torso was hard, with just the right amount of hair curling on his chest like an illuminated letter T. Below that, well, he certainly seemed interested enough. What difference did a guy's equipment make, anyway, as long as he knew how to use it. And he knew how.

In his embrace Melissa was pleasantly crushed to his chest. This was the part she liked, the part where she was indispensable.

One thing about this guy, he was a great kisser. She hadn't met many like that. Some of the men she'd slept with called lovemaking "fucking," as if it were a physical act, like "walking," "jumping," "shoving." Well, she had done her test marketing and she could say for a fact that there was a hell of a lot more to it than the physical. "Fucking," for the animals who knew nothing better, could be confined to the lower parts of the body, but kissing, real kissing, needed a little human feeling.

Eventually, he left her mouth and proceeded to kiss her shoulders and breasts. He would not let her repay his ministrations, but made her lie there for the longest time, swaggering about the pleasure he was sure he was giving her.

Then his kisses grew into teasing little licks and soft bites and went down her expectant body, inch by inch. Until he came to the sparse, sleek black hair between her legs and the licks and kisses became maddeningly insistent. She had to pull him off by the hair of his head. It would be awful to come on a man's head. She was not about to permit him—or herself—that.

She made him lie down and she practiced what he had just demonstrated. Deep, long, lush kisses to the mouth. Playful, teasing, maddening little kisses over his body. Although fellatio was far from her favorite form of love play, when she got to his erect member, she fell to with sportsmanlike efficiency.

The taut skin was silky smooth and tasted clean and sweet. She closed her eyes and pretended it was an ice cream cone. It worked. This time *he* had to pull *her* off.

Then, at last, they coupled. He held on until she began expert climactic throes. Only then did he come, crowing with happiness.

Recovering his breath, he lay facing her. He smiled broadly at Melissa, and he stroked her arm very gently.

His eyelids looked heavy, but apparently he was one of those postcoital talkers.

"Well, well, well, Melissa. I see you're a gal who knows how to please a man."

She smiled and closed her eyes, but he wouldn't take the hint.

"Of course, such a short time, I'm not saying I'm in love, mind you, but if I ever did fall in love, I think it would be with a girl like you, Melissa. Beautiful—really stunning—offbeat, but with an understanding of who wears the pants . . ."

Melissa's eyes shot open and the congenial smile faded from her lips. He wasn't watching, he just kept on talking.

"There are times I think, what the hell, why not go for it? I'm not getting any younger, either, and it gets pretty boring, screwing around. I'll tell you honestly, Melissa, this is one relationship I'm gonna give a fair shot."

How do I handle this gracefully, thought Melissa.

"But, uh, honey, I'm such a slob."

"Well, this place is a tenement to start with. Bet if you had a nice sunny house with some decent furniture, the old nesting instinct would take over."

He got up on his elbows, gave her a teasing wink. "Just watch out that you don't get fat, once you're safe and comfortable and have a bunch of kids."

Now he started drifting off to sleep. She patted him on the cheek.

"How about a shower?"

"Great idea." He disentangled himself from the sheets and clambered reluctantly out of bed.

"Hey, Melissa, aren't you coming?"

"Oh, no. The shower's not big enough for both of us. You go first."

After a quick rinse, he came back to the bed and sat down. She appeared to be getting up for her own shower, but instead she went and gathered his clothes. She handed them to him.

He was as shocked as if she had attacked him with a butcher knife.

In response to the look on his face, she explained, "Gee, I'm sorry, but I have an early day tomorrow. I really need my sleep."

"I don't snore or anything."

"No, really, I need privacy."

He put his clothes on slowly, as if she'd change her mind as he did his reverse striptease.

"Hey, if this isn't what you want, why don't you say so? How come you girls always play mind games?"

"Oh no. You were excellent, really. Just right." She smiled politely.

"I can't believe it. It was just a quick roll in the hay for you, wasn't it? Like, I'm not even a human being, right, just a sex machine."

"Don't be silly," she said, walking him to the door.

"Jesus, you sure made a schmuck out of me. Here I am, practically thinking about introducing you to my mother, while you, you're just *using* me."

"Come on now," she clucked. When was he going to leave? Did he have to wallow in it?

"You know what this reminds me of?"

"No, and I don't . . ."

"It reminds me of the time I was in the service and I went to this off-base party, and I got drunk, and I picked up a tramp. And she turned out to be a transvestite!"

She slammed and locked the door behind him. Then she went to her window, which faced the street, to make sure he was really leaving the building.

She watched him put his car in reverse and screech out of the parking space, scratching the passenger door for his trouble.

"Shit!" he screamed at the dark and hostile street. Then "shit" again. Melissa could see a parking ticket fly up off his windshield and flutter away.

Satisfied that he was gone, Melissa went back to bed. She was pleased at the earliness of the hour. The job tomorrow wasn't much but she'd be fresh and glowing, a bride to perfection.

Chapter Four

MELISSA CROSSED the Pierre's threshold at 8:30 in the morning. She carried a large, compartmentalized bag with a variety of makeup and underwear. Scrubbed clean, her face did not rivet every passerby, as it did when she was made up. Yet it made enough heads turn, and the Pierre's house detective immediately began to follow her discreetly. A female this beautiful could well be a call girl.

Melissa made inquiries at the desk. The Pierre was both large and imposing, but Melissa was beginning to feel at home. The experience at the Stanhope was not for nothing. This little country bumpkin could get used to the elegant life in no time, she thought.

She was directed to a large double suite, where the preparations for the show were to take place. She knocked on the door and a strong, melodious voice answered immediately.

"Come in. It's open."

Melissa looked about in wonder. The suite must have once been a calm and lovely place. Silver wallpaper was gaily festooned with parrots and jungle vines, a charming counterpoint to the fine cherry furniture and the soft blue carpets and upholstery.

But now there were a hundred dresses in the suite, overflowing the closets, piled on the bed, strewn on desks and sofas. The bathtub was crammed with buckets of fresh flowers. Ribbon, lace, and tulle were escaping the dresser drawers. The coffee table was covered with spools of thread, tape measures, and shears. It had been pushed aside to accommodate a sewing machine.

The lady who had spoken was briskly moving things around. She must have been in the suite for hours.

"Hello, I'm Bettina Marshall, chief bridal consultant for Goldsmith's."

Melissa took her outstretched hand and shook it. "Hi! I'm Melissa John." She smiled.

Mrs. Marshall stared. She had seen a great many pretty girls in her lifetime, but this was something else.

Melissa was also impressed. The lady before her—and lady was definitely the term—was somewhere in middle age, tiny, possibly less than five feet, thin as a sparrow, and bubbly as champagne.

Her salt-and-pepper hair was cut short, precisely neat but definitely fashionable. She wore a taupe knit suit—could it be a real Chanel?—whose skirt was hemmed surprisingly short. Her legs, as shapely as those of a woman half her age, ended in Gucci loafers. The short skirt and flat heels served a useful purpose; to get around with her customary speed, little Mrs. Marshall needed to move with a dancer's leaps.

For her part, Bettina Marshall was smitten by Melissa. Mrs. Marshall had, of course, immediately noted the young woman's beauty. But that was with a dispassionate, professional eye. And she was surprised when Melissa shook her hand; most models greeted her offered palm as if it were a dead carp, while Melissa gave a shake as firm as a man's. But it was the smile that struck home.

In most cases, beauty is in the eye of the beholder, but Melissa's beauty was self-contained, complete, as independently gorgeous as an orchid deep in the Amazon jungle. There was something magical, too, that went beyond beauty. Unlike beauty, it was exclusive, undeniable, permanent. Mrs. Marshall sighed, unable to tear her eyes away.

"I hope it's okay that I came a bit early."

"What? Oh. Yes, that's fine. I mean, no, we're paying models by the hour. We're contracted from nine."

Melissa's lips tightened. "I'm not a model. I'm an *actress*."

"Of course, of course. I prefer actresses for our 'wedding

party.' That's why I went to a theatrical agency to hire you, and the others as well."

"Just so we're clear that I'm *not* a model. In fact, I'm a size six below the waist, an eight—maybe more—on top."

"Don't you worry about the fit, darling. I've presented perfect brides at every single one of my fashion brunches, to say nothing of real life. And I always go for actresses. I had another actress set up but unfortunately—or should I say fortunately?—she stood me up at the last minute. I'm depending on you to come through without a rehearsal. Somehow, I just know you'll be terrific."

"I still don't get it. Why don't you get models? They wear clothes well. Frankly, my strength is in looking like it doesn't matter what I wear, as long as the audience thinks there's a chance I'll take it off! Not exactly everyone's idea of a blushing bride."

Mrs. Marshall laughed. "What you must understand is that the secret of a beautiful bride is not in her dress, it's in her feelings. Without that special bridal glow the gown is just silk and beads. I want you to *think* like a bride when you go out there. *Feel* like a bride, *be* one. Models can't do that. They act as if their dresses are fancy ball gowns. The effect is that of a walking hanger.

"But you will *act* like a bride, and every engaged girl in the audience will identify with you completely, will see herself in that dress, on her special day."

Melissa smiled again. "Well, it's a challenge. It's like a role in a silent movie. My acting teacher would like this. Where did you get this idea from, anyway?"

Mrs. Marshall grinned. "In Hollywood, of course. But don't tell anyone. I'm afraid our society customers would consider it very déclassé."

"Hollywood? Really? You worked in Hollywood?" Melissa's tone said, "and you gave it up to come *here*?"

"Why yes, I was assistant in the wardrobe department of one of the studios. As a matter of fact, the first bride I ever dressed was an actress, Mary Astor. Perhaps you remember the film *Veiled Truth*. Miss Astor plays the evil woman who almost marries Ray Milland, until Greer Garson reappears, still alive, despite Mary's schemes."

"No, I don't think I've seen it."

"No, of course you haven't. That was way before your time. But maybe they'll show it on late-night television. Do remember to look for Mary Astor's gown, and think of me.

"Lord, she was beautiful. I loved working with her. I don't think there's ever been anyone as beautiful in the movies, with the possible exception of Louise Brooks."

Melissa gulped. Mary Astor? Louise Brooks? The most beautiful women in Hollywood, and she hadn't even heard of them! Was it possible that beauty wasn't enough? Would that happen to her? Star in a movie or two, be a gilded icon, then a few years later, disappear? No, it couldn't be. Maybe this Marshall woman had weird ideas of beauty.

"You really think they were that pretty? What about Marilyn Monroe, Grace Kelly, Jean Harlow?"

"Oh, *blonds*," said Mrs. Marshall.

"Well, they say gentlemen prefer them." Melissa had toyed with the idea of going blond, but the effort involved in bleaching so much hair, and keeping on top of the coal-black roots, was too discouraging.

"I don't know about gentlemen, there aren't that many of them in Hollywood. Sure, *boys* prefer blonds, but *men*, generally speaking, are attracted to the qualities of brunettes: depth, passion, a certain kind of intelligence."

"Well, how about the brunettes? You know, Liz Taylor, or, what's-her-name, Scarlett O'Hara?"

"Vivien Leigh. Yes, she was exquisite. And of course, so is Elizabeth Taylor. But you know, for both of them that peak of beauty was so fleeting. Taylor will be beautiful forever, but whenever I see her I think, 'Oh how beautiful, but not as beautiful as she was in *A Place in the Sun*.' Do you see what I mean?"

Melissa didn't, or she was afraid to. She wanted to change the subject.

"What was it like, that dress you designed for Mary Astor?"

"Oh, I didn't design it, I'm not a designer. I just put the pieces together. The studio's design head was busy with

Garson's wardrobe. 'Just get some old thing for Miss Astor, and stick a long veil on it,' he said. It was only going to be visible for a few seconds, and he wasn't going to waste any effort on it.

"But I felt then, and I still feel, that a bride—even a pretend one, even an evil one, even one that is seen for a passing moment—should be dressed with the greatest love. And of course, Miss Astor was an inspiration."

"So what did you get her?"

"Well, first I found this bolt of antique Carrickmacross lace. Lace had been out of fashion for years; it had been hidden under a pile of old drapes. In the wardrobe department's old records I found the name of a designer who had made beautiful things for the Gish sisters in the silent era. Amazingly, he was still alive, in a nursing home. He was so happy for the work, that he did it for a pittance—which is what the head had allotted me for this assignment. I ran it up at home, after hours, because I couldn't be spared from my other duties during the day.

"The dress was tight because there was very little of the precious fabric. Its high neckline framed Astor's perfect face. It had natural shoulders, which was unusual for the time. Mary Astor, who often played villainous roles, was especially known for big, padded shoulders and constructed suits. I wanted a long train, but we ran out of lace. In the movie, Astor stands on a staircase, the train trailing up the steps, to look longer. It's a shame, but of course we knew that the details of the material would not show on-screen. Still, I knew how magnificent it was and so did Miss Astor, and I like to think it affected her performance.

"There wasn't enough lace for a headpiece. I made one up from a white turban left over from an Arabian Nights movie. I placed a tiny lace triangle over her forehead and positioned the turban high, behind her head, like a halo. Then I added tulle. I still prefer a tulle veil for most brides.

"Anyway, when Miss Astor came down the stairs to meet the groom, only to find him in the arms of his true love, for a second, just a second, you wondered why any man would go for the Greer Garson character when such a vision of loveliness, no matter how wicked, could be his."

"The blond always wins," sighed Melissa.

"I wouldn't say so," said Mrs. Marshall. "The picture bombed!

"Now how did I get on this subject? We've got plenty of work to do right now without reminiscing about old times. Let's get moving."

Mrs. Marshall leaped over to the largest closet, which was stuffed with muslin-covered gowns. She removed the first gown and stripped off its cover.

"This is the dress I had for the other girl. But I don't think it will do."

She held up the gown. This was no mean feat, as the dress was obviously very heavy, and it dwarfed the small woman who held it. The dress was of double-faced satin, starkly simple, A-line, with a bateau neckline. The severity of the dress was relieved only by a row of embroidery encrusted with crystals and chalk beads at the bottom of the trumpet sleeves.

"This sort of thing has been very popular with the debs, but frankly I'm getting rather tired of the look. I'm afraid that in their effort to avoid too much froufrou, they err on the side of stuffiness."

Mrs. Marshall continued tossing gowns out of the closet as if they were feathers. They landed easily on the sofa, apparently not even creasing each other.

"Mmm, this ivory faille is nice, but I'm afraid an empire waistline would overemphasize your bust, make you look matronly, if such a thing is possible.

"Ah, here's the ticket. A really young dress. Not for Mary Astor, I can assure you. Look, cotton voile, light as a dream. This is just the fashion message I want to project: youth, freshness, adventure. It's not that I approve of rebellion for its own sake, but let's face it, this is 1971. There is something wrong with young people who hew to the old ways without even peeking out from behind the rocks, don't you think?"

Melissa murmured assent. The whole generation-gap business bored her to tears.

• • •

At nine, others began to trickle into the suite. The "brides-maids," and "flower girls," and "mothers" came with their outfits and changed in the bedroom. The men of the party appeared already dressed and repaired to another room to while away the time until the brunch.

The makeup artist did Melissa's face, almost as well as Melissa did her own. The hairdresser put a few rollers in for volume. And the florist hid himself in the bathroom, working furiously and cursing nervously.

Because the gown was very sheer, Mrs. Marshall helped Melissa into a strapless bra. It was tight and boned and manipulated her waist and breasts into mythological propor-tions.

Melissa quickly donned white stockings, white leather ballet slippers, and an enormous taffeta crinoline. Then Mrs. Marshall, standing on the bed, dropped the dress onto Melissa's shoulders.

Melissa could not believe how perfectly it fit. She adjusted the ribbon on the peasant neckline. She puffed out the elbow-length sleeves. She laced the wide corselet tightly. Now there was nothing to do but swirl the clouds of tiered skirts, and admire the ribbon which defined each tier. Looking closely, she saw that the white silk was embroidered with tiny flowers of palest lavender.

"Take it off, Melissa, so the girls can do the adjustments."

"But it's perfect," Melissa protested. She didn't want to part with the dress for a moment. It was bad enough that she'd be wearing it for only a few hours.

"Nonsense. It's a nightmare for the ladies to alter a gown at such short notice. By rights it should be custom tailored to you, just like the dresses at the salon. The seamstresses hate these emergencies."

Secretly, Mrs. Marshall was pleased by Melissa's attachment to the gown. That was just like a real bride, who knows that her tenure in her perfect dress ends all too soon.

Melissa was left in the *Gone With the Wind* underwear while Mrs. Marshall went out to the Cotillion Room for a last-minute look.

The room looked just perfect. They would be having 250

guests—one hundred brides, mothers, sisters, best friends, even an occasional groom—and the Cotillion was a small ballroom just suited for the affair. Its lofty ceiling was hung with an unusual pressed-glass chandelier, and brown-and-white marble columns opened onto a sunken dance floor. Small round tables looked down upon the "wedding" scene on one end and faced the bucolic French *trompe l'oeil* murals that none of the better Manhattan hotels could resist.

Each of the tables was set with a different cloth, china, silver, and crystal, courtesy of the manufacturers who were eager to sell their wares to the wealthy young brides.

At eleven, the guests began to trickle in. The brides were privileged young girls, at an average age of twenty. They wore silk-and-worsted suits in bright colors, with jeweled buttons the only ornament. Most wore their hair in one form or another of a pageboy, as their mothers and grandmothers had done for the better part of the century. Some, it was obvious, had had their hair cut at Vidal Sassoon, but lost their nerve, and set, teased, and sprayed their hairdos as soon as they got home.

This was the cream of Goldsmith's clientele, the debs. Their visibility was important to the salon, but it was the business of far more modest women that plumped up the firm's bottom line.

A substantial part of the clientele was made up of traditional women from the outlying boroughs. There were working-class Italians who came in groups of three, or even four, generations.

The ancient grandmother would lift a piece of beaded lace to her glasses and cackle with pleasure. In the old country every girl worth her salt learned the needlework arts, and many decades later, decades without the leisure for embroidery, they could still recognize quality workmanship at a glance.

"Gramma says this is the best one. This is the one we're gonna get, Teresa," the mother would state.

And Teresa would sulk, preferring the trendier but less noble gown. But she would go with the family's decision in the end. Because the family still meant something to these people. The family was the *point* of the wedding.

The same could be said for the ultra-Orthodox Jews. No matter how fashionable the gowns they chose, they insisted on complete modesty. Great designers would cringe as their gowns were relined with opaque material for these customers. Even flesh-colored silk, which one might hope would serve purposes of coverage while still showing the detail of fine laces and chiffons, was unacceptable.

Yet this insular community spared no expense in beautifying its brides. Penniless girls were often brought in to the salon and outfitted in the most magnificent dresses. Their wealthier coreligionists would pay for the trousseaux, considering it a form of charity. Because they believed that marriage was not just for the happiness of individuals but a blessing for the entire community.

Still, somewhere along the line, these ethnic ideals had ceased to hold meaning for the majority. Fashion, status, snobbery held sway. And Goldsmith's catered to that, too, as today's show would attest.

Chuck Lloyd sat down with his daughter. Lloyd was sixty, his sandy hair receding, and his sports coat hung limply on his torso. One could easily be deceived into believing he was anything other than what he was: Hollywood's foremost agent.

Lloyd's face registered sadness and anxiety, but he was not intimidated by the very feminine splendor of the occasion.

Lloyd's daughter was deep in a discussion with her best friend, who was also a bride-to-be, about which linens were "right."

His daughter had been the product of his brief first marriage to a debutante. The socialite's second husband was the effete heir to a pharmaceutical fortune, a brainless fellow who, however, doted on the little girl and fulfilled her mother's every shallow dream. They had lived in Connecticut all these years and Chuck had seen his daughter only during brief visits.

Now his little girl was getting married. To a jerk, a highborn nitwit whose family would keep him in investment banking and the best clubs, mostly in an alcoholic haze. But, Chuck realized ruefully, he was a pretty even match for this woman, his only child.

She was petty, self-satisfied, and unmotivated; a perfect exemplar of her class. She hadn't even inherited her mother's good looks. But what she was had nothing to do with the intensity with which her father loved her.

Now she had asked him to accompany her to this show, an honor that rightly would go to her mother. Chuck had been in the deal business a long time. He realized that he must eventually pay for any attentions he received from his child.

When she had first become engaged, they, the three of them, had called to tell him. He was thrilled. His only daughter.

"About the wedding . . ."

"Well, you name it, sweetheart. Anything you want, big as you want. Put out all the plugs, don't even think about the bills, I'll take care of them."

"Well, um, Frederick wants to ask you a favor. He'd really like to take care of the arrangements. You know, Daddy, he hasn't any children of his own, and . . ."

Yes, he knew very well. The bride and her mother didn't want some gaudy Hollywood production number. They didn't want his famous clients there, the movie goddesses upstaging the other guests. It would be a wedding of their own kind.

Chuck acquiesced, of course. He wanted to please his daughter. There was no one else for him to please.

There had been his second wife. She was a buxom starlet à la Jayne Mansfield. He had picked her right off the casting couch. Who would have imagined what a fine wife she would make? Patient, supportive, kind, a blessing to come home to every night. Easy to please, and a joy to please. It was all gone now. Gone these ten months, two weeks, and three days. The cancer had lusted for her breasts more than any director had.

Now brunch was served. Cutesy champagne-and-fruit-juice cocktails led into complicated terrines and seafood dishes. Lloyd fasted and watched.

Mrs. Marshall took the microphone and announced the beginning of the processional. The room full of giggling, adenoidal brides-to-be reached a crescendo of noise as the ersatz wedding party proceeded to the altar.

But when the bride appeared, silence descended on the crowd.

"Oh, that dress!" Lloyd's daughter, suddenly whispering, said to her friend.

"*Darling*! It's practically for hippies."

"I didn't say it was appropriate, just that it's striking. Maybe they could make it up more formally."

"Well, it is striking. But maybe it's the model that's making it. She's really something."

"She is not. Goldsmith's can make anyone look like that," Lloyd's daughter insisted with a huff.

Chuck Lloyd appraised the model-bride with a professional eye. He was glad to have something to do, something other than his sorrows to occupy his mind. The woman was luminous. A glowing Gene Tierney, a sensual Vivien Leigh. He had certainly never seen another like her in all his working years.

He would be cautious. What if she couldn't act to save her life? What if she didn't project on camera? But of course, he would take that chance. If she had the vitality of a half-carved Pinocchio, he could make her a legend.

A table of sumptuous, excessive desserts was served. Lloyd could hardly contain himself until everyone had finished eating.

"Sugar," he said to his daughter, "I know you won't mind going home with your friend. I've got some business to attend to now."

"But, Daddy," the girl was puffed up with petulance. "I've something very important to ask you."

"You want Frederick to give you away, don't you?"

"Why, Daddy, how could you possibly have known? Let me explain why . . ."

"If that's what you want, honey, you have my blessings."

"Oh, Daddy! You're the most thoughtful person in the entire world." She gave his hand a quick squeeze.

Oh, thoughtful, he thought. Thoughtful is a wonderful thing to be. Just stick with your lines and show no pain.

Chuck Lloyd excused himself from the ladies, and hurried toward Mrs. Marshall, who was leaving the room.

"Yup," he murmured to himself, "a fine old role. Chuck Lloyd crying all the way to the bank."

"Excuse me," he said, just as Mrs. Marshall was about to enter the suite that was being used as a dressing room.

She turned, surprised to find a man, alone, in such a place.

"Am I mistaken, or were you on the set of *Veiled Truth* back in forty-seven?"

"Heavens, sir. You have the memory of an elephant!"

"Only for the prettier actresses."

Mrs. Marshall blushed. "Oh, I was hardly an actress. Just a wardrobe assistant, I'm afraid."

"Nothing to be afraid of. Some of my best clients would sell their capped teeth for a great wardrobe mistress to dress them."

"Your clients?"

"Oh, I'm sorry. My name is Chuck Lloyd."

"The agent? Oh my goodness, how exciting. And you remember *Veiled Truth*? I thought I was the only one who had reason to cherish the memory of that clunker."

"Are you kidding? It was my first coup. I represented the director. Fortunately, he managed to go on to better things."

"No doubt your doing. Well, all I did was put together an outfit for Mary Astor."

"You did some job."

"Hardly. You didn't need to do much for Mary Astor. She was a deity."

"You can say that again. They don't make 'em like that anymore."

"Oh no? Wait till you see this young woman."

Mrs. Marshall opened the door a crack and stuck her head in. "Melissa. If you're decent, please come out here and meet a charming gentleman."

Melissa came out. She had her jeans on, but her shirt was open, showing the merry widow corset she had worn under the gown.

"I thought you might want to meet Mr. Chuck Lloyd, the

actors' representative," Mrs. Marshall said, with a meaningful look.

Melissa's eyes opened wide. She threw back her shoulders and smiled, as if for an audience of millions.

Chuck Lloyd was now certain that his first impression of her was correct.

"Tell me, miss," he said, "do you have an agent?"

Melissa did not skip a beat. "No. As a matter of fact, I've been looking for one."

Chapter Five

From Thisweek Magazine, June 12, 1971

COMMERCE

A Fifth Avenue Tradition Going Strong

This month, as we approach the heart of the wedding season, it must seem to many that there are fewer and fewer young people tying the knot. The stigma is gone from cohabitation. Old-fashioned parents stand horrified but helpless as the New Generation shirks marital responsibility.

At most, one might think, those few who do marry will be wed on a windswept beach or on a mountaintop, their union blessed by a swami. The bride, and perhaps the groom as well, will be dressed in a colorful ethnic shift, purchased for pennies at a flea market. The happy couple will be toasted with sangria, and more attention will be paid to what the guests will smoke than to what they will eat. Sitar music will mark the festivities, or perhaps a tape of the couple's favorite Beatles album.

The above may be a common impression of marriage today, but it is largely incorrect. More couples than ever—well over two million—will be tying the knot this year, the vast majority in a decidedly traditional way.

Far from writing their own liturgy, reports Reverend Thomas Bascomb of Buffalo's United Presbyterian Church, most couples will, at most, delete the "obey" from the bride's vows. And Seattle's Velvet Violins, a 35-year-old musical ensemble, has had only a few new additions to its dance repertoire in the past decade. Most wedding planners still request vintage romantic tunes for their receptions.

Nowhere does tradition hang on more tenaciously than in the classic white bridal gown and veil. "Business has never been better," says Henry Goldsmith, who has been selling bridal wear since the Depression from the handsome Fifth Avenue salon that bears his name.

"We offer all the most avant-garde designs," says Goldsmith, "but the classic white or ivory gown, in silk or lace, with a veil and a train, is far and away the most popular, accounting for ninety percent of sales in this category."

Tradition does not come cheap at Goldsmith's. Prices range from a thousand dollars for a simple sheath to $10,000 and more for the most elaborate frocks. How can Goldsmith's justify such expense for a dress to be worn only once? Chief Bridal Consultant Bettina Marshall cites the high cost of fabric (Goldsmith's uses only natural fibers), intricate hand-beading by skilled craftswomen, and, in the case of the most expensive garments, antique laces that cannot be duplicated at any price.

"Essentially, all of our dresses are *haute couture*," says Marshall. "The world's greatest designers are at our disposal. And each dress is custom fitted to each bride, with her personality and background, as well as her figure, considered in the execution of the design."

The store includes a stage for modeling of gowns, twenty spacious dressing rooms, three large salons for the selection of headpieces, lingerie, and shoes, and a separate shop for dressing mothers and bridesmaids. Its basement workroom, for altering dresses, is larger than that of many Seventh Avenue manufacturers.

Not only will Goldsmith's completely outfit the well-heeled bride and her retinue, it will, for a fee, coordinate an entire wedding, liaising with the ritziest hotels, caterers, florists, and musicians throughout the country.

Goldsmith's provides its luxurious services on some of the most valuable real estate in New York. The store's property covers a square city block of prime Manhattan retailing space. The five-story building, with its ornate facade, is being considered for landmark status. Less than half of the building space is used for salon activity; the rest is leased, particularly on the Madison Avenue side, to jewelers, fur boutiques, and other high-rent tenants.

The company's revenues are not revealed; it is privately held by Goldsmith, with a small percentage of stock held by long-term employees. But the company will admit that four out of five women who enter the store will purchase a gown there. Considering that in the peak wedding planning months it can take up to three weeks to get an appointment for viewing the gowns, Goldsmith's seems to be raking it in faster than a California guru.

But the salon is more than just a specialty shop churning out big profits, say insiders. Goldsmith's is a garment industry phenomenon.

"They really believe brides are special," says Ted Horwitz of Fabulous Fern, a chic florist that does a "substantial" amount of business with Goldsmith's. "Henry Goldsmith and his entire staff are romantics. After thousands of brides, a girl's love story can still get everybody who works with her misty-eyed. The personal, caring quality comes across for each customer. That's the real secret of their success."

Despite the glamour and the rushing cash-flow,

Goldsmith's is essentially a mom-and-pop operation, and like all such businesses faces a serious challenge in the future: Who will take over the company, and how will that affect it?

What does the founder intend to do on retirement? "Push up daisies," laughs Henry Goldsmith. Whatever the future holds, the present gives Retailer Goldsmith reason to cheer. Flower children or not, for this bridal outfitter, everything's coming up roses.

Chapter Six

July, 1971

Tuesday morning, 7:30 a.m., the day after the July 4th weekend. At that time Fifth Avenue might have been Fargo, North Dakota, for all the traffic there was to be seen. The sidewalk in front of Goldsmith's was bare, and the rested Manhattan air seemed almost fresh.

Mrs. Marshall had walked from her home on West Fifty-seventh Street. It was getting hotter by the minute, and she was sure that she'd be taking a cab home from work. But right now she wanted to walk in whatever pleasant minutes she could get—after all, the whole point of living in the city was to be able to walk from one place to another.

Her spine vibrated pleasantly from the spring in each step. Right now there was nothing on earth she would rather do than what she was doing: starting a brand-new day at Goldsmith's.

She rang for the security guard to open the door for her. As usual, she was the first one at the store. While she waited for him, she looked at the windows with proprietary satisfaction. Although her stock in Goldsmith's amounted to a small fraction of the business, she, and most of the other employees, felt a deep attachment to it. Henry had made it so.

Well, he paid her *well*. Other salons were constantly trying to woo her with offers of great pay raises. But when she told them what she was earning at Goldsmith's, their mouths dropped open. They never did present a better offer. Not that she would have gone with them if they had.

Now a number of bridal salons were closing. Some of the little dressmakers who used to sew up gowns had had to fold. And quite a few department stores had closed their bridal departments, in the general confusion of an era of great fashion changes. Bridal customers wanted to be part of the change, but they wanted, at the same time, to be traditional. It took an almost magical knack to please them. Many failed. Thank God, Goldsmith's in its regal splendor was untouchable.

After all, Goldsmith's was the first and last word in bridal wear. Everyone came to them, not just the rich, as *Thisweek* had implied. Of course the top of the line, the dresses whose prices ran into five figures, could be bought only by the wealthy, but there were many others for whom the bridal gown was the purchase of a lifetime. Entire families worked and saved for this thing of beauty, this symbol of love.

Bettina did not think their spending foolish at all. In fact, she preferred these modest customers to the more privileged ones for whom a wedding dress was little more than another beautiful ball gown.

True, buying a wedding dress, especially a very expensive one, could instigate an orgy of selfishness and spoiled complaining. The occasion could well set off a manipulative mother on a power trip, prod sisters and girlfriends into jealous fits, sink fathers into tightfisted resentment, even scare away skittish grooms.

But all in all, when you had a happy bride—and they did appear regularly—with a nice family and good friends, being a bridal consultant was just about the most wonderful profession on earth.

What better proof of this than this very morning? At the end of the bombardment of June weddings, at the beginning of the heavy season of summer, she could face the day with excited anticipation.

There was endless novelty in her work because each bride was unique. Each had a story of her own, sometimes romantic, sometimes funny, sometimes even tragic. And Bettina Marshall was determined to do her best for every one of them.

She sat down at her desk and began to work through the forest that had piled up in May and June, months too busy for any sort of paperwork. After a few minutes of ruthless weeding, the gold-stenciled top of her antique desk peeked through.

She paged through the albums of winter couture lines that had been gathered on her last trip to Paris. The trends in general fashion would eventually affect bridal lines—you had to stay on top of these.

Since the birth of the couture it had been customary for each designer to climax his showing of the season's line with the modeling of a wedding gown. In recent years, however, the wedding gown had become a vehicle for satire, whimsy, and schoolboy humor.

Mrs. Marshall laughed out loud as she came to the "gown" by the brilliant young Japanese couturier, Tazi. The model wore a classic, floor-length veil of silk illusion. But she held it apart to show a white sequin-covered bikini. The bra had the tips cut off, through which the model's nipples protruded. And the middle string of the bikini bottom was so thin—just a few sequins in width—that tufts of pubic hair stuck out on either side.

In real life, Mrs. Marshall chuckled, Tazi came up with dresses of such purity of design, that the line said "virgin" as emphatically as a Victorian heirloom. How cooperative Tazi could be. "Yes, Bettina-san, *hai*, as you wish," he would murmur on the transatlantic call. And then of course, he would go ahead and do exactly as *he* saw fit. But always in the spirit of her directions, always with a sense of service to the bride.

She leafed quickly through the folders for that of her favorite designer, Sebastian Dupre. She flipped right to the back page, the bridal dress.

She gasped. It was *black*. Black bombazine, a nineteenth-century mourning dress. Now she took a second look. It was an exquisitely cut off-the-shoulder dress that came to a tiny waistline and then shimmered out in yards of silk fabric. The

Queen Victoria veil, also black, came to a point above the model's marble-smooth brow. The design was superb. In white or ivory—which of course Dupre would execute for her—it would walk out of the store, even at $8,000 per dress. Hmmm, blood-red roses. There might be something to that . . .

Nothing wrong with tweaking convention's nose once in a while. Too few brides followed the dictum of "something new."

What was it that she had had new in her own wedding outfit? For heaven's sake, she was getting old, if she couldn't remember that! Of course, it was wartime, hard enough to get *anything* in those days.

Her dress had not been the white extravaganza she'd imagined since childhood. Her mother had been terribly disappointed about that. But the money and ration coupons were best spent on good gray flannel, which would make a long-wearing suit.

She had always been an excellent seamstress, and she put her all into the suit. It had class and sass. Ben had loved the way the jacket curved over her derriere. When she tried it on, he made love to her right there in the sewing room, amid the pins and tape measures. After a moment of ecstasy, she opened her eyes and saw the dressmaker's dummy looming above her. Thinking it was her mother, she cried out in terror. How Ben had laughed! So, she had shown the groom her wedding dress before the wedding.

Bad luck.

They hadn't counted on bad luck. They hadn't counted on anything that happened to ordinary people. They were special, different. Before Ben, her life had been utterly conventional. Before Ben, she was a person unworthy of anyone's imagination.

The widowed schoolteacher's daughter, neither here nor there. Clever with the hands. Doing minor alterations in one of San Diego's first fancy dress shops.

When she met Ben everything changed. Suddenly she was eating the hottest Mexican dishes in cantinas where nice girls didn't go. She was drinking tequila until her head floated like chiffon. They were having sex.

Sex. She thought she was pregnant. Ben was glad. He wanted to get married right away, but she delayed the date. She needed to finish the suit.

Ben was eighteen, she was nineteen. It was, at the time, a shocking secret for the bride to be older than her husband. On the other hand it was exciting to have secrets. It didn't seem as if any of her brides had such things as secrets anymore.

Something old. That was the shell-pink blouse of silk *mousseline*—from her mother's girlhood. It looked so creamy against the black velvet of the suit's collar.

It had been perfect suit weather; a typical San Diego winter day, clear and bright, crisp and clean but with no more harshness in it than there is in a McIntosh apple. She had worn the suit and carried a big bouquet of glorious white camellias from her mother's backyard.

Something borrowed. Time. She'd worn the suit the day after the wedding. And one more day after that.

Something blue. The Pacific. How gorgeous the ocean had been, all sapphires and diamonds. She didn't tire of looking at it, even when her arm got tired, waving and waving, bidding her husband good-bye. And the aircraft carrier! It had seemed invincible, a smoothly gliding Gibraltar. She wouldn't have believed, then, that it would be carrying her beloved off the edge of the earth.

How certain we are of everything when we're young, she thought. Back then she had believed that Life was life with Ben, that United States Navy carriers were unsinkable, and that work was something you did to while away the time until your tummy started to show.

She had gotten her period on the day after the telegram came. She was guilty about how relieved she was not to be pregnant. A baby, it was true, would have been something of Ben. But not enough.

She suspected that if she had had a child she would have ended up just like her mother: respectable and proper, but never quite on the same social footing as other women with the same or lesser educations, women with husbands, women with money.

She left Mother and memories behind, and went to Hollywood. Her needle flew; she got a job right away. The movies were glamorous all right, but the work was hard and not all that rewarding. The head of the studio's wardrobe department was a great designer, but an egomaniac. He was constantly looking over his shoulder at anyone who showed any talent.

He wasn't threatened by her. She never really had the genius of design. But she was good for something better than letting out doublets for overweight Romeos!

Veiled Truth opened briefly, closed quietly, and life went on pretty much as it had before. Then one fine day a dapper man with an Adolphe Menjou mustache came to the studio, and after many inquiries was introduced to her.

"My wife and I sat through that whole boring picture five times, just to see the wedding scene. We want to offer you a position in our company—dressing brides, coordinating their outfits, just as you did for Miss Astor."

Bridal salons. She'd never heard of them before. In San Diego girls made up their own wedding dresses or had a seamstress help them. She imagined the very rich went to designers. But you couldn't retail bridal dresses. No girl would want to marry in a gown she pulled off the rack. It sounded like a crazy idea.

But Henry Goldsmith had convinced her it did work. Of course bridal gowns were not really ready-to-wear. Except for the very cheapest, they were custom altered. Often elements of design were changed for the individual bride, even in the costliest gowns from Paris.

Henry's grandfather started the business, in a way. He went from one Russian village to another selling colored beads and ribbons to the peasant girls, who wove them into fantastic bridal wreaths and embroidered dresses. The czar hounded him over to the New World. Here the girls were less skillful but life was more forgiving. He managed to feed his family on his earnings from a pushcart laden with buttons and bows.

Henry's father was ambitious. He opened his own store on the Lower East Side, selling finer fabrics and trimmings. In those days, overbearing mothers came with their cowed teenage daughters in tow, to buy materials for bridal dresses, not necessarily white, that could be turned out for "best" after the wedding.

As was the custom, Henry began working in his father's store before he'd graduated to long pants. He too was ambitious, but he held his own counsel. After all, his father was doing very well.

Then the Depression hit. Young couples were putting off marriage "until better times," and mothers, less haughty now, found pieces of lace that would serve to upgrade an old Sunday dress.

"I think it's time to do something drastic, Pop," said Henry.

"Sure. Throw me out of a window."

"Seriously, Pop. I've got a great idea. I think we can make more money than ever before.

"See, today the textile industry is so hard up we can get the best fabrics for a fraction of their real value. And first-rate seamstresses are begging for work. Why don't we run up some really nice dresses, and sell them right here?"

"You're crazy! People don't have money for bread, for a roof over their heads. You think they'll spend money on fancy dresses that they wear once?"

"A bride's gown isn't just a fancy dress. It's the dream of a lifetime, it's the one chance for a bit of luxury in a hard, hungry life.

"Look, Pop, I really believe in this. I'm sure it can work. If you won't let me do it here, I'll go to one of the other stores, I'll borrow money . . ."

"Ha! Borrowing money today. From who, Rockefeller? Anyway, there's no borrowing here. We're a family business. You want to invest in this cockamamy idea, okay. Go ahead, prove you're a man. But if you lose the little money we have, it's your loss and your responsibility. Are you really willing to put your old man out on the street?"

Henry gulped. But he went ahead anyway. He sank every penny he could get into two gowns—one lace, one satin. They were barely draped in the window when four young women came into the shop. Two left with gowns; two left disappointed. From that day on he never lost money in providing quality, luxury, and style.

Above Henry Goldsmith's desk in the office with the imposing view of Fifth Avenue there hung a wedding photograph from the thirties. It showed a carefully assembled wedding party of no fewer than fifty-nine attendants. The bride and each bridesmaid and flower girl were exquisitely dressed in the unparalleled bias-cut satins of the period. The men, too, were bedecked in evening wear of long-forgotten elegance. It had been among the first truly luxurious weddings that Goldsmith had coordinated from beginning to end. Everything had turned out marvelously. Even in the forty-year-old photograph the flowers looked fresh.

The bride, the groom, and all of their perfectly posed attendants, were black. Goldsmith was emphatically correct in his prediction that couples throughout the country would want luxury and quality on their wedding day.

Henry's vision was exemplified by his collection of antique laces. It was displayed on the second floor of the salon in specially made cases. These were humidified to preserve the super-fine threads of ancient laces made of Flanders flax. Originally, these designs were made in damp cellars, for the thread was so fine it would break when worked in a dry environment.

Over the years, Henry, and then Bettina, found exquisite examples of old Brussels, made of thread invisible to the naked eye, by craftsmen who worked the pieces by touch. Also preserved were samples of old Mechlin, once a form of legal currency in European countries; rich Valenciennes, so hoarded by the French that the English, in order to get some, stuffed the body of the duke of Devonshire with it before he was brought home for burial; eighteenth-century Venice lace, whose artisans were forbidden to travel out of the city on pain of death and/or imprisonment of closest family members.

There were patterns grouped by convent, from the times when cloistered nuns had a monopoly on production, and abbesses competed with each other in producing designs of greater and greater refinement. There was French "servants' lace," so called because the extravagance of lace just before the French Revolution became immediately outmoded with the beheading of that lace-lover, Marie Antoinette. Noble ladies hastened to give their laces to their maids. Then, with the Empire, lace came back into fashion, but many of the greatest lacemakers had died without imparting their precious knowledge, so the noble ladies were reduced to raiding their servants' quarters for the irreproducible laces.

Mrs. Marshall frankly preferred the modern in wedding attire. She liked a fine antique as well as the next person, but weddings, she felt, should look to the future.

She started at the noise in the hall. The staff was beginning to arrive. She greeted everyone cheerfully, though many were hung over from weekend carousing. Bustling about, she tried to inject some of her energy into the staff.

Mrs. Marshall joined the seamstresses on their way down to the basement workshop. She gave out a constant stream of orders and advice.

"Clothilde, please call Roger Vivier in Paris and have them do up shoes with the brocade from Abraham for the Messenger wedding."

"Oui, oui, Madame Marshall. I hurry before ze time zone difference."

"Please do. And anyone else who needs to place orders to France, remember, you can't get anything done in August. So please, speed is of the essence.

"Darlene, can you find someone to bring a gown up to Boston on the train? The Cartwell wedding is July twenty-second.

"Mrs. Wong, go ahead and order the gown for Miss Simmons in a size ten. There is no way that young lady will be down to a size eight in six weeks. Tell them to leave the seams loose, though, I'm sure she'll lose *some* weight. I know you'll make it fit like a glove, but there are bound to be a lot of last-minute adjustments."

"That's life, Mrs. Marshall."

"Joanne, you said you wanted to see me about something, before the weekend?"

"Oh yes. I'm sorry I ran out, Mrs. Marshall, but I promised my husband we'd get going up to the mountains before the traffic got horrendous."

"Don't apologize, Joanne. I don't expect anyone to work

overtime, except when a customer's needs require it. Did you have a nice vacation?"

"Oh, it was great. Anyway, the problem. You know Dotty Malone, that cute little redhead? Well, she's in tears because her mother and her mother-in-law both insist on wearing minis. She says it's mortifying, and she just won't cooperate about anything else."

"Hmm. Let me handle this. I'm sure I can work out a compromise. Send them to me when they come in."

The lights went on in the workroom. It was a skier's fantasy, mountains and valleys covered in pristine white. Yards of fabric draped languidly from great bolts; multiple layers of rich materials covered every table.

She inhaled deeply of the musky scent of natural fibers, of the citrusy odor of dyes and bleaches. Years ago Mr. Goldsmith had decreed that they would make no dresses of synthetic material. It had seemed an eccentric order back when nylon seemed as good as silk and much more "modern." Now, of course, everyone realized the wisdom of upholding the standards of quality.

When fabric was rationed during World War II, Henry and the other leaders of the fledgling bridal industry petitioned Washington for an exemption. They got it too, on the grounds of national morale. While many brides, like Bettina, made practical outfits for their brief weddings, others marked a day of light in a time of darkness with weddings so elaborate, the very war ceased to exist for a few happy hours.

There was no rationing now, nor any shortage in this balmy young time. And, as that new song promised, "Ooh-ooh, child, things are gonna get sunnier."

Just look at those fabrics. She sighed with satisfaction. Summer fabrics: piqué and voile, dotted Swiss and muslin, organza and georgette, silk charmeuse and crepe de Chine, sheer handkerchief linen. Cool-weather fabrics, perhaps even more sumptuous, waited behind them. Crushed velvet and tissue challis, satin and peau de soie, taffeta and moire and crepe. And the trimmings! Mounds of seed pearls, chalk beads, crystals, mirror and milky sequins, mother-of-pearl paillettes, all brimming in their containers. Dozens of laces from every corner of Europe, spools of silver and gold thread, white mink and fox and ermine, feathery tulle, illusion, and netting, all gathered together like the treasure in a fairy tale.

The sixties had been a time of awe. A generation was getting used to unprecedented material wealth. Now, Mrs. Marshall predicted, it would learn to live more peacefully with the bounty. Mrs. Marshall was sure that classic styles would come into their own in the seventies. The craziness would go, but the materialism and the indulgence—whatever the moral consequences, were here to stay for another few years, at least.

Nine o'clock. The building was humming busily with preparations for the day. On the fifth floor the company's small staff of executives, accountants, and secretaries juggled the financial operations, filed papers, and coped with the jangling phones. On the fourth floor, a "library" of sample dresses, over a thousand of them, all in size eight, was added to and pruned, while dresses to be fitted that day were readied, and models changed into bridal underwear. On the third, maids-and-mothers, inventories and orders were being checked.

On the second floor, the saleswomen in charge of the accessories boutiques readied their wares. The offices of Mrs. Marshall and her assistants were alive with movement.

Only the main salon, where the bridal dresses were presented, remained hushed and quiet even after the doors were opened at ten. As far as Goldsmith's was concerned, the perfect wedding began the moment a young woman crossed the threshold. There, she came upon a magnificent bouquet of ten dozen white roses, replaced daily. She, and her shopping party, were guided to one of the twenty dressing suites. The group was seated on brocade-upholstered love seats and offered champagne. The thick carpeting was a warm coral, a color also included in the pattern of the silk wallpaper. All of the furnishings were fair copies of appointments once ordered for the last three kings of France. Sweet strains of Mozart wafted through the air.

The bridal consultant then entered into a lengthy conversation with her client. When was the wedding? Where? What did the bride have in mind for her dress? What was the budget? Albums with large color photographs were reviewed. At last the consultant spoke with her assistant, who ordered several dresses and a model to the suite.

The model displayed the dress, standing in front of an enormous three-way mirror on a stage raised to show train detail. More batches of gowns were brought down if the bride wasn't captivated by a handful of dresses.

A bride who was within two sizes of an eight could try on the dresses. Otherwise, she made an appointment to try on samples ordered in her size. During the long process of fittings, a dress might be redesigned several times. Sketches would be erased and discarded, if necessary.

The goal was to dress every bride exactly as she hoped to be, and hope was a constantly changing and ever-slippery thing. It was just possible, but highly imprudent, to begin this process less than a year before the wedding.

"Mrs. Marshall!" a shrill voice demanded. Bettina turned to see Melissa John shaking a wedding gown angrily. "I absolutely refuse to show this to Cookie Peters!" said Melissa, tossing the gown contemptuously.

Bettina caught it effortlessly, although it was a heavy, beaded dress. It was the dress Mae West might have worn, had the actress ever chosen to marry.

"What's wrong with it?"

"*Tina*. The girl's such a little mouse. I mean, she's sort of a shy violet. This get-up would be ridiculous on her."

"But her mother loves . . ."

"Swell. Let the damn mother wear the dress. She's doing everything else—including fucking the groom, for all I know."

"Melissa!" A gentle warning sounded in her voice. Then, because she was a pushover for Melissa, and because Melissa was right, "Let's find some other lines for Miss Peters."

Thank heavens for beautiful, beguiling Melissa. She had brought a new breath of life into the salon. Bettina had convinced her to model part-time for Goldsmith's. It paid better than waitressing, and she could continue with her acting lessons.

In the beginning, of course, they were all certain Melissa would be going to Hollywood—hadn't Chuck Lloyd practically promised her a screen test? But the weeks went by, then months. No word from Lloyd, and calls to his office were answered with the standard "I'm sure he has your number, miss. He'll call you."

Melissa's terrible disappointment did not keep her from making the most of the modeling job. Each time she modeled, she thoroughly studied the bride-to-be, then projected herself into the part. What a difference from the cool aloofness of the average model.

But the best of it, for Bettina, was her personal connection with the young beauty. Melissa usually left at two for her classes, but, the very first week, she reappeared at six, waited patiently by Bettina's office. Melissa smiled as she held up two tickets.

"Look! Freebies from the workshop. You like Shakespeare, don't you, Mrs. M.? Are you free tonight?"

She was. And then, on other nights, it was Bettina's treat, introducing Melissa to the ballet, to the opera. Melissa wouldn't be working at Goldsmith's for long. She had talent, she'd get her break soon. But for now . . . Tina felt a sweet pang in that place below her breasts, that place where nature and fate had declared nothing would quicken.

An assistant called from a phone, her hand over the mouthpiece, "Mrs. Marshall, are you free to see Mr. Goldsmith now?"

She went up to his fifth-floor office. A coffee service was already waiting on the table between the two sofas.

"How was your weekend, Teeny?"

"Marvelous. Rubinstein played 'Eroica' Saturday night." And Melissa had been poised half out of her seat in astonishment for the whole performance.

"The old guy is still tops, huh?"

"The best."

"Some of us feel our years more than others."

"You've had a few rough ones lately, Henry. It takes time to heal." Millie Goldsmith had died recently, after a long illness.

"I don't know, a lot of guys my age are thinking retirement. Enjoy life a little, while you can."

Bettina made a face.

"Oh, all right, I'm not the guy for retirement. Not that I could if I wanted to."

"Why do you say that?"

"Jeff is going to business school."

"That's wonderful. The financial world is much more complicated these days. The young people need the training."

Henry shook his head. "You can't keep 'em down in the *schmatte* business once they've seen Wharton. He'll want challenge, he'll want to use all that fancy training. Some conglomerate for Jeff, maybe. Or a multinational. Not Goldsmith's wedding gowns."

"There's money in them thar gowns, enough to impress the wage earners in a conglomerate."

"The money he gets anyway. Like Steve."

"Well, Steve is another matter. A Rhodes scholar—it would be criminal to force him into business when his heart is in literature."

"So tell me, who is going to run this place after me?"

Bettina's throat tightened. "You'll be running the ship for decades. You don't have to think about that now."

Henry smiled wryly. "Hell of a way to run a ship. Let's face it, Tina. You and me are the last of a breed, the business being our life. We'd go down with the ship—and the ship will go down after us."

Bettina shook her head adamantly. "You're perfectly fit. There are youngsters half your age who would gladly trade their bodies for yours. As for me, I'm almost fifteen years younger—practically a baby. Anyway, we're eternal!"

Henry came over and hugged her. Bettina's heart jumped. The smell of his soap, the smooth feel of his tropical wool suit, these sensations loosened feelings held in check for decades. What was she doing?

"Bettina Marshall," Henry said, and there were tears in his eyes, "you're the best friend I've ever had."

Bettina's heart expanded in pride and then sharply contracted with disappointment. Best friend. That's it?

She could take him up on it, she could say those words out loud. Ever since Millie's death he'd dropped a lot of little remarks like that. Not quite double-entendres, she thought of them. But she never took it further.

It had been too long since she had been that kind of woman. There were two kinds of women: women who loved and women who worked. There was no doubt which kind she was. Those women's movement people were saying a woman had the right and ought to have the opportunity to be both. God's truth. It's just that she, Bettina, had never seen a specimen like that in the flesh. And as a woman who worked, she couldn't gamble with her life's investment.

Besides, at their age . . . Did a man his age still . . . Did she . . . ?

Bettina flushed fiercely. "Look at that, I'm late for my appointment," she said, jabbing at her watch.

Henry didn't hide his feelings, his chin fell to his chest.

"Don't worry," said Bettina. "Nothing will happen to the store. Goldsmith's will be in business as long as there's such a thing as love."

She walked down the five flights, collecting herself along the way. Matters were exactly the opposite of what she pretended to Henry. What was between them would be controlled. Isn't it true that she controlled herself all these years, as would any sensible woman who . . . loved . . . yes, loved a decent married man. And she was still sensible, even if he was no longer another woman's husband.

But the business, that was a problem, and she could not think of a solution. Yes, the two of them were still in charge and still capable. But nothing was forever. Who would take over after Henry? And who would take over after her? They had good employees, sure, but no one who cared the way they did. No one with the heart and the guts to put everything on the line for Goldsmith's.

Her meeting today was for the wedding of the Lloyd girl. A shallow, silly thing rather obviously marrying someone closely matched for money and status. Why was it that people who already had enough of it continued to sacrifice so much for money? Was love utterly without value because it wasn't listed on the New York Stock Exchange?

But you never knew, sometimes the most unlikely couples

ended up happy. This pair knew exactly what they were expecting from each other, and because those expectations were clearly defined, neither of them was likely to be disappointed. Any shared interest or emotional warmth would be a surprise—and all the more appreciated. Wherever there is a wedding there is hope.

Mrs. Marshall was suddenly startled out of her ruminations. Miss Lloyd and her handsome mother had just come in for their appointment. Chuck Lloyd's daughter! There just had to be a way to find out the reason that Melissa had been abandoned by the agent.

Bettina could hardly wait to get through the preliminaries before she could broach the subject.

"Let's discuss the ways in which we can incorporate the stepfamilies into the wedding. It's a very common occurrence nowadays, and I have several suggestions for you to consider."

"Oh, no need for that," said the mother of the bride. "There will just be my people and Frederick's."

"Forgive me," said Bettina. "I met Mr. Lloyd briefly, and . . ."

"Oh, he won't be at the wedding," said the Lloyd girl.

Bettina was shocked and she looked it.

"We invited him, of course," the young woman hastened to explain, "but he can't possibly come. He's had a really major heart attack."

"How awful!" cried Bettina.

Both women nodded polite agreement.

"But please don't tell anyone, Mrs. Marshall. You see, Daddy won't be allowed to go back to work, and if word got out, his entire agency would collapse. We mustn't let that happen to the business."

No, we mustn't, thought Bettina. How cold blue blood could run. Poor Mr. Lloyd, poor in so many ways. But there was one silver lining, at least, although she could never say so out loud. Melissa would be staying in New York for a while.

Mrs. Marshall carefully planned out the Lloyd affair. While it wasn't the kind of wedding she enjoyed doing, being a professional meant you did a good job of it anyway.

Tomorrow would be a fresh new day. Who knew what happy

new brides she might meet, what joyful celebrations she would be called upon to orchestrate? Why, even as she stood here, disgusted with unfeeling aristocrats, worried about the future of the business, and mulling over her silly spinsterish crush, there were young people out there feeling the first stirrings of fresh, pure, *perfect* love; there were men and women pledging their hearts to each other with a simple, uncomplicated honesty. And eventually some of them would find their way to her door. And she would take care of them. So long as she breathed, she'd take care of them.

Chapter Seven

Cripple Hollow, Arkansas
September, 1971

P LEASE.

    Please, Daddy.

Please, Daddy, don't.

Don't, *don't*, please.

I'll be good, Daddy, I promise. I'll be the best girl in the whole wide world. If you don't.

Oh, Daddy, don't. *Don't*. It hurts.

I *do* love you, Daddy. But I hate when you do it. I *hate* it. It's wrong, Daddy. I just know it's wrong.

I know the Bible says to do everything you say. But, Daddy, it can't be right. And it hurts.

I'm so tired. Oh, Daddy. Please stop. Let me sleep, let me sleep.

Stop!

Please.

It was morning. Looked like the day would work out cloudy. Too early to tell. Supposed to be, summer was still here, but the cold bit into her nose and throat, making her feel like she was about to cry.

"Earline, wake up." Her ma at the door. All dressed in her

black dress with the little gray bells all over it, the thick brown sweater, two pairs of socks, and the Red Wing work boots, smallest men's size. Earline could not recall ever seeing Ma in a nightgown or a robe.

"I'm already awake, Ma."

"Well, then, get your lazy body out of bed. If you want to get to that kindygarten of yours, you'd best finish all your chores afore breakfast."

Earline got dressed as fast as she could, but quietly, so as not to wake her little sister, Ruthie.

Earline followed her ma out into the farmyard, their feet crackling on the frost. Ma barked out orders without looking back at her. Earline didn't mind. She looked up at Ma like a thirsty plant.

"When you done with that, come into the pighouse. I 'tend to butcher that old hog, like I been aiming to."

Earline hesitated. She gulped. Slaughtering horrified her.

"I ain't much help to that, Ma. I'll run in and get Mary Beth. Or Martha."

"Don't need your help, girl. Just want you to watch. Yer gettin' on to six, now. Should be learning women's work."

"But, Ma. They don't like me, see . . ." Earline couldn't understand it. Her ma loved those pigs, loved them more than her and Mary Beth and Martha and Ruthie. But it didn't bother her to kill them. Earline hated them, hated their mean eyes and their stubborn behinds. And she hated the pighouse, where Ma spent all her time, cooing and tending to the stupid things.

"They don't know about likin' or not likin', they're *pigs*. They're dependable. Now you just watch, girl. Watching will do you good, put some color into yer cheeks."

"Oh, Ma, it makes me sick to my stomach!" Earline blurted out.

"Don't see why. Sure don't get sick when they pass the chops to you at dinner. Nor ham or bacon, neither."

Earline cast about desperately for a way out.

"My shoes. I got my school shoes on. They'll get blood on 'em, Ma."

"Well, take 'em off," Ma said, her teeth clenched. "You can wash your delicate little white feet off at the spigot, missy."

Earline walked into the kitchen. Her face was the color of homemade soap. She clutched her shoes to her chest. Her feet were wet and blue.

Mary Beth was at the stove, with two iron skillets that were smoking up the kitchen. She had already set the table, packed lunches, and tenderly wakened Martha. Martha was helping Ruthie get dressed. Mary Beth was sixteen; there was a year between her and Martha, same as there was between Earline and Ruthie.

Daddy was sitting at the table, banging his fork against his coffee mug, as if the noise would make the coffee perk faster.

Mary Beth glanced at Earline, at her feet. She wore the same old-woman face she always wore. "Dish towel's clean. Dry your feet before you catch your death. I'll get another in a minute."

When Earline had finished putting on her shoes and socks, she helped Mary Beth serve breakfast. Martha came in. She had on two plastic bangle bracelets that made a fancy clacking sound when she moved her arm.

Little Ruthie fed herself scrambled eggs with a spoon. Her hair was the color of the eggs. She seemed to Earline like a summer field full of buttercups.

Ma came in. There were dark maroon stains on her sweater and dress.

Greeting no one, she sat down heavily and began to devour the plate of food that Mary Beth had put at her place.

Without looking up from her plate or turning her head, she spoke. Except for orders, she never addressed anyone but Daddy.

"I hear old Cunningham needs some lumber hauled. Why'nt you take the pickup into town and do it for him."

Daddy squirmed in his chair. "Waaal . . . I was figurin' on doing some planting today."

Ma snorted, loud as a horse in cold weather. "Plant what?"

Daddy shook himself a little, mustering his pride. "Sorghum, like my daddy did. And his daddy afore him. And maybe some of this here new stuff, soybeans."

Ma laughed. It was a caw-caw sound, like crows make. "You ain't planting nothing, Earl. Ain't nothing gonna grow on this land but the sage grass. You know as well as I do that the soil is shot all to hell. You just makin' up excuses not to go into town. Lord never made a man as scared of a day's labor as you, you piece of manure."

Daddy seemed to shrivel in his chair, like a weed protecting itself in time of drought. Mary Beth and Martha exchanged glances. They knew why Daddy hated to go into town. People made fun of him. "Paaa Prewitt," they drawled at him. They knew what he did. There weren't many secrets in this neck of the woods.

After breakfast, Mary Beth washed the dishes and Earline dried.

Earline was exhausted. Daddy at night and Ma in the morning was more than she could bear. A dish slipped out of her hand and crashed to the floor. Earline started crying in great gulping freshets.

"Never you mind, Earline, I'll clean it up in a jiffy," said Mary Beth. "Now, baby, you stop that. No cause to go on so, nobody's riled about that old saucer. Earline, come on, we got millions of 'em in the attic."

"It's not that. It's, it's . . . Daddy."

Mary Beth looked quickly around the empty kitchen. "Now you hush. No sense saying something you'll be sorry about later."

"Mary Beth, Mary Beth, I've got to tell you, I've got to tell *somebody*. I need help. Daddy does something bad to me. Somebody's got to make him stop!"

"Shh, shh," said Mary Beth, with the unconvincing bluster of a threatened chicken.

"If you knew, Mary Beth, what he . . ."

"Hush! I do. Hush! Don't talk about it. Don't say one word. But for your information I know more about it than I'd ever want to know about anything as long as I live."

"Well, then help me!"

"Child, child," said Mary Beth. She had lifted her hands to

her face. Suds dripped down to her elbow. She looked at Earline with her old-grandmother eyes. "You make him stop with you, Earline, he'll just start up on Ruthie. That's what happened with . . ." Mary Beth went back to the dishes.

Earline thought about what Mary Beth said. She thought about it all morning at the Head Start. She thought about it at her afternoon chores. After supper, she dried the dishes with Mary Beth and stared and stared at her. But their parents and Martha were watching television in the parlor, so they couldn't talk.

But that night Daddy came to her again. This time she kicked and bit him and fussed so that Ruthie almost woke up.

"You don't want me to hold you," Daddy whined.

And she *did* want him to hold her. She did want him to love her. She wanted somebody to love her and it made her sick.

And when she lay still and let Daddy do it, she kept quiet, even though it hurt.

She swore to herself: I'm gonna tell.

I'm gonna tell.

I'm gonna tell tomorrow.

Morning at last. She followed Ma into the pighouse.

"I got something important to tell you, Ma." Now that she had made up her mind, the words came easily. She'd tell now, before Mary Beth made her change her mind.

Ma didn't look at her, in the same way she never looked at her.

Earline placed herself squarely in front of the pig Ma was dealing with. Finally, she had Ma's attention, the way a piglet gets a sow's attention.

She told.

Ma's face swelled up. The skin around her eyes puffed up so that her eyes looked like tiny blue buttons sewn into a stuffed animal.

"Liar!" she screamed. The pigs squealed their agreement.

"Jesus will punish you for your filthy lies. Little whore liar! I'll clean your filthy mouth out!"

She picked Earline up by her hair and dragged her over to

the part of the pighouse where there were shelves with supplies. She snatched a bottle off a shelf. It was the disinfectant used to clean the pens.

She pulled Earline's hair back. It forced her mouth open. Ma poured the disinfectant into her mouth.

Earline howled. It was a sound so fierce, so long, so frightening that it rose above the squealing of the animals. From the house, Daddy, Mary Beth, and Martha—still in her nightgown—came running.

Mary Beth tried to wash away the stuff with water from the spigot, but Earline kept screaming.

The two girls hoisted up their little sister and ran with her to the truck. Daddy drove hell-bent to the doctor in town. Mary Beth cradled Earline's head in her lap and tried to drown out her screams with crooning.

When they reached the doctor's office, their hearts sank. Doc Bailey's car was not parked in front. However, there was a new young doctor who immediately began to treat Earline.

Mary Beth had had the presence of mind to bring along the bottle of disinfectant.

"I doubt that she swallowed any of this stuff," said the young doctor. "One hit of it stings so bad that it cures all curiosity. Still, I'd like to keep her here in the infirmary for a few hours, for observation. And don't worry, when the burn heals, there won't be much scarring. At most, her lips will look a little swollen and red. Could be kinda sexy when she grows up," he said, winking, man to man, at Earl Prewitt.

Mary Beth helped Earline, who had received a sedative, into a paper examination gown, and tucked sheets and blankets around her. The doctor looked at Earline.

Her hair was so light and fine it seemed to be made of cellophane. Her skin was so pale that her face seemed a film on the white pillowcase. Wrapped in the big paper gown, she was like an angel planted on a Christmas tree. Pale blue eyes painted on a papier-mâché face, frail wire holding up the robe and wings.

"Why don't you stay with her a little," the doctor said to Mary Beth and Daddy. He indicated that Martha come with him to his adjoining office.

"That's more for the parents' benefit than for little Earline's," the doctor confided to Martha.

"Mmm," said Martha, amused that the doctor thought Mary Beth was Earline's mother.

Martha pulled the belt on her robe tighter. She was still in her gown and robe but had already put on her eyeliner and teased the top of her hair.

"So, ah, you're the big sister, right?"

"Yeah, I'm Martha." She smiled a very sweet, slightly spoiled smile.

The belt accented her narrow waist and rich hips. She could see the doctor exploring her cleavage with his eyes.

"So, you're what, nineteen?"

"Mmm," she said. There were two kinds of Prewitt women, the ones who ripened before their time, like her and Aunt Thelma, and the ones who never ripened, just grew like boys and then shriveled away, like Mary Beth and Ma.

"I'm from the Chicago area," the doctor confided.

Martha looked at him as if this was the most fascinating information in the world.

"Up there, if a kid like Earline came in with a burn like that to an ER, they'd assume she was trying to commit *suicide*. You see, kids from the ghetto have no childhood. They have adult problems from the start."

"Sounds just terrible," said Martha. The word "terrible" came out like a purr.

"It is. It's just like the movie *Midnight Cowboy*. Have you seen it?"

"No, I haven't," said Martha, her lashes sweeping her cheeks coyly. "But I understand it's going to be showing next week over in town."

"Yeah, that's what I hear. Maybe we can catch it. I wouldn't mind seeing it again, terrific film. Gee, it's about two years old, though, and here it is, just coming into the local Bijou. I guess that's the price you pay for all this rustic tranquility."

"It isn't called the Bijou, it's called the Imperial."

The doctor laughed. "Right. Heart of the Ozark entertainment center. Say, hey, I don't mean to be insulting. I really admire you mountain folks. And not just compared to the concrete jungle. Even compared to the suburbs.

"I spent my whole life in suburbia and let me assure you, it is not what it's cracked up to be. I mean, our parents moved out from the cities to raise us in a supposedly decent environment, and you know what we got? Hypocrisy, materialism, conformism, that's what. Behind every decorator drape and color-coordinated window shade there's a dirty secret. Oh, the stories I can tell you. Well, maybe I'll get a chance to tell you one of these days. Now I better get back to work.

"But just let me leave you with this: Thank your lucky stars that you got to grow up in a place like this. The people here are rooted in the land, they're tuned into authentic things. The air is pure and the people are pure, know what I mean? Authentic.

"It's maybe one of the last places on earth where honest folks can raise girls as wholesome as you are. And just look at that little sweetheart of a sister you've got. I get positively misty. In a little while she's gonna feel better. And having learned her little lesson about experimenting with unknown liquids, she'll go back to the farm, and grow up with sunshine, with the smell of the rain-soaked earth, with the smell of apple blossoms.

"She's gonna be one of the very few of the Vietnam Generation, one of the *very* few to grow up free, happy, and strong."

Chapter Eight

Brooklyn
September, 1971

THIS WAS IT. Two more days and Erica was going up to Radcliffe. For a while, after she had agreed to go, she had gotten used to the idea a bit and even relaxed. But now, as D-Day approached, she felt panicky.

She hadn't eaten a bite in two days, and she felt light-headed. What had she gotten herself into? Harvard had not been created for the likes of America Valenta. Cliffies were supposed to be the kind of girls who were photographed in head shots in the wedding section of the Sunday *Times*. When Harvard went slumming in the middle class, they generally went for smart-as-whips, like Buzzy Alpert, who talked politics in Greenwich Village coffee houses.

The Founding Fathers never had in mind a grind from the Crest Motor Lodge. Well, damn it, she grinned suddenly, she would make them stand up on their Persian carpets and take notice! Watch out, Harvard!

She sat in the kitchen with a cup of tea, feeling warm and cozy, relishing the fleeting comforts of home.

"E-rrri-ca!"

It was her mother, with the singsong, flirtatious tone of voice she used when she was happy. Her white head popped into the kitchen.

"Are you busy?"

"Of course not, Mama. Just thinking."

"Well, if you're not too bu-usy, I want to show you somethi-ing!"

She took her daughter by the hand and led her to Erica's own bedroom.

"*Ta-dum, ta-da,*" she announced, throwing the door open with a flourish. "For you, Miss Radcliffe Lady. Straight from the September college issues of the high-class fashion magazines."

Erica's mouth dropped open. There on her bed, in geometric array, was an entire fall wardrobe.

There were stacks of wool sweaters with patterned yokes, there were pastel cotton blouses with Peter Pan collars and roll-up sleeves, there were kilts with safety pins and wool skirts with accordion pleats. There were even plaid tams and tasseled knee socks.

It would have made a perfect send-off to a Seven Sisters school—in 1962. But now it was ridiculous! Now everyone wore jeans and T-shirts and sweatshirts. The neat little coed didn't exist anywhere but in the minds of threatened fashion editors. Erica wanted to scream.

"They're gorgeous, Mama, but they're much too expensive. Please take them back."

"Ooch, I knew you would say that. I said to Papa, 'You'll see, all she say is too expensive.' But I fix you, Erica! I buy on sale—one-third off—and no returning. Now you must take them and enjoy no matter how much you complain."

Erica stretched her lips into a smile. "Thank you, Mama."

"What kind of thank-you is that? For the scholarship man you say 'thank you' like that. For your Mama you bend down and give a big hug to squash the ribs!"

Erica buried her face in her mother's hair, white as scouring powder. She wouldn't cry. That had been her graduation present to herself. She'd never, ever cry about anything again.

Dinner that night was very quiet.

Afterwards, her father hemmed and hawed. Mama left the last of the dishes to dry in the rack and announced she was going back to work. Papa shifted in his chair.

"Please, Erica, sit."

She sat down next to him at the table. The marble design in the Formica had faded and been polished away to milkiness.

Erica made her heart do its new, all-purpose grown-up routine. Nothing could make her cry. Nothing could hurt her. *Think of him as a stranger would. He is old. That's a fact. It need not affect you. You are going away, you are going to be separate. He is old, but that has nothing to do with you.*

Jaroslav Valenta's callused hand swept through his hair. The hand was not really that of a workman. The fingers were slender, the movements graceful. He had been a master craftsman, an artist. His hands would never forget that.

He is trying to tell me something, thought Erica, forcing herself to be dispassionate. His farewell speech.

Jaroslav stopped his fidgeting and looked at her. He was trying to span the great divide of years and language and culture, to tell her, and teach her, and warn her, and protect her.

"Mama and me, we are so proud of you." Emphasis and emotion made him roll his r's even more than usual. "Your grandparents, you know, did not even know what is a university. But Mama and me, we know, we know. And we are so proud!"

"It's nothing, Papa. If times had been different, if it hadn't been for the war and the communists and having to come here, you both would have gone to college. Why, you'd both be Ph.Ds, I bet."

"No, no," her father waved his supple hand in dismissal. "We have not what it takes. We have never had your mind or your spirit, my darling America.

"Now you will enter another world, a wonderful place for your talents."

Jaroslav hesitated. "It will be nice, also, to meet boys on your level. Fine boys from intelligentsia."

Erica stared at the floor. Her father was shifting uncomfortably in his chair. Oh God, please, not a boys-only-want-one-thing lecture. Especially at her. Imagine, a girl who can't get a prom escort in Brooklyn, the subject of lusting young gods from Harvard! She'd be lucky to get a date—ever.

She wondered if there were any male equivalents of a working-class, ordinary girl who got into Radcliffe by accident. Why not? If the admissions committee at Radcliffe could screw up, so could the one at Harvard. Of course, what was the likelihood that there would be a really *tall* one . . .

Jaroslav finally managed to tear the words from his lips. "I am not so smart, like university."

"Oh, Papa," Erica sighed.

"No, please," he continued. "You must find advice from other people, people who know how to live American. This I do not know.

"But other things I know. I know how to live in bad places, bad times. I have seen many things with my eyes, many not nice things. And this, this I have to tell you, my beautiful Erica.

"In the world of men, my Erica, a woman must always be . . ."

He had half risen from his chair. His face was red with effort, with the extreme frustration of trying to find the right word in an alien tongue.

"A woman must always be . . . Arrogant!"

He sat down, satisfied.

"Arrogant?" asked Erica. She was confused. This wasn't what she expected him to say. Not at all. What on earth was he talking about? She had to shake her mind free of its own reveries. Let's see, what could he have meant?

"You mean . . . proud . . . or honorable."

"No, no. I mean *arrogant*. Exactly."

He looked so pleased, she did not have the heart to argue with him.

They hugged each other, long and hard. His mind was somewhere else, thought Erica, somewhere in Europe. She would never understand where it was coming from; she'd long ago given up the effort. But what did it matter? They loved each other. Even if they didn't understand each other, love was enough.

Erica wished there was some way to tell him. To tell him that she felt what he felt, believed what he believed. That,

Harvard or no, she would never abandon the values he had taught her.

Although she could not say it in words, she wanted to promise that she would be all the things he wanted her to be. Be the woman he would be proud to call daughter.

She opened her mouth, but the thoughts became tangled before they became words, as if she too were attempting to speak in a strange, baffling language.

"I love you, Papa," she said in Czech.

Cambridge, Massachusetts
December, 1972

Erica twitched with impatience as she listened to the speakers in the vast library of Spence Hall. She calculated how long she would have to stay before she could respectably leave. Other girls would be doing that, too, girls going on dates.

That, unfortunately, was not her reason for going. Over a full year at college and not one single date. She just couldn't prettify that statistic. Why did her height mean so much to the guys? The girls didn't mind, the professors didn't. Why were boys so prejudiced?

It wasn't her attitude, either. Freshman year she had rushed over to Buzzy Alpert at a mixer. He looked up at her and cocked an eyebrow, "Have we met?" And Buzzy knew her, really knew her personality. If he could be that way, what could you expect from strangers?

Academically, Radcliffe was just as competitive as she had expected. There were brilliant golden girls who confounded you with their easy intelligence and their great looks. There were intense bookworms, ruthlessly aggressive. There were the "artists" whose shortcomings were excused as eccentricity. Erica couldn't match their style, but it was amazing how far you could get by applying your rear to a library chair.

At least she could honestly say she was too busy to socialize. She had to study hard and long for good grades, and now she had to take a part-time job, as well. The scholarship was supposed to cover everything but incidentals. The "incidentals" were what did her in. Others might have been embarrassed to write to Daddy to cover these expenses, but Erica couldn't even allow her parents to *know*.

After the first semester, she dropped her original intention of majoring in math. She wasn't disappointed; in the adult world, you had to be flexible. She now concentrated on American History. That seemed much easier, and it was more, well, feminine. Besides, her folks were enormously proud of her studying it.

She'd pretended to her parents that the subsidies were adequate, otherwise they would have started sending her money, and she knew they couldn't afford to. They would force her to take it, though, if they knew she supported herself by waitressing in a crummy roadhouse.

And now, sitting in this stuffy formal library, enduring a boring scholarly exercise, she couldn't help thinking that she could be at the Dew Drop Inn instead, making tips. No, she mustn't think that way. It was a low-class, dirty job, and it was embarrassing to realize she liked it so much more than going to classes in the finest university in the country.

On the other hand, she stood a chance of making seventy-five dollars here. Seventy-five bucks was the honorarium to be bestowed on the maiden who would present the best undergraduate paper in American History. Old Mr. Spence, the benefactor of this great hall, had so provided in his will.

She was the second to read her paper. It was about Thomas Jefferson. She had always admired Jefferson, and even back in Czechoslovakia, Jefferson had been her father's boyhood hero.

Her voice rang out confidently, as she read the paper. And then, right in the middle, she came upon a terrible realization. Everything to be said about Jefferson had already been said. There was nothing to explore but ridiculous minutiae. Was she going to spend her life doing this? And academia paid so little!

She forced a cheerful note into her voice as she came to the little joke that ended her presentation.

The professors guffawed as if she were George Carlin. Erica beamed at them. She might win the seventy-five dollars after all!

There was another gentleman with the profs who was being

honored tonight for his addition to the library of some newly discovered letters of Chester Arthur. He looked terribly bored. Well, it was all kind of silly.

Erica listened politely to the other speakers. It was a good opportunity to do a bit of mental review. What was she going to do with her life? An academic career wasn't really what she wanted, even if she could make it big there. But what was it that she *could* do? Right now she was barely making a living at unskilled labor. How foolish it had been to assume that reasonable goals would just materialize at college.

A wave of laughter rippled over the audience. The speaker, a naturally cherry-lipped blond in a real Irish fisherman's knit, had said something witty about the Civil War. Erica rolled her eyes. She reviewed the portraits of generations of Spences, which lined the walls with pompous gloom.

A refreshment break was announced. Now, thought Erica, getting to her feet like a sprinter. She murmured politely to the two profs and the department chairman and made a point of shaking hands with the savior of Chester Arthur's letters. He was introduced by the chairman as Mr. Whittaker Spence Eaton II, whose grandfather, not so coincidentally, was the benefactor of the undergraduate papers.

She apologized for leaving early.

"Quite all right, Miss Valenta. Excellent paper, excellent."

Erica resisted making a face. She had glanced at him once or twice, and he hadn't even been listening.

Brian Mulligan, owner of the Dew Drop Inn, was waiting anxiously for her.

"Hey, Erica, forget the hopheads for a minute, I want you to see the stuff the accountant screwed up. Jesus, if I get taxed on the . . ."

"I'm sorry, Brian, I really need the tips tonight. Why don't I take a look at the books when business levels off?"

"Aw come on, Erica, I can advance you what you need. I'd rather close the office up early tonight and get to the Drop Inn Two."

Erica mumbled something else. She didn't want the advance, she wanted the extra money in the tips. Sure, it was more interesting to do the books and gab about business with Brian, but she needed a new winter coat. She finally agreed to take the books home with her and do them at night.

She sighed. More hours shaved from studying time. But she had to do it. Brian had been very good to her. And he *listened* to her. And the business underpinnings of the bar were fascinating.

It was weird, but of all the successes she'd had at Harvard none made her prouder than having advised Brian to open another tavern. He had, and it was thriving. And he didn't hesitate to give praise where it was due, and—more to the point—a gift of cash.

Just her luck that Brian was gay.

Erica rushed to change into her uniform. She cringed at the odor of the ladies' room. Stale booze and vomit, no deodorizer could mask it.

She'd just delivered her first order when three young men in expensive ski jackets walked in. It happened fairly often, rich guys coming in to slum along the townies who made up the bread-and-butter clientele. She moaned as they sat down at one of her tables. Rich guys were lousy tippers.

One of the three was handsome beyond belief. He was very tall, maybe six-five. He moved with easy, muscled grace. His strong-jawed face was freshly tanned. The burnished color made his eyes glow like polished stones and his shining white smile irresistible.

Erica felt a violent clenching in her stomach. Just because she had no dates didn't mean she was a stranger to desire. How nice it would be to go up to him, flirt and tease like the other barmaids. But whoa, she had to keep her mind—and her body—on the goal. Right now, that was financial survival.

And dear God, survival wasn't enough. Soon her parents would have to retire. What would they live on? And what would *she* do? She wished she had gone to Brooklyn College, as she had originally planned. By now she would be on her way to a teaching degree. Not the most lucrative of callings, to be sure, but safe and secure. What did she have now? A handful of tips and uncertainty.

The tanned giant hooked into her eyes. Erica became acutely conscious of her untrimmed hair and clodhopper shoes. Well, the shoes were comfortable, she argued silently, and she was the number one girl in the place. One of the other barmaids looked like Farrah Fawcett, and you would think she made plenty in tips. She got plenty of hassle, all right, but not enough tips to make any of it worth her while.

Erica's eyes bounced back to the bronze god.

"Hey, gorgeous," he called.

Erica whipped around. She saw the Farrah-twin going off with an order.

"I mean you, Veruschka!"

Her cheeks burned. She didn't look anything like the famous model, except for her height. She wanted to die of shame.

The teasing smile disappeared from the boy's beautiful mouth. He searched her face.

Erica felt her tongue swell in her mouth. She had to say something, it was her job.

"Can I get you a drink?" she managed to choke out.

"Got any Heineken?" asked one of his companions.

"We only carry domestic brands," she said. Now go away, all of you. Please.

"In that case," said the god, "how about your phone number?"

"What?" said Erica.

"Your phone number."

"I don't understand." Was she back in Spence Hall, day-dreaming?

He held out his hand and grinned, clearing the smoky lounge with Aspen sunshine.

"I should really introduce myself. Whittaker Spence Eaton. The Third. People who love me call me Whit."

It was Erica's third winter in Boston. Before, she had always thought of the season in that city as something to be endured. It was the device of a Calvinist God who would test the mettle of the Elect, see if they were worthy of mastering New England.

But with Whit the Boston winter took on a luminous, fairy-tale face. The sky, she discovered for the first time, was a certain sharp shade of blue, just so, that could not be seen anywhere else or in any other season. The cold itself, once her sworn enemy, was now a bright lens through which she could see the crystalline days and the star-sequined nights as never before.

He was her savior and Erica worshipped him. He gave of himself constantly, his attention, his love, and asked practically nothing of her in return. All her projects, at school, at the Inn, seemed like dust compared to Whit's brilliant presence. She abandoned everything gladly to spend every minute she could with him.

Her grades began to slip, Brian complained, but nothing mattered. Whit's love created a shield of armor around her, and a buffer of goose down. The dean sent her terse letters, her bankbook gathered dust. Still, it didn't matter. How petty both the academic dog-paddling and the money-grubbing seemed now.

Whit was the first man she had ever slept with, but it would have been wrong to say that he deflowered her. Quite the opposite. He had gently broken the shell around her, and she had emerged, wet, rejoicing, ready to fly into the sun.

For Erica there had always been one thing more important than love. Simon and Garfunkel didn't sing about it, and Erich Segal didn't write about it; still, in the romantic reaches of her mind, she cherished the dream of *respect*. And Whit realized the dream. He respected her. More than that, he honored her, he was proud of her. For the first time in her life, Erica felt proud of herself. How could she fail to? Didn't Whit Eaton, the golden, beautiful, aristocratic boy, adore her above all the women he knew, all the highborn women who would die for a crumb of his attention?

She had no secrets from Whit. He knew about the Crest, about Tangee, about how she'd hustled the professors shamelessly to get the seventy-five-dollar honorarium in history. And still, he honored her.

Whit took her to elegant places and instead of acting ashamed of her unsuitable clothes and Brooklyn manners, he went out of his way to introduce her to his friends. Once he spotted a relative at the opera, another time he hailed his father's top banking client at a restaurant. Both times he pushed his way over to introduce Erica, his hand possessively around her shoulders.

And he didn't ask her to change. He did not urge her to quit working as a barmaid and find a more genteel job. He did not insult her by offering her money to buy clothes more suitable to the companion of a Boston Brahmin.

And when he made love to her, finally, after a long courtship that left Erica aching with desire, it was with such solemn tenderness, such worship, that you would have thought it was he who was the handyman's son, privileged and lucky beyond dreams, to melt in union with a princess.

Oh, the loving. It was so sweet, sweet as if life before that had been lived in brine. Erica would look down at her thin legs, tangled in after-love with Whit's shapely, muscular ones, and wonder: What was she doing here? How could she deserve this? She had given nothing to anyone in this life. How could she deserve to be the recipient of so much? First from the most wonderful parents in the world, now from the most wonderful lover.

She loved him. She adored sleeping with him. She wanted desperately to marry him and make it last forever.

"I'm planning to get married," Whit told his parents at breakfast. There was a long minute filled with the tinkling of sterling on china and the rustle of starched linen napkins. Crystal goblets, filled with orange, tomato, and cranberry juice, glowed like jewels.

"Wedding plans? Again?" said his mother, pronouncing the last word to rhyme with "rain."

"Yes, again," said Whit, very deliberately.

"Who, or shall I say, what, is this one?"

"Her name is Erica Valenta. She serves drinks at the Dew Drop Inn. Her people are from Eastern Europe. They work in this, uh, transient's motel in Brooklyn. You wouldn't know them."

The senior Mr. Eaton looked up from his egg substitute and asparagus vinaigrette. "Why don't you have her come for dinner tonight?" he said lightly.

He threw a furtive look at his wife, signaling her to keep quiet. It was all she could do to keep a wad of toast from falling out of her mouth.

After their son was safely off to work, Mrs. Eaton hissed, "Spence! What in heaven's name are you up to?"

"I know the girl."

"Dear God!"

"It's not what you think, dear. I heard her in December in Spence Hall, at that American History business. Spoke about some southerner, I believe. And afterwards, damned if she didn't come right over and shake our hands like some sort of Irish politician! Tall as a lamppost, she was."

"It doesn't sound like the right one. You know as well as I that Whit hardly favors intellectual girls."

"Well, she's something of a Radcliffe charity case. You know, get them away from their deprived environment and all that."

"Even so, Spence, you know how Whit is about his female companions. If he discovers that we consider her even faintly acceptable, he'll drop her immediately."

"By now our Whit may be too besotted to recognize that. After all, she does have the two qualities he most values in a woman. She *is* both needy and pitiful."

"Well, she sounds every bit as horrid to me as the 'dancer' and the K mart girl, though a tad better than the Negress from Roxbury, to be sure."

"My dear, I think we should let him do it this time."

"Spence, are you mad? You know he never goes through with his threat to marry against our will. Eaton: name, house, and fortune, will always be his true love. This infatuation with common types will pass."

"I don't think so. I think our boy has got himself a serious problem here."

"Well, perhaps we should encourage him to see a, a

specialist, then." Wild horses could not induce Mrs. Eaton to use the word "psychiatrist."

"It could take them years, perhaps forever, to set him straight. By that time Whit will undoubtedly have married someone even less suitable than this girl. I say, let's take advantage of this fluke of fate—a girl obscure enough to pass, or at least keep covered—and have him marry the chit. With full legal precautions, of course."

"Perhaps you are right, dear. And I do so want the boy to be happy."

"Mama, is Papa there?"

"Yes, darling, he's right here."

"Good. I don't want him to miss this."

"Why you calling today, Erica?"

"This can't wait till Sunday! I have some wonderful news."

"Oh. About that boy you go to fancy places with?"

"Yes, Mama, Whit. He's asked me to marry him. And I said yes. Subject to Papa's approval, of course."

"Oh my goodness! Here's Papa, you put your young man on over there."

"No, he's not here now. We're going to come down next week and Whit will ask him personally."

"Come here, to the Crest?"

"Yes. Don't worry, I've explained everything to him. He's wonderful, he understands completely. You never have to be ashamed with Whit."

"But, Erica, a boy like that in such a place . . ."

"I said don't worry. You'll see. Everything will work out like a fairy tale."

"I don't know, Erica. I am still worried. You sure everything is okay? This boy comes from such a high-class family, he is so handsome, he has such a good job . . ."

"In his father's bank, as a matter of fact."

"Yes, yes. Just like in fairy tales. But life is not a fairy tale . . ."

"What are you trying to say?" Erica could feel something

cold rise in her. "That he's too good for me? That I don't deserve a man who is handsome and rich!"

"No, of course not, darling, it's just that, just that . . ."

"That there must be something wrong with him if he wants someone like me!"

"No. No, I can't explain in English. Oh, Erica, you know Papa and me want the best for you. We want to be sure you'll be happy . . ."

"I *am* happy. I'm in love with the most fantastic guy . . ."

"Really, darling? It's not just the money and the family, yes?"

"Of course not!" What an infuriating conversation. Why couldn't her parents just be happy, for once? Why couldn't they accept that she had realized her dream? *Their* dream. Why couldn't they give her credit for doing anything by herself, for once?

"Look. We're coming down next week. You'll meet him and you'll see. You'll fall in love with him just as I did."

"Yes, yes, I'm sure you're right, darling. Now here is Papa, he congratulate you personally."

"You congratulate the man. It's proper etiquette to say 'good luck' to the woman." She'd been doing some reading. As Mrs. Whittaker Spence Eaton the Third, she'd be expected to know these fine points.

"Oh yes, Erica, you know that. You know we wish you good luck a million, trillion times!"

"Well, this *is* a surprise! My star pupil apparently remembers her old school with a shred of fondness. So how are you, Erica? How is Radcliffe? You're doing us proud, I bet. We've got two girls, excuse me, women, in this year's senior class who are following in your footsteps. Can you keep a sisterly eye on them?"

"Sure, Mr. Birnbaum." Whit had just assumed that Erica would be dropping out of college to get married, and, the way her grades were going, she was almost relieved to do so. But it would be difficult and embarrassing to explain that now.

"Great! And while I have you on the hook, when will you be able to address the student body at Assembly?"

"Oh, I don't think I can do that, Mr. Birnbaum. You see I'm getting married . . ."

"Isn't that nice. Congratulations, Erica. I wish you all the best."

"Thank you." Erica felt just a twinge of disappointment. Mr. Birnbaum wasn't as excited about the impending wedding as she would have liked. If only there were some tactful way to describe how handsome Whit was, how prestigious his family . . . Then Mr. Birnbaum would shut up about those imaginary academic exploits. Boy, would he ever be surprised to find her succeeding at winning the Big One, the one that counted for women, not some bookworm Women's Libber's consolation prize.

"Actually, the reason I called was because I was wondering if you have an address for Tangee White. I haven't been in touch with her for ages, and I was hoping to invite her to the wedding."

More precisely, Erica wanted to ask Tangee to be her maid (matron?) of honor. Her future mother-in-law would probably spring a leak when she saw Tangee. She was willing to accommodate Mrs. Eaton in virtually everything, but she would stand firm on this one. Tangee was the best friend she'd ever had and that was that.

"Gee, Erica, I'm sorry to disappoint you, but I've been unable to get in touch with Tangee. At one point I even drove into East New York to her old apartment. The people there, and the neighbors, either didn't know where she went or were unwilling to tell me. I must have knocked on half the doors in the project, and had my car radio and hub caps stolen for my trouble. The city agencies were unwilling to help me contact her. Frankly, I've given up the quest. Like so many welfare mothers, she seems to have been swallowed up by the system.

"I can't tell you how much this hurts me, Erica. Tangee— like you—was one of the best hopes of my career as an educator."

"Well, thanks anyway, Mr. Birnbaum. It was good talking

to you. If you can make it to Boston on the day before Election Day . . ."

"Oh, a school day. No, I'm afraid I can't. But please keep in touch. One of these days, I'll be the hit of some party because 'I knew Erica Valenta back then.' "

Erica hung up. The conversation left her both guilty and relieved that she wouldn't have to introduce Tangee to the Eatons.

Maria Valenta shimmered like a pearl. This was her moment of glory. This was the day she had dreamed of since she first discovered the fantasy land of Fifth Avenue.

The bronze doors opened before her like waves in a biblical epic. Erica followed behind her, diffidently.

"I am Mrs. Valenta and this is the bride, Erica Valenta. We have an appointment!"

Her pronouncement was made without the slightest hesitation. After all those years of mooning on the outside, one would have thought she would be intimidated by Goldsmith's. But she spoke with the self-assurance of a Hapsburg empress.

"Ah yes, Mrs. Valenta, Mrs. Marshall will be with you shortly. Won't you have a seat? May I get you some champagne? Or perhaps coffee?"

Maria settled herself comfortably on a gilded love seat. She winked at Erica as if to say, "Didn't I always tell you this is what it would be like?"

Mrs. Marshall soon strode forward to greet them. Erica usually mistrusted overly energetic short people, but she liked this lady immediately. Mrs. Valenta sized her up, then broke into a wide smile.

"It is so nice to meet you," said Mrs. Marshall. "I've heard a great deal about both of you. Mrs. Eaton and I were on the phone for hours yesterday."

Mrs. Marshall made it sound as if they had had a delightful chat. In truth, there had been lots of acrimony, with Bettina doing her utmost to modify what were, in her eyes, Mrs. Eaton's outrageous demands.

The bridal consultant continued to explain the upshot of

the conversation. "Mrs. Eaton insists that I send her the bill for your ensemble, Erica, as well as for the dresses of the other ladies in the bridal party."

Erica and her mother stared at each other. The Eatons had volunteered to foot the bill for the wedding, with the understanding that it would take place in Boston. That was fine with the Valentas—they had few relations, and those relatives also made up the larger part of their social circle. The main advantage, however, was that they could pull out all the stops in choosing Erica's gown. But now Mrs. Eaton had offered to pay for that, as well. Such extraordinary generosity. How could they refuse?

"Let's look at some dresses," said Mrs. Marshall. Bettina led the Valenta women into one of the suites. They were reseated, facing a raised platform nestled by three ten-foot mirrors. On the carved table at their side was a silver tray with two china cups, a coffee service, some dainty glazed fruit tarts, and a Polaroid camera.

No sooner were they settled than the door to the suite flew open and in came a stranger with the force of a hurricane. Erica and her mother were astonished. It wasn't the intrusion; the interloper was the most beautiful woman either of them had ever seen.

"Rehearsal's been canceled," she announced.

"Why?" asked Bettina.

"Show closed before it opened."

"What a shame! And this is the second play, too."

"Yeah. Fame and fortune will be on hold a while longer. Speaking of which, can I get in any extra time this afternoon?"

"I'm afraid Carrie will be modeling for Miss Valenta. Oh! Pardon my manners. Ms. Erica Valenta, Mrs. Valenta, please meet Melissa John. Melissa is one of our models, but remember that face. One of these days she will be a famous actress."

Melissa took the introduction with no sense of irony. She smiled and shook hands all around.

"Hey," said Melissa, as Erica rose at the introduction, "*you* should be modeling here."

Erica's face burned. She thought of herself as plain and

gawky, despite Whit's protests to the contrary. But Melissa's compliment seemed completely sincere.

"Well," said Mrs. Marshall, recovering her professional cool, "we need to talk about the play, Melissa, but these ladies have an appointment, so I'm going to ask you to wait . . ."

"Oh, no," said Erica and her mother simultaneously.

"Please stay," Erica begged.

"You give us second opinion," said Mrs. Valenta.

Melissa kicked her shoes off and cozied up in the stuffed pink satin chair next to Erica's. She looked like Venus on the half-shell.

"So," she said, leaning over to Erica, "who you hitching up with?"

"He's from Boston," said Erica, hesitating. "A banker. His name is Whittaker Spence Eaton the Third."

Melissa whistled low. "Sounds like big bucks."

Erica was somehow very pleased by Melissa's reaction. Perhaps it was the candor of the other woman. "Yes. I guess so. But we're very much in love."

Melissa ignored the last remark. "Guess nothing, honey. You need to check these things out. Have you got yourself a lawyer?"

"Oh no. A lawyer? For heaven's sake, Boston people aren't anything like that. Are they, Mama?"

Mrs. Valenta said nothing, but she was looking very thoughtfully at Melissa.

"Carrie will be modeling a few dresses that I thought might appeal to you, and that conform to Mrs. Eaton's, uh, suggestions," said Mrs. Marshall.

Erica and her mother smiled silently. The room, and Mrs. Eaton's invisible presence, finally combined to intimidate both of them.

The parade of gowns began. Goldsmith's had really provided a surprising variety, considering the limitations posed by Mrs. Eaton. All the dresses were relatively informal, all were tea-length, hemmed at the ankle, and all were in a deep ivory shade or ecru.

On the phone, Mrs. Marshall had asked, "Will this be a second wedding?" That's what the length and color suggested.

Mrs. Eaton had sighed, then responded, "Not really."

Mrs. Marshall could swear she saw tears through Maria Valenta's lashes. Erica's face was determined, grim. How sorry she felt for them! This experience could be such a blissful time, when mothers and daughters squealed with delight, as one delicious gown after another passed before them. Perhaps she would call up and have them bring out some yummy new numbers, and to hell with the old biddy!

Silence.

"What the hell was *that*?" muttered Melissa. "Pre-widow's weeds?"

Bettina shot her a withering look. None of your damn business, it warned.

Maria and Erica whispered to each other, in Czech. Mrs. Marshall rose to leave. "Why don't you discuss this between yourselves. Take your time, I'm available whenever you like."

"No, no," said Mrs. Valenta firmly. "Erica will try on the turtleneck dress, the two-piece, and the one with the fringed shawl."

Mrs. Marshall secretly hoped that Erica and her mother would protest Mrs. Eaton's choices in bridal wear. Why, Erica was a perfectly lovely young woman, regally tall, fashionably thin, with a sweet, heart-shaped face. Bettina would have loved to dress her in something utterly romantic, with dramatic details—a cathedral train, for sure—that would make her an absolute queen on her wedding day. But there wasn't a peep of complaint from mother or daughter. And Mrs. Marshall had no choice but to play the tune called by the one who paid the piper. She shuddered involuntarily. Overbearing mothers were bad enough, but obnoxious mothers-in-law were positively hounds from hell.

Erica was a perfect size eight, and each sample dress she tried on fit almost as if it had been designed for her. But there was something missing. The bridal glow, the sheer magic that takes over when a woman puts on the most special dress of her life.

"You need some blusher," said Melissa. But everyone just looked down.

The turtleneck was an A-line, elegant but without a shred

of ornamentation. Erica's face was expressionless, her mother's, hesitant. Melissa clutched her throat as if she were about to vomit. Bettina shook her head in an emphatic "no."

The two-piece was shaped like a suit. It had a gored skirt, which showed off Erica's good legs, but the top was a bouclé knit with a shawl collar, tied by a belt. It was almost like a sweater.

"Too casual," pronounced Mrs. Marshall, before anyone could express either interest or contempt.

The third dress was silk knit, an exceptionally heavy fabric, which only a woman as large as Erica could carry without seeming burdened. A wide belt emphasized her narrow waist, as well as the Grecian folds of the dress. It was adorned by a scarf of the same material, deeply fringed, forming a cape in back.

It was a magnificent dress, even more magnificent on Erica. Its workmanship was superb, its fabric exceptional. It was one of those dresses that cost a fortune—four thousand dollars—and showed every penny in its quality.

"This is it," said Erica, but there was no excitement in her voice. And why should she be excited, thought Mrs. Marshall. It was a dress that could just as well be worn to the theater.

"Oh, how proper," jeered Melissa.

Erica ignored the sarcasm. "Yes, it is," she stated quietly.

The business of the dress being done, the four women proceeded up to the second floor. First they entered the lingerie boutique. "Oh, look," cried Melissa, holding up a red lace nightgown. "This is you, Erica."

Erica's mouth dropped open. It was! How could Melissa have known that? It was as if she'd read her secret thoughts.

Erica loved sexy underwear—and so would Whit, she decided. But the thought that her future mother-in-law would be paying for it froze her desire. All of Melissa's pleading couldn't get her to buy it.

At the shoe salon Mrs. Marshall, with Melissa's help, talked Erica into getting high-heeled silk pumps with thick platform soles. The very tall groom would not be dwarfed, and she needed to look *superior* in some way, Mrs. Marshall felt.

There could be no such ploy with the headpiece; the veil had to match the gown. It would be absurd to put an elaborate, long veil over what was essentially an ivory cocktail dress. Mrs. Marshall did her best with a youthful cap of flowers, ribbons, and organdy butterflies. Erica tried on the frivolous little cap, with its tufts of veil, and Mrs. Marshall saw her really smile for the first time.

With Erica's outfit complete, they all went up to the third floor to choose a dress for Maria.

Mrs. Eaton had generously allowed the mother of the bride to wear whatever she wished—so long as it was beige or gray. It was clear to all that Mrs. Eaton was afraid that Erica's mother would wear something loud and peasant-like, if her inclinations weren't checked.

Maria did not care; she had very little personal vanity. After a short time, she chose a beige wool dress with a brown velvet collar.

"Mrs. Valenta, you look so *distinguished* in that dress," Mrs. Marshall declared.

She looks *distinguished* in her maid's uniform, too, Erica thought.

Erica and her mother made appointments for fittings and thanked Mrs. Marshall.

"It was delightful meeting you, Melissa. I hope we—you and Whit and I—can get together sometime," said Erica. She meant it, too. Maybe some day Melissa would become a famous actress. She and Whit could entertain the Hollywood star in their elegant house. Wouldn't that be nice? Of course Melissa might be a little, oh, *obvious* for the Boston crowd. But she was beginning to catch on to Whit's people. They loved celebrities.

"I like you," said Melissa, giving Erica her firm, sensuous handshake. "And I know we'll meet again."

Melissa couldn't wait to get Mrs. Marshall alone. She was willing to bet that Erica's marriage wouldn't come off. Long, tall Erica had her head up in the romantic clouds. Didn't know how to handle deals. And those Boston types were shrewd and experienced in the art of negotiation.

It was a tiring day. The Valentas staggered out to Fifth Avenue, exhausted. In silence they made their way to the subway station, and in silence they rode home. The noise of the city and the train allowed them to keep their own counsel. Only in the relative quiet of the walk from the Brooklyn station did silence seem awkward.

"You know Mrs. Eaton has no daughters," Erica pointed out. "So of course she wants to do everything, have all the fun of planning a wedding."

"I'm happy she is so generous," Maria allowed. "Still, I wonder, because she has no daughters, maybe she has wrong ideas about what a bride should wear. A bride, especially a pure one like you, my angel, should wear snow white, with a train, and meters and meters of tulle."

Erica bit her lip. There were some things she just couldn't explain to her mother. Like what understated Bostonians considered proper fashion. Or what young people did today, if they were in love.

The wedding clothes were a drag, but money gave Mrs. Eaton the moral authority to dictate the style of the wedding. It was infuriating, but a fact of life nevertheless. But soon she too would have money, and she would show the Eatons that it could be used for good purposes, and without hurting the feelings of others. She would teach them the gift of the poor people: to share. She'd take the musty old Eaton name and snap it smartly in the wind.

Erica Eaton, that name would mean something in the world!

Chapter Nine

ON HER WEDDING DAY Erica was so excited that she woke before dawn. After she bathed, she inspected the sky. It was gray; it suggested that the day might turn out in any of a number of ways. Perhaps it would rain. It might even snow. Or it might turn out brilliantly sunny. As it was, Nature rejected all these possibilities, and the overcast but dry weather stayed the day.

The wedding was small, because Mrs. Eaton had inexplicably scheduled the ceremony for a workday morning. Erica sighed. It would take a lot of self-control to bend with her mother-in-law's eccentricities. But she would do it. Being nice to Mrs. Eaton was not such a great sacrifice, after all, since it meant pleasing Whit.

Besides, *her* relatives were present in full force. They had driven up—a bunch of them had piled into Cousin Jiri's RV—or taken the train. They had taken the day off from their jobs as longshoremen, printers, and cops, sacrificing a sick day, or forfeiting the day's wages. Most of Whit's relatives had sent their regrets; they would not take time off from their work, even though they were, almost without exception, in positions where they did not have to account to anyone for their time. Yet another way, concluded Erica, that the rich were different.

Mr. Singh, her parents' employer, regretted that he could not come to the wedding because, of course, he had to man the desk at the Crest. As a wedding gift, however, he arranged to have all of the Valentas' guests stay free of charge at the Berkshire Palms Motel, owned by his brother-in-law. The only stipulation was that they check in after midnight.

That turned out to be just fine, because of a wonderful surprise. Brian Mulligan and the staff of the Dew Drop Inn had thrown a fabulous rehearsal dinner. Whit's parents had begged off, but the Valenta clan had a smashing time.

Brian had located a Bohemian band that played lively folk tunes and there was dancing all night. The Dew Drop provided only simple chops and drinks, but there was plenty of both. The tavern staff and the Czechs from New York got along famously, and laughter reverberated through the building. Erica looked nervously at Whit. This was surely not the sort of partying his family did. Thank God none of them had come.

But Whit returned her look with a bright smile. "This is absolutely terrific!" he said. "I just love your family and your friends."

At midnight Brian presented a special performance by a friend of his—a female impersonator. Maria and Jaroslav were shocked, but they couldn't help laughing at the actor's riotous routine. Finally, everyone went off to get a few hours of sleep before the wedding in the morning.

At last the hour of truth had come. Erica alighted from a limousine. The church was old and imposing; generations of Eatons had been married, christened, and buried there.

Mr. and Mrs. Eaton met her at the door.

"Come, dear," said Mrs. Eaton, "you must meet the Reverend Mr. Quimby, our assistant rector."

In the study, she was introduced to the young minister, who seemed more nervous than she was, if that were possible.

He said something to her, but his nasal Boston accent was so heavy, she barely understood what it was. He held a pen up to her. She took it. He indicated the papers on his desk. She looked down. It was a form of some sort. Mr. Eaton looked anxiously at his watch. It was getting late.

"Please sign this now," the Reverend Mr. Quimby said through his adenoids.

Erica quickly did so. Must be more license-type things. She was glad Whit had handled all that stuff. Who wants to deal with the Commonwealth of Massachusetts when you have all the details of a wedding to attend to? Of course, there weren't that many details, because Mrs. Eaton had insisted on planning the whole wedding herself.

It took some getting used to, all this self-sufficiency of the rich.

The ceremony itself was beautiful. She felt like a fairy-tale princess, going from the arm of her father—enormously handsome in morning dress—to her gorgeous bridegroom.

The assistant rector intoned, the bride's side of the church echoed with the sounds of crying matrons and blowing noses, the groom's side rustled with reserved curiosity. And when Whit kissed her, she felt as if she had passed into Paradise.

The reception was held at the Eatons' home, in a room large enough to accommodate a ball. The Eaton kin dropped in to congratulate the principals, sip a quick glass of champagne, and dash off to their important appointments.

The Valenta clan held delicate tulip champagne flutes gingerly, as they looked in vain for some solid food and merrymaking booze. There were only silver platters of limp little sandwiches, and more champagne.

The room was prettily decorated with delicate bouquets of pink sweetheart roses and baby's breath. Erica felt awkward and big, lumbering among the daintiness. She escaped as quickly as she could to change into her going-away outfit.

When she came downstairs, she found her father and Mr. Eaton in conversation.

"I understand you are in the hotel business," said her father-in-law.

"Is no business," said Jaroslav sadly, "is slowdown in the work. But we are lucky. My wife works hard, and together, we make good money."

Mr. Eaton looked about for an avenue of escape. Finding none, he opened another gambit.

"I understand you are Polish, Mr. Valenta."

Jaroslav looked at him, incredulous. How could this cosmopolitan man make such a ridiculous mistake? A person of refinement and education must surely be able to distinguish one nationality from another. "We are Czech. Bohemian. Before we became citizens of United States, by the grace of God."

Eaton blushed uncomfortably. Patriotism, like other emotions, confused him.

"Hey, look at this," said Whit, as he and Erica unwrapped wedding presents.

"Oh, let me see," said Erica.

It was a magnificent pewter bowl, its finish like a blend of silver and pearl, with the soft patina of age. Its shape was simple, yet distinguished, as if it were the primeval bowl, which all other bowls would forever imitate. She turned it over in her hands, its weight balancing perfectly at every angle. On its base was the hallmark of a great colonial smith.

It was the sort of gift one might have expected from the blue-blooded Spences. But it was not. The Spences had sent a set of four carved ducks that were of no earthly use.

Whit frowned. It was a very slight frown, but it seemed to scramble the features of his perfect face. "It's from your dear friend, the *homosexual.*"

The way he said it, made it sound so obscene. Yet it was a respectable word. Somehow, it wouldn't have been so cutting if Whit had said "fag," or some other epithet. A nasty name could be said in a joshing way, and would lose its sting. But Whit's comment dripped contempt.

Erica felt sad. Brian was perhaps the only person she knew "from before" who would fit in in her married life. His dress, manners, and speech were impeccable. And he had money and leisure time. But now she could see that Whit wouldn't want anything to do with Brian.

"I'll send the thank-you note, honey, but we're not under any obligation to use it."

Whit smiled at her, which, as always, made her melt with love and desire.

Erica hid the offending bowl deep in the cavernous Eaton silver pantry.

The wedding was over, the last guest gone, the gifts disposed of. It felt like late at night, but actually it was only three in the afternoon.

They got into Whit's car. Erica snuggled up to Whit, as much as she could, anyway, in a bucket seat, and with Whit's safety harness already in place. She sighed with contentment.

Once again Whit flashed her his dazzling smile. Even when her husband would be old and gray, she would never get tired of that marvelous smile!

And now the honeymoon. Surely they would be going on some wonderful surprise trip. To some hidden Caribbean cay. Or maybe a darling little chalet in Switzerland. Or was this the right time of year for Monaco?

"We're going to one of those Poconos places. God, it'll be a gas," said Whit.

The interior decor of the resort reminded Erica of the Crest, except that the toilet seat in their room was heart-shaped. At dinner, there was dancing to a Lawrence Welk–type accordionist. A greasy, unfunny comedian made jokes about virgins, reducing some of the younger brides to tears, and their husbands, probably, to impotence.

Whit insisted on buying Erica some clothes from the hotel shop. She pretended that the scratchy nylon baby dolls and horrid polyester pants—already bagging—were amusingly campy.

They spent two days screwing, because that was what they were supposed to be doing. In all that time she didn't have a single orgasm. The very first time she failed to come Whit had made such a fuss that she was upset and embarrassed. After that, she pretended.

It was her fault, after all, not his. He had always managed

to bring her to the top before, and his style hadn't changed now. Maybe she had some subconscious guilt about not waiting till marriage, the way she had been raised to do. Maybe the guilt was coming home to roost now, since she hadn't felt it before. Maybe she was resenting the kind of honeymoon they were having, and not wanting to express that resentment to Whit, she was probably turning her spite on herself. Either way, she figured, it was her own fault.

At last the honeymoon was over, and they returned to Boston. Erica was doubly thrilled, for they were moving into the Eaton mansion. No newlyweds' apartment could compare with the glamour of this historical house. And it was so big that Erica figured there would be just a few polite interactions with the senior Eatons each day.

From the day of the wedding—perhaps before—Erica wondered how soon she could do it. How soon could she suggest that her parents move up to Boston? How long would she have to wait so that it would no longer seem as if she were elbowing her family in crudely? As it happened, the opportunity came up naturally.

"I visited the cottage today," said Mrs. Eaton after dinner one day, "and it's terribly run-down."

"Mmmm," said Mr. Eaton and Whit and Erica.

"It's really quite impossible for our staff to run over there all the time. It needs a person, perhaps two, to maintain it properly."

"Well then, hire a couple," said Mr. Eaton.

"But it's horribly expensive. Especially since we never use the place anymore."

"Perhaps we should sell it."

"Spence, how could you? It's from your mother's family property."

"May I make a suggestion," said Erica. Everyone looked at her in surprise, as if an inanimate object had spoken. "My parents. My parents would be great at caring for that house."

There was silence.

"Of course, I'd like to contribute to the expense. I was

thinking, perhaps I could come into the firm. I'm good at accounts, I can make myself useful around the office."

"My dear," said Mrs. Eaton icily, "that simply isn't done."

"But having her parents maintain the cottage, that's a great idea," said Whit. "The basement rooms would be just right for them, after they clear out the trash and stuff."

Erica smiled gratefully at Whit. But instead of smiling back he looked at her in the oddest way.

The subject was suddenly dropped. The next time Erica tried to bring it up again, Mrs. Eaton informed her that she had already hired a Filipino couple to care for the cottage.

Erica was concerned. When her parents retired, how would she care for them? While Whit did not question her expenditures (Mrs. Eaton did remark once that designer clothing was for people who "did not know whence they came"), Erica could hardly support her parents as an "expense." And Whit didn't seem to understand her little hints about the matter.

Being rich was not as simple as Erica had imagined. It wasn't hard, it didn't suck your soul, the way poverty did, but it took up a lot of time. Shopping for clothes and having her hair and nails done, and exercising and being massaged, and attending luncheons and charity teas, these tired her out as if they were actual labor. And they didn't leave her time to do all the things she once imagined she would do if she had the money: reading, volunteering for political candidates, working in amateur theatricals. On Beacon Hill, she could swear, they watched the same television shows they did in Tangee's project.

About three months after the wedding, Erica came to a sickening realization. Her marriage was in trouble. She could feel it without suspecting anyone or anything specific. They made love as frequently as ever, perhaps even more frequently, and certainly—as far as Whit was concerned—more vehemently. But every time she spoke to him, Whit's attention wandered, and his fabulous smile, which he still beamed at her frequently, seemed disconnected from his eyes.

Erica determined to stop this downward spiral. She had concentrated on pleasing Whit's parents, and had ended up taking her husband's affection for granted. That was foolish. From now on, she would work on becoming the wife Whit wanted. The thing he resented—of course, he was too well bred to point it out—had to be her style.

You can take the girl out of Brooklyn, and with a little effort, you can take Brooklyn out of the girl. She began to imitate the mannerisms and conversation of the people in Whit's social set. She took up their sports. From the invitations that began coming her way, she could tell she was succeeding. Hell, it wasn't that hard to imitate the privileged. As long as someone else did the work of *becoming* rich, *being* rich did not take much talent.

"The Allardyces are having a do Sunday evening," Whit mentioned casually. It was late Thursday night. He had just come home after a late squash game and dinner out with his father, leaving her to dine with Mrs. Eaton. Whit seemed to be doing that a lot lately.

"What? And they didn't invite us?" Erica was hurt. She thought she got along very well with the Allardyces.

"They did. I guess I put the invitation somewhere. It was a few weeks ago."

Erica resisted the urge to snap at him. Nagging was not going to put the bloom back on their relationship.

"What a shame, Whit. The Allardyces are really nice to me. Besides, I'd get to meet more of your friends there."

"So let's go, honey."

"But it's so rude."

"Oh, just call Bitsy tomorrow morning and tell her we're coming. I'm sure she won't say anything."

No, thought Erica, but she'll *think* I'm a total boor.

"Okay, darling. If you think it's all right. By the way, what should I wear? Did the invitation indicate how formal?"

"Oh, honey, you don't need an invitation to know how to

dress for a party at the *Allardyces*. They do it every year. Strictly black tie. You know. Have you got anything for, say, opening night at the opera?"

Erica gulped. She sure didn't. She had exactly two days to get an evening gown. And it had to be sensational. It had to be good enough to make Whit proud of her.

A systematic attack on Boston's best shops resulted in a dress by eleven Saturday morning. It was a slinky, strapless sheath of dark red silk, delicately embroidered in gold with a long matching jacket encrusted with the same embroidery. It made her look like a million dollars and cost just a few zeros less. She bought a pair of shoes to go with it. They had the highest heels she had ever worn. Why not, she figured, Whit would still be taller. That was a freedom he had given her: the right to be tall and feel good about it.

After a late breakfast on Sunday Whit left for the club to play tennis. He'd meet her at five at the Allardyces, he said. That suited her fine, because she had arranged for a hairdresser to come to the house at noon. She wanted time and privacy to dress. The aim was magnificence, with a touch, perhaps, of what Papa called "arrogance," she thought fondly.

At a quarter of four she examined her image in the mirror. She was a long, narrow column of flame, from her glinting slippers to the complicated sculpture of her auburn hair. Oh, thank you, God and Oscar de la Renta!

She sang "If They Could See Me Now." Wouldn't that really be something, if she could line them all up here in the dressing room. Buzzy Alpert and the man who had mocked her mother at the bank. All the people who had ever thought she was nothing and no one.

At last it was time to go. The senior Eatons had gone out in the chauffeur-driven car. Erica had not been given keys to a car of her own, and so had to phone for a cab. The taxi driver grumbled all the way to the Allardyces; he resented having to go out to the country with no fare back. But nothing could destroy Erica's high mood of confidence.

She rang the ornate bell near the door. There was no answer. She rang again. How strange. While the Allardyces did not keep a permanent staff, they would surely hire a butler for a gala party. After the fourth ring she heard a female voice from the side of the house.

"Over here! Everybody's in the back. Hurry, or you'll miss all the food."

Erica followed her hostess's voice to the back garden of the house. The second she came into view, she and everyone at the party were struck dumb.

It was a barbecue.

The men wore brightly colored sports clothes. Whit still wore his tennis things, clothes that particularly suited him. The women wore divided skirts or Bermuda shorts, mostly in pink or green cotton. Many of both sexes wore boating shoes without socks. Even with her heels sinking into the sod, Erica stood at least a head above every woman there.

Bitsy Allardyce broke the silence. "It's so good of you, Erica, to drop by . . . before your party tonight."

Bitsy's gracious line fooled no one. Erica was too spooked to reply. Her blanched face heightened the brightness of her dress and her hair. Like an automaton she accepted a plastic plate heaped with spare ribs and ears of corn. The party had become so quiet, the twittering of birds could be heard as they pecked for crumbs at the garden's edge.

"I'm going in to call for a cab," Erica told her husband hoarsely.

"Don't be ridiculous, darling. I'll drive you home."

He smiled, and his face was radiant. Poison, too, could be radiant.

There were several people Whit just *had* to speak to before he could leave. Erica felt as if she had been crucified with the plate of food in one hand, a cup of diet soda in the other, and the evening slippers nailing her feet into the ground. Whit let her hang there until the last drop of living blood oozed out of her.

A millennium later they left. Well, that was it. The people at the Allardyces had grudgingly let her intrude into their world, in tiny little steps, because of Whit. But it was all over now. Two things had happened. The fiasco had inflicted her with the social equivalent of cancer. And it was abundantly clear that Whit was letting her go.

The minute they reached their room, Erica ripped off her dress and left it on the floor. She had no bra on because the dress had its own support, but it didn't matter. She knew even the sight of her bare breasts no longer turned Whit on. On her dresser was a chased silver vanity set that her aunt had sent from Prague. The wedding present was the last antique heirloom in the family, and had been dangerously illegal to send. Despite that, she began to brush her hair violently with the delicate silver brush. She wanted to get every one of the curls out, out as if they were vermin.

Whit stood and watched her. A bare-breasted woman brushing her hair. But there was no lust in his smile.

"Enjoy the party, Erica?"

She exploded.

"You son of a bitch," she roared, not caring if Mrs. Eaton could hear her.

Whit was stunned. Never before had she contested his opinion, to say nothing of *cursing* him. He took her by the shoulders and shook her, as if she was a malfunctioning machine.

"Stop that," he ordered in a quiet but malevolent voice. "You're forgetting who you are, gutter girl, and where you are—in the *master's* house. If you don't learn your place, I'll have to call up the agency and replace you."

"Well, well. So now it all comes out. Why you married me. And why I disappoint you, too, right? Only a 'gutter girl' makes you feel like a man, Whit. Just as soon as she crawls up on the sidewalk, you lose interest. Well, I'm sorry to disappoint you. But, you know, I have a feeling that a harem-full of 'gutter girls' wouldn't make you into a real man."

He slapped her.

If Erica had taken the time to think, she might have started to cry. She might have continued cursing and insulting him. She might have blamed herself for provoking him to violence.

But she didn't stop to think. She reacted from the well of her being, from deep within the primitive part of her brain.

Her hormones commanded: fight or flight, and she wasn't the type to fly.

She smacked him with the hairbrush with all her might.

Erica dropped the brush as if it were a live coal. The head was bent back from the handle of the brush.

Whit stood in shock. He looked as if he had seen the marker for his own grave. A huge welt was already forming across his perfectly tanned cheek.

He shuffled over to the door, his back bent, like a refugee carrying his sad bundle of worldly goods. He was a man absolutely aware of his own smallness.

Even with their marriage irretrievably finished, Erica made no move to divorce Whit. How could she explain any of this to her parents? And *divorce*. They would die of shame, they would be unable to face their relatives.

Then Whit started seeing other women. First there was the former receptionist at the family firm, who had been fired for not using deodorant. Then there was the next-door neighbor's obese cook. Still, Erica hesitated. There would be a sign, there would be a time, when she could tell her parents in a way that would spare their feelings. The months inched along.

Finally, Whit himself asked for a divorce.

"Why now?" asked Erica. They had just gone through the charade of their first anniversary.

"I want to marry someone else."

"Who?" asked Erica, her feelings overpowered by simple curiosity.

"Sydney," said Whit.

"Oh," said Erica. Sydney was a Spence cousin with emotional problems. Two years earlier Sydney had thrown herself off the roof of her family's town house with the intention of killing herself. She had succeeded only in paralyzing herself from the waist down.

The sting of pain and the sense of relief were equal and simultaneous.

After a sleepless night, Erica was summoned to the library.

Mr. and Mrs. Eaton were sitting there on a leather sofa, on the edge, as if they were guests.

"Well, well," said Mr. Eaton, "it's time we discussed the terms of the, er, dissolution."

Already? thought Erica. She had hardly assimilated the fact of divorce. She hadn't thought about the money at all.

"You realize, of course, my dear, that you have agreed not to profit financially from this marriage," said Mrs. Eaton.

"What, *what?*"

Mrs. Eaton continued. "No alimony, no settlement. No family jewelry."

"But that's ridiculous. The state would never allow that. You are so wealthy, and I've got nothing."

"You've signed a written agreement. You're an adult . . ."

She handed Erica a set of papers. It was a premarital agreement, stating that the undersigned would never make any claims on the espoused's property. And on the last page was her clear, flowing signature, with the date of the marriage. This was what she had signed in the rector's study!

"Isn't this your signature?"

"Yes, but I had no idea what it was. You, you tricked me into signing that."

"Did we?" said Mr. Eaton, raising his eyebrows. "It seems to me that you are perfectly capable of reading. And the language is hardly impenetrable, for a Harvard student."

"But you knew I was nervous and excited about the wedding. You knew it was no time for me to look at a fine-print contract."

Mr. Eaton shook his head. "You people are so impulsive. And of course, you would like more prudent souls to pay for your impetuousness. You can, of course, contest this document, but you will have to pay for the lawyers yourself."

Erica looked down at the Aubusson. She had never regretted as much her vow not to cry. At the same time, she sensed that the Eatons would be totally unmoved by tears. Weeping would even increase their contempt for her.

"*We people* would die of shame before doing something this

indecent to one of *our* children. I suppose you feel very proud of yourselves. You really outsmarted the girl from Brooklyn, and her whole refugee clan, to boot. You aren't losing a daughter-in-law, you're gaining an antique vanity set. A bunch of shrewd Yankees *you* are!"

"Look here, Miss, you're free to take the wedding presents, for heaven's sake," Spence Eaton sputtered.

"That's *Mrs.* Mrs. Eaton, and let's see you do something about *that.*"

"Don't you try to be morally uppity with us. We assured protection for our son, and we're very glad we did. We've done our duty by shielding our boy from those who would exploit his little problem. We're not unaware of your motives for marrying him, you know.

"We have a responsibility to our son, to our family, even to our ancestors. Do you think we achieved what we have by falling prey to every con man—or woman—who comes along? We intend to pass on our heritage, intact, to our grandchildren."

"Married for money, ha ha," Erica laughed, the sound ugly with rage. "Well, you may have some insight there, Mr. Eaton, which is more than this blushing bride ever did. And since you are so insightful, sir, won't you figure out why it was that *he* married *me*? Whatever it was, I guess we can conclude that I delivered.

"I guess you don't really want to think about Whit—what, who, why, he is what he is. I'm sure you'd rather think about your great-grandfather. Who wouldn't? At least he *made* his fortune, honestly or not. Which is more than you can say for you and your friends, sitting around your stuffy old clubs, preserving the money in formaldehyde, safe from the people who had the gall to come in steerage.

"Sure. Think about the grandchildren. They will be a tribute to you, the offspring of a basket case and a gelding. Watch that money, Mr. Eaton, the grandchildren will need it. Those institutions aren't cheap, you know."

Mrs. Eaton sprang to her feet. She was not exactly red in the face—she was probably incapable of blushing—but the granite bones of her tough ancestors strained against her skin.

"That's enough!"

Erica had never heard her speak so loudly.

"Pack your bags immediately. Get out!"

Erica smiled in bitter triumph.

"I guess that means I can take my clothes."

Chapter Ten

ERICA SAT in the employment agency with a clipboard on her lap. She hoped that she had not yet applied to this one. It was hard to tell. After the first dozen, they all looked the same. The application form on the clipboard was exactly the same, too.

Her hand and forearm were cramped from writing, but she bent to the task. She needed a job, any job. She needed it now.

When she first came down from Boston, she had been in a state of shock. She would venture down to the lobby of the Crest, intent on a day of job hunting, only to realize that she had no idea where to go. She sat in the lobby staring at the wall, letting the fear and the anger fester in her stomach. Where could she go to find work? What could she do?

After a few days Mr. Singh took pity on her. There was a big motel in Queens short a maid. They would hire Erica on Mr. Singh's say-so. It was a long ride, true, but she would be paid well, better than her mother was. After all, she wasn't getting a room. Besides, she was young and strong. Erica accepted.

When Maria found out she was furious. "Over my dead body," she stormed, "you work like maid. Not for this we come to America."

Her father was even more upset. He said nothing, but his face went ashen. She noted for the first time objective signs of his aging. His hair, once so richly red, had faded to a dull tan.

Erica hated to go back on her word to Mr. Singh, but he accepted her reversal cordially. Secretly, he was relieved. He owed the Valenta family this favor, but the truth was, he doubted Erica would make much of a chambermaid. This second generation, it just didn't have the backbone of the immigrants. Often, he had noted with chagrin, even among his own kin, they were little better than old-time Americans. Lazy, unmotivated, no pride in the lot of them.

Erica had no other contacts to help her find work. She had burned her bridges at Radcliffe; they had been on the verge of suspending her before her marriage, something she had laughed about at the time. Even if she could get back into school, her scholarship was gone forever. It would take thousands to pay the tuition.

Returning to Mr. Birnbaum would be excruciatingly shameful, and her relatives were in no position to help. So, after exhausting the want ads, she went down the list of employment agencies in the phone book, applying at each. She was now up to "Windward Elite."

"Print legibly. *Name*: ERICA EATON." Yes, she had kept her married name. Partly, to spite the Eatons (they couldn't cheat her out of their name, at least), partly to be rid of the immigrant's stigma, for once and for all.

"*Address*": Yes, the Crest Motor Lodge. What choice did she have? It no longer felt like a humiliation. And she didn't know anyone who cared enough about her to mock her for moving back in with her parents.

"*Experience*": One and a half years serving beer at the Dew Drop. It wasn't fair; on paper that seemed pathetic, but it *hadn't* been in real life.

The receptionist at the agency smiled at her. Erica could tell the look of pity. She tried smiling back. The muscles of her mouth could barely recall the movement. It must seem like a grimace.

The hollows beneath her eyes were deep enough to store nuts for the winter. She didn't sleep well. She kept going over and over the events of the last year. What had she done? She still relished the memory of her one glorious minute of defiance, but now she wondered: Was there perhaps truth to the accusation of the Eatons? Did she really marry Whit for his money? Had she agreed to devote her life to a man she should have known was imbalanced? But how could she have known? When you're in love, you're not supposed to see clearly!

"Mr. Bixby will see you now," said the receptionist.

Why not? She had been cooling her heels for an hour and fifteen minutes already. That should be enough to put anyone in her place.

"Thank you!" said Erica, trying desperately to sound enthusiastic, although she could tell precisely what would happen next, as if she were an actor in a long-running play.

Mr. Bixby did not ask her to sit down while he skimmed her application form. Erica shifted from foot to foot. It was funny, when you had self-confidence, height was a terrific asset. When you lacked assurance, being tall made you feel like a sore thumb.

"Have a seat, Erica," he said, finally.

Erica pursed her lips. A few years ago she had thought Women's Lib a waste of time. When she began seeing Whit, she felt uneasy, even threatened by feminists. Now she couldn't help but wonder, was there any place on earth where a woman was respectfully called by her last name, while *she* addressed men by their first, without their permission?

Bixby yawned loudly, not bothering to cover his mouth, then he stretched. There were large, disgusting stains under his arms. He probably knew they were there, but what did he care? *She* was the one who had to impress *him* favorably.

"So," he said, "you're not interested in work as a waitress?"

"No," she answered. She had found the competition in New York fierce. There were gorgeous would-be actresses and models, who liked the flexibility of waiting on tables and waiting for the big break at the same time. And there were the older, wiser, coffee-shop pros, who could serve lunch to a hundred customers, crack jokes, and clean the counter, all at the same time, and without breathing hard.

"Well what *do* you want to do?" he asked irritably.

"Work, in an office." *The sign on the door said "Office Personnel Employment" didn't it?*

"Take dictation?"

"No, sir."

The "sir" mollified him. At least he wouldn't harangue her about her incompetence.

"How about typing?"

"I can type." The words were carefully chosen.

"How fast?" Her subterfuges never worked.

"Not that fast." She had tried stretching the truth on that one but it didn't work. They had given her typing tests in several places and she had been slow and inaccurate. If she ever did improve, she wouldn't know what to do, typing really hurt her back. Too bad, really, because there was something to be said for typing. Your hands would be doing something skilled and competent, and your brain was free to do its own thing.

She couldn't understand how others could do it. Her back began to ache after a typing *test*. Could people really type for eight hours straight and not be crippled? Or was this another of society's coy little lies, that anything women did was by definition physically easy. Like cleaning, or dragging little kids around.

Mr. Bixby snorted. "You college girls! You think you can just waltz in here and the world will lay itself at your feet. For what? We don't have that many requests for gals experienced at attending fraternity blasts. And what's this, Miss *Radcliffe*. You didn't even finish? What's the matter, got bored? Daddy let you come home and go shopping, instead?"

Erica's face went red. There was no point in fighting back. It wasn't going to help her get a job.

"I left school to get married. But it didn't work out."

Now he really sneered, and shook his head, as if it was the first he had heard of this loathsome depravity.

Traditionalists always chuckled obligingly when girls dropped out to get married. But in the end they had contempt for the women who did it, just like everybody else.

"What makes you think you can be successful in an office?" The subsequent words were unsaid but there: Considering you failed at something any moron can do, like marriage.

"Well, I like numbers. I'm pretty good with financial records."

"Oh, are you? Too bad they're full up at Price, Waterhouse. Ever take a bookkeeping course?"

"No." Courses took time and money. She needed a job *now*.

"Well, I have to be frank with you," *after coddling your ego all through this interview.* "There is nothing available for girls of your, uh, talents, right now."

"Well, thank you anyway. For your time."

"You're very welcome. And good luck."

"If something should come in . . ."

"Of course. We'll keep your application in the active file." *You know, the one under the desk, with the plastic liner.*

After leaving ZZZ Temporaries, Erica began a new plan. She would simply walk into major office buildings and, one floor at a time, enter every single office and ask if there was any work available. There had to be hundreds of thousands of places of work in New York. Somewhere there must be a job, any job, for her.

Well, there certainly were a lot of businesses in Manhattan. By mid-March she had barely gone through a small part of the Wall Street area. Trouble was, she hadn't found a job anywhere. She would walk in, ask the receptionist if there was a job available. The receptionist would say no. Or she would call someone in who would ask about her credentials, and that woman would say no. Or the second woman would call in someone else again, and *he* would say no.

On a Friday afternoon, Erica "finished" a skyscraper and crossed the street. A new street, a new glass tower. She looked up at it. The big buildings no longer intimidated her. It was pouring rain and dark clouds hid what she guessed was the upper half of the building.

The rain had soaked through Erica's raincoat. Her shoulders felt chilled and her back was clammy. Her hair was flattened to her head and mascara streamed down her face. Erica started to cry. It was okay. She wasn't breaking her promise to herself.

They weren't tears, they were raindrops. Nobody could tell in a million years.

It would be okay to quit now. It was 4:50, all the offices were starting to close up for the weekend. At best she would get to one office—and just look at the size of the building! It was daunting. But something forced her to go on.

Erica entered the building. People were already pouring out of the elevators. She pushed through the throng. Going up, she had the elevator all to herself. Belatedly, she realized that the elevator served floors thirty to fifty-nine. What the hell, it was time for a change. What difference did it make if you started on the first floor or the top one? She pushed fifty-nine.

She opened the door to the first office and immediately felt like Snow White. But instead of a messy little cottage with seven little beds she saw a tidy little room with thirteen steel desks. Behind twelve desks sat twelve oriental men in white shirts and black ties. The thirteenth desk was bare.

The office manager asked her her business.

"I'm looking for work. Would you happen to have a position available?"

"You type?"

"Yes!"

"We need not much typing. Small amount."

"I sure can do a small amount!"

"What we really need is someone who can explain things in simple language. You see, our people come on four-year tours from Japan. Their English is not so good."

"I'm good at that! My parents are from Europe and their English is still not great, and I'm always explaining things to them in a clear way! What kind of things would you like me to clarify?"

"Business reports, newsletters, magazines . . ." He was thrilled that she could start on Monday.

The descent from the elevator was like floating down from heaven. The roar of afternoon traffic was like the swelling of a symphony, the exhaust of the subways was suddenly a sweet perfume.

She had a job. A place to be, useful things to do. A job, a mutually agreed upon function. It didn't matter what the pay was or the hours or the tasks. She was an adult, with the responsibility and the earned respect of adulthood.

Erica shivered with joy. She had never felt like this before. Gowned and jeweled in the Eaton mansion, she had never felt as rich as she did today.

Work for money, it was a covenant. When you labored for your wages, you knew where you stood, and so did your employer. It was not like the shifting sands of marriage, totally unlike the ephemeral promises of love.

Erica raised her chin in pride. She was no starry-eyed bride dreaming of a future that would magically descend on her. She was a grown-up woman creating her rightful place in society.

From this day on, her work would be a sacrament.

And from the very first day, Erica loved her work. Her firm turned out to be one of Japan's largest, an Oriental equivalent of Du Pont. She got to read an immensely varied number of newspapers and magazines, and soon found herself gaining an excellent grounding in business news. Since the company produced so many different products, she was introduced into commercial worlds she barely knew existed. And there were some nice perks, too. A free supply of soy products convinced her mother to vary her heavy European cuisine. And every day a sushi restaurant catered the office lunch.

Erica soon learned to type rapidly, but she was rarely asked to do much of it. And she really enjoyed reading and précis-writing, the major part of the job.

Every day she would rise early, while her parents slept after their long night's labors. She dressed quickly in one of the inexpensive, simple outfits she had bought with her first month's salary.

Pressed in the subway, flowing with the great crowd of working humanity that flooded Wall Street in the morning, there seemed to be an almost spiritual camaraderie, a brotherhood of employed New Yorkers.

Perky or bleary-eyed, enthusiastic or shuffling, out to make a million or struggling to pay for the groceries, together they made up a great, powerful whole.

She loved it. From the wait in the morning for doughnuts and coffee at a corner take-out shop to the five o'clock throng that made even sleazy neighborhoods—for a single hour—as safe as a living room.

She loved being part of it. Knowing her place, not in a put-down way, but as in *belonging*. There was a certain democracy in working. No, of course the best workers were not necessarily rewarded. Office politics, nepotism, who-you-know, these still dictated the pecking order in most businesses. But there was a reward system beyond money and position. There was a satisfaction in knowing you did your work well.

The caveman whose flint knife came to a perfect edge, the bookkeeper whose entries balanced exactly, the salesman whose latest customer was satisfied, the doctor discharging a patient from the hospital, they all knew the feeling.

The grateful look on her boss's face when she handed him a memo, the way the department manager dry-washed his hands gleefully when she reported that *Barrons, Forbes,* and the *Wall Street Journal* all favored legislation that would serve the company's interests, the telexed "thank you" from the Frankfurt office—these were the rewards Erica savored.

She loved it. She loved every minute from nine to five, five days a week. The rest of the time she lived off the work week, the way a cactus lives off its internal water supply.

One of these days, she thought, she would look up some of her old friends from high school, *some* of them must be single or divorced. But not just yet.

One of these days she would seriously join a church group or a political party or an evening class in how-to-do-your-own-taxes, someplace she might meet some men. But not just now.

One of these days she would really spill her heart out to her parents, discuss her marriage, and with their wisdom, figure out what actually went wrong. But now her wounds were too raw. It would have to wait.

Meanwhile, she loved work. Loved it. Was in love. Because it wasn't a man, or a child, or money, she could not speak her love. But even silent, even hidden, it was still love.

Slowly, from the inside, it began to heal her.

* * *

Oddly enough, the first person she looked up wasn't a high school friend. One day, on a mission to midtown, Erica passed Goldsmith's. The familiar windows made her heart ache, but, she suddenly wondered, whatever happened to that beautiful model, Melissa? She had invited further friendship, hadn't she?

Erica approached the receptionist. "Excuse me, do you know a house model called Melissa John?"

"*Melissa John!* What do you want from her?"

"Uh, nothing, I'm just an old friend . . ."

"Wait here, please," said the receptionist. She left, and soon came back with Mrs. Marshall.

Bettina quickly surveyed Erica's simple dress and unjeweled left hand. "Forgive me, your name . . ."

"Erica Eaton."

Erica paused, the heat rising in her cheeks.

"I got my wedding gown here a year and a half ago. But I'm divorced now." Would the shame last forever? Would it always be her fault?

Bettina waved a hand in dismissal. "You're in New York now? Wonderful!"

That single movement, that short phrase changing the subject. Erica thought she'd love Mrs. Marshall forever for that.

"I was wondering if Melissa John still worked here."

The older woman's shoulders dropped just half an inch.

"I'm afraid Melissa left a few months ago for Hollywood."

"Oh, how thrilling!"

"Yes," said Mrs. Marshall, but she didn't sound thrilled. "There's this agent with a lot of faith in her. He's semiretired now but . . . Say, I bet she'd love to hear from you, let me write down her number for you."

Erica thanked her but looked at the little slip of paper doubtfully. She had thought that Melissa might be a good friend to have in the city. Sophisticated, full of fun, and probably with access to eligible men. But a continent away, what was the point of connecting?

Just as Erica left, an assistant came with an urgent message for Bettina. "Mr. Goldsmith needs to see you right away."

Henry's back was toward her, as Mrs. Marshall entered the office. He was bent over a credenza, studying the papers piled on it. Bettina closed her eyes and breathed. The familiar scent of his aftershave, sweet and fresh, filled her lungs. It would be so much easier if he smelled like an old man.

"What's up, Henry?"

"Look." He pointed at the papers. His voice sounded as if he were carrying a boulder on his back.

"That financial stuff is just gobbledygook to me."

"All right, I'll sum it up." Henry was now facing her and she could see the full range of his fears in his expression. "We're in trouble. Very deep trouble. The store may not be able to make it."

"What? Just a minute! We show a profit, a good profit. What's going on?"

"It's not the salon, it's the building. Tuck & Tuck is going out of business."

"That's impossible. They've been here forever. They were here before Goldsmith's." Tuck & Tuck was an expensive specialty department store featuring classic clothing. It took up three floors of the Madison Avenue side of the building.

"It's the young people. They don't want to shop there anymore. And the mothers can't force them."

"Well, there must be dozen of shops dying for that location."

Henry shook his head sadly. "No. We haven't been able to find even one. Even if we permit the space to be broken up, we can't find enough tenants."

"But we own the building, we can stick it out for a while."

"Bettina, do you know what the taxes are on this building? And we can't leave the space empty. Reputation is everything in an older building. When Tuck & Tuck closes, if there is no tenant ready to come in, the other tenants will panic, we can become a ghost building within weeks."

"Is it hopeless?"

"Nothing is ever hopeless. You know that, Bettina."

Tina's heart filled with warmth. This was the old Henry. She stood up as tall as she could.

"So what is it we can do?"

"We're going to have to fill the space up ourselves."

"But it's so large! I could think of an extra boutique for garters and whatever, but three whole floors . . ."

"No, not a boutique. We've got to think of something new, a new service for the bride. Something we don't have now at all. Something special. Put on your thinking cap, Bettina."

"You bet I will," she said. She went back to the door, biting her lower lip in concentration.

"And, Tina," the urgency in his voice made her turn back and look at him again. "Think as fast as you can."

By nine Sunday morning Erica was already bored. Weekends were the worst. Saturdays could be taken up with various chores, shopping, laundry, haircuts. But Sunday loomed before her. On an impulse she rummaged through her pocketbook and came up with the note with Melissa's phone number. Well, Sunday meant inexpensive long-distance rates.

"Hello? This is Erica Eaton. May I speak with . . ."

"Well, he*llo*. Tina Marshall told me you would call."

Her effusiveness caught Erica by surprise. "G-gosh, you sound so chipper for nine o'clock on a Sunday."

"Nine? Honey, it's 6:00 A.M. out here."

"Oh my God. I forgot about the time difference. Gee, I'm so sorry, oh . . ."

"Don't be silly. I'm wide awake. You have to be up before dawn for filming. And then on weekends it's hard to change your sleep rhythms."

"You're filming? You got a part in a movie?"

"Yes! Isn't that fantastic! It's just a teeny role, but everybody's got to start somewhere. But I get to the set early, before the star. Hell, if she ever comes down with leprosy, I'll be right there."

"Just like in the movies, huh?"

"Not exactly, it's kind of a long day and nothing much happens."

"Do you get bored?"

"Never! Hey, I mean, it's *work*."

"Yeah! I know exactly what you mean."

The knowledge of it bridged the continent, bound them together.

"Erica, this call must be costing you a fortune, I'll hang up in a minute, and it's my treat next time. Actually, I know this place I can call from for free . . . How about next week sometime?"

"That would be great." Erica flushed with pleasure. She'd made a friend.

"Just one thing, though."

"Oh, anything."

"Can you check up on Tina Marshall once in a while?"

"Mrs. Marshall?" Erica couldn't imagine anyone less likely to need checking up on.

"Yeah, see the business, Goldsmith's, is up shit's creek, and it's practically Bettina's whole life. She's got no family or anything."

"The business . . . her whole life . . ." Erica couldn't believe how stupid she was sounding.

"Yes. Of course I strongly suspect she has the hots for old Mr. Goldsmith. But she won't admit it to herself."

Erica nodded dumbly at the phone. She couldn't believe what an *interesting* conversation this turned out to be. Definitely worth the long-distance toll.

"The business . . ."

"Yeah, well, I don't understand all the details. But please, Erica, try and be there for her, will you? She'll do it for you someday, I'm sure."

"Well, I don't know what I can do, I don't really know her . . ."

"Just see her, will you please? I'll call you next week and we'll hash over everything, okay?"

"Sure!"

"Yeah. And we'll talk about men."

"Not much for me to talk about on that topic. There is no such thing as an ummarried Japanese male."

"So?"

Erica laughed. "Oh, you mean sex? Gee, let me see if I can remember what it's like."

"Never mind. I've got enough to make up for both of us."

Chapter Eleven

A POWER LUNCH.

Erica swept into the Café des Artistes on the arm of Brian Mulligan. Every head turned to stare. They certainly made an outstanding couple. She, statuesque, tanned, dressed in crisp peach, cut down to there. He, blond and perfectly barbered, debonair in a raw-silk suit. The lushly romantic restaurant, with its pastel frescoes of cavorting nudes, and window boxes overflowing with flowers, formed a perfect setting for them—or what they appeared to be.

It filled Erica with sadness. Oh, why did Brian have to be gay? He was so charming, so good-looking, so clever at business. In his company she was always relaxed, she always managed to say the smart thing. He knew her mind well and he liked her for all the right reasons. If only he were straight, her problems would be over.

Really, the rotten luck she had with men defied logic.

It might be petty and materialistic, but she loved this sort of place and everything it stood for. To feel at home here, to be admired by people like those who frequented the Café des Artistes—wouldn't that be wonderful!

The memory of her most recent tentative dates made her cheeks burn through the tan. Awkward conversations, hasty, unsatisfying sex.

Whatever was the matter with her? What on earth had happened to her values, the bedrock her family had provided for her? Why did she fall for all these superficial things, status and money in Whit, a bunch of sexy bodies. Could it be that she was incapable of love, and not just unlucky in being loved?

"So what's new in your life, Erica?"

"Wait a minute. *You're* the one who is staying at the Plaza for a month. You tell me what's new with you, first."

"Okay," said Brian, grinning with pride. "The Drops —there are now six of them—have skyrocketed. I've gained a partner, some solid capital, and we're moving down to the Big Apple. This is the big time, this is where it counts. New York, Erica. It's the only real *city* there is."

"Tell me all about your plans!"

"We're opening a club. Not a bar, a real club. With blond hatcheck girls, and crystal martini glasses, and members who feel comfortable attending in dinner jackets and evening gowns, the chicest boys, the trendiest heteros and, and . . ."

"Wow, Brian, how are you financing this?"

"I knew you would ask me, so here, I brought along the prospectus. Read it at home, there are some *very* interesting little items hidden between the lines, if you like gossip. Which brings this conversation back to you."

"Well, nothing as dramatic as your ventures. I'm working, what else can I tell you? Oh, hell, Brian, I'm working and I *love* it. You have no idea how much I've wanted to say this. I'm crazy about my work, it's absolutely the best thing in my life."

"Kid, you always loved work. Christ, some people obviously don't know how to have fun like normal human beings. Just do me one favor. Never work for my competition. Please. All right, tell me all about this great lay, your job."

So Erica told him.

Afterwards when the veal and sea bass had been consumed and they were forcing themselves to make room for fresh raspberries, key lime pie, and whipped cream thick as cheese, Brian slipped in the little question.

"So what are they paying you for this labor of love?"

Erica's face fell like a soufflé that would have to be returned to the kitchen.

"Okay, that's the only bad part. It's a hundred and fifty a week. There just isn't anything I can do about it."

"What?" shouted Brian, loud enough to draw curious looks from nearby tables.

"I know it's pathetic, but . . ."

"Pathetic? Erica, I'd pay you more to draw beer."

"But I don't want to draw beer. It want to be in business, I want to make things work in the company."

"I know. You're in love, and love is blind. But let's just sit here for a minute and look at things realistically."

"You can't tell me anything I don't know."

"I don't want to tell you anything. I want you to admit the truth to yourself. Just what *is* your future in this great Asian enterprise?"

Erica shrugged her shoulders. She had no words to answer him.

"There's no future in it, is there, Erica? Not even if they were paying you twice as much—which they should be. There's no place to promote an American, much less a female one. Erica, what the hell are you doing with your life?"

"Just a minute," she answered defensively. "The company has been great to me. They let me in when no one else would give me a broom to sweep the floor with, they've taught me tons about business, they appreciate my efforts. And I don't have to deal with any stuffed egos around my office, either. You should see the desk that the vice president has—not a bit more luxurious than mine. We're all in this together. For the company."

"Very touching. All you little bees working together for the production of the honey. But you haven't answered my question. Where do you go from here? You've been at this place, what, six months? How long, do you think, before it's time to move?"

"I can't get through to you, Brian. You just don't understand what it means, company loyalty."

"Oh, I understand too well. Safety before all else. Really, Erica. To all appearances you're just another little secretary working to keep herself in nail polish, waiting for the white knight to come and save her from this cruel world, set her up in the tract-castle with the all-electric eat-in kitchen."

"Brian, you don't know me as well as you think. There's a

part of me that really longs for the ordinary joys that make life worth living for most of this race. If you could shoot someone for wanting a family and kids, I'd be dead twice over."

"But that isn't what you really want the *most*, is it? If it were, you'd be the set designer for the church production of *My Fair Lady* or dating the guy who came in to fix your telephone line."

"No, I'm not 'circulating,' but not because I don't want to. I need time to heal from a catastrophic marriage. Besides, once burned, ever careful."

"Aww, poor Erica. Somehow, it doesn't quite gel, 'Erica as victim.' Have you ever considered that your whole relationship with old Whit-less Eaton was a scene you yourself created?"

"Oh, please!" Erica was angry. "You sound like one of those est people. Everything is the victim's fault. Cambodia, world hunger . . ."

"Take it easy. I'm not blaming you for that awful mess with the Eatons. I'm merely suggesting that you are one of those people who need to get their mistakes over with. You do the things others expect of you, and when that proves disastrous, you're free to do what you really want."

Erica sighed. "All this analysis is very clever, but it doesn't really get me anywhere, does it?"

"That depends. Where do you want to get to?"

Erica was about to shake her head in despair, then she stopped herself. "I want to get to . . . to a point where I won't have to worry about my parents' security ever again."

"Bravo, Erica! Nice choice. Although, if you're going to talk about security, be honest. Talk about your own. Now. How do you propose to get to your goal?"

"There's the rub. You know that I know that I can't get there working for the Japanese."

"Exactly so. All right, we've progressed, we agree that it's time to make a move. Now, what will it be?"

"I could try to find work at another company. My experience here should be worth something. I could try the major chemical companies, Du Pont, Dow, Nox . . . But oh, Brian, the idea of looking for a job again . . ."

Brian waved his hand in dismissal. "You're thinking strictly short-term, Erica. That's always a mistake in business. If you headed for the chemical big boys you'd certainly get a better-paying job. But, your chances of rising in the corporation are almost as infinitesimal as where you are. Eventually, you'll learn shorthand and move up to being some hotshot's assistant. But forget real responsibility. And without responsibility, my dear, you'll always be just another little bee."

"Well, what can I do? Come on, Mr. Realist, do you think I can walk in somewhere and demand the key to the executive washroom? Let's face it, this little bee is pretty much stuck in the wax."

"Oh, Erica, Erica. Open your eyes. This is a new world here. Business is discovering America, and vice versa.

"Look at me. Ten years ago I was considering entering the seminary. What else could a poor Irish sissy with good grades aim for? But I let the current carry me instead, and here I am, stringing my bars and restaurants all up and down the coast. And who do you think is financing all this, dear student? Guess. No, not the savings and loan around the corner, not some hip young venture capitalist in a pastel suit. No, no. None other than Spence, Eaton, and Chalmers."

"No!"

"Oh, yes. And they were *begging* for the business. Times must be getting hard for the blue bloods, don't you think, if they're panting at my Irish lace curtains and falling all over themselves to spread cash on the disco floor."

"My God, you mean Whit and his dad know that you're opening *gay bars* with their money?"

"They sure do. And old man Eaton is just about smart enough to be grateful. Not any smarter, to be sure . . . And your ex, Whit, he'll appreciate it too, when he comes down from his high. What is it he does, coke?"

"What?"

"Cocaine. He's into nose candy, isn't he? I can tell."

"Brian, don't be ridiculous. Drugs? He's an *Eaton*, for heaven's sake."

"Every inch of him. And a Spence as well. He might as well be a Chalmers, too, for my money. All of them together don't know enough about modern economic life to scrape the wax off a lottery ticket."

"Oh come on, Brian. They are rich and getting richer. That banking house makes tons of money. *You're* making them rich after all, aren't you?"

"Sure, but it's not thanks to the firm's heads. They can always find two Jews and an Armenian to run the show and keep it in the black. And times are changing, Erica, as I said before. Those three young guys will wake up one day and say, 'Hey, we don't have accents, we don't use brilliantine, but we still can't make partner in this company. Only Whit Eaton and his fellow tootin' polo players can rise in this bank. Let's make tracks.'

"And eventually, there will be nothing left but those old farts sitting in leather club chairs and reminiscing about how wily old Chalmers the first made a killing in the volatile markets of 'ought four."

"Well, that's very interesting gossip, but I've got no connections with them, as you know. Whether the bank rises or falls is nothing to me."

"Ah, but it has a lot to do with you. There are no vacuums allowed in the game, Erica. The old order is fading and a new one will take its place. If the Mings fall the Manchus must rise."

"What makes you think I'm a Manchu, rather than just another coolie?"

"Got a feeling about you, girl. Always did. I think, Erica, that the only one who doesn't feel the heat from the fire in your belly is you."

"You think I'm ambitious. Boy, that's funny. Well, maybe I am. So what? Wishful thinking is so cheap even I can afford it."

"Training, on the other hand, is more expensive. But, Erica, you can afford that, too."

"How do you mean?"

"Business school. Don't you see, that *has* to be your next move."

"But Brian . . . well, I did see a pamphlet about Baruch, and it's not too expensive. Maybe I could go at night."

"No, Erica, you can't. You can't go to Baruch and you can't go at night.

"You must go to one of the top schools, Stanford, Harvard, Wharton . . ."

"How? They're expensive! And I bet they admit about two and a half women among the bunch of them. Besides, I didn't even finish college. And my grades stank to high heaven. Don't you see, it's hopeless."

"I don't see it at all. As far as I'm concerned there's only one prerequisite for *anything* you want in life: the desire and the energy to go out and get it.

"Now, here's how you start."

Brian took an eelskin checkbook out of his breast pocket. He wrote a check, tore it out, and stuck it between the vanda orchid and the Turk's-cap lily in the table vase.

Erica looked at the check. Her eyebrows shot up. "It's generous of you, Brian, but really, I can save up the money for school myself, that really isn't the issue."

"That's not for school, honey, that's for clothes. You're going to spend that entire sum on one outfit, understand? One perfect outfit for your interviews. You can pay me back in, oh, four years. You should be making decent money by then."

Brian glanced up and down her revealing peach summer dress. His survey was the physical but nonerotic gaze of a gynecologist.

"You look great, Erica. But you have to know that there's a difference between *great* and *right*."

The interviewer wore a bow tie and smoked a pipe with tobacco that smelled edible. He looked like a man who had been asked once too often, "If you're so smart, why ain't you rich?"

He cleared his throat. Erica forced her body into composure. She smoothed her perfectly tailored skirt and crossed her perfectly shod feet at the ankles.

"So, Miss Eaton, is it?"

Erica did not correct the honorific.

"Any relation to Cyrus Eaton, the great industrialist?"

"No, and many are the regrets I've heard about *that*, for all the Spence and Eaton snobbery about midwesterners!"

She smiled in what she hoped was an impish way.

"Oh," he laughed nervously, "Spence, Eaton, & Chalmers. *Those* Eatons."

"The very same," said Erica. "Ha, ha, ha."

The interviewer shuffled her application forms. "Now, I see here that you left Radcliffe prior to completing the course of studies. Why would you interrupt so promising an academic career?"

"I was impatient, sir. I felt I had to go out into the world of business. The real world."

"Well, I can certainly sympathize with that. And I see here that you found an immediate executive position with Mulligan Restaurant Associates. Quite an achievement in itself. But why didn't you enter the family firm?"

"Oh, that wouldn't have been very challenging. And after all, challenge is my raison d'être for going into business in the first place."

That and eating regularly. Did you get the French? See how well-rounded I am. Not your usual money-grubbing applicant, right? An unusually promising young lady, right? And you get points for every woman and minority, so might as well take this one, right?

"My, Mr. Mulligan's letter of recommendation is certainly enthusiastic."

"He's very kind. It was he who encouraged me to apply to your school in the first place. Of course, my family would prefer that I attend Harvard, but . . ."

Where's your school pride? Here's your chance to steal away one of the heirs to the Harvard Patrimony.

"And is this letter from Toshiro Ozu, *the* Japanese managerial innovator?"

"Mr. Ozu has been a great inspiration to me. Working with the Japanese has given me a whole new perspective on management."

"Your business experience is most interesting. Ah, what exactly did you do for this Mr. Singh, the president of the motel chain?"

"I'm helping computerize the chain's reservations and accounting system. I do that in my spare time, in the evenings."

Oh, what a whopper! Imagine Singh keeping electronic records of his cash.

"Marvelous. We need more young people like you, unafraid of technology. We look to the future here, Miss Eaton.

"Well, this is not a promise, Miss Eaton, but I like the cut of your jib. You're courageous and innovative and energetic, without being, you know, unfeminine. I like that and I think the committee will, too.

"So, if I may say so, in the event that you are invited to attend the Graduate School of Business at this great university, and you accept, I am certain that you will have at least as rich and rewarding a learning experience as at the, ahem, institution your family has previously endowed."

He stood to shake hands.

Chapter Twelve

From Thisweek *Magazine, October 15, 1977*

GOSSIP

"A" PARTIES . . . BLAST OF THE YEAR . . . was the nuptials of Superagent CHUCK LLOYD, 67, and Sexy Starlet MELISSA JOHN, 26, he for the third time, she for the second. All Hollywood turned out for the rollicking event, where the triumphant bridegroom put to rest all rumors that ill health was leading him to retirement. Lloyd's deal-making behind the scenes of *Star Wars* was a big factor behind the movie's astonishing success, and no one at the wedding was likely to overlook it. Ewok "bridesmaids" attended the bride—she of E.Z. Shave commercial fame—who wore a Princess Leia gown of sueded silk and carried a "bouquet" of flashing laser-beam bulbs. Which may all point to the fashion of the future—all but the forties-style shoulder pads, which mode pundits agree, haven't a chance. . . .

Beverly Hills
September, 1978

Nina was an excellent maid. She had been "stolen" by one wealthy matron after another, each paying her more and more, until she had ended up at the Lloyds' house. Her salary supported an entire Guatemalan village.

Nina padded into the room and woke Melissa. Melissa came wide awake immediately. If Nina came in to wake her, it must be important.

Nina pulled the tassels that moved the billowing curtains from the French windows. Light poured in on Melissa's bed, as if it were a stage at Caesar's Palace.

Melissa bolted up to a sitting position.

"What's the matter?"

"It is Señor Lloyd's doctor on the phone, Señora."

Melissa pulled the phone from one of the bedside tables. The voluminous skirts of the table rustled from the movement. The earpiece of the phone fell on the floor and was lost among the satin dust ruffles.

Damn it! She hated that stupid phone. It was a fake French "antique," gilded and pink-enameled. She couldn't imagine it being useful as anything other than a prop in a screwball-heiress comedy.

"Hello?" Her voice sounded worried. Hell, she *was* worried.

An impersonal female voice. "Dr. Lederer for Mrs. Lloyd. Please hold on."

Then, a small man's voice. "Mrs. Lloyd? Sheldon Lederer here. Mrs. Lloyd, I don't mean to alarm you, but I do think it's advisable to discuss your husband's condition before we proceed further in his treatment."

"Well, sure. When can we talk?"

"I thought we might discuss it over lunch."

"I'm afraid I already have a date for lunch, how about earlier."

"Uh, eleven-thirty, then? At my office?"

It was 9:30 already. Time to get moving.

First she tip-toed across the hallway to Chuck's room. She opened the door carefully and stuck her head in.

You could tell Chuck was sick. He never rose after eight, even on vacation. Most days he was in his office by seven, the better to start negotiations with the East coast. That's why they had separate bedrooms. His wife—the one before Melissa—liked to sleep late.

Chuck's face was covered with a film of sweat, despite the active air-conditioning. His face looked like clay melting in the rain.

He was really sick, there was no kidding about it. The alarms first rang in her brain when the doctor ordered plenty of bed rest and Chuck hadn't protested at all. Now here was the doctor calling her in for a little talk. It wasn't likely to be good news.

He couldn't be dying. He couldn't *do* that to her. They had this pact, this unspoken agreement. He was going to make her a star; she was going to make him young again.

The truth was she'd never been turned on by older men, she hadn't been on the prowl for a father figure. Her own father had been distant and uncommunicative but he had been daddy enough. Still, she loved Chuck more than any human being on earth. And she would be the first to admit that that wasn't anywhere near what he deserved.

Chuck deserved a real wife. The second was the only one he could really think of as a wife. Melissa was the beautiful girl he'd married, and the silly society woman was his "ex," but only the middle one really registered in Chuck's mind as "wife." Melissa didn't hold it against him.

She loved being married to Chuck.

The wedding had been great fun. *Everyone* was there. The caterer's tables were paved with beluga and champagne flowed like the Johnstown flood. Cold-hearted Hollywood made an exception for the popular and powerful groom. And for the first time, they really *noticed* Melissa.

All these strangers with faces more familiar than your own flesh and blood! Yet their warmth and good wishes seemed genuine.

Only one thing gave her a start. The icy stare of Diana

Tremain seemed to follow Melissa all day. She *couldn't* remember, could she? It was so long ago, that scene in the Stanhope. Then why did she keep looking at her that way? Diana's bloodless fingers grasped a champagne flute, and she chatted with many guests, but her eyes didn't leave Melissa for a moment.

And since the wedding, every time they ran into each other, which was often, Diana gave her the same look. The bitch! Melissa admitted to herself that she resented Diana. What had that cold, *old* woman ever done to deserve a husband like Paul Tremain? That stuck-up attitude really was repulsive. Just who did she think she was, anyway? She ought to be down on her hands and knees in gratitude for being married to the world's number one dreamboat. Instead, she was acting as if she owned the universe, even at *Melissa's own wedding*. Melissa wished she had the nerve to tell Diana off. But of course, she wouldn't. She would never embarrass Chuck that way.

Melissa took lovers. In the beginning she was very secretive, then she realized that Chuck was fully aware of what was going on. After all, he was no fool. She began to notice that there were many Hollywood couples who maintained their kind of relationship, that a standard existed, as in the European upper classes, of neatly separating marriage from sex.

She was always discreet; in her way she was loyal and respectful to her husband. She'd make love with a man in some nook or cranny of the sprawling house. Never would she mess around on her own bed, despite the fact that it looked like a hooker's fantasy, a raised cupcake of pink satin with a padded peacock-tail headboard. Suspended above it was an enormous chandelier that would have been at home in the lobby of a Miami hotel. Perhaps, Melissa feared, it might fall vengefully on her and one of her lovers.

She really had to redecorate the bedroom one of these days. She liked to keep the drapes open. "I didn't come to California to sit in the dark," Melissa often said. Now the room— carefully matched in cameo pink by Chuck's wife—was streaked and faded to the shade of an old lady's face powder.

She'd have to get a decorator one of these days, though she

had no head for any of it. Why, it was weeks before she realized that the dining room that Chuck had ordered wallpapered with pale apricot silk, had mistakenly been painted maroon. She could never quite get the point of any of those things—decor, food, social manipulation—that marked the successful matron.

Now it was time to get dressed. In this she certainly *was* expert. She sat down to her dressing table, which was built into a Plexiglas unit that cataloged her cosmetics the way chemicals were stored in a professional laboratory. Then she entered the fifty-foot closet. It had been built to the specifications of the "wife," in whose day it was stuffed with hundreds of fantasy gowns in chiffon, lamé, and other silly fabrics.

Now the cavernous closet was virtually empty. Melissa kept exactly a dozen outfits, each one perfect. She did not hesitate to add to her wardrobe—but recycled an outfit to charity with each acquisition. To Melissa, dressing was a science.

She chose a white cotton dress, whose utter simplicity did not hide the fact that it was very expensive. On a less-voluptuous figure the dress would have seemed stiff, forbidding. But on Melissa it was seductive and at the same time, refined.

She glided out of the driveway in her turquoise Ferrari. What pleasure she had from that car! The truth was she loved a bargain, although she *wasn't* cheap.

The car had belonged to a doomed actress, a beauty who had died in a drunken accident. At the auction that followed, the actress's house sold for a record price, and her memorabilia went for ludicrous amounts of money. But the car was shunned.

Melissa laughed in derision. Superstitious idiots, these Hollywood people. It was the foolish actress, not the car, that had courted death. And it wasn't as if there were bloodstains on the beige chamois interior.

She gunned the machine toward Dr. Lederer's office.

Melissa had been certain that there would be a long, humiliating wait. She cringed at the thought of patients eyeing her, asking her, "Are you somebody?" "Have I seen you on TV?"

But she was wrong on both counts. First, the receptionist waved her right in. And, when she thought about it, the people likely to be waiting in that waiting room, patients sick enough to need a specialist of Lederer's standing, had little stomach for celebrity games.

It was clear that the doctor's decorator had been given a free hand. The office resembled a restaurant with a South Seas theme. Huge-leafed plants sprang up in the waiting room, seashells, nets, and other nautical paraphernalia drifted all over the walls, tropical fish swam in six-foot tanks.

Sheldon Lederer, M.D., P.C., Fellow of the American Colleges of Surgery, Cardiology, and Internal Medicine, honorary professor at the Karolinska, Hadassah, and Pasteur institutes, rose to greet her.

"Melissa! If I may call you that. Come, let's sit on the lanai."

They passed through to an adjoining porch, shaded by jungle foliage.

Dr. Lederer was of medium height, pudgy, with the look about him of the bright but overlooked student. His hands were beautiful, slim and expressive as a ballerina's.

"The operation," began Melissa.

"We simply could not perform it at this time."

"But you said he'd had a mild heart attack. I've heard of people having quadruple bypasses. Why couldn't Chuck have just the one?"

Lederer placed one of his exquisite hands on Melissa's forearm. It was light as a butterfly, but she knew lust when it touched her.

"Mrs. Lloyd, ah, Melissa. Would to God it were only the cardiac problem. Were it so, we would have performed the bypass and the condition would have been alleviated, as you said.

"But I very much regret to tell you that preoperative radiology revealed a shadow on the lower left quadrant of Mr. Lloyd's right lung."

"A shadow?"

"And, I'm afraid, further examination showed metastasis to the liver."

"Cancer!" she said.

He lowered his head. There was no need to repeat the obscene word.

"But he doesn't even smoke," said Melissa, helplessly.

"I'm afraid virtue is not always rewarded," the doctor said, folding his lovely hands modestly in his lap.

"What now?" asked Melissa.

"Under the circumstances—the advanced stage of the disease—I would think that chemotherapy would do more harm than good. However, I urge you to consult with an oncologist before you decide on a course of treatment—or the absence of any."

"Have you told him that he's *dying*?" Surely the bastard didn't expect *her* to do his dirty job.

"I don't believe that's necessary. In my experience, most patients of his intelligence already know. Let him indicate if he wants to discuss it in greater detail."

Although Melissa felt in control of her feelings, she wobbled slightly on her heels as they went back into the office.

Lederer caught her by her bare upper arm and wouldn't let go.

"I want you to know, Melissa, that in the coming weeks and months, a time of great stress and anxiety for you, you must always remember that you have a friend who is happy to lend whatever support you might need. Truly, a friend and not just a physician.

"I mean that. Call me for whatever reason. For any reason at all. Or none."

"Thanks so much, doctor," she said, unclamping his hand, and leaving. "I will."

Bro-ther.

The horror of the morning's meeting swelled it out of realistic proportion. She was amazed to find that although already exhausted by the day's events, she was early for her lunch date at the Polo Lounge. Melissa's face burned crimson as she told the maître d' her name.

"Mrs. Chuck Lloyd."

She had no choice. "Melissa John" meant nothing here; she had to use her husband's good offices if she wanted to eat at the trough of the mighty.

The Polo Lounge was one of the few places in the world where few heads turned when she entered the room. The wheelers and dealers of moviedom had gorged on female beauty to the point of nausea.

Melissa watched cautiously as a stunning young blond entered, wearing a crocheted dress with nothing underneath. Men noticed her only if they were otherwise unoccupied. Few were at such leisure.

Her lunch date arrived. Throughout the room people nodded slightly to Shirl Kaufman. She held little power of her own, and Hollywood was notoriously reluctant to bestow any attention at all on the *spouses* of the powerful. But Shirl Kaufman was the daughter of the legendary studio head, Aram Akullian, the Fresno raisin farmer who first exploited the true power of the talkies. Her father, and the studio system, were long dead, but people paid homage to Shirl. She was as Old Hollywood as they came.

Shirl looked like a woman with half a century behind her, much of it well spent.

"Darling! You look wonderful," said the two ladies simultaneously. Melissa kissed the air between Shirl's necklace and earring.

"How's Chuckie doing, Melissa?"

"Wonderful. I just saw his doctor and the reports are excellent." *The kiss of death was the kiss of death in this town.*

"I'm so glad. I just love that man. So does Josh," said Shirl sincerely.

"Don't we all." *Already the eulogies.*

Shirl placed a hand on one of Melissa's. "Lederer's the man you want to be seeing. He's the tops in cardiac."

"Yes, he's our man. I really do feel very confident about him. A top-notch doctor." *And, of course, Forest Lawn. We wouldn't want him buried in a losers' cemetery.*

The waiter was standing above them.

"Oh, good. I'm starving," said Shirl.

Melissa stared at the menu. She had to concentrate. She

couldn't let what was happening to Chuck scramble her careful plans for the day. It had been hell getting Shirl here in the first place. Now she had to turn the conversation to serious purpose.

Shirl's husband, Josh Kaufman, was one of the most successful independent producers anywhere. His power could be belittled only in comparison with his late father-in-law's. Melissa was determined to get herself a part in his latest movie, *Shades of Gray*.

The waiter was looking at her, politely but insistently.

"Oh. I'll have the same."

Melissa was appalled when the double Scotches arrived. Shirl downed hers like a thirsty hiker hitting the canteen.

There was an awkward pause in their conversation.

Now. Do it now, thought Melissa. But words wouldn't form in her mouth.

"Well, if you aren't having this, let's not waste it," said Shirl, tossing off the second generous glassful.

Melissa's eyes bugged. The woman must have the Loch Ness monster in her stomach!

Shirl slammed the glass down with a satisfied "Ahh."

Melissa froze in terror. What could she talk about now? She could hardly start discussing Shirl's husband's movies out of the blue. It would be so baldly calculating. She'd been so confident last night, as she imagined this scene. Now she felt like she was drowning. Oh, damn that doctor and his evil tidings.

The waiter arrived, a personal savior.

Melissa dug into the salad with false enthusiasm. They'd come up with all these different kinds of lettuce these days. All of them tasted like diet licorice.

Shirl ate heartily. "So," she said, her mouth full of food, "sleeping with Josh was a very shrewd idea."

Melissa choked.

"Take it easy, kid. Doesn't bother me in the least. Never has. Not in the last thirty years, at least. But seriously, it was very smart.

"See, Josh knows anything he can give you, Chuck could

give you for free. So, he figures, you must be screwing him because you really like him. God, is he flattered.

"But tell me, what *do* you want from him?"

Melissa put down her fork. She wasn't embarrassed anymore. "I want a part in *Shades.*"

Shirl grimaced. "That piece of *dreck*? Whatever for? Besides, Bujold's got the part. She'd like to get out of it, to be sure, but she's probably stuck."

"Not that part, I mean the part of the wife."

"Oh come on, Melissa. Who's going to believe that any man would leave *you* for another woman?"

"But Genevieve Bujold is prettier than I am."

"Don't fish for compliments. It's bad for your image."

"Damn it. I need the part, I need *something* in a major production."

"Well, *something*, maybe, but not *anything*. Besides, *Shades* is less a 'major production' than an expected flop. I can't believe Chuck would let you do it."

"Oh, he disapproves of my being in it. But every time there's a part I could get, he tells me to hold off. At this rate my big break will come as a *grandmother.*"

"Well, whatever Chuck told you, he's probably right."

Melissa said nothing. She was angry and tired. This day had turned into a nightmare; she yearned for sleep. She pointedly refused dessert and coffee, and did not insist that Shirl have any. She was in no mood to play hostess.

As they waited outside for their cars to be brought round, Shirl faced Melissa in the harsh sunlight.

"Well, you've made it clear why you invited me to lunch. Now aren't you curious as to why I accepted?"

Melissa stared.

"Have you ever slept with a woman, Melissa?"

Melissa thought she would sink right down on the driveway. She tried to recall every remedy for stage fright that she had ever heard of.

"No. As a matter of fact I haven't."

"You don't sound disgusted."

Melissa giggled nervously. "Why should I be?"

Shirl smiled. It made her face look ten years younger. "Would you like to sleep with me?"

Melissa looked down at her Maud Frizon sandals. Think fast! She'd never for a minute thought that way about women. Certainly she couldn't dream of lusting for Shirl Kaufman! But here was the opportunity to get exactly what she had wanted from the producer's wife. God, she was turning into such a whore. But, hell, she did it with men for no better reason.

"Sure."

Melissa drove carefully behind Shirl's white Cadillac. It was not a trendy car, but Shirl's father had always warned that Rollses attracted kidnappers.

Melissa was awed by Shirl's house. It was beautiful, really beautiful. Very showy, obviously expensive, but, unlike her own home, not gaudy, undeniably beautiful.

They went to Shirl's exquisite boudoir, done in lilac and yellow. They undressed. Melissa felt a curiosity she knew could make up for a lack of desire.

The sheets on Shirl's bed looked as if they were painted by Monet to match the decor.

"Pure silk, right?" asked Melissa, touching the softness of a pillow sham.

"No, cotton. A special kind they grow in only one place. An island off North Carolina, I think."

"I've got to get some for Chuck. All our linens chafe him."

Naked, Melissa contemplated Shirl's body. It was in good shape, but it was a mother's body. Why not? Shirl had two grown children. Her breasts were generous and soft and wholesome—like the pillow shams.

Melissa now realized she could never get it up for Shirl, and her acting talents would once again be called for in her role as lover.

Soon Melissa figured out the angle, just as she did with every lover. She could love a woman's body, yes. Her *own*.

As Shirl's hands moved down the sides of her torso, Melissa identified with them. Oh, divine skin! Oh, flesh full of joy and life! Precious, precious thighs.

Vulva, rose red, unfolding like the radiant rose. Sweet petals of the rose, moist with the morning dew, stirring in the warm breeze of love.

Unfurl, unfold, delicious flower! Give up the sweetness of your perfume, the richness of your flavor. Oh, the incomparable pleasure of loving Melissa John!

She groaned in genuine ecstasy.

Shirl was delightfully surprised. She laughed a girlish laugh. Melissa hadn't noticed whether the older woman had had any other pleasure from the encounter.

They dressed. Shirl was quicker and sat in an exquisite tufted *fauteuil*, gazing at Melissa with adoration.

"Come," she said, "let me hold you in my arms."

Melissa went over and sat next to her hostess.

Shirl held her tight, cradled her head in her bosom, rocked back and forth, back and forth, cooing softly.

Melissa felt a terrible pity for her. Sex was one thing, but trading in love was pathetic.

As she pulled away, Melissa noticed that Shirl's eyes were wet.

"Will you come here again?" asked Shirl.

Melissa shrugged. She couldn't lie to the poor woman, she couldn't. "We'll see."

Fear passed over the face of Shirl Kaufman.

"Josh was talking the other day . . ."

Melissa straightened, electrified.

"Aldo Brandini has a new project he's very interested in."
Brandini. Europe's greatest director.

"Brandini intends to do a very expensive, very big production. Josh thinks it's worth it. He says the audience is there."

"What? What is it about?"

"It's a biblical epic. A retelling of the story of Christ.

"Oh, Melissa, I think you'd be just perfect for it."

"I would? As what?"

"As the Virgin Mary, of course."

Melissa on the way back from her fateful rendezvous. A flash of turquoise lightning in the Hills of Beverly.

She was flushed, as if with sex as she raced through the house. She leaped up the ostentatious staircase, three steps at a time.

She rushed into Chuck's room, pushing the door wildly before her, not bothering to knock.

Her heart stopped. The bed was empty. The bedspread was absolutely geometrical, like a bedspread in a chain hotel.

No, God. No, no, no!

She was being ridiculous. Of course he wasn't dead.

She raced back downstairs, leaving the Maud Frizons on the staircase, like Cinderella. Through the huge, overchilled, overdecorated rooms, to the kitchen.

Nina was chatting with the cook, her back to the door, but turned instantly when Melissa entered. She sensed Melissa's fear.

"Señor Lloyd, he was feeling a little better, Señora. I told Ernesto to help me bring him over to the pool. The sun, it is good for him, no?"

Melissa remembered Ernesto. He had the most beautiful eyelashes she had ever seen, and he was lithe as a fish. But it was a mistake to screw with the help. They got cocky, so to speak. They stopped doing their jobs. And it was a lot harder to get decent domestics than a decent lay.

The pool area was a riot of hibiscus, hot pink, gold, flame. The blooms, brazen as harlots, were at their peak.

Chuck was lying on a chaise. His color was even more ghastly against the yellow fabric, against the emerald grass, against the lapis blue pool.

"Hi, honey," she whispered, "are you sleeping?"

His eyes opened immediately and he smiled his familiar sad smile.

"Oh, Chuck," she babbled, as if her chatter could sustain him. "I heard the most exciting thing today." She pulled a chair up to the chaise.

"I had lunch with Shirl Kaufman—it went on *forever*—and what do you think the little birdie told me? Aldo Brandini is doing a movie about Jesus, and Josh Kaufman is backing it one hundred fifty percent! Shirl says she thinks, well, she feels I'm a shoo-in for the role of Mary. What do you think, honey? Be honest."

There was a pause. Melissa thought that Chuck was falling asleep on her. She shivered. But suddenly he responded with animation.

"I think it's a wonderful idea. Perfect. This could be it, darling."

"Really? You really think so? I always thought I was more the Mary Magdalene type, actually," she winked.

Chuck was too tired for coquetry. "It's a great part, and you'll get it. If it were a real starring vehicle you wouldn't have a chance. Brandini and Kaufman wouldn't bank on an unknown quantity. But Mary is not an official lead, while still the most important female role. It's a golden opportunity, Melissa.

"Just think, every Easter they'll show that movie on TV and everyone will be reminded, again and again, how beautiful you are, and that you're a *serious* actress."

Melissa's heart was pounding. "Are you going to call Aldo Brandini, Chuck?"

"Oh, darling, I'm so tired."

"Oh, honey, I didn't mean *now.*"

He ignored her protest. "Go call Ted at the office. He's a very competent man. You'll get the part. You'll get it on your own steam."

Melissa beamed. "Thank you for your confidence, honey. But I'm not ashamed to use your pull. You're my man and I'm proud of it."

She should kiss him on the forehead, she thought. But she hesitated. That cold, clammy gray skin, like something out of a cellar.

"The sun's not too hot for you, is it, Chuckie?"

He had closed his eyes. The conversation had worn him out. In answer to her question it was all he could manage to shake his head.

"Okay, I'll go up and change. Be right back, so don't go away, hear?"

Melissa headed up to her bedroom. She felt sick herself.

Sick with guilt. Sick with loneliness. Chuck was dying; she was at the dawn of her real life.

She would get the part on her own steam. She really didn't need Chuck now, not for that. And he didn't need her now. This was a journey he'd be going alone.

From her dressing room Melissa looked out at the pool.

Chuck had managed to raise a hand, and signaled to Nina. Nina approached him, put her ear to his lips. A minute later she came back with a manuscript in floppy covers.

Melissa was incensed. Imagine! Giving the man scripts to read when he was so exhausted! What the hell was the matter with that Nina?

She pulled on a sundress and marched furiously out to the pool. Chuck's head had fallen down to his sunken chest. Her heart stopped for a terrible instant. But he wasn't dead, of course, only napping.

She glanced down at the open manuscript in his lap. It wasn't a screenplay, after all.

It was a Bible.

Chapter Thirteen

MELISSA HUGGED Erica hard. After a second's hesitation, Erica hugged back.

"Thank you for coming out to the airport to pick me up, Melissa. Frankly, I was a little hesitant about calling you."

"Whatever for? Aren't I one of your best friends in L.A.?"

"You're my only friend in this city. But you're a *movie star*, for heaven's sake. And, well, it's one thing to gab on the phone once in a while, another to impose on your hospitality."

Melissa grimaced in disdain. Her beautiful face was amazingly elastic. "Come on. We've been buddies for a long time, ever since you came into Goldsmith's. Not that I'm not permanently pissed at your not coming out for my wedding. Chuck had two planeloads of easterners flown in. It wouldn't have cost you a dime."

"Oh, Melissa, you know I would have loved to come. But how could I—the term had just started at business school. There's a limit to how many times you can mess up at school."

"But Chuck . . . Erica, he was probably the best man who will ever come into my life, and you never even met him."

"I know, I'm sorry. Believe me, I would have loved to be there. You in Bettina's most glorious getup, even with all those movie stars, you, the most gorgeous movie star . . ."

"Aw, cut out that 'movie star' shit. I'm just a working woman, just like you will be, Miss Fancy Pants Executive Trainee."

"Get out of here."

"I mean it. I've even got to go in today to shoot a short scene over. Want to come and watch?"

"Watch one of your movies being filmed? Seriously?"

"Sure. We'll drop off your stuff at the house, then go right over."

Melissa grabbed Erica's bags and headed for her car.

"Melissa, what are you doing?" cried Erica.

"These are nothing. You ought to see what I lift at the gym. Greatest thing for toning."

Soon they were riding in Melissa's convertible, a lime-green Excalibur. As the wind blew through Erica's hair and the sun shone down brightly, Erica experienced a sensation of physical freedom such as she had never felt before.

"Is it true, Melissa, that California is the edge of the world? Is it true this is Paradise, or as close as we're likely to get to it?"

"Buckle your seat belt," said Melissa.

At the studio, Erica accompanied Melissa to makeup.

"This is Lacey, the woman who made my career. Lace, this is Erica Eaton, my old buddy, a business whiz from New York."

Lacey and Erica both began to protest at the same time.

"Nobody created Melissa John but Melissa John. She knows more about what look is right for her than anyone does. And besides, she's got talent, not just that face."

"And what's this nonsense about me and business, Melissa? I'm just starting out on my first job after school."

"False modesty is such a lot of crap, you two. Come on, Erica, you practically pulled Goldsmith's out of bankruptcy."

"Get out of here! I made one teeny suggestion. Ideas are a dime a dozen."

"You'll love this, Lacey. Erica came up with the idea of a skin-and-cosmetics salon at Goldsmith's bridal shop."

Erica blushed. The new salon had been an almost instant success. She changed the subject. "This is certainly different makeup from the Goldsmith salon. What kind of goddess are you making today, Lacey?"

Melissa shook her head. "No goddesses. See, the character I play, Nora, has just lost the love of her life in a flying accident. She's having a tense face-off with the lover's sister, who believes that there was foul play and Nora had something to do with it. We can't have Nora looking like she spent the morning in front of her mirror!"

Lacey smiled indulgently as she sponged foundation on Melissa's face. "She's really something, our Melissa. The only actress I know who doesn't think her beauty is the point of the picture. Ironically, it probably *is*."

Erica found a shadowed seat from which to watch the filming. She was immediately disappointed. The set, which was supposed to be the library of an elegant house, was made of the cheapest cardboard. She could tell, even from her distant seat, that the table between Melissa and the other actress, supposedly of marble, was slapdash plywood covered in Con-Tact paper.

"What brings you here at a time like this?" said Melissa, as the shooting began. Erica immediately felt on the verge of tears. Melissa was that sympathetic in the role.

"You know damn well what I want to talk about. And so does that son-of-a-bitch Watson."

"Cut!" yelled the director, so that Erica jumped.

"Think we can do that with a little feeling, Doreen? Say, enough to convince us you wouldn't rather be elsewhere?"

The actress pursed her lips.

"What brings you here at a time like this?" said Melissa, bringing tears of sympathy to Erica's eyes again.

"You know damn well what I want to talk about. And so does that son-of-a-bitch Watson."

"Cut!" yelled the director again. His criticism and his sarcasm increased by several degrees.

Three more times the scene was repeated. After the fifth cut, Doreen burst out, "I've had it! Watson isn't the son of a bitch here, you are!" And she stormed off the set.

Melissa ran after her. She put both hands on the actress's shoulders. "Come on, don't let him do this to you. You're a professional, don't let him bug you out of doing what you know you are capable of."

"No, it's impossible. I'm through with this picture."

"The hell you are. Look. It's like falling off a horse. You've got to get right back on again, or you spook yourself. It may be the horse's fault, but you can't lose your own assurance. If you walk off the set, you're through with this director, but what about the next temperamental one? Come on, let's go back there and kill him with how good we are."

The actress consented and the next take crackled with taut acting. It was a print. Erica settled back to watch the rest of the show. But the director now found fault with something else. The second scene, too, was endlessly repeated. So was every scene that followed.

At last, they broke for the day. As Lacey removed Melissa's makeup, Erica sighed. "I don't know if it's my jet lag, or what, but that felt like Chinese water torture. I may never go to another movie again!"

Melissa opened her eyes in consternation. "You didn't like it? Oh, I thought you would really love it. Oh, that's awful . . ."

"Maybe it was just today, doing the same thing over and over."

"But it wasn't over and over. Each repetition was different. Could you see how Nora kept opening up, how she was slowly finding courage within herself? And the sister, did you notice how, as Doreen got into it, not only the evil but the self-pity comes through?"

"Uh, no, I didn't. But boy, the director sure let her have it with both barrels."

Melissa frowned. "She had it coming. God, what a baby. Really, I was ashamed for her. It wouldn't be so bad if she weren't so talented. The worst thing would be for her to get a reputation as a hard case and never get a chance to develop. It could be tragic! Also, this is not her living room. Everybody involved with the movie has to think of the big picture, pardon the pun. Oh, don't repeat a word I said here."

Erica laughed. "Don't worry, I think I've watched my last movie filming. And I don't expect the trainees at Nox, my big boring chemical company, will be hobnobbing with the stars."

"Well, I'm sorry there's no greasepaint in your blood, but say, maybe you'd like Lacey to do your face before we go?"

"No thanks."

"Just a drop of blusher, some contouring maybe?"

"No," said Erica, smiling. "Glamour is not the real me."

"You've got terrific bones," said Lacey, "and wonderful skin. With a little . . ."

"Thanks but no." Her jaw was set.

Melissa looked at Lacey and shrugged.

Dinner was served at Melissa's house, not in the awesome dining room, but in the comfortable breakfast room.

They relaxed with decaffeinated coffee—Melissa was going to bed soon, since the next day she was due at the studio before dawn.

"So," said Melissa, "what news from the romantic wars?"

Erica went to the curved Art Deco window. Early evening sunlight flowed in with a purifying power. "I've done my darndest, but frankly, I've had it up to here with men, all of them. From now on I'm strictly a company woman. A corporate nun."

"Yeah, I tend to agree. Men are basically good for only one thing."

"Sometimes I wonder even about that. I tell you I've really had it with the whole gender. I'm seriously thinking of becoming a celibate."

"Oh, yes! Save a bundle on nightgowns."

"How about you? I bet the immediate universe is plying you with flowers and diamond bracelets."

"Not exactly. Work and widowhood are two things that give men the creeps. But there is one guy panting at my feet."

"Really? *Melissa*, why haven't you told me before?"

"Must have slipped my mind. He's been around forever."

"Who is it, you tease?"

"Sheldon. This doctor who was treating Chuck. If you met him you'd realize why I never mentioned him before. Eminently forgettable."

"So why do you keep seeing him?"

"I don't know. He makes me feel safe, I guess."

"What do you need to feel safe from?"

"From . . . you know. A girl's got to have some protection."

"She does?"

It did seem ludicrous. Melissa broke into laughter. Then her face, with its ability to fluidly turn one emotion into another, became grave. "Maybe I'm attached to Sheldon because he was there when Chuck died. He was there in that terrible, ugly time."

"Oh God, I'm sorry I was so flip. How awful."

"No, it wasn't really all that bad. The worst part was before Chuck died. Afterwards, well, what can I say, he's just gone. And dead, let me tell you, is really gone." Melissa took a sip of coffee.

Erica gaped at her hostess.

"You think I'm cold, don't you, Erica?"

"N-no. Maybe a little cool."

Melissa grinned. "The highest praise in this town. Well, it's the real me. I won't bullshit about that. I forge bonds, but the bonds are cool."

"Gee, I hope they're strong, though. I plan on settling here, bringing my parents over. A good friend will make it seem more like home."

"I'm that good friend, you can count on it. But I have to tell you, I'm leaving town next month. I've got a three-picture deal I'm shooting in Europe. It'll take more than a year."

"Oh, that's terrible! I mean, I'm glad for you . . ."

"Say, I've got an idea, Erica. Why don't you move into my house. It's got plenty of room for your parents, and anyone else you want. You can throw parties here, I don't mind. And I'll keep the staff's salaries going anyway."

"No. I can't do that."

"You'd be doing me a favor. I hate the idea of no one in the house. Say, I can pay you for house-sitting."

"It's fantastically generous of you, Melissa. But I don't think so."

"Why not? It's awful not to have *people* in here. It's bad

enough with just me. Why, it was even kind of lonely when it was me and Chuck. Come on, Erica. Please."

"I'm sorry, Melissa, but you see, I've never had my own place before. I've never had even a tiny little apartment of my own, and I'm kind of looking forward to it."

"Oh, I see. Yes, I can relate to that."

Erica could see that Melissa was trying hard not to show her disappointment, that she wanted her friend's dream to come true, despite her own need for a presence in the house. Soon a radiant smile graced Melissa's beautiful face.

"Well, okay, but I still think you should get a fashion makeover."

"Melissa, Melissa. I'm not looking to be a movie star—I'd rather dig ditches than go through that acting business—and I don't need to look like one to do what I want to do, which is a man's work on a man's turf."

"Okay," said Melissa, her face full of love and acceptance. She raised a crystal goblet filled with sparkling water.

"To our hopes and dreams and ambitions, great or small."

Erica strode with purpose to the office of Roy Little, director of personnel in Nox's Century City headquarters. The secretary gave her a slow going over. There were no women executives at Nox, and secretaries just didn't know what to expect. Erica herself was at a loss as to how to dress. She decided to play it safe by wearing conservative wool suits, skirts that covered the knees, and medium-heeled pumps. The outfits always looked dowdy against the brilliant prints and bare midriffs of the clerical staff. But her clothes were a close approximation of executive men's haberdashery. Besides, it was always freezing in the building. Its temperature—and everything else about it—was adjusted to the pleasure of those who wore suits.

"Mr. Little will see you now, uh, miss."

Roy Little was a stocky man with pale, receding hair and a highly florid complexion. His thin lips protruded and his colorless brows overhung his eyes in a ridge, giving him a distinctly simian appearance, a blond ape.

Erica felt sorry for him; with looks like that he must really have talent to have risen so high in the corporation. He would have to have sympathy with her, a person discriminated against because of sex, because of an irrelevant factor. Ugly people must understand prejudice.

"Well, dear, come on over and sit down. Tell me what's on your mind."

Erica winced at his patronizing tone. Her complaint wasn't just "on her mind." She had evidence, documentation.

"Mr. Little, I have had occasion to compare notes with other members of the Executive Training Corps here. It appears to me that I am being paid a salary one thousand dollars less than is being paid each of the other five persons I spoke to. As I am the only woman in the program, I can't help but conclude that I am being discriminated against because of my sex."

Little leaned back in his chair until it creaked. "Heh, heh, heh. It's hardly as simple as that, my dear. But first things first. Aren't you aware that all salaries at Nox are to be kept confidential?"

Erica's face burned. "If you penalize me for disclosing my salary, you'll have to get the other five guys on the same charge. I'll provide their names, if you wish. Now, let's return to the subject at hand."

Roy Little's eyes narrowed, creating a thin culvert under the overhanging brows. "Let's not get hostile, shall we? I'm here to help you, Erica, to explain how we do things here at Nox Industries."

"Fine," said Erica, fighting to keep herself under control. "Please explain, then, why I am getting a thousand dollars less in salary than the males in the exact same job category!"

"Job category isn't the only factor in determining salary. An employee's background and previous experience have a great deal to do with determining what contribution he—or *she*— will bring to the corporation."

Erica felt her temper slip like a loose chain. "Just a minute, Mr. Little. I graduated twelfth in my class, Gerry Crosby graduated ninety-first in that same class. I've had extensive business experience, Jack Johnson went to business school straight out of college. None of the others has worked for a chemical producer, I have. None of the others has inside knowledge of our Japanese competitors. I do.

"This 'background and experience' crap is nothing but a deceitful tactic to cover up bald, shameless, and illegal discrimination!"

The hotter Erica got, the cooler Little became.

"Now, my dear, let's not fly off the handle. Company policy is implemented with good, solid, legally waterproof reasoning here at Nox. Let's look at the record, shall we, and get to the bottom of this misunderstanding."

Roy Little had her file ready on his desk. Erica's heart dropped. The lies and exaggerations she had told to get into business school had been toned down considerably when she wrote her job résumé. Still, that document wasn't something she'd swear her mother's life on.

He opened the file portentously. It looked rather silly. The file contained only two sheets of paper, one of which was her job application.

"Ah," he said. "There we are." The tone was that of a surgeon who had just discovered an elusive tumor.

Erica craned her neck to look at the résumé, trying to figure out which fanciful entry had been caught out.

"You see, dear," he said, his voice hearty. "It's all quite obvious. Erica, by your own admission, *you never graduated from college.*"

"*What?* That's the most asinine thing I've ever heard. A year of college did not stop one of the best business schools in the world from accepting me. It didn't stop me from winning honors at that school. It didn't stop this company from hiring me. But all of a sudden it justifies the most outrageous behavior since Jim Crow."

She rose from her chair. "Well, *dear*, you can tell it to the court!"

Little got up and blocked her way out of the office. He indicated the chair she had just vacated. "Now, now. Let's discuss this like reasonable people. Please sit down.

"Well, Miss Eaton, you've made some very strong pronouncements here, and frankly, I feel they are totally without justification. I know it can't be very comfortable to be the only woman here . . ."

"I prefer to think I'll be the *first* woman executive at Nox," she said pointedly.

"Yes, of course. Right. Well then, let's see what conclusions *the facts* lead to. Miss Eaton, do you know how much Nox Industries made in profits last year?"

"Yes. One point two billion."

"Actually, closer to one point five."

"So?"

"So does it make sense to you that a company that makes one and a half billion dollars a year would fiendishly plot to deprive *one* employee of a measly thousand dollars?"

"Mr. Little, a thousand dollars is of much greater importance to me than a million dollars, apparently, is to Nox. So let's not call it 'measly.'

"Let's not pretend, shall we, that we don't know what is going on here. This company has finally hired a woman for executive training—a more than qualified woman—not because it wants to but because it can no longer avoid doing so. Yes, Nox complies with the law, superficially. But it makes it clear to women, to minorities, that they are not welcome, that they are considered outsiders. That they don't really have a chance of making it here.

"A thousand dollars. No profit at all for a company of this size. But it's the corporate equivalent of a slap on the face."

"Oh, I think you're reading a lot into this that simply isn't there . . ."

"Maybe. We'll let the courts decide. We'll let the public decide, if that's what you prefer."

A moist haze formed above Little's chimp's lips. Erica saw it and thrilled.

"*Please*, Miss Eaton." No more "Erica dears." "This company has made a great investment in you, an investment in money—well beyond a thousand dollars—and an investment in training time, and an investment in the future. You, after all, are the management leadership of tomorrow. There is not a shred of justification in your argument, of course, but the Nox family really wants you to be happy."

At this he smiled with great insincerity. It was such a funny look that Erica couldn't help smiling back.

"So you're going to increase my salary retroactively, to bring it up to parity with the others."

"I didn't say that. I can't promise you anything . . . It isn't in my hands . . ."

"Isn't it? You know I overstepped my boss and several levels of management, because all the arrows lead to you as the decision-maker. Am I wrong? Are you just another paper pusher? If so, who *is* responsible? I have a right to know."

"I, um, uh, will discuss this case with . . . I have every confidence that this will be satisfactorily resolved . . ."

"Great!" said Erica, seizing Little's hand from his side and pumping it heartily. "I look forward to my adjusted paycheck next week. Thank you for your help."

"You're welcome," he said, between clenched teeth.

Erica felt like a kite soaring above a perfect Malibu beach. She left the office and shut the door behind her.

But even so, she could hear Roy Little's last words.

"Fucking bitch."

Bert Hickey called his group of executive trainees into the thirtieth-floor conference room. Hickey was in his early fifties. He had worked his way up from the mailroom at Nox, putting in twenty-three years. He was pleased by the title and salary of his current position, but he felt insulted by the job itself. Shepherding a bunch of snot-nosed kids around, teaching them how to tie their shoelaces.

Business school was what they had. College. Bah. Old man Knox, the founder of the company, would have spit on all that. He would have sent them out to sell paint, distribute pesticides, put a year or two in in a plastics factory. But you didn't get that anymore, not with this generation. Easy riders, that's what they were. Forget about earning your spurs, forget about an honest day's work for a day's pay. These kids wouldn't know what you were talking about.

The worst of them was the girl. He'd heard all about it in the twenty-second-floor men's room. The bitch had gone and ignored five levels of chain-of-command, busted into Roy Little's office, hiked up her skirt and got herself a big fat raise. Five, ten thou, the guy in the men's room had said. Not a bad piece of change for a little nookie.

Hickey threw a stack of vinyl-bound folders on the table.

"Your next assignment, should you choose to undertake it. Of course some of you people may find it to be Mission Impossible."

Erica and Jack Johnson exchanged glances. Here goes Hickey with another long, bitter diatribe.

"What? No one's quitting? Must be too hot for tennis today. Water polo, anyone? No? Well, then, let's play at business. What we've got here is a little manufacturing dud called Arrowhead School Supply. We picked it up with the big Northern Wood Products Company acquisition this past spring.

"Arrowhead's a piece of shit. Always has been. It lost money for Northern Wood, and it's still losing money. The hemophiliac's story is in your folders there.

"So, boys and girl, do you know what Nox does to losers?" He smiled thinly at each trainee, then he slowly drew his finger across his neck.

"You try to figure out what to do with the carcass. Maybe you can find some sucker to buy it. Maybe you can find someone who just wants the Mr. Coffee machine. Just dump it someplace so it doesn't leech the company any more. Nobody wants the little fart in the annual report next year.

"You've got about three weeks to get this done. Then we have the annual New Executives get-together with whichever senior honchos want to attend. You can each present your solution to the assembly. It'll be *fun*. Make a fool of yourself and you get the shaft along with Arrowhead. Or maybe you'll prove yourself a big genius, and Nox will actually take your advice. Anything can happen."

With a final sneer, Hickey turned on his heel and left the room.

Erica took her folder to her desk. The desk was in an open cubicle in an office that resembled a maze for not-too-bright laboratory mice. She could hear her colleagues joking nervously about the assignment. Hickey had made it very clear: their future at Nox depended on what they did with this no-win challenge.

Erica read through the document. It didn't take long. Arrowhead School Supply of Golgotha, Idaho, was indeed a loser. It had operated at a growing loss in the past twelve years, ever since it had been acquired by Northern Wood. Now that Nox had swallowed the parent company, the losses were obviously intolerable, at least on paper. Logic dictated that they spin it off—or end its miserable life.

But what a shame. It was unpleasant to preside over the death of a factory; choosing the means of execution was not going to be her brightest hour, no matter how skillfully she did it.

It wasn't as if Nox needed the money, either. Sometimes companies would "spin off" parts of new acquisitions to help pay for the takeover. That wasn't the case now. It wasn't as if Arrowhead was some flaky, fly-by-night enterprise, either. The company was over eighty years old, it produced a staple product (kids still went to school, didn't they?), and it was practical and efficient for the Northern Wood subsidiary to supply it with raw materials.

So why was Arrowhead in such deep trouble?

It really wasn't any of her business, was it? The numbers spoke very loudly, the powers-that-be at Nox had already decided to terminate it, the die was cast.

But it didn't make any sense.

Hers was not to question why, though. She had already gotten herself a reputation as a troublemaker. Why not just go ahead and do the assignment as best she could.

Because it went against her grain as a businesswoman.

This was not the time to wave flags, not when their work was going to be paraded before Nox's hot-shot executives. She shivered, thinking of Roy Little and the way he would be lurking around waiting for her to make a mistake.

Coward.

She remembered the day, a year before, when one of her professors had intoned: "Business is like poker. Twenty-five percent luck, twenty-five percent skill, and fifty percent sheer balls."

He glanced at Erica and the other two women in the lecture hall (they always sat together). "Oh, pardon me, ladies."

Erica bristled. The professor was an elderly man, the sort from whom you expected, and dismissed, mild sexism. But the comment really irritated her. Its connotations seemed greater than a quirk of slang.

"Don't apologize," Erica yelled out. "We've got balls too, you know. Deep inside, where it counts."

Laughter waved through the hall. The professor wasn't laughing, however.

"That may be so," he said quietly, "but you're going to have to prove it."

Erica picked up her phone. She dialed Idaho information, got Arrowhead's number. Her fingers paused above the buttons. She really didn't know what she was doing here. Gathering information, that's what. Let's find out what's wrong with the patient before we administer euthanasia.

She dialed.

"Yup." A male voice. Accent like a cowboy.

"Is this the Arrowhead School Supply Company?"

"Yup."

"May I speak with the manager, please?"

"The manager's in Houston, interviewing for a job. He ain't been here since the first rumor about Nox."

"How about the assistant manager, then?"

"Hoo wee. If he's awake yet, he'd be out fishin'."

"I see," said Erica tartly. "Who's in charge of the plant, then?"

"That would be the foreman, Quentin Shining Blue Stone. Same as always. Ya want to talk to him?"

"Yes, please."

The phone clattered and bumped. It had, perhaps, fallen off the desk. After a while, another western accent answered.

"Quentin here."

"Good morning, sir." How the hell did one address him, Mr. Shining————, Mr. Blue————, Mr. Stone?

"My name is Erica Eaton. I'm calling from Nox headquarters in Los Angeles."

"You a secretary?"

"No, I am not. I am a member of the Executive Training Program."

"What's that, a boss lady?"

"Yeah, I guess it is!"

"Okay, shoot."

"We recently received some of your plant's P and L's. Uh, that's profit and loss statements."

"Yeah, I know what it means. I ought to. I been preparing them for the past fifteen years."

"Oh. Well, uh, the last report we have ends with May. How have operations been since then?"

"They suck. Same as always."

"I see."

"Sure you do."

"Sir, I resent your attitude. I think you realize that Arrowhead is in very deep trouble. In confidence, I'll tell you that there's a very strong possibility that the plant may be closed down. Now I was puzzled as to why the situation should be as grave as it is now, but considering your attitude . . ."

"Oh sure, it's my attitude. All this trouble was caused by my *attitude*. Now you bring down Norman Vincent Peale and we'll all be hunky-dory."

"Okay, I apologize. But I really want to know. What the hell is going on there?"

"You really want to know."

"Yes, I do."

"Why?"

"Because I can't sit by while a business goes under. There are hundreds of employees who would be seriously hurt."

Quentin Shining Blue Stone laughed. It was a horrible laugh, a wail of anguish, a sadness as deep-cut as a ravine.

"You want to know, lady, then you come up here. You come here and you'll see. But you won't, will you? Ain't Nox ever sent *anyone* here, and Northern Wood's sent us nothing but low-life executives that don't know nothing—and care less."

"I'm coming."

"The hell you say."

"I said I'm coming and I'm coming. Just tell me how to get there. This Golgotha isn't even on my road map."

"You authorized? How come I haven't heard . . ."

"I said I'm coming. Now give me the directions."

"Mr. Hickey, I'm taking next Monday as a vacation day."

"You can take it and shove it."

She felt funny about taking a vacation day so soon after she had started working, but she didn't want to call in sick. Yes, she had learned to lie; she even enjoyed it sometimes. But it was one thing to bluff, quite another to cheat. She couldn't do it.

It wasn't the only unpleasant thing about this little adventure. The cost of flying to Idaho was high—for the same money she could visit New York three times.

She drove to the airport in the dark. She was exhilarated just to be leaving Los Angeles. She just didn't like the city, she was out of sync with it. Drove too slow and walked too fast. She *ought* to like it—it was Nox's headquarters and it was a wonderful place for her parents to retire to—but she didn't.

On the flight to Boise they served orange juice with the stale flavor of melted ice. Also a Danish. She owned earrings bigger than the Danishes.

There was a connecting flight to a small airport called Carlton. Everyone else on the sputtering little plane was carrying fishing gear.

Carlton was just a runway on an open field. The terminal was the size of a large garden shed. All she was carrying was her attaché case, so Erica didn't even go in. She looked around for Quentin, who was supposed to pick her up.

Not far from the tiny terminal was a group of five men. They wore plaid shirts, jeans, thick boots. Two of them were heavily tattooed, all wore hats or caps.

"Quentin?" asked Erica tentatively.

"Yup."

Erica shook his hand. She extended her hand to the next man. He looked at Quentin questioningly. Quentin nodded and the man shook her hand. Quentin introduced each of them. They wiped their hands on their jeans before they dared shake hers. It was apparently a novel experience.

Quentin indicated a pickup truck. It was badly painted powder blue. Three other colors showed through in patches. Quentin got into the driver's seat, and the other men got into the back of the truck. Erica climbed up to ride shotgun. Boy, was she glad her suit had a longish, generous skirt. She pulled her sexless jacket tightly to her chest. The crew here looked like the characters in newspaper pictures captioned, "Five arraigned in gang rape case."

The truck had no seat belts. While the roads weren't bad, the pickup apparently predated the invention of suspension. Erica's head repeatedly bumped into the roof of the cab. Finally she anchored herself down with the window handle.

They rode for a long time. The scenery became spectacular. Lakes and rivers glittered like Czech crystal. Magnificent forests loomed up before them, engulfed them in velvety green. She gasped at breathtaking mountains studded with flowers she had never seen before. No bumpkin viewing the Empire State Building had ever been more awed.

At last they came to the factory. It was the first eyesore she had seen all day. Gray, windowless, a blight on the gentle valley it hunkered in. Decrepit vehicles that made the pickup look like a Rolls in comparison peppered the parking lot.

Quentin gave her the grand tour. At least two-thirds of the machinery was still. Rust and corrosion were everywhere. The workers were so dulled by their labors that they didn't even turn to look at Erica—as if tall redheaded women in power suits were always dropping in on the Arrowhead factory. Protective ear coverings and safety goggles lay at the work stations in their original wrappers. A woman with two missing fingers worked a machine that spewed out spiral-bound notebooks at a frantic rate. Every minute or two she stopped the machine and pulled out mangled notebooks.

The place was pathetic.

Erica was relieved to be let into Quentin's office, which was so tiny he could be accused of statutory if he ever invited a teenager in. Fortunately, the door couldn't close. His desk was piled high with papers. The paper clips were bent out of shape. An ancient typewriter held down some Workman's Compensation forms. Erica had recently seen the same model typewriter used as a planter in a trendy Los Angeles garden.

Erica held up her hands. "How?"

Quentin smiled a lopsided smile. "That's what they all say to Indians. Well, it's a long story."

"The plane out of Carlton doesn't leave till seven. And I didn't see any first-run movie theaters on the way."

Quentin leaned back against the wall. The paint was scaling, or perhaps a fungus was growing there.

"The Reverend Oscar Wright built this factory in 1897. His motives were charitable. He did it for the Indians. The Reverend Wright was convinced that he was saving the souls of that lost tribe of Israel, the Shoshone. The souls of the Shoshone were in a sad state, all right. They had lost just about everything by then. There are stories that the old ones just wrapped themselves in blankets and sat down, waiting to die. The young didn't have much to live for, either.

"The Reverend decided to succor the dying race through that great lifeline of salvation: hard work. He put the men to work in the paper factory, women and children—some as young as six—in the pencil plant. They worked fourteen hours a day, six days a week. On Sundays, they were required to come to the factory for religious services. Reverend Wright's sermons were four or more hours long.

"In a short while, many of the workers came down with tuberculosis. After that came the Great Influenza Epidemic. And then there was deadly measles. All the great gifts of the white man. The Reverend started getting scared, his supply of workers diminished, while the demand for school supplies went up. It never occurred to him, though, to change conditions in the factory.

"In 1930 the Rev went to meet his Maker—or something—and the company was inherited by his son, Charles. Charles was not a religious man. At least the Sunday sermons stopped.

The Depression started then. The pressure mounted. Poachers picked our forests clean and fished out our waters. The factory became the only source of sustenance for the Indians."

"Now, wait a minute. Times were tough for everyone. What do you mean 'your' forests and 'your' waters? What else could landless farmers do, other than harvest public land."

"Public land! Lady, this is a reservation!"

"What do you mean? There's an Indian reservation near here?"

Quentin knocked on the wall behind him. "*This* is the official border of the Sacajawea Reservation."

"But I didn't see . . ."

"You didn't see. Nobody sees nothing," Quentin drawled slowly, but fire flashed in his eyes.

"The Indians didn't see either, but now our eyes are opening. This land the plant is on, for example, we didn't see that the surveyors had registered it falsely. This land belongs to us, according to your own cheating treaties. But the Indians have had it up to here. We're taking this to court. We're gonna get our land back! There's a civil liberties organization that's promised to pay all our legal expenses. We're gonna take this all the way—even the Supreme Court."

"Please get back to Charles Wright."

"Yes. Well, the factory muddled through the Depression. The Indians managed to keep the factory jobs—there weren't any white men who wanted them."

"What about the town?"

"There is no town. Golgotha is just a make-believe. The Rev always wanted a post office of his own. Anyway, things moseyed along through the war. Then there was the postwar boom in school supplies and Charles decided to cash in by selling out to Northern Wood.

"In the beginning, things were okay. There were a lot of little kids going to school in the fifties and more big ones going off to college than ever before. But Northern Wood was not exactly an enlightened employer in the best of times. They let the equipment go to seed, they played mean-spirited games with the workers—I always expected them to hand us colored beads on payday. Worst of all were the managers they sent out here. An assignment to Arrowhead was a *punishment* for their executives.

"Then about ten years ago, the school supply business started to change. Licensing became the big rage; you had to do it to stay in competition. But Northern Wood wouldn't budge. Why pay good money to put Snoopy on a pencil, they said, when a pencil worked just as well without it.

"Our market share was wiped out, and the only reaction from headquarters was 'cut losses.' Now the ball's in your court, lady. My guess is, Nox will finish us off."

Erica sighed. She sure didn't see any call for optimism.

"How about some lunch?" asked Quentin.

"Can't wait to see the cafeteria," said Erica.

"Been closed since sixty-seven."

"But there's no town, no place to eat!"

"Come on, we'll drive over to the reservation."

"I thought it was right next door."

Quentin laughed. "You're from New York, right? You're the only people in this country who figure they can *walk* someplace. Sure the reservation is next door—or right here, according to our calculations—but it goes on for a way. Nearest place to eat is forty miles east of here."

Erica gulped.

"Yeah. It's a real problem for the workers. See, if a woman's baby is sick, the medical service is way over, more than a hundred miles. She's gotta drive there, gotta drive back. Gets paid the minimum wage, so it's hardly worth it. And the bastards from Northern Wood say 'lazy work force, can't do a thing with 'em.' Well, what the hell do they expect? Bad pay, no chance for advancement, lousy working conditions. What the hell do you expect?"

Neither the situation nor Quentin's anger did much for Erica's appetite. But her mood lifted when they got away from the factory and back out into the magnificent countryside.

After another bumpy ride they came to a settlement, of sorts. The group of buildings was dominated by a large, wooden one. After they parked the truck, Erica noticed that one side of the large building was faced with an enormous fresco.

The painting was striking. A beautiful young woman, copper skin glowing, berry eyes determined, pointed into the distance. Erica could not move from the spot. She felt a thrill of recognition, an absolute knowledge of the woman's strength and courage.

"Who is that?" she breathed.

"That is Sacajawea," Quentin answered. His studied drawl could not hide his pride.

"She was the guide for Lewis and Clark, right?"

"Among other things."

"Did she live on this reservation?"

"No. But she was Shoshone, they say. Anyway, it doesn't matter."

"No, it doesn't." The woman in the painting reached out: across time, across tribal lines, across the races.

Quentin moved to go into the building, but Erica didn't budge.

"Who painted that? It's an incredibly powerful piece of art."

"Our young people did it. They built the whole community center. They decorated it. They did it all together. They cooperated, the way our people did in the old times."

"Still, someone must have made the master drawing. There's an artistic presence behind this. An individual."

"Yeah," Quentin admitted grudgingly. He was more enamored of the idea of a group effort than of art. "Kid's name is Wendell Corey."

He finally tore her away and showed her into the center's cafeteria.

Erica looked around. All the walls were covered with splendid murals depicting scenes from ancient legends and Indian history. They all bore the unmistakable stamp of the same artist.

On the way to the center, Erica had fantasized about the fresh trout she imagined leaping in the crystalline brooks and lakes they had passed. But there was no fish on the menu. She had stringy chicken in a bland cream sauce. At least there were baked Idaho potatoes. But one bite proved that hers had been sitting on the steam table too long.

"Hey, we drove all the way out here and you aren't even eating."

"I'd just rather look at the murals. They're really outstanding."

"Well, if you want to meet the artist, he's over with that bunch of young fellas near 'The Buffalo Hunt.'"

Wendell Corey was certainly unmistakable. Of the half dozen young men, he was the only one who looked like an Indian. He wore his long hair in two braids, plaited with cowhide thongs. His feet were moccasined, and he glittered with silver and turquoise jewelry. He was glaring at her, at her white skin.

Erica felt a stab of the liberal's free-floating guilt. It hardly mattered in the great context of things, she knew, that her own ancestors were indentured to the European soil when other whites devastated the Native Americans.

"No. Thanks just the same, Quentin. Let's get back to the plant. This will be my only chance to examine Arrowhead. If you don't mind I'd like to see whatever books you have, your internal accounting. I want to learn all I can today."

All the way back to Los Angeles, the striking visage and pointing finger of Sacajawea followed Erica.

She shivered in the warm, static air of the covered parking lot. Could it be that the spirit of the Bird Woman followed her here? Was she being designated by forces greater than her to save the Shoshone remnant—or, anyway, one of their major sources of livelihood?

Was she, like Sacajawea, standing at the brink of a new America?

I've got to find the courage, thought Erica. I've got to succeed.

That, or bury my career at Wounded Knee.

Chapter Fourteen

S UNLIGHT POURED through the fifteen-foot windows that circled the top floor of the Nox Building. Century City swam in the heat below, like fabled Xanadu. The heat rose from below and beat down from above, baking the smog like a convection oven. Yet the party in the penthouse was cool, even chilly. The electronic, state-of-the-art climate control must have been set at Antarctic.

Erica had been checking the carved ice swan for an hour and it hadn't melted a bit. Each feather was still carefully delineated. The swan was set in a deep silver dish, aswim in a lake of caviar, surrounded by the traditional toast, lemon, eggs, and vodka. In an hour, the lake had emptied.

Not that Erica had had any caviar. She was wearing a white suit and did not dare risk scooping the black fish eggs up with fragile toast points. Nor had she risked the prawns in red-hot sauce, the deviled eggs, the asparagus hollandaise, the tiny pizzas with pesto, or the curried artichoke hearts. She had become acutely aware that everything edible at this party dripped a brightly colored sauce. Nowhere was a stick of celery or a cube of cheese to be found.

It wasn't coincidence. Nothing at Nox happened by chance. Nor was it her imagination about the drinks. She had ordered ginger ale, and she tasted liquor in it. She refused to drink it, and asked the bartender for some tap water. He had *argued* with her.

Everything was planned here, for the Day of Judgment at Nox. Nothing was left to serendipity, much less the will of such pawns as the hapless members of the Executive Training Program.

Bert Hickey stood with his back pressed against an elegant structural column, watching and leering. He was a hyena, waiting impatiently for the lions to make their kill, gorge themselves, and leave the easy leftovers for him.

Erica caught a glimpse of Roy Little. She shivered. The only reason *he* would be at this joyless "party" was to get *her*. Well, for a thousand dollars she had made herself one permanent enemy. But she had no regrets. There was no going back.

She caught a reflection of herself in a mirrored panel. The white suit was serious and severe, yet its color demanded attention. She had prepared her presentation out on the little terrace of her apartment and even in the shade the California sun had tanned her to a rich peach, making up for the lack of makeup. She smiled. Her teeth sparkled. Nox had a great dental plan.

The murmur of the assembled rose like harmony from a church choir. A man with an entourage emerged from an elevator.

"Look at that," whispered Jack Johnson to Erica. "It's George Steel, the top honcho! What the hell is he doing here?"

"Which one is he?" Erica whispered back. It had to be the tall, powerfully built man, but he was only in his forties.

"The gray-haired guy is Steel."

"Our chief executive officer?"

"And president. Capo de capos. The boss man."

The official host of the gathering was Oscar Barnes, vice president, Corporate Relations. Barnes was fat, bald, and bespectacled, the very image of a benign grandfather—were it not for his shrewd eyes, which seemed to see everything in the room.

Barnes was clasping a colleague warmly. George Steel

glanced at his Rolex. Immediately Barnes raised both his arms in the air and the room fell to attention.

"I'm sure our trainees realize what a special consideration it is to have the president of this company attend our meeting. On behalf of our executives of tomorrow, George, gentlemen, welcome. We know you're heading back to New York this afternoon, so without further ado, let us adjourn to the conference room and get on with our business!"

It was the largest table Erica had ever seen. Nureyev would have felt comfortable doing *grandes jetés* on it. There must have been forty of them seated at the sides, yet no one's elbow touched his neighbor's.

Barnes summed up the assignment. "Our trainees were asked to dispose of an unprofitable company, Arrowhead School Supply, which Nox acquired as part of the Northern Wood Products package.

"Everyone here knows Bert Hickey, right? Bert's taken on the guidance of our trainees this year, along with his other yeoman duties. Bert, I speak for the entire Nox family in thanking you for the great contribution you are making to the future leadership of the company."

Polite applause. *Very* polite from the trainees' side of the table.

"Bert, will you introduce us to these fine young people, as they speak."

"Thanks for your kind words, Oscar. Our first report is from Jack Johnson. Mr. Johnson was first in his class at Wharton, and I'm sure *everyone* here is anxious to find out how that wisdom is applied to a *practical* business problem."

Jack rose nervously to his feet. He was painfully young. The pale plaid jacket he wore was all wrong, and a brilliant yellow curry stain showed itself on one lapel. He could have been the Portrait of the Absentminded Professor as a Young Man.

He coughed. "Excuse me. Well. I'll make this as brief as possible. So, okay.

"It is my informed recommendation that Nox approach Zellerhauser Industries as a potential buyer for Arrowhead.

"Zellerhauser would be the natural home for this company. It is the largest producer of paper in the Northwest, its two school supply companies already have the lion's share of the market, and it has a good record in diversifying and distributing its consumer products.

"In short, Zellerhauser would know what to do with Arrowhead. Consequently, it is worth a great deal to them, while it is worth nothing—or worse—to us.

"The natural and most beneficial sale would be to Zellerhauser. Thank you."

He sat.

Silence.

"Mr. Johnson," said an executive seated on Steel's right. "How much, would you say, could we expect from Zellerhauser for Arrowhead?"

"Um, uh. I don't know."

"The reason I ask is so that we might compare that figure with that which might be offered by other, less 'natural' potential buyers. After all, once Arrowhead is sold it could hardly matter to us whether it becomes profitable or not. The sale itself, sir, its benefit to us, is all that should concern us here."

"Yeah," said Bert Hickey. "Who gives a shit if they go under. It's the new owner's lookout."

Jack shrank in his chair. To Erica's horror, he began to cry. She would never do that, *never*. She'd sooner cut her wrists on the lacquered table.

"All right," said Bert Hickey. "Next on our list is Gerald Crosby. Gerry's shown himself to be a can-do kind of guy these last few months. I'm sure he'll tell us something interesting now."

"Thanks, Mr. Hickey. The pleasure's mine."

Gerry mugged and smiled, attempting to ingratiate himself with the executives at the table. Soon it became apparent that two large beads of caviar had lodged themselves between his two upper teeth. Almost everyone was distracted from his words. They kept staring at his mouth, waiting for the two black fish eggs to appear in his grin.

"So my advice to you, gentlemen, is to hang on to the property. The factory would have to be torn down—whether by us or the competitors—so we won't realize any profit on it.

But the land! Jesus, that's prime hunting and fishing land. It's only a few miles from huge expanses of federal parkland, and the deer don't know from 'No Trespassing' signs, do they? Let's send a task force out there right away, and figure out what we can put up there. Time-share condos, an amusement park? The sky's the limit.

"Thanks for hearing me out, guys."

The silence followed. The novelty of the caviar in the teeth had worn off. Most of the men were fidgeting, figuring this was a waste of their time, wondering what was going on back at the office.

"Well and good, young fellow," said Barnes, "but Nox isn't in the vacation home or amusement park business. A company must think long and hard before diversifying. Many a sound business has gone under taking a flyer on something it knows nothing about. Diversify can mean 'deworsify.'"

The lecture was over. George Steel checked his watch again. Gerry Crosby shrugged. He'd already lined up a job under Roy Little for next year. It didn't matter to him whether they liked his idea or not, you got ahead in a company the way a guy got ahead in the Kremlin.

Trainee after trainee made his little speech. Erica's mind drifted as she looked over the company president.

George Steel's hair was completely gray, but its thickness and stylish cut indicated youthfulness. He had a craggy face and hands that did not look as if they had been folded on blotters all his life. His pale blue eyes looked through each person seated at the table.

Steel was indeed what the man looked to be made of. Not a shaft of unbending backbone, but a coiled spring, biding its own good time.

Steel was perfectly dressed. In fact there was something forced about it, as if he were a model wearing the perfect outfit for a powerful executive—rather than the executive himself.

Erica stared and stared. She felt a knot form in her stomach. One loop of the knot was sexual attraction, the other loop was fear.

The parade of trainees came near to its end.

"Now we'll hear from Mr. Robert Greenspan," Hickey mumbled.

Bob rose and said, "My colleague, Francis X. Touhy, did half the research on this project. He shares the conclusions with me. We would like to present our findings as partners."

"That is not acceptable," hissed Roy Little. As VP, Personnel, it was his policy to keep the young execs lean and hungry, competing against each other, suspicious of each other. When any showed an excessive fondness for cooperation, he felt it best to divide and conquer.

"Yeah," said Hickey, "you were supposed to do all the work yourself."

"Well," said Greenspan, "we've done the work together . . ."

"And," said Touhy, finishing Bob's sentence, as he often did, "we'll give the report together."

Erica's ears perked up, not only because Roy Little had shown his hostility—and the enemy of her enemy was her friend—but because Bob and Frank were two very bright guys whom she liked and admired. But, to be honest, they were not organization men.

"From what we could conclude," said Bob, "Northern Wood was unable to make Arrowhead viable. It's even less likely that their managers will do so now that they're a part of Nox, and have so many other opportunities to seek new challenges."

"As Jack Johnson pointed out, and Mr. Barnes underscored, Nox has no expertise with this type of business, and might be foolhardy to try to save it."

"But," said Bob, "there are those who are experts at salvaging just such basket cases."

"Or disposing of them, when necessary," said Frank. "In fact," he continued, "we have cautiously approached one of these 'specialists'—Sir Carl Connaught."

George Steel sat up in his chair as if he had been jerked back by the hair.

"Mr. Greenspan. Mr. Touhy. We at Nox do not deal with men . . . like . . . Carl Connaught," said Barnes.

"The man is a rattlesnake," spat Roy Little. "He swallows companies whole and spits out the bones!"

Oscar Barnes nodded. "It would be healthier to do business with the Mafia."

George Steel looked at the two from under veiled eyes. "And what did Connaught offer you for Arrowhead?"

"It wasn't actually Connaught," said Bob.

"It was one of his right-hand men," said Frank.

"We could have gotten to Connaught himself."

"But we knew we weren't authorized, so we didn't push for a meeting."

"Anyway, the deal his people presented was this: They're ready to pay—cash—pretty much our asking price for Arrowhead. But they also want to buy another Northern company, Rainbow Resins."

"That's preposterous," said Oscar Barnes. "Rainbow is one of the main reasons we bought Northern Wood Products. Industrial resins and solvents are right up our alley, why should we sell to Connaught—and at his prices, too!"

"Look, it's just the concept," said Touhy. "If we want someone to swallow Arrowhead, we'll have to sweeten the mouthful."

"Besides, everything's negotiable. We didn't even sit down to the table yet. Maybe Connaught would go for another company, or we can tie this to something else. The point is, he's listening," said Greenspan.

"You know the old story about Bernard Shaw."

"Not again," groaned Greenspan.

Touhy ignored his partner. "It's like this. Shaw is sitting at dinner with some high-society woman. 'Madam,' he says, 'will you sleep with me?' 'Certainly not,' says the lady, 'what sort of woman do you take me for?' 'Well,' Shaw persists, 'will you sleep with me if I give you a million pounds?' 'Oh my,' she says, 'for a million pounds I suppose I would.' 'Good,' says Shaw, 'now that we have established the principle, let us negotiate the price.'"

"In short," said Bob Greenspan, "we've established the principle that Connaught could buy Arrowhead. Maybe you could get a better buyer, maybe you could get a better price. But as for us—Frank and I—we feel we've fulfilled our assignment."

Steel's second gritted his teeth. "Bert, are there any more trainees to hear out? We're leaving L.A. in half an hour."

"Just one more," said Hickey, relishing the way he had put Erica in the spot.

Erica rose, planted her feet squarely on the floor, and placed her briefcase on the table. The nervousness had vanished from her stomach. She had worked and worked on her project until every detail was resolved to her satisfaction. Fortune favors the prepared.

"Gentlemen. Each of you has before you a pad and pencil."

They looked down at the table in surprise. Of course there was a yellow legal pad and a new, sharpened pencil at each seat. There always was, at every official meeting. But no executive ever used these things.

"Would you please use those pencils to write the word 'pinpoint.'"

Every man present picked up his pencil and did her bidding, as if she were a second grade teacher.

"Now will you please use your erasers to erase the dots on the *i*'s and the crossbar on the *t*."

Again they did as told, getting a certain childish satisfaction in doing the task, brushing and blowing eraser crumbs off their pads.

Now Erica opened her briefcase and took out a bright plastic pencil case in the shape of a school bus. There were cartoon children waving merrily out of the bus's windows. She began handing out pencils to everyone present.

"Once again, please. Write the word 'pinpoint' with these pencils, then erase the dots and the crossbar, just as you did before."

They complied with her direction. Now everyone realized that their new pencils were different. The erasers were shaped like the feathers of an arrow, with little rubber points that made it possible to erase the dots and crossbars on the shaft of the *t* without erasing any of the neighboring letters.

The pencils began to disappear into the breast pockets of many nicely tailored suits.

"Say, Roy," said Barnes, "I see you aren't taking your pencil. Mind if I have it?"

"I think you have convinced yourselves that the Arrowhead pencil is a truly superior product," said Erica. "Now let me show you some other original items from Arrowhead School Supply."

She drew a notebook out of the briefcase. Its cover looked as if it were embroidered with Indian beading.

"You all remember composition books from school, don't you? They were dull little things bound in coated cardboard. But look at this beauty! Its cover is made of blistered plastic with the three-dimensional feel of original Ojibway Indian decorative design."

She handed the notebook to Frank Touhy, who sat on her right and he passed it on to the next person. No one could resist touching the glistening cover with its eagles and owls made of "beads" of black, white, turquoise, red, and gold.

She took out another notebook. This one was a large spiral-bound notebook with a magnificently photographed cover. It showed a waterfall in a wooded mountain vista. Deer drank from the lapis pool at its foot.

"Notice how the quality of this notebook cover is brilliantly clear. It's as sharp as a museum print."

She handed this notebook to Jack Johnson on her left, who passed it along for inspection.

"And here is Arrowhead's college-ruled notebook, part of a planned American Heritage series."

The notebook she raised had a cover that was a replica of the giant mural on the Community Center wall, except for slight changes. Sacajawea's buckskin dress was tighter, and cut to show a little cleavage. Her outstretched arms still directed "go yonder" to the unseen Lewis and Clark, but there was something about her that also hinted "come hither." These refinements were not lost upon Erica's audience.

The notebooks ended in a heap before the executives, on the other side of the table.

"Ladies and gentlemen. (Well, there were some secretaries sitting behind the most senior executives.) Until now, my colleagues have taken for granted that, in the name of fiscal sanity, we must rid ourselves of Arrowhead School Supply. I intend to convince you otherwise, that Nox would be wise to keep Arrowhead, that, indeed, it has the potential of becoming a small jewel in our industrial crown.

"Before we address how this is to be done, you have a right—in fact, a duty—to ask why Arrowhead has performed so poorly in the past, and why it appears to be such a hopeless case today.

"This company was founded by a missionary, and however fanatical and perverse his vision was, at least it was a vision. But after his time, Arrowhead has been managed like a corporate stepchild by everyone who's owned it. First, an indifferent heir, then Northern Wood, a company with deep identity problems of its own—why else did we pick off that rich plum so easily?

"The labor force at Arrowhead is composed entirely of residents of the adjacent Sacajawea Indian Reservation. Arrowhead's management and absentee owners have had one thing in common: contempt for the Indians' dignity, culture, and special relationship to the land. No more than a handful of workers at the plant earn more than the minimum wage. No rewards or incentives are given for productivity, yet the manager and assistant manager of the plant attribute its losses to the 'lazy, drunken Indians.'

"Characteristic of Arrowhead leadership has been the stubborn refusal to exploit any of the natural resources unique to the place. Magnificent scenery, unique Indian craftsmanship, easy access to supplies—all these advantages have been ignored. Myopic leadership, a demoralized and resentful work force, valuable resources tossed out in the trash. Is it any wonder Arrowhead loses money?

"But Nox does not have to continue this miserable tradition. Nox is not a befuddled medium-size wood supplier, Nox is not a dynasty that treats a factory like a personal fiefdom. Nox is the most efficient, the most farsighted, the most innovative—let's not be ashamed to say it, the *best* damn company on the Fortune 100!"

Oscar Barnes whistled and banged on the table. His assistant clapped and cheered. Some of the others laughed at this display. Everyone seemed to be loosening up.

Erica cleared her throat loudly. She was glad they were

being entertained and grateful to have their attention, but she wanted to make certain that they understood the seriousness of her point.

"What, then, can be done, to make Arrowhead a more productive, *profitable* part of Nox?

"The first thing I would recommend is the immediate firing of the manager and assistant manager. We've got to make the message perfectly clear: Nox will not tolerate incompetence."

The men glanced at each other in surprise. They had taken the woman for a liberal softie. Apparently the lady had a little iron in her too.

"Second," she continued, "we must begin a vigorous training program of all Arrowhead employees. Arrowhead must become technologically competent. We must make that demand of it, just as we have made that demand of every sector of the corporation. Workers who work *well* are workers who *want* to work. I think each of us can testify to that from our own experience. The squandering of talent at Arrowhead is a shocking waste. The people who painted the notebook covers, invented the plastic-blister design, photographed the waterfall, and thought up the arrow pencil erasers are all current employees at the Golgotha plant. Their jobs are, respectively, packer, binding-machine operator, truck loader, and sweeper. Every suggestion they have ever made has been rejected, often with a racial slur, to boot.

"Third, machinery at the factory is antique. Believe it or not, most Arrowhead products are at least partially handmade. Not because they are meant to be, but because the machinery is broken down. Now there is always considerable capital outlay in machinery, and this factory needs a lot of it. But one of the advantages of being part of a giant outfit like Nox is the ability to obtain the finest machinery and parts at the best prices. So let's do that post haste.

"Finally, morale needs an immediate and visible boost. You may not have heard of it yet but the Sacajawea tribal counsel is already suing Nox, claiming that the land occupied by the Arrowhead plant was granted to the Shoshone in an 1880 treaty. A messy court battle looms ahead, and the issue has the reservation radicals inflamed. We can turn this into a win-win situation. If we offer to sell the land to the reservation for a nominal sum, they will lease it back to Nox, also for a trivial sum. If everyone's face is saved, company morale will rise. It seems a small price to pay for the good will of our own employees.

"Now we must come to the strategic planning of Arrowhead production and marketing. It is foolish to continue competing with Zellerhauser, which produces quality school supplies at a modest price. But we *can* find a profitable niche in the market for innovative products.

"Today's school children and college students have an enormous disposable income. Increasingly, they are status-conscious and competitive in their acquisitions.

"Arrowhead can become the Jaguar of school supplies. An Arrowhead notebook may cost two or three times as much as a plain old Zellerhauser one—but wouldn't you rather day-dream about that waterfall or Sacajawea's adventures, than listen to an organic chemistry lecture with no visual escape other than raw cardboard?

"I posit this to you, sirs: Nox is not only a viable corporate home for Arrowhead, it is the best company for guiding Arrowhead to a future as the leading edge of quality school stationery.

"World-famous Pigmento paints and artists' supplies have given us entrée to the best art supply stores in the country. Arrowhead can ride in on that for an introduction to the quality-conscious consumer of notebooks and pencils. Once a profile is established, it's a hop and a skip to the drug and variety stores, the college bookstores, and finally, the upscale supermarkets for the saturation market. Who, if not Nox, can get the best shelf space in all of these?

"Who, if not Nox, can provide the finest quality raw materials to the factory? Who, if not Nox, can safely guide the expected growth of Arrowhead, and provide expert financial and management support?

"Who, if not Nox, will recognize the qualities that are already present in Golgotha—such as the gifted and dedicated foreman of the plant, Quentin Shining Blue Stone, who deserves to be promoted to the managerial level.

"There are outfits, like Carl Connaught's, that can squeeze gold out of the dead and dying. That isn't our specialty. What we *can* do, and do very well, is find and develop the products this country—and nations abroad—need, want, and like. And we have the corporate culture to motivate our people to produce those goods, and produce them well."

Erica paused for a sip of water. It did not break the spell. She had bet everything on her point of view, on the gamble that Nox executives would believe in Arrowhead, in the Arrowhead she envisioned. Now it was time to stand back, to see which way the chips would fall.

"I have had the honor to be hosted at lunch at the Nox executive dining room. As all of you know, it is one of the finest restaurants in Los Angeles. The view is stunning, the decor is lovely, the service first-rate. And oh, the food! But you all know that. What you may not know, or have forgotten over the years, is that the rest of the workers in this building eat in the basement cafeteria.

"Way down there, there's no view, the most you can say for the decor is that it's clean and cheerful, and you serve yourself from the salad bar and the steam tables. But, gentlemen, *the food is the very same as it is upstairs.* With the company's generous subsidy, every employee can dine like a prince every day—and for pennies. That is one reason the employees at Nox headquarters have the lowest absentee rate in the industry. That is part of the reason you rarely hear a grumble when you ask a typist to finish one more letter after five o'clock. That is why people say, 'I'm lucky, I work for Nox.'

"We're all lucky to work for Nox, and we all make that special effort to show it. This is a spirit that must reach out from headquarters and touch every part of Nox Industries. It can touch Arrowhead School Supply and it can change it forever.

"Let us not give up before we have faced the challenge. Every organ in our corporate body cries out for Arrowhead. The nose for profit, the eye for growth, the heart for our employees. All, *all* say we must make the effort at Arrowhead.

"Thank you."

• • •

Silence reigned in the room, like the silence that must reign in Antarctica. At last, George Steel turned slightly in his chair, addressing the woman who sat behind him.

"Beatrice, would you call the pilot now? Tell him we'll be late."

Again silence.

"Miss Eaton," said an executive, "I'd have to quibble about some of your financial predictions, but, I must say, that was a nicely turned report."

Erica thanked him. "What financial aspects . . ."

"Hell!" boomed Oscar Barnes, "talk about the details later! That was one terrific presentation. It does this old geezer good to hear a young gal like you bring some heart into the business world. Yes, sirree, I'm glad now that they took you into the program, I definitely am. Don't know when I've heard a speech so impressive. Honey, I'd like to give you a big kiss."

He stood up and began to approach her.

(*A woman must be arrogant.*)

"I'd rather you didn't."

Silence again, and then, quickly, an eruption of congratulations from her peers.

Triumph welled up inside her, as the hands of the trainees reached out to shake hers. Despite her efforts to repress it, a big grin burst out on her lips.

God, it felt great! No wonder men preferred this to romance.

When the congratulations died down, George Steel moved forward in his seat. Immediately, the absolute silence fell again.

"Ms. Eaton." The soft *zzz* sound at the end of the word made Erica aware that he was not calling her "Miss." The *New York Times* might reject it, but, by golly, the president of Nox Industries was calling her by a free woman's honorific. Progress was being made after all.

"Ms. Eaton, how, exactly, did you come by all this information on the Arrowhead plant?"

"I went up to see the place for myself. You see, our folders didn't have much information, and the principals were reluctant to speak frankly on the phone."

"I see. And when did you make this trip?"

"I took a vacation day."

"How did you get there?"

"I flew."

"Who paid for the tickets?"

"I did."

"Why?"

Erica blushed. "I wasn't authorized, and, uh, I didn't think Mr. Hickey would authorize the trip. After all, it's just a learning exercise, hypothetical. Isn't it?"

Steel ignored her question. "Do you have the receipts for your trip?"

"Yes, I think so."

"Hand them in to Hickey before you leave the building today. You'll be reimbursed fully."

"Oh, thank you. I really appreciate that."

"This is not a gracious act, Ms. Eaton. I have to protect Nox's interests. If you compile this information on your own time, come to the conclusions on your own time, and pay the expenses yourself, what's to stop you from selling your report to Zellerhauser or Connaught?"

Erica was shocked. "Mr. Steel, I wouldn't dream . . ."

"Of course you don't. You're still touchingly naive. But everyone loses their virginity someday.

"And speaking of the loss of innocence, tell your friends on the reservation that the buffalo will be roaming the plains before they get their fingers on a square inch of Nox property. Nobody plays Nox for a patsy. Nobody."

Steel got up. Every other chair in the room instantly scraped back.

"How long do these trainees have to finish this jerk-off program?" he asked, addressing Roy Little.

"Ah, just a few months more, George."

"It's a goddamn waste of time. Just gives them more time to stick their noses where they don't belong.

"Send Erica Eaton to Strategic Planning. Pay off the rest of them."

Without waiting for a response or saying good-bye, George Steel strode to the elevator.

In the ladies' room at last. Erica splashed cold water all over her face. She was so excited that she had to do something to cool down. Strategic Planning! Why, the bottom position in that department was just three down from vice president. How could it be? Oh God, what if Steel was making her a secretary there? No, of course not. How paranoid.

Could he really have fired all the other trainees? Gee, Roy Little would never stand for that, not after he'd promised Gerry Crosby a spot in his own department . . .

A woman entered the restroom. She was sixty-ish, trim, stylishly suited.

"That was a super job you did in there. Steel is rarely that impressed, I can tell you."

"You work for him?"

"His executive secretary. Would have been fifteen years, next January."

"Oh, are you retiring?"

"No. Unfortunately, I'm quitting because of the move to New York."

"What move?"

"You mean the news hasn't trickled down to your floor yet? Steel is moving headquarters."

"To New York? Why? Everyone says it's a dying city."

"George doesn't think so, he's hot on the Big Apple. And he thinks it's crucial for Nox's future to be near the world's financial center."

"So why don't *you* want to go?"

"I can't. My husband's a veterinarian, he's got a Beverly Hills practice. And I've got three grandchildren in the San Fernando Valley."

"Sounds like you have a lovely family. Of course you wouldn't move at this point just for the job."

"At this point, no. But twenty years ago, when I started working for George, I would have followed him all around the world—dragging my husband, kids, and the pets with us."

"You sound like a loyal employee. I bet Mr. Steel will be sorry to lose you."

"He better writhe in pain! I'm just joking, he's the greatest. You'll see when you work for him. Everybody gives him one hundred and five percent and feels privileged to be doing it. Of course the people who work directly for Steel are a very special crew. Hand-picked, with the guts to really perform. I guess you could call us the Palace Guard. Definitely elite. He just doesn't tolerate less than excellence."

"Gosh, you scare me. I'm not sure I can measure up to those standards."

"Well, Steel seems to think you will."

"At least he hasn't been swayed by Roy Little's opinion."

"No, he hasn't. And not by the rumors, either."

"Rumors about *me?*"

"Yeah. You're on the boys' turf and they're already playing dirty."

"Oh no. How awful."

"Well, it's a jungle out there, better get yourself a shotgun."

"Okay," Erica laughed. "I will."

The other woman laughed too. "Well, let's not talk too much politics in here. If I know those men, they'll be putting a bug in the tampon dispenser."

Beatrice left, and Erica decided to wash her face with warm water. The steam fogged up the mirror above the sink.

The warm water softened all the tense muscles. There was nothing left but pure happiness.

She had had a wonderful success.

She was being promoted to the winner's circle.

She was going back to New York, back to where she could keep an eye on Mama and Papa.

Absently, Erica traced some letters on the mirror. Even after she left the ladies' room, the word remained, faintly, on the glass.

"*Yippee!*"

Chapter Fifteen

From Thisweek *Magazine, May 22, 1981*

COMMERCE

George Steel Forges Ahead at Nox

W HEN MADELINE STEEL came to review the paint job on her 48-room mansion in Englewood, New Jersey, she found the shade of ecru she had chosen to be not quite right. Her husband, George, just shrugged and said, "Have them do it over, dear. They'll get it right eventually."

An especially indulgent husband? Maybe, but Steel, 44, President and Chief Executive Officer of Nox Industries, can afford to throw the paint around. His company, after all, is the world's largest producer of the stuff, as well as thousands of other chemical and related products. And Steel's generosity may well have been affected by his company's record earnings this year, $8.46 per share.

That's just one of the records Steel has achieved in his six years at the helm of Nox, the nation's ninth largest company. As the youngest CEO of a major corporation, he beat the odds in what industry analysts call a mature market. He has successfully staved off foreign competition in many sensitive areas, including synthetic fibers and pharmaceuticals. And he has tightened the huge company's operating budget without initiating mass layoffs or plant closings.

Which is not to say that Steel has made no enemies. He was included for four of his six years at Nox's helm in a major business newsletter's "Ten Most Difficult Bosses" list. He pruned the company's senior staff of its "Old Guard" executives and replaced them with energetic, brash young men in his own mold. And some Wall Street analysts fear that his hungry reach—he has acquired more new subsidiaries during his tenure than Nox did in the previous twenty years—will exceed his grasp, leaving Nox cash-poor and with satellites outside its proven area of expertise.

But Steel's supporters brush aside such possibilities. They point out that Steel has brought a once stolid and conservatively managed company into the leading edge of production, and that he has done so while keeping the stockholders happy.

His interest in the shareholders' welfare is such that he recently moved executive headquarters from Los Angeles to Manhattan to hew close to the financial world. Nox now occupies forty of the sixty-three floors of a historic Art Moderne skyscraper on the Avenue of the Americas.

Despite a manner often characterized as brusque, Steel's management strength is in his ability to attract the right people and keep them happy at Nox. From the bottom—he's won several awards for aggressive hiring and promotion of minorities and women—to the top (he instituted decentralized cost accounting, a procedure that saves the company millions annually and is being widely copied by other giant corporations), George Steel keeps Nox employees performing at a lively clip.

Steel is also noted—and imitated—for his assertive role in seeking markets outside the U.S., and for computerizing offices early and effectively.

An Ohio native, George Steel dropped out of college to work for Osborne Knox and ended up both marrying his daughter and assuming his mantle of leadership on Knox's retirement. Old Nox watchers were somewhat surprised, it had been assumed that the position would fall to Cockburn (Coby) Knox, 51, Osborne's son, who had been groomed for leadership of the family-founded business virtually from birth. But, as Coby Knox admits with a hearty laugh, "When I see those dividends I have to admit that I couldn't have done it better myself!"

An admitted workaholic, Steel relaxes with his wife and daughters, Sophia and Hilary, in their art-filled homes. These include a ranch near Santa Barbara, an apartment in Manhattan's River House, and an estate in Palm Beach, as well as the fresh-painted Englewood manse, which Madeline has filled with museum-quality furniture and paintings.[]

Chapter Sixteen

New York City
June 1, 1981

E VEN THOUGH Erica got to her desk at eight on Monday morning, there was already a message on it from George Steel to see him immediately.

She walked through the darkened, hushed floor which the clerical workers would soon enliven. Her sensible heels clicked on the polished tiles.

Mr. Steel's new secretary was Janine Shapiro. She was competent, doggedly loyal, and sassy.

"He's busy. Go right in," she said without looking up from her word processor.

"Good morning" didn't get out of Erica's mouth.

"You've been seeing our comptroller?" he demanded.

"I, I, I . . . beg your pardon?" Her dates were casual—and none of his business.

"Are you going to Lorillard with him?"

"Not Lorillard, Reynolds."

He grinned malevolently. "Just checking."

Erica blushed furiously. She had just given away a confidence! "No, sir. I am not going. I'm not sure Doug is leaving Nox, either, for that matter."

"Well, I am sure."

"What can I do for you, sir? Other than espionage, that is."

"Now, now. You're paid much too well to be a mere spy. How would you like to move over to Development?"

"I really like it in Strategic Planning. You told Jim I was doing a good job, didn't you?"

"I terminate those who don't. What I had in mind was Assistant Vice President for Development."

Erica's mouth dropped open. "Mr. Steel! I don't know what to say." She had been with the company less than a year!

Steel gave her a cut-the-crap look. "Are you in or not?"

"Yes, sir! I'm in!"

"Fine. Go move your stuff. You can take your secretary with you."

"Can she get a raise?"

"Does she deserve it?"

"Oh, absolutely."

"Then you should have given it to her before. All right, do it now."

"Thank you."

"Oh, by the way, Eaton."

"Yes?"

"Don't expect any special treatment up here."

"Oh, I won't, sir. Any time the male assistant VPs need to haul cases of Nox-Out off the back ends of delivery trucks, you can bet I will do it too!"

He gave her a searching look.

Erica felt his pale blue eyes pierce the core of her very being. On the way down in the elevator, she wondered if the core of her very being wasn't located somewhere between her legs.

The Steels were having a civilized divorce.

Everyone was dressed very nicely, as if for church, sitting in George Steel's divorce lawyer's pecan-paneled conference room.

Nothing would be decided today, of course. The gargantuan task of dividing the couple's property was done, thanks to the devoted labor of two teams of the very best lawyers money could buy. But there were papers to be signed, formalities that had to be gone through. In other words, a big waste of time.

It drove George Steel crazy. He kept looking pointedly at his watch. The gesture always got his staff at Nox hopping, but nobody here moved. Madeline was having an Experience and was savoring every minute, memorizing details to sift through in future lunches at La Grenouille. As for the lawyers, they billed by the hour.

"I feel this is dragging on unnecessarily," George said.

"Feel?" Madeline jumped in. "I doubt that you've ever felt anything in your entire life, George. You wouldn't know the meaning of that word."

The lawyers ignored her. They'd heard such sentiments so many times that the words no longer registered. They had become subliminal, like the buzz of fluorescent bulbs.

George found himself with Madeline in a situation that had become as inevitable as taxes and death. It had been agreed that she would receive the ranch and the Palm Beach estate, as well as the contents of the apartment and the house in New Jersey. Good riddance, thought Steel, to the overwrought junk the antique dealers had conned her into.

Of course Madeline was left with enormous wealth. Old Osborne had provided well for his daughter. A huge chunk of Nox stock was vested equally in Madeline and her brother. This didn't seem to concern Madeline much. She knew money as something to spend or something to show off. She never considered it as something to wield.

They both nodded to the fiction that she was divorcing him because he was too dull and too hardworking a husband, unsuited to escort her in a life of privileged leisure. In truth he knew that he was divorcing Madeline, she who had thoughtlessly ceded the power of her wealth. He was divorcing her because she was weak and lazy.

In September Erica pulled off a major coup by coming up with a plan for the organization of the national staff. The division between New York and Los Angeles left the company in an operational quandary. Erica's solution catered to Steel's directions while soothing egos down the line and promoting efficiency.

It would have been unthinkable to promote her within the department so quickly after her extraordinary ascent to the position of assistant vice president. But Steel rewarded her with a bonus and a personal commendation.

Erica stood uneasily in his office until invited to sit, then *sat* uneasily.

"You did a magnificent job," said Steel.

"No, it was nothing," stammered Erica.

"What is that, one of the handicaps of womanhood?"

"What is?"

"The inability to accept praise. Either you treat it as your due, or you make a convincing argument that you don't deserve it."

Erica smiled. "I always learn so much from you. And it always hurts."

"You have intelligence and energy but just not enough of a tough streak. If you don't watch it, you'll end up with nothing more than a mildly successful little start-up, selling cosmetics or underwear."

"No way, not me. I'm devoted to Nox."

"Burning out, mini-entrepreneuring, that's what happened to all the promising women executives I've ever heard of."

Erica's eyes blazed. "Well, I'm not one of them."

After she left, he wondered: Was there enough raw material there for the making of an heir?

It was one of the historic days of the Valenta family. After more than a quarter of a century, they were leaving the Crest.

Erica's heart swelled with pride. She had bought them the apartment—fiercely expensive—in the Yorkville neighborhood, not far from her own condominium on the Upper East Side. It was a solid neighborhood, with enough elderly Europeans around to make them feel at home. And their building was only yards away from a library.

When she'd bought her own apartment, the mortgage banker's eyebrows had shot up at the information under the heading Employment & Salary. But now, for a second apartment, the heads started shaking. Fortunately, Brian had come in as a cosigner and the mortgage was approved.

Now that her parents were retired, Erica rested easier. They were in good health, and they had interests to keep their minds occupied. They also had each other.

Erica was more proud than she had been of anything she'd ever done, taking care of her parents in their old age, providing well for them. It was a satisfaction that all but buried her doubts about debt.

Those fears, after all, were a working-class superstition. Debt, she had learned in business school, and in the world of high finance, was not, per se, a bad thing. Indeed, it could be very good, a sign of economic vigor and health.

"Hello, my darling!"

"Papa, what's up? Did the moving van come? Don't lift *anything*, do you hear? The moving people are being paid plenty to pack and move everything themselves. When do you think they'll be ready? I need to call for a car so I can come and get you."

"Ho, ho. Surprise! I am talking to you already from here, Manhattan, New York. Soon is the moving people going to be here. Mama and I are enjoying the quiet and the beautiful view."

"What? How did you get there? If you took the subway . . ."

"*Subway*. Ha, ha. America mine—we took the Rolls-Royce!"

"Papa! I've told you a million times. The subway is no place . . ."

"No, Erica, is true. We really came in a Rolls-Royce. With champagne in the backseat, like in a fancy restaurant."

"How on earth . . ."

"Is your Mr. Steel. He came with a chauffeur. He keeps asking is there anything we need. But we didn't need anything else, Erica. At least Mama and I couldn't think of anything."

"Is he still there? Can I speak to him?"

"Mr. Steel, I don't know what to say . . ."

"Don't say anything. It's been ages since I've had such a good time in the Rolls. You ought to see their faces. Your folks are absolutely wonderful. You don't realize how lucky you are to have them."

It was the Sunday night after Thanksgiving that Erica was awakened by the buzzing of the doorman's intercom.

"There's a man here, name of Steel, says he wants to come up," said the doorman skeptically.

"Mr. *Steel*? Of course, of course. Send him up right away."

Her doorbell rang. She jumped to answer it, realized she was in her pajamas, and ran back to get her robe from the bedroom.

"I'm sorry," she began, as she opened the door. Then it hit her. Steel was standing there with something huge in florist's paper. It was almost midnight.

"Please come in," she said, feeling silly about the formality of her tone. But what *was* the right tone in a situation like this?

Steel handed her the bouquet. She unwrapped the paper. It was stunning, three dozen anemones, the most spectacular flowers she had ever seen. Where on earth did he get them, late on a Sunday night?

She looked about vainly, knowing she didn't own a vase big enough for the bouquet.

She felt a hand as strong as stone on her shoulder.

"Erica," he said, turning her around.

It was the first word he had uttered. He said no more but took her face in his hand, like an appraiser at Sotheby's evaluating something priceless.

She was barefoot and had to pull her head back to look him in the eyes. His eyes, those soul-raking things, what shameful things might they find in hers?

For the longest time she had been thinking about what she would do with him in exactly this position. But it had been fantasy. It had been perfectly safe to let herself go in the bedroom of her mind. This was different, this was real. This was dangerous.

He pulled her into the bedroom, made her pajamas vanish, as if he were a magician.

"I don't know if we should be doing this," she said.

"Oh?" he raised an eyebrow.

Another man might have laughed—it was already much too late for her to be playing coy.

"Why not?" he asked, perfectly patient, perfectly sincere.

"Sex is so . . . I mean, within the company, the ramifications . . ."

"You're a very self-controlled woman, but I had no idea how far that discipline extended."

"Well, I'm no prude! But I don't sleep around, especially with company . . ."

"I wasn't suggesting you sleep around."

"Well, what the hell is this conversation about?" Erica giggled nervously. They were both naked.

"It's about sex, about the cement that binds two perfectly suited people together."

"And if they're not so perfectly suited?"

"Then it's Krazy Glue. And they shouldn't be surprised if their skin tears and bleeds when they come apart."

It sounded like an ominous warning. But she didn't care, there was only one thing on her mind now. She wanted him furiously, and right now.

Soon he was on top of her, pressing her deliciously against the extra-firm mattress, directing her with his hard-muscled body, freeing her from every decision.

Possessed. The way the female is possessed by the wolf in the forest, not with violence but with absolute mastery.

His body was extraordinary, ageless. It was massive but lean, with a wolf's quick and dangerous grace.

Erica saw herself, as if from a distance, being sucked into the vortex of a tornado. She was whirled about madly, pulled down, and, finally, submerged.

Breathless, blinded, she tried to come up, tried vainly to make sense of her sensations. What was this? Something unlike any of her experiences. The brief sexual episodes since her divorce seemed as brisk and shallow as the charge of masturbation.

And what did the feelings elicited by George say about her passion—lost and mourned—for Whit? Compared to this, even the greatest (premarital) joy with him had been no more than a passing drift of perfume.

But she couldn't think now. Wouldn't. No thinking. No talking. She gave herself up utterly, and was lost to the night.

The next morning, her biggest surprise was to find that she had slept soundly. Erica woke refreshed and relaxed, stretching sensuously.

George Steel wasn't there. There was no impression of his head on the pillow, no muss of the sheets, no wrinkling of the blanket. No scent of him, lingering. No hairs. No toilet seat raised. For a hallucinatory moment, she wondered if last night had happened only in her imagination.

She walked out into the living room. Never before had she walked like this, naked and proud, her hair wild on her shoulders, her feet sure upon the floor.

There on the sofa, on the coffee table, trailing on the carpet, were the anemones. Their brilliant petals, blue and scarlet, and their pitch-black hearts were at odds with the thin stalks and lacy leaves. Already, the flowers had weakened terminally from their night's drought and the purity of their color was compromised.

The room, scattered with a riot of anemones, looked like the scene of a lethal childbirth. Blood, venous and arterial, sank silently into the ground.

Two weeks later she was summoned to the president's office.

"What can I do for you, Mr. Steel?"

"You can shut the door and cut out the 'Mr. Steel' crap."

She slammed the door. "I'm *trying* to be discreet. I always called you that before."

"It sounded bizarre before, too. This is still a California company. Senior executives call each other by their first names. You sound like a character in a sitcom."

"If I begin acting familiar now, it will start the rumors flying."

"What do you mean, 'start'?"

"Oh no! And we've been so *careful*."

"Erica, there were rumors months ago. Long before we

touched. That's corporate life. You ignore it, or preferably, you exploit it."

Erica shuddered. "Not me. I'm an old-fashioned girl. Besides, that sort of thing is bad for the company."

"Suit yourself. But right now your virtuous reputation and the squeaky Nox image on the annual report are the least of your problems."

"What do you mean? What problems? You didn't like the way I handled Osaka Textiles? I'll get back to . . ."

"Calm down. The Osaka deal is the best anyone can hope for, considering they're Japs.

"There's a board meeting scheduled for this afternoon. There's an item on the agenda that you should be aware of—a request for your dismissal."

"What! Why? I haven't . . ."

He raised his hand to stop her. "Irrelevant. *Who* is the question. And the answer to that is, Coby Knox."

"*What*? I've never even met the man."

"How could you, you're at work all the time. Besides, he's got nothing against you. It's me he wants to needle."

"Oh, George, what am I going to do? Can I come to the meeting, to defend myself?"

"No. You are going to do nothing. Don't worry, I'll take care of it. You don't think I'd let a dumb prick like Coby Knox pick and choose my senior staff? I'll let him state the case in his slurred, alcoholic way. Then I'll take care of the little shit—out where the whole board of directors can enjoy the show."

"Please, George. I wish you wouldn't. Can't you just call him now and convince him to withdraw the item from the agenda?"

"No, I can't."

"Please don't be stubborn, George. For my sake."

"I didn't say I wouldn't. I said I can't, and I can't."

"George, you've had that guy in your back pocket since I was in grade school. Don't tell me you can't make him shut up."

"Erica, pay attention. This is the reality of the matter. Coby Knox is a fart enclosed in a British suit. Coby Knox gets tachycardia when I sneeze. But understand this: Coby Knox votes thirty-five percent of the stock in this company. If he puts an item on the agenda, it gets discussed. But I said I'd take care of it. Just remember who did."

Erica shuffled back to her office. She had her secretary hold all calls, so she could brood in peace.

So, it had come to this. The end of the line. The meteor's burnout, the belly flop into the cistern.

What would she do now? The story would reach the ears of every corporation in the country. She'd never find an entry-level job, much less duplicate her quick rise at Nox.

The mortgages would be foreclosed, that was for sure. What would she do with her parents? The worst nightmare of her life was facing her now.

She didn't have a chance. The board would be glad to sacrifice someone like her to appease Coby Knox. Throw this bone to him and maybe the old coyote will go back to his vodka-soaked yacht for another ten years and let them live in peace.

Erica sighed. She should have resisted the man. But he was fire, he was flame. And now she would have to pay through the nose. The world hadn't changed a bit since the days of Hester Prynne.

Would George really come to her defense? As a gentleman and an officer of the corporation, he'd make polite noises, but would he risk his career for her honor? Most fool women would do that for a man without thinking twice. Vice versa was a different story.

Chapter Seventeen

Zebra stripes lined the room, as dawn light streamed through the broken slats of the shutters. Earline smoothed the hair of her sleeping sister, Ruthie. It was like a child playing with a doll. At sixteen, Earline's near-albino coloring and delicate build made her seem prepubescent; Ruthie's bright yellow hair, rosy cheeks, and lips pouting in sleep, as if suckling, lent her the air of a plastic baby.

"It's gonna be all right, sugar, I promise," whispered Earline. "Joe says we'll bring you over just as soon as I'm settled into New York City. That won't be but a few weeks, I know it.

"See, I gotta be a married lady, take care of you proper.

"It'll be so great, Ruthie. You just wait and see. You're gonna go to school in New York City, a good city school, not like Haywood. And then college. I swear I'm gonna get you to college. Just be patient, sugar pie."

Earline got up and checked the locks on her little valise. She felt confident. Ruthie would be okay—she'd made sure of that before taking a step northward.

For years Earline had "tended" Daddy. She worked powerful hard to please him, and it worked, because he never did touch Ruthie.

A few months earlier Daddy had a mild heart attack and

after that, he stopped bothering Earline, so she figured Ruthie would be safe from now on.

Ma was doing poorly, too. She'd lock herself in with the pigs, make all these strange noises. But Mary Beth didn't mind caring for her.

There had been one success in the family. Martha had married a doctor and moved to Little Rock, to a house with a swimming pool. She played tennis in a country club, wearing real diamond bracelets. But Martha had said, "Don't ever come here, don't ever call me. I don't care if you win a lottery or the Academy Awards, Barry and I just don't want to have anything at all to do with you people. Get that clear."

That had hurt Mary Beth something awful, but Mary Beth had her hands full now, taking care of Ma, trying to eke out a living even with the welfare. Earline figured she was doing her a kindness too, by going.

Joe Tully was the fourth or fifth most popular boy in the senior class. Joe was a singer and guitar player and had high hopes of making it as an entertainer someday. Folks around Haywood kept urging him to play country/western, but Joe insisted rock was where the big money was.

Nobody, least of all Joe, doubted his eventual success. He was, after all, the son of fine people; his daddy owned the biggest drugstore in the county. His daddy did not much care for guitar playing and would not contribute a penny to the development of his son's career. But Joe had always been sure of himself, and even a year before graduation, he had plans for leaving town. Sure enough, the day after the senior prom Haywood saw his Camaro's exhaust for the last time.

Joe always knew what he wanted, and was ready to take whatever opportunity came up, no matter what people said. When he asked Earline Prewitt out the first time, the topic dominated the girls'-bathroom conversation for a week. *Earline Prewitt?*

Those who had predicted that Joe Tully would dump Earline as soon as he had gotten into her pants were proved wrong. She became his steady, even going to the prom with him. His senior year passed quickly, and then he left town, as planned.

"You'll write to me as soon as you get to New York, right, Joe?"

"Nah, honey, you know I hate to write letters. I'll call you, though. Just as soon as I get a place of my own."

"You'll call. And you'll fix it so I can come, okay, Joe?"

"Sure. Sure, I will. And you'll settle in real nice there, I know. Just as soon as those recording contracts come in, sweetie, we'll be living in clover."

"Can we get married then, Joe?"

"Yeah, sure. Why not."

"And can Ruthie live with us?"

"Yeah, sure, why not?"

But weeks went by, then the summer, and Joe didn't call. Earline asked in the drugstore as to his whereabouts, but either his daddy didn't know or he wouldn't tell her.

Then in late October, when the dying year brings a touch of sadness in even the sunniest weather, he phoned.

He told her he hadn't gotten a place yet, that's why he hadn't called before. He was staying with some friends, but thought he might be moving soon, so he couldn't leave his number. He said that the big time was tougher to get into than he'd expected, but that he was finding work, here and there, in the entertainment business.

When she asked him if they were still getting married, he said sure, why not.

After that he called infrequently, every three weeks, maybe four. But he did call, and he still wanted to marry her and still wanted Ruthie to live with them. So Earline knew for a fact that his love was true.

At last, in June, during a suffocating, dry heat wave, he called, telling her to come.

Earline was disturbed by the changes in Joe. In a single year, the one between his nineteenth and twentieth, Joe had developed *wrinkles*. Deep rays came from the outer corners of his eyes and furrows bracketed his mouth. Even his Camaro was dusty and defeated, the tape deck gone.

The apartment he took her to was okay, but very dirty. He introduced her to Dwayne, who sat in the filthy kitchen, silently, and nodded agreement to everything that was said.

Earline spent her first two weeks cleaning the place. Joe was almost never there, but Dwayne, unfortunately, never left. Dwayne didn't talk at all, and on the rare occasion when he moved it was so slowly that he seemed like a robot on half-dead batteries.

"What's with Dwayne?" Earline whispered. "Is he retarded or what?"

"Hey," Joe snarled at her, "he owns the place. What do you want, to be out on the street?"

"No, 'course not, honey. But why can't we rent our own apartment?"

"With what? Do you see a lot of money rolling around here? And if I had any extra I'd invest it in the business."

"Sure, honey, you know I'll do anything to help your career. But where are all of your instruments? And the amps and stuff?"

"They're in the studio," he shouted. "What the hell are you bugging me for? Don't you think I've got enough problems without your nagging? I mean, shit, we're not even married, and you're nagging."

"I'm sorry," she said, and determined to go job-hunting the very next morning, whether she could finally scrape that stuff off the sink or not.

The search for work was dispiriting. Every time she applied for a job as a waitress or a receptionist or a shampoo girl there were a dozen girls there, all hoping and training and beautiful enough to be actresses. There wasn't anything for someone with Earline's modest ambitions.

Every morning she scoured the want ads, but by noon she had exhausted the possibilities. Not wanting to return to the apartment and the nodding Dwayne, she window-shopped the afternoon away.

The best place for this was Fifth Avenue, of course, and she especially loved to moon at the bridal gown displays at Goldsmith's. You could get lost in them, they were like little sets for a play.

One day they had photos of the wedding of Melissa John. Earline hadn't seen any of her pictures, but she had read all about the star in movie magazines. The dummy in the window wore the exact same dress as Melissa John had. It was all tight and sequin-ny, like a mermaid's, and you could see a lot of her breasts. Melissa John looked so beautiful and happy in all the photos, and you could bet her husband, a doctor, was happy too, even though there were no photos of him. It must be so nice to have a lot of money.

"Well, she'd be just as happy with a plain, everyday white dress. But Joe hadn't said a thing about marriage since she'd arrived in the city, and she was afraid to press him. After all, he was working in the studio all day and into the night, and *she* hadn't done a thing to ease their money troubles.

"We've gotta talk," said Joe. Earline noticed that the callus on his guitar hand was gone.

"I've gotta be honest with you, sugar. The music business just isn't going the way I hoped. Geez, hon, I am so sorry. I wanted things to be really great, I wanted to bring up your sister and buy you furs and nice stuff . . ."

Earline's eyes filled with tears. It had been a long time since he had spoken so sweetly to her.

"Joe, I don't need none of that fancy stuff. Just as long as I'm with you, honey, it doesn't matter if we're rich or poor. Whatever happens, I know you'll be a big success. At least to me, you'll always be one."

"Yeah, Earliny, you have always been real supportive. That's what I love best about you. But, babe, we have got serious cash flow problems here."

"You're smart, Joe. I'm sure you'll find a way over."

"Yeah, I think I have, but, sweetheart, I need your help."

"I'd do anything! Oh, Joe, you know it isn't my fault that I haven't found a job . . ."

"Of course not, sugar. Anyway, I've found some work you can do."

"Great, what is it?"

Joe swallowed. "Well, it sounds bad, but really it isn't as bad as you might think. After all, you're a country girl and this is the big city, big time. We've all got to change our hick way of thinking. Okay, it's like this. I want you to go out on some dates with some guys I know."

"What do you mean, 'dates.' You mean . . ."

"Sure, okay. Sleep with them. Whatever."

There was a long silence. Sheets of tears flowed down Earline's face. Joe avoided looking at her.

"Oh, Joe," she said at last. "Is that what you think of me? That I'm a . . . a . . . a prostitute."

"How can you say that, Earline?" He held her tightly by the arms. "How can you say that to a man who asked you to be his wife?"

"Oh, Joe. Do you really mean that? Are we really getting married?"

"Of course, babe. Hey, what do you think? You think you're engaged to a liar, huh?"

"No," she giggled. Then she sobered. "But, Joe, how could I do it? Men who do that are sleazy. They're creeps."

"No way, hon. Like I said, these are friends of mine. Handpicked. And listen. Any time you don't want a guy, just say the word. I'll get rid of him in a minute. Okay?"

Earline bit her lip. "I don't know. I just don't think I could do it."

"Hon-ey. It'll be a cinch. You know how when you make love you kind of tune out? Not tune out like Dwayne but sort of go into a dream world, right? Well, just do that with these guys. You won't even know they've been there. I swear, you'll forget their faces as soon as they leave the room.

"Please, babe. Just for a short time. Till we've got enough to get our own place, settle in. Then we'll get married. And we'll bring your sister up."

The months stretched on. Joe was right about one thing. She forgot their faces. She forgot them before she even saw them.

She and Joe moved into their own place. Joe got a stunning new car. He bought her whatever she wanted, but she never asked for anything expensive. She had a feeling that if she asked him to bring up Ruthie . . . But no, this wasn't the right time. First she had to finish with this business. The whole point, after all, was to make a decent, respectable home for Ruthie.

She began to suspect that Joe had other girls. Still, she told herself, he loves only me, *I'm* the one he's going to marry.

"I think it's time we got married," she announced one day.

"Oh really?" said Joe.

"Yes."

Joe was more upset by the insistence than by the proposition itself. It wasn't like Earline to put her foot down.

A few weeks later, she made him set the date. He got the license. They went for blood tests.

Earline did something she felt very guilty about. Every day she would take a customer or two on her own. She wouldn't tell Joe about it and she kept all the money. She was saving up for a trousseau.

At last it was her wedding day. Joe woke up in a rotten mood. He swore at everything from the coffee machine to the cat. He wanted to go to City Hall "first thing in the morning" (it was already eleven) and get it over with.

"No," said Earline, "I'll meet you in City Hall at two o'clock. I've got some things I want to do."

"What the hell," said Joe.

She got to Goldsmith's as fast as she could. A saleswoman looked her up and down, then pretended she had some other task elsewhere. But an older woman quickly ran over to her. The woman's smile took the intimidation out of the fancy salon.

"Hello, I'm Mrs. Marshall. How can I help you?"

"Well, I was wondering if you had anything simple."

"We can always add or remove ornamentation. Tell me more about your dream gown."

"No, it really has to be very plain. You see I'm getting married in a cl . . . judge's office. During the day."

"Certainly. I'm sure we'll come up with something absolutely appropriate, yet perfectly charming. If you'll step this way to a dressing room. I'll bring in a first group of selections. You're a size four, I'd guess."

Earline stood on a pedestal, breathless at her own reflection.

Mrs. Marshall looked on approvingly. Nine times out of ten a bride ended up buying the first dress she tried on.

It was a clean-cut cotton dress, plain enough to wear to an office, fine enough to say "quality" anywhere. The chalky whiteness seemed to bring out what little color there was in Earline's skin; its artful tailoring accentuated her few curves.

She pretended to try on the next dress. Instead she sneaked a peek at the price tag on the first. Dear Lord. Three times as much money as she had saved.

"I think I'd like to look around some more," she told Mrs. Marshall.

Earline refused to be disappointed. She was wearing her best outfit for just such a contingency. White pants, the only white garment she owned, but at least they were real slacks, not jeans, and a very pale pink pullover that looked like a sweater but was made out of something cool. She bought herself a bunch of pink daisies and treated herself to a cab to City Hall.

Oh, but it was beautiful. What a graceful building, with a dome and fluted columns and a grand flight of stairs to walk up. Brilliant sunshine poured down on it, there was a soft blue sky above it and a little patch of grass in front of it. And politicians and protestors and TV cameras! Earline got into a group of picketers and smiled shyly into a minicam. Maybe someone would recognize her on TV tonight! But, of course, she didn't know anyone in New York who would recognize her.

She walked into the building, which was deliciously cool inside. A guard gave her a shrewd look, another examined her handbag. Then they nodded her in.

The building was almost deserted. She wandered around a bit, looking for the room where marriages were performed. It wasn't a big building, and after a short while she found the room. It was breathtaking. There were rows of polished wooden pews, a magnificent chandelier, and enormous windows draped in tassled blue silk. The carpet was of rich blue, and the altar was gilded and draped.

The light honeyed the somber faces in golden-framed portraits. She recognized George Washington. The glorious pictures made her feel all tingly inside. She took a seat near the back and waited patiently. It would feel lonely in here with just the two of them and the clerk. Her kin and Joe's would have easily filled the room. But of course, there wasn't anything this pretty back in Arkansas.

The clock on the wall showed 2:05. Where were they? Joe was so antsy about being on time, if he was late, it meant that something must have happened to him. Or perhaps he'd changed his mind after all. But no, they were destined to be married. But what about the clerk?

Suddenly she had the terrible sinking feeling that the wedding had been called off. Joe had found her a false I.D. because she was still under age for marriage in New York State. It was foolproof, he said, but what if the bluff were called after all? Still, someone would have come to tell her.

An hour passed. Earline did her best not to cry. She didn't want to look silly on her wedding day! Another half hour.

This isn't right, she thought. And why aren't other people getting married on a beautiful summer afternoon? There must be tons of people in a city the size of New York . . .

Finally, at 3:45 she stepped out of the room. A uniformed guard was pacing up and down the hall.

"Excuse me, sir. Isn't there supposed to be a clerk here now?"

"Clerk? Why would there be a clerk here? The board isn't in session."

"Board?"

"Sure. Board of Estimates. That's the room where they meet. Over on the other side is the Council chambers. Pretty, ain't they?"

"But, but where do people get married? I mean, when they get married at City Hall?"

"Well, it ain't actually City Hall. What they do, see, is marry at the Municipal Building. That's over across the street, in the big building . . . Hey, where you goin'?"

Earline ran down the marble staircase. Then she ran back up again. She had forgotten her pink daisies in the glorious meeting room of the Board of Estimates.

She ran back down again, out the building, down the front

steps. In a different mood, in a skirt, the descent would have been glamorous.

The big Municipal Building was ugly and unmistakable. But how to get there? Between it and City Hall was a torrent of cars rushing to get on to the Brooklyn Bridge. She circled round City Hall, looking for a way to cross the street. There was a light, but she waited and waited and it just wouldn't change. There was no letup in the swift stream of traffic. What was there in Brooklyn that they were in such a hurry to get to?

Earline closed her eyes tight. I've just got to do it. She stepped down into the street. She promised herself not to open her eyes until she was either dead or on the other side of the street.

The horns screamed as if the cars were being tortured, but she managed to get to the other side, safe and sound.

She ran and she ran and she asked directions and she ran some more. At last she was at the door to the clerk's office where marriages, a sign proclaimed, were performed between nine and four o'clock.

There was a shabby waiting room, done in government, institutional green, decorated with mismatched plastic molded chairs. In the one directly facing the door was Joe, fast asleep.

"Thank God," said Earline, trying to catch her breath and wake Joe gently at the same time.

Joe woke, shaking his head and looking up at the clock.

"Oh Joe, honey love, I am so sorry. I was over at . . ."

"Christ. You stupid bitch. What the hell is this? Whose idea was this in the first place?"

"Oh, Joe. I apologize. A million, trillion times. We can get married now. The clerk will take us, it isn't four yet."

"He can take a flying fuck . . ." Joe went off into incoherence.

Suddenly he picked her up—literally raised her off the floor—by her pullover, and threw her against the stained wall. Then he smacked her, hard, across her cheek.

A summoned guard was on his way, but Joe was already leaving the room.

"No wait, Joe! Wait for me," she cried, picking herself up and running after him.

He turned a corner without looking back at her. When she turned it, she faced the closed door of an elevator.

She turned back. The guard was closing the door to the marriage office.

"It's four o'clock," he said.

But when Earline walked past him into the room, he didn't protest. While the door had been shut to newcomers, those already seated would be married that day.

Earline slumped in a chair, trying to figure out what had happened, what was going to happen next.

The waiting room was crowded and noisy. It was, after all, a beautiful summer day, a perfect day for a wedding. Bored children whined and fought with each other. Many of the couples tying the knot were parents, finally legitimizing their union.

Slowly the waiting room emptied, and the newly married were let out by the guard.

Earline sat. She didn't have the strength to get up. She didn't know where to go.

The last couple approached the receptionist. The groom was a grizzled man of sixty with an ash-black face on which deep creases were indistinguishable from scars. His posture showed habitual rage and defeat.

The bride was very young, very thin, very blond. There was something so needy about her face that it could never be said to be pretty. An unbecoming dress hung from her sharp shoulder bones. She wore a corsage of many white ribbons and one feeble white orchid sprinkled with silver glitter. Earline was shocked at how much the girl resembled herself.

After conferring with the receptionist, the couple looked around the room. The bride came over to Earline and asked shyly,

"We need a witness. Could you be ours?"

"Sure," said Earline.

"For free?"

"Sure."

The girl smiled at her groom in relief. The groom didn't smile, but he reached into his pocket and came up with a wrinkled five-dollar bill, smoothed it carefully, and handed it to the receptionist.

The receptionist smiled wearily, nodded, and directed the bridal party into the next room.

The room was like a spaceship cocoon, with the same dark carpeting covering floor and walls. There was scant, indirect lighting and a stained-glass panel showing some innocuous, vaguely pastoral scenes.

The clerk stood behind a simple wooden lectern, flanked by the American and state flags.

The ceremony was over before Earline realized that anything had happened.

They all filed out of the room, and Earline heard the receptionist tell the clerk, "Good timing, thirty-five seconds for that one."

"Yup," said the clerk, "shaved ten seconds off the average."

Earline followed the couple out to the hall. The woman had a shopping bag and she took out a quart bottle of malt liquor and some plastic champagne glasses.

"Have a drink with us?" she offered nervously, looking to see if anyone official was coming into the hallway.

"No, thanks," said Earline.

She wished the couple good luck, knowing as well as they did that they would never have any.

Down in the street it was still bright and sunny, but the streets were covered with moving human beings, freshly released from their jobs.

Whatever was she going to do now? Obviously Joe Tully would never marry her, and if she didn't think of something soon, Ruthie would stay in Cripple Hollow till hell froze over like their mother's heart.

Chapter Eighteen

New York City
December 23, 1986

I T WAS A HEARTWARMING SCENE. Dozens of young mothers were wheeling their babies in strollers. They bent down to fix hoods and pick up dropped mittens and tissue off runny noses with gentle, practiced swipes. The mothers chatted with each other about diaper brands and washing powders and local pediatricians.

But this was not a typically pretty picture of maternal care. For one thing, it was six o'clock on a December evening, hardly the time most mothers would choose to give their babies an airing. The location, too, was unusual: Eighth Avenue and Forty-second Street. In fact, the young women (a majority were in their teens) were taking their children to babysitters on the way to work.

They were prostitutes, street hookers. From the central point of the sitters' apartments they fanned out over mid-Manhattan, each taking her place in the area she had staked out like a territorial animal.

Separated from the strollers, they no longer looked sweet. In fact they barely looked human.

Earline walked past scores of them on her way to her own station, way over west near the river. Their skin was pockmarked and slack and sallow. Their eyes were wet with infection and heroin and fury. They were still children, but theirs was a race with a short life cycle.

They say that one way or another, most hookers commit suicide.

The wind blowing off the Hudson was like acid on her face. Yet she pushed on. She didn't have a pimp, she didn't *have* to do it. She could have taken one night off, a cold night like this. But hooking was what she *did*. She didn't know what else to do. She didn't know what else to be. She had never survived any other way.

She liked it over on Twelfth Avenue. Business was slow there. There was less competition. There were fewer police busts. Far fewer pimps. A girl could make do there on her own, if a girl wasn't greedy, and she certainly wasn't.

On Fortieth and Ninth a potential john was arguing with a pimp. Near them, slouching against a long-abandoned gas pump, was the hooker in question. Her face was adolescent but her body drooped like a worn-out old whore's. The girl was in the worst throes of teenage acne, her skin festering with pustules, her hair saturated with grease. Her makeup was applied like that of a five-year-old playing dress-up: without knowledge of seduction or intention to seduce.

"She ain't worth no ten dollar, man. She a piece a shit," the would-be customer said.

The pimp glanced back at his woman. She wore the same expression she had worn before, as if she would just as soon be part of the nameless ooze in the gutter, frozen on its way down to the sewer grating.

"Yeah," said the pimp. "But I gotta make a livin', man."

Earline fought back her nausea. As degraded as the girl was, the john was worse. Imagine spending money to squirt into the mouth of a pathetic stranger. Imagine touching a sick-looking girl like that of your own free will. *That* was the lowest.

If only she couldn't see it all so clearly. If only she could live like the other girls, hooked on a dream of riches, or the imaginary love of a fancy man, or the illusion that she was doing it for kicks. If only she were like the others, spaced out on drugs, slightly retarded, or raised to believe there was no choice.

What had happened to the dream of bringing Ruthie up? To what? To what? Was this any better than what her little sister had at home?

So here she was, a day before Christmas Eve. What do hookers do for Christmas? Is there some great whores' Christmas party somewhere, with children, pimps, babysitters, sleazy hotel owners, and other hangers-on attending?

Or did everyone just take the night off on their own? Did girls go back to places like Minnesota and South Carolina and Jamaica, Queens, and pretend they were home from regular jobs in the great city of opportunity?

Twenty-four hours later, Earline found herself on the same street she always walked. Christmas Eve had changed nothing. If there was a Christmas Ball for her colleagues, no one had invited her to it. Returning to Arkansas was out of the question—she would rather slit her throat.

In case of emergency, she could go up to the motel on the corner, go to her usual room and watch pay TV. She'd noticed that the usual desk clerk was on duty. He was from India. Probably Christmas didn't mean anything special to Hindus. He was a nice man and would often come and chat with her when she took a break at the soup machine.

See, she told herself, the desk clerk proved that the world wasn't full of rats. Most people in his position would have thrown her out, but he let her ply her trade, shocking the tourists.

"Don't worry," he'd say, "they go back to their home towns and tell all the other chaps about their adventures in New York, about the bargain motel—nice and clean, though—where you-know-what goes on. And all their friends want to come here too!"

After the soup she forced herself to go out and do her thing. The street was utterly empty, it could have been in outer space. She bared her leg in a come-on pose. She thought about the unthinkable. The complimentary razor in her hotel room, the depth of the tub.

A silver limousine slithered down the block. A customer at

last. Earline hurried out to the curb. The back window rolled down. A woman sat in the seat, a brandy snifter in hand. Earline sighed. She didn't like to entertain lesbians or be used like a gadget to please a husband.

"It's not what you think. Come in."

"What is it, then?"

"A job."

"What kind of job?"

"A pleasant, well-paying job."

"That's not what I asked."

"Get out of the cold. I'll tell you anything you want to know."

Earline hesitated. The woman laughed a throaty, cultured laugh. "Well, what exactly do you have to lose?"

Earline shrugged and got into the car. The door closed with a rich click.

"Welcome aboard, Cindy," the woman said.

"My name is Earline."

"I like Cindy better."

Earline looked at the paneled bar and at the driver's uniformed back.

"Yeah. So do I."

And from then on it was Cindy.

The woman's name was Rae, and she was something else. The scion of a genteel family whose fortune had come to ruin through generations of messy divorces, Rae had outmaneuvered the police, outsmarted the moral guardians of the City, and outnerved the Mob, to run the most sophisticated and most profitable call-girl operation in town. Rae was proof positive that blood will tell (her ancestor had made the original family fortune by ripping off the Pilgrim Fathers).

Cindy was awed and intimidated by Rae's stable of girls. The majority were tall, blond, and fabulously beautiful. Many were college educated, some were witty, all were carefully groomed and trained by the madam.

Yet Cindy had a special place among them. Of all the girls, Rae said, she alone had a special quality of innocence and freshness. It helped that she looked much, much younger than her nineteen years, but her unique attraction was more than mere youth.

"She looks untouched," noted Rae shrewdly, "a reusable virgin."

Cindy proved to be a very popular attraction. Soon Rae began to refine her with carefully chosen clothes, speech and elocution lessons, and dance classes for poise. As usual, Rae's investment paid off handsomely. Cindy's basic appeal moved a wide range of men. Moreover, she was hard-working, punctual, and free of the common vices of the profession: love, drugs, and the entrepreneurial impulse.

One day, after two successful years, Rae called Cindy into her office. As always, Cindy was awed by the combination of fine English furniture and the computer banks.

"Cindy, dear," said Rae, "whatever shall we do about your money?"

Cindy shrugged. "I don't know."

Rae threw up her hands in exasperation. "You needn't actually *be* innocent, dear. Looking the part is enough."

Cindy gave the carpet a bitter look.

"Shall we look into, oh, some commercial properties for you, downtown? My friends in the municipality inform me of some good buys there."

"Whatever you think, Rae."

"Of course, I must charge you for my financial services, Cindy, you do understand that?"

"Sure, anything you say is fine."

"Excellent! Cindy, dear, we're going to be very rich women someday."

The prospect seemed to thrill Rae much more than Cindy, and Rae was *already* rich.

Rae rubbed her hands. She loved doing financial management. Sometimes she thought about giving up this racket and going into bond trading.

"Oh, Cindy. One more thing."

"What is it? I've got a date at the Marriott in twenty minutes."

"It's just that I've noticed that you have some pimples, dear. Can't let the clients know you're heading toward puberty, you know."

"Oh, these dumb things on my chin? I think I'm allergic to some of the foods in these fancy restaurants. They put everything but the kitchen sink into those sauces. And you know how much the clients hate it when you fuss with food, so of course I have to *taste*, at least . . ."

"Okay, okay, okay. But get it taken care of. Take a day at Goldsmith's."

Cindy blanched. "The bridal salon?"

"Don't be ridiculous. The skin-care salon on Madison."

"Oh, come on, spend a fortune just to sit under some hair dryer all day?"

"Trust me, they're worth the money. Look, it'll be my treat. I owe you."

The Madison side of the building didn't look anything like the traditional brass-and-glass on Fifth. Two silver-plated doors opened to a vast, Art Deco hall of white marble and cobalt blue.

Gorgeous women of mixed race, dressed in evening gowns, loped around the great hall carrying dossiers, while the subjects of the files, inevitably less gorgeous, followed like baby ducks.

A woman in Thai national dress, the eyes under her slanted lids disarmingly blue, greeted Cindy with cool oriental politeness. She whisked Cindy out of the hall to the elevator bank.

The oriental woman presented Cindy to Olga, a cosmetician with heavy shoes and a heavier accent. Like all of the Goldsmith cosmeticians, Olga had come from somewhere shrouded in the mists of the Danube and of time. Dressed in the starched white uniform of a prewar nurse, Olga began her ministrations.

"Disrrrobe, if you vould," ordered Olga.

Cindy did as she was bidden, then wrapped herself in a

cobalt blue towel secured under her arms by Velcro panels. The color, Olga noted, was sensational against Cindy's white skin.

Cindy reclined on what looked like an operating table. Above her were huge arc lamps, reflecting mirrors, magnifying lenses and other surgical appliances. Olga smoothed back Cindy's hair and wrapped it in a small towel. She poured some lotion into the palm of one hand, warming it, then spread it deftly onto Cindy's face. Olga was surprised when she tissued off the lotion to find that Cindy was not wearing any makeup.

She lowered a powerful magnifying lens and peered through it critically.

"Ah, yes," intoned Olga, "ze pimples und ze blackheads." Her tone intimated that the patient might have, at most, six months to live.

She smoothed another lotion on, then lowered a contraption to frame and enclose Cindy's face. An undulating mist, scented with rosemary, engulfed her.

Cindy was unaware that Olga had left the room until she heard the door click when Olga returned, and felt the removal of the device.

"Excellent. It is vunderful to have such small pores, yes? But now ve open zem for business, yes?"

Cindy relaxed. Obviously Olga was one of those people who expect no response to their questions. She sure didn't want to have to mind her p's and q's when she wasn't even working. None of Rae's "behave like a lady" now. She could just lie back and relax . . .

"Ouch!" she cried out.

Olga, amid her meaningless incantations, had expertly squeezed a pimple, releasing trapped sebum and sending knifelike pain slashing into Cindy's sinuses.

Olga nodded sagely. "Yes, yes. To be beautiful ve must undergo pain."

Cindy determined to show no weakness during the rest of the treatment. Each time Olga applied her flat, strong fingers to a blackhead it felt like pincers were being used in some exquisite medieval torture. Yet Cindy forced herself to relax.

The pain remained, but Cindy mastered it, floated above it. That, after all, was one thing she was really good at.

Under the punished skin, Cindy's muscles were as smooth and soft as the stuffing in a quilt.

"Bravo!" said Olga at last, finishing up. "You vere magnificent. I have never seen such self-control. And now a revard, yes?"

Using a thick sable brush, Olga painted a cool paste, smelling faintly of almonds, on Cindy's face. The throbbing flesh screamed gratitude. Soon all sensation died, a state Cindy found delicious. After placing soothing pads on Cindy's eyes, Olga left the room again, leaving Cindy in her pleasant void.

After a time—Cindy had no way of knowing how long—Olga returned. She removed the hardened mask and sprinkled flower-water on Cindy's face. The process of a facial was like an idolatrous ceremony, precisely detailed and basically meaningless.

Next, Olga produced a glass wand that sizzled with a purple flash of electricity. The air smelled of ozone and sparks flew as she passed it ritually over Cindy's face. Finally, she brought out a smooth lump of heated metal, very much like a toy iron.

"Is for pressing out ze wrinkles," said Olga. Now even she felt ridiculous. Cindy's face was no more wrinkled than a toddler's.

The facial done, Olga escorted Cindy through a passageway to the baths. What was done to her face was simple compared to the series of massages, sprays, masks, and treatments applied to her body, hair, and scalp.

Cindy was growing impatient. It must be late afternoon by now. Rae might be paying for the beauty treatments, but she certainly wasn't paying for time lost from work. Cindy felt anxious whenever she wasn't working regular or even extended hours.

"Just vone more bath," promised Olga. She smiled. They all loved this one.

The bath looked like an Egyptian sarcophagus. It was specially adjusted to each woman so that it fit perfectly up to her neck. The bath was as viscous as honey, although it contained other esoteric skin-softening ingredients as well. Tiny jets made the thick concoction whirl and pulsate.

Cindy stood upon a platform in the bath, but standing took hardly any effort. The thickness of the honey kept her suspended. She felt like a floating astronaut.

When Olga turned the switch on, Cindy could feel the jets pulse against her skin. They beat strongly but pleasantly against the muscles of her back and shoulders and calves and hips. The effect was wonderfully relaxing. The only trouble was, an insistent jet was throbbing directly between her legs.

Cindy cringed, trying to position her body away from the jet. But the shape of the bath held her rigidly, if weightlessly, in position. Nor could she close her legs. Her feet were deeply imbedded in the bath's adjusted platform.

"Can you adjust this, please?" she asked Olga.

"No, no, madame, it is exactly correct, yes?" Olga smiled warmly.

Cindy was too embarrassed to tell Olga exactly what the problem was. The jet kept beating thickly, insistently, between her legs.

She felt a heat and a slickness and a rushing—very much like, but not exactly like, the heat and the slickness and the rushing of the honey bath.

She felt her nipples become erect, as they did when she was cold or frightened. Yet the bath was definitely warm, comforting, unthreatening.

It seemed as if the jet was deafening in its pounding. Her heart beat along with it, drumming out a jungle rhythm she couldn't stop.

She felt her clitoris grow alarmingly, extending outward to the jet, exposing itself to the soft punches.

Suddenly, she felt an almost painful stab. The long muscles of her legs tightened and a lightning blast of sheer pleasure coursed through her. Her body pulsed harder than any jet. Hot blood rushed into every vessel. She grunted twice, aware and ashamed of the animal-like noise, but unable to suppress it.

Olga looked at the flushed face above the bath. Cindy's eyelids were lowered in embarrassment. Her ears burned red. Despite the moderate warmth of the bath, her face was wet with perspiration.

"Very good, very good," nodded Olga, satisfied with her charge.

Cindy had never climaxed physically before. She'd come close, when first caressed by Joe. But now she knew for sure. This was no "almost," "kind of," or "sorta." This was the real thing; as unmistakable, simple, strong, and satisfying as a good hard sneeze. She was perplexed and a bit humiliated by what had happened. Weren't you supposed to be in love? Wasn't it supposed to be romantic and dreamy?

She was awfully glad to get into the privacy of the cool, rinsing shower. Nevertheless, she had to admit to herself, her body had never before felt so good.

As she dressed, Olga wrote lengthy notes in Cindy's dossier. The slinky Eurasian returned to shepherd Cindy to makeup.

The makeup man wore a full-length caftan of purple brocade. His left ear was outlined by a semicircle of pierced diamond studs. He chattered nonstop in a tonsiled tone that made Olga sound like a Greek philosopher in comparison.

Cindy could hardly wait to see what face a guy like that might paint on her. But when he was done she looked at herself in the mirror and was surprised by what she saw. Staring back at her was the face of an angel.

A wide, procelain brow came down to soft brown eyebrows that wouldn't know how to frown. Underneath them were two eyes, blue and bright as a perfect June sky. The nose, the last facial feature to develop to its mature state, looked as if it had not yet done so. It was a child's delightful little button. Delicately bruised rosebud lips perched on a sweet little chin. Her cheeks were soft and rosy as cotton candy.

What a lie! A Kate Greenaway illustration hiding a monster. A witch. A creature who had seen and done the filthiest, slimiest things. Cindy wanted to cry.

The Eurasian came once again. The makeup man scribbled furiously in the file and handed it to the exotic lady.

Cindy was led to the first floor, to one of the marble counters. She was seated on a tall stool, from which vantage she could see her reflection in three large mirrors.

"We recommend," said the lovely Thai behind the counter, "that you acquire the following products for skin maintenance between salon visits . . ."

She then reeled off a long list of potions and lotions from the notes in the ever-thickening dossier. The employees got a commission on sales; they tried to get the bill for a first visit to the salon up to four figures. Cindy nodded, agreeing to each item. After all, Rae was paying. It was in Rae's interest alone to maintain that false angel in the mirrors.

At last Cindy found herself at the heavy doors, weighed down with two enormous shopping bags loaded with silver-and-blue bottles and jars.

"Just a moment, please," said a six-foot-tall black woman wearing tribal jewelry. "Our directress wonders if she might speak with you for a minute."

The directress's office was decorated in the same motif as the establishment, but with a refinement and subtlety evident at first glance. The thinnest threads of silver flashed through fine fabrics. An impressive collection of crystal, some of it in cobalt, lined one wall. And who should be standing there—Cindy recognized her immediately—but Mrs. Marshall.

Cindy blushed deeply. "You probably remember me. I once shopped at the bridal salon. I didn't buy anything." Her voice trailed off in a whisper.

"Oh? I don't think I remember."

Cindy gave her a grateful look. Sometimes forgetting was the greatest gift.

Bettina invited Cindy to sit, then explained the reason that the salon employees had brought her in.

"You see, our skin salon, which is rather a new business for us, has been doing very well. A friend, that is, a *consultant*, has suggested that we expand into selling the skin-care products at other outlets. At first, we'll just be doing it experimentally, of course, but we hope to eventually have our creams in every major department store! Anyway, for purposes of advertising, we need someone who will personify the line of products. Someone very lovely who hasn't modeled before, who will become recognized as the 'Pure Innocence' face."

Cindy burst out laughing. "As the *what*?"

"That's the name of the product line, 'Pure Innocence.' I think you look perfect for it. Of course, I'm not the last word here. We'll have to consult Mr. Goldsmith, our president, and

Ms. Eaton, the consultant, and a few other people. But I think you may have a job offer."

Cindy shook her head. "Mrs. Marshall, you have no idea how crazy ridiculous this is."

"Why do you say that?"

"For starters, I'm no model. I came here because my skin was a wreck. Without makeup no one even gives me a second look in the street!"

"But makeup is the whole point. And with it you look just sensational!"

Cindy scowled. "If only you realized how ironic this all is. Pure Innocence! Mrs. Marshall, do you realize what I am?"

Bettina reddened, much to her own annoyance. She liked to think of herself as sophisticated. "Now, now, we—and most businesses around here—have many patrons who are, are, in unusual lines of work."

"Mrs. Marshall, I'm a whore. A whore! A hooker. A prostitute who caters to pederasts."

"Mmm. Well, it isn't exactly tattooed on your forehead. You could be a model, as far as I'm concerned. Look, why don't you leave your home number and I'll call you next week for an appointment with the other people. That way, you can think about it, okay?"

Well, thought Cindy, in the taxi to Rae's, it sure has been an interesting day.

Could she really do something else, something other than the work that made her want to tear her soul out of her body? Now? Now that she had gotten good at what she did? Now that she had been trained by Rae into the sleekest of the sisterhood? And what did modeling pay? Not as much as hooking. Big deal, who cared.

If all this was for real (could it possibly be?) she could bring up Ruthie.

Yes, that's what she'd do. Even if it turned out that the modeling thing fell through, still it was a sign. She was good for something else in life.

Even if she didn't get the job, she had her savings. And Rae's real estate! She'd call for Ruthie tonight!

Chapter Nineteen

From Thisweek *Magazine, November 29, 1989*

COMMERCE

America's Top Woman Executive

WHILE WOMEN have been entering the work force in a deluge for more than a decade, only a handful, so far, have managed to reach the upper echelons of corporate management. There is just one Fortune 500 company headed by a woman, but then Katharine Graham inherited her publishing position from her father and husband.

You would have to go one level down to find the highest women achievers in business. A handful head their own companies. Another small group has reached the summit of smaller corporations. The most exclusive sorority of all is women in the second level of command at the largest corporations. Of these, few have had careers as spectacular as that of Erica Valenta Eaton, Executive Vice President of Nox Industries, Inc.

Born to a family of motel entrepreneurs, Eaton always wanted to be a businesswoman. Radcliffe and an M.B.A. were natural moves to that end. Yet Eaton showed unusual gumption in joining Nox. While most ambitious women cut their teeth on such "traditional" businesses as apparel, cosmetics, and advertising, Eaton plunged right into the male bastion of Nox—the country's leading producer of chemicals and other "macho" products.

Her rise at Nox has been more steady than rapid. Like many successful women, Eaton acquired—and retains—a powerful male mentor. From the beginning, she has been championed by George Steel, longtime president and CEO of the company. One of the first corporate advocates of promoting women and minorities, Steel enthusiastically supported Eaton throughout her rise, and against the opposition of stodgier voices in the corporate hierarchy.

Too enthusiastically say some Nox executives, off the record, noting that Eaton's arrival coincided with the breakup of Steel's longtime marriage. Tongues were set wagging by the frequent round-the-clock conferencing between the firm's two executives. But a crisis in morale has long since been averted. Eaton and Steel are engaged to be married, and Nox hopes to profit happily ever after.

Eaton's managerial style is tough and driven, "the typical castrating female boss," says one junior vice president who insists on anonymity. Yet others find a feminine streak in her concern for Nox's 200,000 employees (the company has the most generous medical plan in America and a few of its plants have on-site day-care centers) and her sensitivity to the human factors of company markets (she engineered a flexible financial plan for the purchase of Nox fertilizers and pesticides that eases the burden on independent farmers).

Eaton is fiercely protective of her privacy, refusing to grant interviews on anything more personal than company policy. Close members of her staff insist that she has a subtle sense of humor, but her appearance is definitely dour. She wears her hair severely tied back, eschews makeup, and favors conservative suits. Low-heeled shoes do not lessen the impact of her 5' 11" height.

Where does Erica Eaton go from here? Will she become the first woman to rise to the head of a major industrial company? Certainly she has the expertise. At Nox she has manned every major post, mastering strategic planning, development, marketing, finance, and operations. But while Erica Eaton may be ready to be the first woman at the helm, industrial America in the 1990s probably isn't.

Besides, George Steel retains a youthful, firm, and much-hailed grip on Nox, and Erica Eaton has never shown an interest in moving elsewhere. It's quite possible that America's top woman executive is perfectly content in the number two slot, and it seems the company prefers her in that position.

Quips Gerald Crosby, VP Personnel, "Nox is like a mom-and-pop grocery these days." "Sure," winks Roy Little, VP Finance, "Erica gets along great with the boss!" []

Chapter Twenty

NOTHING BUT THE BY-NOW UNBREAKABLE HABIT of getting up and going to the office every single weekday morning got Erica to Nox headquarters on Monday. She had spent the weekend in an agony of humiliation. On Friday evening, she'd picked up a copy of *Thisweek*, fully expecting to be mildly thrilled by becoming a minor celebrity. She'd been profiled before in business magazines, of course, and she figured this would be a similar experience.

She was stunned. The article slapped her around brutally. Why, it insinuated broadly that she had slept her way up the executive ladder, it had just about stated that she was *ugly*, it had made her out to be some kind of corporate Mamie Eisenhower, content in the shadow of George Steel, happy to serve on the sidelines.

Those mean things people said! Did no one have a kind word for her? She didn't expect much better from Crosby, whose entire career was nothing but office politicking. And she figured her old enemy Roy Little could have done lots more damage, but she knew that the *Thisweek* reporter had interviewed so many others. Why had they been so cruel?

"Morning, Ruthie."

She couldn't even look her own secretary in the eye.

"Hi, boss. Five reactions so far. Oscar Barnes says it's an eight on the P.R. scale—for the company, of course. *Family Circle* wants to know your favorite recipe. Melissa John says she's flying in next week and will take you for a makeover at knife point. And two headhunters want you to call back."

"Oh, screw 'em all. What's in the news?"

Every morning Ruthie Prewitt read the *Times* and the *Wall Street Journal* and gave Erica a précis of relevant news. With each new level of responsibility Erica had found her time more and more concentrated. She had none to spare for perusing the papers and depended on her secretary to digest public events for her.

"Market's up again."

"Shit."

"Why, you selling short?"

"No. It's just that it's been going up too much."

"I can think of worse news."

"What goes up must come down."

Ruthie shrugged. She didn't play the market herself. "Want me to call your broker?"

"No. Yes. No."

Ruthie shrugged again.

"Sorry, Ruthie. I'm just real uptight this morning because of that *Thisweek* crap."

"Want something to loosen up?"

Erica looked meaningfully at her secretary. "No, thank you." She knew what Ruthie was offering and she was horrified. But she didn't want to offend the woman. No, her secretary was a jewel.

Erica had been through a dozen during her Nox career. In the beginning she favored bright young women with the glint of ambition in their eyes. She opened up opportunities for them, they were deeply grateful, and Nox gained some excellent new middle managers. But it left Erica with no secretarial support.

Then there was a series of insolent gum-chewers. She could take the rudeness, but not the incompetence. How she had longed for a secretary like one of George's, experienced, responsible, and motherly. But such classic executive secretaries were rarely willing to work for a woman.

And then she found Ruthie. Or rather Cindy, who was the hottest thing at Goldsmith's these days, had begged her to give her baby sister a try. Baby? Hah! Cindy was the vacant little angel-baby. *Ruthie* was a dynamo.

Usually, a woman like Ruthie would be competing with Erica for her own turf. Fortunately she was from the South, the Land that Feminism Forgot. Thank God, Erica thought selfishly, for the hidden heartland of American with its great labor resources: secretaries, nannies, and wives.

Ruthie had an I.Q. as high as her own. Ruthie had a brilliant file system even Erica could access. Ruthie was as one with every computerized innovation.

This secretary took direction but had a brain of her own. She accepted Erica's authority without being servile. She was a close-to-perfect assistant.

Erica chose to overlook Ruthie's eccentricities. So what if she had inky tufts of hair emerging from her platinum crew cut? So what if she wore ten pierced earrings in each ear? And so what if she smoked marijuana?

Ruthie smoked a *lot* of marijuana. In the Nox elevators, where the men exuded Polo and the women were drenched in Red, all eyes turned to the passenger who reeked of Eau de Woodstock.

Each time the question of mandatory drug testing came up at a Nox executive meeting, Erica would fight it tooth and nail. Everyone thought she had a highly developed feeling for constitutional rights. In fact she was terrified of losing Ruthie. Ruthie's urine sample would probably float to the ceiling of the laboratory.

However, the effects of the weed did not influence her work.

"Mail call," Ruthie announced. Naturally, she had taken care of everything but the two envelopes marked "Personal."

The first letter was imprinted with "Robert Alpert, M.D., P.C." Erica raised an eyebrow. She hadn't had a checkup in years. She opened it.

> *Dear America (see, I didn't forget),*
> *The article in* Thisweek *sure brought back a lot of memories about all our old times together. I sure am glad you made it after your unhappy start at Radcliffe, where we all felt so sorry for you. It seems you're doing well for yourself, especially with this guy Steel, who sounds like a real winner and who we'd love to meet one of these days.*

Actually, your career and personal success are what lead me to write. I couldn't help but note the picture in the article, which shows that the stress of clawing your way to the top has left its tell-tale signs. Puffiness around the eyes, lines at the mouth, etc. Erica, you don't need me to tell you that these are not enhancing your image!

Perhaps you are among the old-fashioned folks who think that cosmetic surgery is morally wrong or needlessly dangerous. But such work, for someone in your position, could be vital. We all know that men and women at the top need to stay as young-looking as possible, for there are always ruthless competitors who would have others believe that one is losing vitality and sharpness along with one's youth. And of course, marrying a successful man, as you are, you are aware that there are an awful lot of young girls out there competing for his attention.

Now, Erica, perhaps you figured that you are too young for enhancing surgery. As a board-certified Plastic and Reconstructive Surgeon, let me assure you, nothing could be further from the truth! My secretary would be happy to make an appointment for a consultation, and, in strictest confidence, we can further explore your options.

On the personal front, I don't know whether you've heard, but I married the former Pam Harris. You remember, she was in your Radcliffe class. Used to write a lot of poetry, ring a bell? Blond and petite, I'm proud to say Pammy hasn't gained a pound since we married! We've got two little boys, regular sluggers, and they sure keep Pammy busy.

Anyway, it was great to hear about you. I always knew you would make it, despite your background as the daughter of "hotel entrepreneurs."

Sincerely,
Robert "Buzzy" Alpert, M.D., P.C.

"Say, Ruthie,"

The secretary appeared at the door. They used the intercom only when there were others in the office.

"Yeah, boss,"

"What does 'P.C.' stand for?"

"As in what?"

"What is it, some kind of medical degree?"

"Oh that. No, it's for 'private corporation.' You know, so doctors can deduct their mothers' dinette sets."

Erica laughed, crumpled up the letter and threw it at a fake malachite trash can in a corner of the office.

"Basketball's your sport," said Ruthie. "Who's that?"

"A guy I last saw at a freshman mixer. Apparently he never got out."

The second envelope bore a return address in Brooklyn Heights, but no name.

> *Dear Erica,*
>
> *When my book first came out, I thought you would be the one person from my past who would look me up. I was so hurt and so pissed when you didn't. But now I saw that article about you and realized I could look you up so easily, so I swallowed my pride . . . Can we get together soon?*
>
> *Oh, Erica. There have been so many times when I needed to talk to you. But I'm projecting too much. I'm not the girl I was then, and you, too must be a very different woman.*
> *But love,*
> *always and anyway,*
>
> *Tangee*

"Ruthie," Erica shouted, so loud that Ruthie came running.

"Have you ever heard of a book by someone called Tangee White?"

Ruthie shook her head.

"Are you sure? Tangee, maybe Tangerine White? A book about civil rights maybe?"

"What, are you kidding? Tangerine White? You mean *In Darkest Africa*?"

"Yes, that's it! How do we get a copy of it?"

"How do you *avoid* getting it, you mean?"

"What do you mean?"

"I mean, don't you check the paperback racks at the airports? Or are you waiting for the movie."

"You know I usually go on the corporate jets. But, you're kidding, this is really a popular book? A book on Africa?"

Ruthie sighed. "It's not about Africa, it's a love story about a welfare mother and a crack addict in a New York slum. It's been on the best-seller list for ages, it's won the National Book Award and it's going to be filmed by Oliver Stone."

"Oh, my God!" The best friend she'd ever had had become a brilliant success but she was too locked up in her own narrow world to notice! What on earth had become of her? She'd given up every interest but the concerns of Nox. Would she delegate her entire life, her heart, her mind to Ruthie?

"Listen, Ruthie. Get me five hardcover copies of *In Darkest Africa* and a copy of any reviews or interviews with the author that you can get your hands on. Okay, do it now!"

Ruthie turned on her heels.

Erica hardly got any work done while Ruthie was gone. At least she was no longer upset about the article in *Thisweek*. That public drubbing was nothing compared with the shame she felt inside herself.

At last Erica had a copy of the novel in her hands. She turned to the back. For a moment, she thought there must have been a mistake, but no. It was Tangee all right.

Even seated, Tangee was obviously a big woman. She had grown stout, too. And she had the same idol's face that revealed nothing.

The dashiki and wild jewelry were gone. Tangee wore a matronly knit suit with no adornments, not even a wedding band. Erica stared at the hands. The hands were skinny, the knuckles knotted. They reminded Erica of her mother's hands.

Erica turned to the inside back cover.

"TANGERINE WHITE is Associate Professor of English at Kingsborough Community College. She is the author of *The Shakespearean Perception of Africans* and *A Syntactical Analysis of Early Gospel Songs*. This is her first novel."

"You'll break Cindy's heart if you don't show up for the lunch at the Carlyle today," said Ruthie.

"What?" said Erica. She had been disturbed in the middle of her thoughts.

"And you wanted to see the promotional displays at Goldsmith's first."

"Right. Thanks, Ruthie. I'll be done with this in a minute."

A fast look at the book reviews. There was a front-page article from *The New York Times Book Review.*

"The publication of 'In Darkest Africa' is a milestone in the development of American literature. It does for the black woman's urban experience what 'The Color Purple' did for the rural one. Yet it is more ambitious than that ground-breaking book . . ."

Erica skimmed through the article, greedy for news about Tangee, hating her schedule.

"Into the life of Pudding McGee, orphaned, scarred, illiterate, and pregnant, comes Vondell Washington, handsome, charming, gifted—and doomed . . ."

Erica skipped some more paragraphs. She didn't want them to give away the story. She planned to stay up tonight to read the whole book.

". . . Laugh-out-loud humor that leaves you in painful hysterics, as if you were laughing during open-heart surgery. And underneath it all, the unbearable pathos of a nightmare world from which all exits are sealed . . ."

Erica forced herself to shut the file and get moving.

It was only a few blocks to Goldsmith's, so Erica walked. All the while her thoughts were boiling. So Tangee had made it, after all. Not just made it, but accomplished her highest girlhood ideals, made a difference in the lives of black people, in the way the world looked at them. And Tangee had done so against virtually insurmountable odds.

A few fat lazy snowflakes were beginning to fall as Erica approached Goldsmith's. Her throat tightened. There had been enough nostalgia for the day, and she hated nostalgia.

Goldsmith's familiar front made her happy to be safely delivered to the present.

In the right display window was a classic, virginal lace gown, high of waist and morality. Underneath it was a promotion for "Pure Innocence" perfume, being introduced today, Goldsmith's first venture into national distribution. In the other window there was a mannequin with Cindy's face dressed in an off-the-shoulder satin dress, surrounded by bottles of the new fragrance. "Good luck to the staff of Goldsmith's on your 'maiden voyage,'" a sign declared.

Both windows also had huge posters of Cindy, whose photo-magnified skin was as nacreous as the inside of a seashell. Her eyes, guileless as an infant's, expressed simple wonder. She was, of course, beautifully tiara-ed, necklaced, and veiled. Erica laughed out loud. Cindy looked about twelve years old.

The minds of advertising people really amazed her. Crafty as Eden's snake, they penetrated deep into your psyche and got you where you dreamed. She took another glance at the dresses and felt a ridiculous urge to cry.

Her wedding dress hadn't been like either of the two in the windows. She shook her head vigorously. God, if there was one thing she didn't want to do, it was think about her marriage to Whit!

Her mother had been pressing her to set a date for the wedding to George. Neither she nor George was in much of a hurry. This time, she wouldn't rush through the wedding plans. This time it would be different. For one thing, she and her mother would get the dress *they* wanted.

It was more than a mile to the Carlyle, where the coming-out party for the perfume was to be held, but Erica didn't mind walking. The snow was picking up momentum and it would be impossible to get a cab, anyway. Of course, she was free to call for George's chauffeur-driven Rolls, but she wanted to walk. Those shoes that *Thisweek* found so dowdy were good for something!

By the time she reached the hotel, she felt refreshed. She slipped off her chinchilla coat, shivering with the sensual thrill of the furs. For Christmas George had told her to choose any fur she wanted. But he made her return the seven-eighths mink she had selected.

"If they won't take it back, give it to charity," he said.

They did take it back, and Erica decided to get the coat she really and truly loved the most, the softest one. George approved of the chinchilla, although he said *he* would have gone for a Russian sable. How cuddled Erica felt, by the warmth of the coat, and by her fiancé's generosity.

At the ballroom entrance, Mr. Goldsmith stepped away from a group of important-looking men to greet Erica. She was secretly pleased to be shown the deference. Her advice to Goldsmith was worth a fortune, but couldn't be bought because, of course, she could do official business only on behalf of Nox. She gave it free, out of friendship to Bettina. She liked Henry, too, and learned a lot herself from his old-fashioned common sense.

He kissed her on the cheek. "Tina is back there, helping Cindy get dressed. You'll be sitting at the front table, there. Shall I introduce you to the others?"

"I'll just look around a little first."

The Trianon Suite was decorated to simulate a wedding. Sets of twin doves held back drapes, centerpieces featured silver bells, bouquets of white flowers were ringed with blue garters.

"We're having the food first, then a fashion show of bridal gowns, then we'll give out the freebies."

"Sounds great. Good luck, Henry, I'll see you around later."

Erica next poked her head into the room where Bettina was putting the finishing touches on Cindy.

"Hey, aren't you guys going to party?"

Both women groaned. "Some party. It's work, work, work, for us," said Bettina, in her best imitation of a growl.

"Is Ruthie here?" asked Cindy.

"Now, Cindy, you know how she feels about these shows," said Bettina. "She's bored by 'high society,' she hates fashion shows, and she gets all the cosmetic freebies she can use, anyway. Besides, I'll bet she actually prefers slaving away for Erica."

"This may not be the right time to say it, Cindy, but she really is a capable adult now, and she deserves to have a life of her own," said Erica.

"Oh, Erica, you only say that because you see her in an office environment. If you saw her at home, you wouldn't be so convinced about her maturity. The *men* she dates! Unbelievable. No college, no class. I just can't talk any sense into her."

"How about you, Cindy? We never hear about your dates, professors or otherwise," said Bettina.

"Me?" her tone was shockingly bitter. "I'm not the dating kind."

"Nobody's the *dating* kind," Bettina laughed lightly. "You young people today have no idea how to court. What a meat market! I'm surprised we've stayed in business this long."

"Yeah, tell us about how your generation courts, Tina," Erica teased.

Bettina and Henry Goldsmith had been a romantic item for years, yet continued to insist that they had nothing but a very close working relationship.

"Yeah," chimed in Cindy.

"Don't change the subject," snapped Bettina. "Cindy, you've used up your last excuse for your lonely life-style. Ruthie has adjusted very well to New York life. Now it's time to look after yourself."

"I'm just fine," Cindy protested.

"No, you're not," declared Bettina. "You need to get married."

"Married? *Me?*"

"Why not?" ventured Erica. "You'd be a natural at it. Unlike some of us bitchy career woman types."

They all laughed.

"Why not indeed?" said Bettina.

"Well, for one thing, this job is a jinx," Cindy kidded nervously.

"Nonsense," declared Mrs. Marshall. "Put your mind to it, young lady, and I'll bet you'll be wearing one of these confections, for real, within the year."

"No way . . ."

"It would make wonderful publicity," said Erica.

Henry guided Erica to her table. All the men rose as one.

"Mrs. Erica Eaton," said Henry, at his most urbane. Erica expected to hear trumpets any minute. "May I present your luncheon companions?"

Goldsmith first introduced the portly president of Kensington Department Stores. The man smothered Erica's hand in a huge, cigar-scented paw.

"Howah ya, Ms. Erica? I hope you're ready to make some bucks this month. God knows, it can't hurt any of us in this damn—excuse my French—economy. I read that *Thisweek* article about you. Underneath all that crap they wrote, I can see you're quite a gal. Anytime you get tired of those whining bastards in the poison gas business, you can come sell schmattes for me.

"Nah, just kidding. I can't afford you. But seriously, come down to the Fifty-seventh Street Kensington and check out our promotion. The 'Pure Innocence' cosmetics has legs. From the new fragrance, I don't know. Perfume is always another kettle of fish, y'know?

"But come down and check it out. Whadda ya say, tomorrow? And pick up a couple of outfits for yourself. My treat, okay?"

Erica laughed uncomfortably. Another volunteer to "make over" America's top dowdy woman exec. But she liked the fellow anyway. The type of man who, if you asked him, would say women should stay home and have babies, but, if you worked for him, would pay you to the penny what a man in the position earned.

Henry continued introductions round the table. "Mrs. Albertina Nelson." Erica nodded graciously at the extremely chic wife of an indicted savings-and-loan president.

Henry went on. "Of course you know Mr. Ronald M. Davis of Wellington, Parks."

Indeed she did. Davis was the investment banker who'd helped pull off a recent, important deal for Nox. He was shrewd, the best in the business, and Erica would use no one else for the job. But what an unctuous pig. He didn't miss a single opportunity during the deal-making process to insult Erica and every other female with the misfortune to be present. He acted as if he were judging a small-town beauty contest, rather than earning his company 1.5 million dollars in fees.

Erica managed to get through the negotiations with Davis, but just barely. If the acquisition hadn't been so important to her, she would have *decked* the fat creep.

"Good to see you, Ron," Erica lied amiably.

"Sugar!" he yelled across the table. "You're still the cutest piece of ass I know, what likes to play boys' games. Come here, you big tomboy, and give ol' Ronnie a fat, wet kiss."

Erica ignored him and turned to the empty chair next to his, reserved for Bettina, as if she would be introduced to an invisible presence.

At last they came to the man at Erica's left. He was shorter than Erica and not handsome. His hair was receding and his face was notable only for a pair of large, rather mournful black eyes. But his form was what could only be described as imperially slim, and he was wearing the most marvelous suit Erica had ever seen. Erica could hardly tear her eyes away from the hand-stitched lapel. His shirt, tie, and shoes looked every bit as exquisite as the suit.

Probably gay, thought Erica with a sigh, so many of the good ones are. Stop it, her inward voice admonished. You've already got a terrific man of your own, enough of this sobbing singles routine.

"May I present the Commercial Attaché of the Consulate of Belgium," Henry said, "Baron Jean-Luc Marie de Gramont."

In a single graceful gesture the consul kissed her hand. It was an authentic European ritual, his lips meeting the air above her hand in silence. It was as respectful as a handshake, but somehow more civilized. Could there be room for this lovely sort of thing, wondered Erica, in an egalitarian world?

"Please," he said, addressing the table, "just Jean-Luc."

"Pleased ta meetcha, Jean," said the department store magnate, pronouncing it "John."

The consul didn't seem to mind at all. Soon the two were busy conversing about Belgian fabrics and import tariffs. Of course, Erica reminded herself, Goldsmith cosmetics were manufactured in Belgium. The aristocratic Jean-Luc was probably a dollar-a-year diplomat, but he was plugging his country's commercial interests like a pro.

Lunch was now being served. Erica noted with some

amusement that almost everyone at the table had lit into the food with gusto. They were all aware that there was no such thing as a free lunch, but they were determined to enjoy themselves anyway.

But Erica had no appetite. She stabbed a giant prawn with her fork, marveling at how much it resembled Roy Little, but she didn't feel like eating it. And what was this salad? What sort of lettuce were they using these days? She was so out of it. Life was passing her by, bubbling along in the green valleys while she was preoccupied with climbing a raw mountaintop and hanging on the sheer face with her fingernails. Was it worth it? Was "because it's there" reason enough for the struggle? Was "because *men* do it" reason enough?

Dessert was a Sylvia Weinstock wedding cake, a multistoried edifice covered with sugar flowers—roses, lilies, hyacinths—each perfectly shaped and tinted, and indistinguishable from fresh blossoms.

Erica took a bite for tradition's sake. It was surprisingly good, and she finished her slice. Not a smudge of cake or a petal of icing was left on the table when she looked up. Except Jean-Luc's portion, which was intact. He had barely touched any of the dishes. Not a man who indulges himself, she decided. Even the clothes were probably a matter of doing his job, his duty.

A single violin pierced the luncheon noise. The fashion show was about to begin. The freeloaders edged to the door.

The models came out in Goldsmith's finest. The profusion of rich fabrics and ornaments sated even the most dedicated romantic-fashion junkies.

Afterwards, the applause was more than polite. At Erica's table, Mrs. Marshall was heartily congratulated.

"Excellent use of Belgian lace!" said Jean-Luc.

Attention now returned to Henry Goldsmith, who had risen to the microphone. His obviously personal excitement kept the audience attentive despite the banal content of his spiel. He waxed ecstatic over the youth-retentive contents of the "Pure Innocence" cleansing and moisturizing regimen. He enthused over the tender shades of the line's lipsticks and eyeshadows. The perfume, he suggested, was practically born of a religious epiphany. The audience ate it up like so much wedding cake.

The solitary but effective violin struck up Mendelssohn's Wedding March. Shimmering curtains parted and out stepped Cindy of the posters. She had about her such an authentic aura of innocence, that the jaded watchers, overfed on a diet of New York sophistication, were quite captivated.

The young woman walked delicately to the sentimental beat of the music, while the company president went on with an almost subliminal recitation of the cosmetics' virtues. At the end of the processional, Cindy handed a basket, a lovely thing trimmed with tiny flowers and silk ribbons, and heaped with sample boxes, to Bettina, who beamed proudly.

Cindy then distributed similar baskets at each table. The room filled again with self-serving chatter and the sounds of wheeling-dealing.

"Sweet, isn't she?" said Erica, making conversation with Jean-Luc. But Jean-Luc didn't answer.

She turned to look at him fully. What sort of diplomat would act so rudely?

Jean-Luc de Gramont looked like a man who had just witnessed the detonation of a nuclear bomb. His eyes were opened sightlessly, like someone suffering retinal burn. His Adam's apple bobbed rapidly above the perfect knot of his perfect tie.

Erica craned her neck to see what it was that had transfixed Jean-Luc. Cindy was serving a table on the other side of the room. Her movements were so self-contained that only the skirt of her gown moved with little ripples. Above it her tiny waist was cinched in satin; above that, a fluff of blouse ended with a bit of her shoulders and her swan's neck bare. Her pale blond, almost colorless hair had been caught up in a loose braid, and bound with a circlet of tiny flowers. The nape of her neck seemed especially vulnerable.

Erica looked back at Jean-Luc. She smiled. Oh no, she thought, he's fallen in love at first sight. Wow! Cindy must be exuding some chemical that registered as "I'm ready, able and willing *now*." Good for Cindy! Erica felt a little worm of jealousy crawl in her heart.

Now Cindy came toward their table with baskets of favors. She walked with the mincing step of a geisha. As she approached, Jean-Luc grew as red as a drunk.

As Cindy leaned over to deposit a basket between Mrs. S&L and Ron Davis, the latter "accidentally" brushed his hand against her breast. Cindy recoiled instantly, as if from a flame.

Jean-Luc all but threw himself across the table.

"Apologize," he hissed.

The young woman looked at him, her eyes as blue and surprised as a doll's.

"Okay, okay," said Davis. "Geez, and there's hardly nothin' there."

Erica and Bettina began to chatter like birds in the effort to relieve the tension. Cindy hurriedly headed for another table.

"Do you ladies know her?" asked Jean-Luc breathlessly.

"We certainly do," said Bettina, "and she's as good-hearted as she is lovely."

"Mon Dieu, but how old is she?"

"About twice as old as she looks," snapped Erica.

"Oh," sighed the consul happily.

Reporters first, the Trianon Suite soon emptied.

Bettina helped the models undress, but abandoned them when she saw that Cindy was about to go.

"Wait."

"Oh, Tina, I haven't had lunch. And I've got to eat this special diet gook, too. After seeing that cake, it's so depressing."

"You poor thing. I've just the thing for cheering you up."

"What?"

"Shopping, of course."

"I already have tons of clothes."

"Oh, but we both could use some new evening things."

"We could?"

"Sure. We've been invited out tonight. Erica Eaton insists we join her and Steel at eight. For a *very* elegant dinner."

"Where?"

"The Belgian consulate. Hurry, darling."

Chapter Twenty-one

ERICA HAD INVITED Tangee to lunch at the Four Seasons, but they had agreed to meet first in front of the Seagram Building. They had spoken only briefly on the phone, and each was nervous about seeing the other after so many years.

Erica was early, but in the distance she saw a tall black monolith, like Cleopatra's Needle, waiting. Without a word, the two women fell in each other's arms, kissing each other—and not in the manner of lunching ladies, either, but smearing lipstick and laughing and crying, just like the long-lost friends they were.

In the vestibule of the restaurant they sized each other up. Erica's suit was nothing to cause a retraction from *Thisweek*, but she knew she looked every inch the executive, and she felt proud.

"Well, let's take a look at you, Tangerine White." Tangee's dress was a navy St. John knit, very refined, very becoming, yet so conservative that Erica, who remembered Tangee in the wildest print dashikis, thought it was a put-on.

Tangee guessed what she was thinking. "I teach, you know. I learned a long time ago that no one takes your scholarship seriously if you don't dress the part."

"Tang, don't tell me that stunning brooch is standard issue for professors."

"Oh this?" said Tangee, touching a cameo in which a black head was outlined against white shell. The head was a black woman's, in profile. Her hair was caught in a delicate gold net, studded with diamonds. A sunburst of diamonds radiated from the pin.

"It was my reward to myself for completing the screenplay for 'Africa.' These cameos are portraits of African aristocrats. They were made in the early nineteenth century by European imperialists trying to bribe their way into tribal territories."

"But don't you feel, uh, politically . . . funny about it?"

"No. It's a piece of art. I believe the artist was sincere in his admiration for African beauty."

They went to their table in the Grill Room. It was, probably, the most high-powered eatery in the world. Money, influence, or breeding, by themselves, would not cause much of a stir in this room. But two statuesque women, one black and one red-headed, whose achievements had been widely covered in the press, caused neck-craning even on the part of persons who were themselves household words.

Erica and Tangee ordered aperitifs.

"Come here often?" asked Tangee.

"Practically the Honey Bowl of adulthood. When you take a client to the Four Seasons, it always softens them up. I'm usually over at the Pool room, it's prettier and the food is fancier. But the Grill is where the publishing honchos gather, so I thought you might prefer it."

"Yeah, this is really editorial heaven. See the guy with the beard and the bifocals? That's Daniel Nagy, the most famous editor since Perkins. He holds the floor in the bidding on my next, not-yet-written book. And the lady with the curly gray mop? That's my current publisher, Betsy Thrasher."

"The one who's talking to Lola Sage?"

"Who's Lola Sage?"

"Geez, Tangee, and I thought *I* was isolated. Lola Sage is probably the top woman ever in advertising."

Thrasher noticed their stares and whispers and came over to their table.

"Hi, Tangee. How's the book coming?"

"Almost done. Treating myself to lunch out with my old pal, Erica Eaton. Erica, my publisher, Betsy Thrasher."

Betsy shook Erica's hand with a man's strength and a man's sense of authority.

"I've been meaning to give you a call," she said.

"Oh?" said Erica.

"Yes. I thought you might be interested in doing a book."

"Me? About what?"

"About women in business. Or anything business. Business is a very hot topic. Been strong for years. Japanese win tactics? A leveraged buyout story? An overview of the economy? Whatever."

"But I'm a terrible writer. And I never write anything longer than a memo."

"That's all right. We'll send you someone to help with the organization of your thoughts. A professional."

Erica tilted her head impishly. "Well, I could trust a ghost if it were to be, say, Tangee."

"Forget it," said Betsy, squeezing Tangee's shoulder. "We don't use caviar as hamburger helper. Tangerine White is very dear to us at our house. We're loyal to our writers' interests, and they repay us in kind."

Betsy's eyes wandered ever so slightly in Daniel Nagy's direction.

After Betsy returned to her own table, Tangee said to Erica, "Don't take it personally. Betsy would do anything to butter me up. The house needs my books. They sell well *and* they're what passes today for 'literature.' Both those things mean a lot in publishing today. Especially the former.

"But God, sometimes I wish I could just take my books back to the university press that did my nonfiction."

"Why don't you?"

"'Cause I have the same values they do," she said, gesturing to the tables at their side.

It is the custom, at the Four Seasons, to visit at the tables of others. Erica, too, had a visitor.

Ron Davis, the much-too-personal banker, had been on his way into a meeting in one of the private dining rooms, when he caught sight of Erica.

"Honeybunch!" he drawled. He leaned down and kissed Erica on the ear, letting his tongue slide into it. Erica wanted to retch. Unfortunately, Davis's bank, Wellington, Parks, was one of the main players in financing. Erica forced herself to smile.

"I said to myself, what the fuck is Erica Eaton doing over with the *artistes*? Wait till I tell my wife. Sugar, won't you introduce me to Alice Walker."

"She's not Alice Walker."

"No, suh," said Tangee, "no way. Don't you recognize yo' Aunt Jemima? Fahn son of Dixie, lak you, don't you know nothin', boy? You got somethin' there for Miss Erica? Well, Ah gotta take care of her. Ah gotta make sure she don't keep the wrong kind of company. Come hyar. I'll just put my little hand in yo' fly. We'll see if you got anythin' to back up yo' promises in Miss Erica's ear."

There was a stunned, silent second. Then Davis burst into laughter.

"Oh Lord, oh, oh. I tell you," he said, wiping tears away from his eyes. "You and Steel, Erica. You really live the life. Dinners with Jackie Onassis, okay. But this takes the cake.

"Christ," he said, moving toward the private party room, "*that's* something. Imagine, lunch with *Whoopi Goldberg*."

The waiter stood patiently until Erica and Tangee had stopped laughing.

"Let's order," said Erica, trying to compose herself.

They looked over the menu.

"I'm going to choose from the Spa Cuisine," said Tangee ruefully.

"I've got the opposite problem. Can't seem to gain weight no matter what I do."

"You never did eat much."

"Hey, you were even skinnier than I was."

"Yeah, but now I've got this occupational hazard."

"Writing?"

"Yes. Writing hurts. Some writers drink to ease the pain. Some eat.

"I'll start with the grapefruit, beet and endive salad. Then, the escallop of veal with mustard seeds and braised endive."

"Let me try the carpaccio with pecorino and arugula. Then, hmmm, the medallions of venison with red cabbage and chestnut puree."

"What the hell is that stuff, Erica?"

"Beats me. I figure at an easy hundred bucks for lunch, I should be entertained. I can always pick up a tuna sandwich in the cafeteria at Nox, after all."

They sat quietly and looked at the napkins in their laps.

"You first," said Tangee.

"No. I was first last time. *You* first."

Tangee shifted in her seat. "Where do I begin?"

"Begin with the baby. Did you have it?"

Tangee smiled so that her face glowed. "Yes. It was a girl. Nowadays she's a freshman at Sarah Lawrence. Want to see some pictures?"

"I sure do."

Tangee took some photos from her bag. They were professional glossies. Some featured products. All showed a gloriously beautiful girl with café au lait skin and the tawny eyes of a lioness.

"Oh, Tangee. She's incredibly beautiful."

"Yes. The Ford agency wanted to sign her up, but no way would I let her interrupt her education. Still, for some reason, having a beautiful daughter makes you feel *successful* like nothing else."

Erica raised her eyebrows at this bit of feminist treason.

"Don't you have any kids, Erica?"

"No. And I probably never will." She swallowed. She hadn't intended for that to come out as bitter as it did. She cleared her throat.

"I don't see how I could ever be a good enough mother—I don't have enough hours in the day as it is. Besides, my fiancé has children from his former marriage. What's your daughter's name, Tangee?"

"Ricky."

"That's nice. Simple. I'm glad she didn't get saddled the way we were.

"It's short for 'America.'"

"Oh, God. Tangee."

She tried to blink back the tears. She looked up at the ceiling. There was a chandelier made of chrome icicles. She pretended it was fascinating. But then she could see that the people at the next table, a former secretary of state and the father of modern American architecture, were giving her puzzled glances.

Her self-control returned. "This is really none of my business but, I've been wondering all these years, who is Ricky's father? You said it was someone I didn't know, but that never rang true."

Tangee laughed. "Right again, Erica! It was that nerdy guy, Buzzy Alpert."

"Buzzy Alpert!" she shrieked. The ex-secretary, the architect, and half a dozen publishers looked up in alarm.

"Why yes," said Tangee matter-of-factly, "I wanted the baby to be good at math and science."

"And is she?"

"Not very." They laughed and ate their appetizers.

"Is there a man in your life, Tangee?"

"Yes." She rummaged in her purse again. This time she drew a simple snapshot. It had been taken in front of a Christmas tree; ribbons and wrapping were scattered about. A gigantic bear of a man had one hand around Tangee, the other around Ricky. Ricky looked like a doll next to him, and even Tangee in a tentlike robe was dwarfed by his size.

"Tangee, forgive me. His face is familiar, but I am such a rube. I'm sure he's very famous . . ."

"His name is K.O. Tolliver. He was the world heavyweight boxing champion when we were in third grade."

"Of course!"

"Of course nothing. He lost his title, he lost his health, he lost his money, his self-respect, everything. When I first met him, Howard Cosell wouldn't have recognized him."

"You must love him very much."

Tangee shrugged. "He has his faults. I wish he were better educated. I wish he hadn't got hit in the temples so many times. But he's there for me. We both know what it's like to play the white man's games. And he treats Ricky like a daughter—and not like anything else."

"Are you going to marry him?"

"I doubt it. At this point it would just make things messy."

Erica laughed. "My fiancé, George, says every woman really wants to get married."

"Oh yeah? What does he know?"

"Usually, everything."

"Ain't that somethin'. Tell more."

"Not yet. Tell me how you did it, Tangee. When last we met, you were at the bottom of a pit in East New York, poor, pregnant, and alone. How did you get out? How did you do what your character Puddin' couldn't? How did you get to be a college professor and then a writer that everyone but your best friend has heard of?"

"I wasn't at the bottom of the pit. My grandmother and her husband sent me money. My senior year in college they took Ricky, so I could go to school full-time.

"Nobody who's really at the bottom ever gets out. I was already on the rim when I started. And sometimes, I wonder if I really got that far at all. Maybe I'm still tethered to some invisible anchor."

"Hey, no self-pity in this restaurant. Achievement is the god here. The people you see, especially the women, did it all themselves. Not one of them came up the road without regrets. And you're young, Tangee. If things don't suit you, you can still change them."

"I guess. It's just that I get so depressed sometimes. Another occupational hazard."

"The trouble with you writers is you think too much."

"No joke, Erica, I'm on lithium."

"Oh. I'm so sorry."

"Don't be. It beats crack. But let's get off my cheerful case and get on to yours."

They continued to talk and eat until the plates and the past were cleared away.

"So," said Tangee, "that's George Steel. Sounds like a paragon among men—or is that a parallelogram?"

"He *is* great. You know what they say, 'You can't be too tall or too rich.'"

"Something like that."

"Dessert?" said the waiter.

"Oh, I couldn't," the two women said simultaneously.

They looked at each other and the love and the lost years shimmered in the air between them, waiting to be recaptured in words.

"I'll have the Grand Marnier soufflé," said Tangee.

"And I'll have the vanilla ice cream with espresso and bourbon."

"So, about Superman."

"What?"

"The Man of Steel."

"Right. George. What can I say, Tang, I've found Mr. Right."

"What's he like in bed?" whispered Tangee.

"What a question, Tangee. You mean you're not a virgin anymore?"

They shrieked with laughter. Heads turned to stare.

Erica bent over to whisper. "He's fucking fabulous!"

They shrieked again. The other diners shook their heads.

"The vital thing is, he's wonderful to me, and, most important, he knows what my goals are and he keeps me to them. When I get discouraged, he's there, shoring me up. Also, this is terribly reactionary but I can't help it, I love it that he's *more*. More successful than I am, more experienced, more sophisticated—taller! And he's great to my parents. Sometimes, I confess, he's better to them than I am."

"How are the Valentas?"

"Well and kicking. Come for dinner Tuesday, they'd love to see you."

"I'll bet! Can I bring K.O.?"

"Of course. This will be just great."

"So, what else do you do to keep busy?"

"Cut it out. I do take a break. I have this project, do you know Goldsmith's Bridal Salon?"

"Of course."

"Well, for years I've been hanging around—I made a number of friends there—and helping out with financing ideas, whatever. We've all gotten very close. Especially one former model there (you're not my only celebrity friend, you know), Melissa John."

"Melissa John? I know her!"

"Really? What a coincidence!"

"I don't know her well, or anything. But she was at a Hollywood party for 'Africa.'"

"Oh, wait till I tell her."

"I doubt if she'll remember me. Or anyone else at the party. She was all over this guy—you know, 'Barkley' from the nighttime soap?—I mean it was *obscene*."

"Oh God, no. And she's married."

"You're kidding? What is he, embalmed in Australia?"

"No. He's this famous doctor, Sheldon Lederer."

"Jesus, he was there! He's her *husband*? Man, I thought I'd seen everything."

"Oh, poor Melissa!"

"Uh huh."

"No, seriously. She's a wonderful human being. But men, men drive her crazy. Anyway, Melissa and I met at Goldsmith's when I went to get my first wedding gown."

Erica told Tangee the succinct but now honest version of her failed marriage.

"So anyway, Goldsmith's has been really important in my life. I'll be devastated when it closes."

"Goldsmith's is closing?"

"Well, not now, but it is essentially a mom-and-pop shop, a very personal, service-intensive business. The principals are getting old, the kids are in the professions, there are no apparent heirs. Taxes go up and the business gets more demanding. I'm afraid it's doomed."

The hours flew by.

"So we're set for Tuesday evening, Tang. I'll tell my mother today."

After lunch, Erica turned down Tangee's offer to share a cab. "Nox is just over on Sixth Avenue. I need to walk off all that food."

"As long as your shoes don't hurt," said Tangee with a wink.

The noise in Ruthie's office startled Erica. It was unusual to hear voices raised out there. She came to the door.

Her secretary was arguing with a young man.

"Get your coat right out of the closet and get out of here, or I'll call Security," Ruthie said.

"You're threatening me with the cops? With what you've got stashed in your desk, ma'am? That would be unwise."

"What's going on here?" said Erica.

"This cowboy wants to see you 'raght now,' Mrs. Eaton," Ruthie reported.

"Let's not get out of hand here. My secretary is doing her job. Why don't you state your business to Ms. Prewitt. She'll make an appointment for you, or, more probably, refer you to the right party in the company."

"Ms. Eaton, you are the right party—I know because I've been chasing around this building for almost two weeks, and all roads lead here. I've got to see you today."

"I'm afraid that's impossible. But Ms. Prewitt will make an appointment for you."

She gave Ruthie a knowing look. There was zero possibility of his having any business that would interest her.

"Ma'am, I've just blown my whole vacation trying to get through to you and I've got to be at Kennedy airport at four today. Please, let me state my case and I swear, I'll be out of here in less than ten minutes."

It was taking her longer than that to get him out of Ruthie's office—and she couldn't risk the security guard in Ruthie's vicinity.

"All right. Ruthie, time this."

She led him briskly into her office.

"My name is Andy Fairchild. I'm from San Jose, California."

"How may I help you, Mr. Fairchild?"

She folded her hands on her desk but the index finger tapped impatiently.

Despite his pushiness there was a comfortable, boyish charm to the man. Glasses rimmed big brown eyes. Corn-yellow hair cascaded to his collar. He wore a tie with obvious discomfort, the way an average man would wear spats. His casual pants and sport jacket were in tones of brown. No one in New York wore brown for business.

Fairchild took his seat—for about two seconds. He seemed eager to keep his ten-minute bargain and he was bursting with information, just as his battered briefcase was bursting with papers. His body, short and compact but muscled, wasn't made for sitting still.

"My training's in biochemistry. Here's my c.v., but don't read it now."

Erica scanned it anyway. Impressive degrees from Stanford, steadily rising research positions at a small-but-solid veterinary products laboratory.

"You're from Idaho?"

"Yes. Ever been there?"

She nodded slightly. A million years ago. "Your résumé is very impressive, Dr. Fairchild. Why don't I send this along to Personnel . . ."

"I'm not looking for a job. I've got something to sell you. Maybe something to change the whole company, its focus, its image, maybe even the world . . ."

"Dr. Fairchild . . ."

"Just call me Andy. Anyway, take a look at this." He handed her a large glossy photo featuring a loathsome fat caterpillar, a furry cocoon, and a rather nondescript brown moth. "Portrait of the enemy!" proclaimed Andy.

Erica didn't know whether to break out laughing or call Security, after all. Fairchild didn't give her time to make up her mind.

"The Tussock moth, scourge of California's fruit orchards. Over one hundred million dollars' worth of damage annually. And I've got the way to zap it." He made a pistol of his index finger and pretended to shoot the creature.

Erica shook her head. "Nox is the world's leading producer of pesticides. I'm sure we've got something farmers can use against this pest." If he heard the arch tone of the word "pest" he pretended he didn't.

"Sure you do. Nox-Out 479, as potent a bug killer as ever came out of a test tube, and probably a big money-maker for the company."

"So? What's wrong with that?"

"So it's poison. It kills the moths, but it also pollutes land, water, you name it."

"And your solution?"

"Wouldn't hurt a fly. It's totally natural."

"If this is one of those sex hormone lures, I must tell you that we maintain a laboratory researching them, but so far, the results have been limited. The idea may be clever but it doesn't always work. Maybe sex isn't such a powerful drive for everyone. I mean, everything."

She blushed at her slip, and she was furious with herself. It made her blush more.

Fairchild didn't seem to notice. "You're right. We can't always transfer human attitudes to animals. In this case, though, it does work. I've found an instinct even stronger than sex. The little buggers' Achilles' heel is *hope*."

"What do you mean?"

"Okay, now that you're listening . . ." He pulled more photos and papers out of his briefcase.

"This is the Tussock moth's life cycle: In summer the eggs hatch into this lovely furry creature, which munches its way through fruit and leaf until the fall. Then it builds a cocoon around itself. Comes spring, it emerges as the moth, eats, mates, eats, lays the eggs, eats, and dies. Control has been in the form of spraying at the caterpillar stage. You get them that way, but you also ruin the year's crop. There are no known natural enemies.

"Now here is my solution. As autumn deepens into winter, you spray the trees with my non-toxic spray. What's in it? Nothing but tree pollen and a little mineral oil to hold it in place. The pollen triggers the moth's urge to pupate. It emerges from the cocoon—completely immature and into the hostile winter. Unprepared for life, it dies an untimely death. Voila, moths are dead, the crop is saved, and, best of all, the land and waters are left clean."

"Well, it sounds great, if it works as well as you say. Since I'm no biologist, I'll have to present this to our research staff. Okay, let's say it works, what then? You say you don't want a job."

"That's right. All I'm saying is give my spray a chance. If it works, let me have a lab with decent equipment and a good staff. I bet I can come up with harmless analogs for many of Nox's poisonous and invasive chemicals."

"Dr. Fairchild . . ."

"Andy."

"Andy, have you applied for a patent for your spray?"

"No, why should I? It's only pollen and mineral oil."

"Let me advise you, first thing, to apply for a patent. Someone could easily rip off your idea. If it's as safe and effective as you claim, it could be worth millions."

"But if Nox buys it from me, won't they get the patent?"

Erica didn't want to tell him that Nox would offer him a pretty small sum for the idea; they'd have to pay a percentage of sales or millions in a flat sum for a patented product.

"It's just sound business practice, as a rule." She hoped she wasn't being disloyal to the company, but it would be a shame to take advantage of the man. He might be naive, but he was idealistic, public spirited, and it *was* a good idea. Nox would make plenty of profit from it, in any case. Besides, she always liked to see Nox putting people and their environment first.

"Anyway, I will speak to our biologists and *if* it pans out, we'll take it the next step as a Development project, that is, under my wing."

Andy leaped up from his chair and pumped her hand. "Oh thank you, *thank* you. This is so much more than I'd dared to hope for. How can I thank you? Can I send you some flowers?"

"No. That's really not necessary. Hopefully, before too long it'll be Nox that will be thanking *you*."

"Look, these are flowers I grow myself. Actually, I'm hybridizing some new ones. They're gerberas, kind of like daisies. Please let me send you some."

"Well, if you insist."

"I do. In fact, I'd like to fill your office with them, and to hell with feminist sensibilities."

She laughed but also, unmistakably, led him to the door.

Back at her desk she put aside his résumé. Twenty-nine. God, he was young. She was only five years his senior, but she felt well into middle age. Why was that? How did her youth slip by unnoticed?

Her secretary came in. "George Steel called."

"Why didn't you buzz me?"

"But you were in a meeting with that *insistent* man."

"I always take calls from Mr. Steel, Ruthie. No matter what. He's the big boss, you know."

"If I didn't, he'd let me know," Ruthie said dryly. Erica ignored her sarcasm. George Steel probably wasn't a heart-throb from Ruthie's point of view. But George was the right man for *her*.

The next day George got back from a trip to Korea, Japan, and San Francisco. When Erica entered his office, she was shocked. George looked exhausted. For once, he looked every day of his true age.

"Honey, you're a wreck. You've been in the air much too long. Will you please go home and get some rest?"

"Oh, does it show?" He ran a hand through his gray hair, which was no longer perfectly in place.

"You know better than to do this to yourself," said Erica, giving him a hug.

He raised a finger to his lips, indicating silence. He went over to his desk and pushed some buttons. The lights went off and a wide-screen TV went on. A promotional video for Nox began, and George turned the volume up high.

He took Erica to the farthest corner of the room.

"We can't be too careful," he whispered. "There are bugs, and probably cameras monitoring my office."

Erica strained to hear him above the hearty, booming voice of the video narrator.

"I heard a rumor in San Francisco. They say Carl Connaught is planning an unfriendly takeover of Nox."

Erica blanched. "What?" she blurted out loud.

George's index finger came out of the dark and touched her lips in warning.

"Don't worry," he whispered in her ear. "I swear upon my mother's grave that son-of-a-whore won't touch my company."

Steel went back to the desk, turned on the lights, and terminated the video.

It was now Erica who looked like death. She sat heavily on a sofa, trying to recover from the terrible news.

"I think you're right, darling. I'm going right to my apartment to get some shut-eye."

He kissed her pale cheek. "See you first thing tomorrow morning."

Erica sat at her own desk in stunned silence. Sir Carl Connaught, the toughest, the richest, and the meanest of all the corporate raiders. He borrowed billions of dollars to buy companies, then shredded them to pay off the debt. He made a fortune off these deals—but at the cost of thousands of jobs, of chaos in management, of the destruction of companies.

In the flash of a blitzkrieg takeover Erica—and George—could lose everything they had ever worked to build. Everything would disappear down the funnel of corporate debt. It would be a disaster.

But wait. Erica pulled herself together. Connaught's greed might be limitless, but realistically, no company even half the size of Nox had ever been bought out in such a maneuver. There were, after all, limits to this financial game.

What's more, if Connaught was tough, George Steel was ten times tougher. There was no question in her mind about that.

Thirdly, it was only a rumor. Rumors were cheap to start, easy to spread. Chances were nine to one there was nothing behind it.

Fourth: Nox was as solid a company as could be found in the United States. Its stock market value was fair, its productivity was excellent, it was in healthy financial shape. With all due modesty, its management was superb.

If Nox could be bushwhacked by the likes of Carl Connaught, no company in America was safe. Well, things hadn't come to that pass yet!

Erica shrugged her shoulders and got back to work.

Chapter Twenty-two

"**H**OLA, LUIS. How did Madame's examination go?"

"Oh, Mr. Gramont, she did real good. She's gonna get a job in Lincoln Hospital now. A real good job."

Luis was impressed. This Gramont guy must have a hell of a memory. The morning doorman said he was some kind of prince, and from the suits you could believe it. But so friendly, like a regular guy, not like most of the cheap shits in the building.

And Gramont didn't even live there. He'd just been coming around the last few months to see Miz Prewitt. *Nice* guy.

The elevator man helped Gramont with his many packages.

Cindy answered the doorbell.

She was a sight. A wrinkled flannel nightgown hung down from under a ratty terry bathrobe. Her unwashed hair was pulled back with a rubber band. Her eyes were rimmed in red and the sides of her nostrils were raw.

"My angel!" exclaimed Jean-Luc with such enthusiasm that the doorman looked up in surprise.

"Oh, hodey, you didn't have to cobe agaid. Odce a day is edough, eved if I were *really* sick."

"Nonsense!" he said, bringing the packages to the kitchen. "How could I leave you all alone at this time?"

"But, Jead-Luc, it's odly a cold."

"Hardly! It is the flu."

"Big deal. Is that a reasod to baby be?"

"I love to baby you. I love to spoil you. I like doing that more than anything in the world—with the possible exception of making love to you."

"Oh, Jead-Luc. Probise you won't disappear whed the codeide wears off."

He kissed her. "I shall be with you until the sun rises in the west."

He was good with words, always had been. A natural at the diplomatic game. But he had always been awkward expressing his feelings. Especially to women. His relationships had been so shallow and so short-lived that his own mother was convinced that he was gay.

But it had all changed with Cindy. From the first moment he knew that he would love her with all his powers. With his heart, with his words, with his money and his influence and his place in society. Everything was dedicated to her. She had made his heart sing.

"Oh, Jead-Luc! Don't you have didder todight with the people frob Kodak?"

Jean-Luc waved a hand in dismissal. "I sent Henri Brinker instead. He's a very able man."

"But, hodey, they're expecting sobeode at a higher level. They'll be furious. It isn't like you to shirk your duty like that."

"Well, am I a slave? Do I not get sick days off like any worker in a civilized country?"

Cindy shook her head. But she was pleased that Jean-Luc was here with her.

"Chérie, why are you not in bed?"

"It's too hot. I was sweating."

"You are supposed to sweat. It brings the toxins out of your body."

Jean-Luc went to the bedroom and began to redo the bed as efficiently as a veteran housewife. That very afternoon he had bought her a huge down comforter, ordered from Europe, where, he insisted, they had more experience in making featherbeds. He fluffed up the shams and pillows so she could sit up.

"Is the television okay?" he asked. That afternoon he had installed a hospital-type pole that held the TV up so that it could be watched from an angle on the bed.

"It's fide but I'b bored with TV and bored with reading and bored with everything but you. If I didn't look so awful I would have gode to beet Karl Lagerfeld with Bettida. Such a fabous desigder. It's a first for Goldsbith's."

"Hummph. Like many people with iron constitutions, Tina apparently has no sympathy for the sick. Now then, it's time for your dinner. I've brought a few things.

"Lots of liquids, that's what the doctors recommend. These are blood oranges, lots of vitamin C. Let me just squeeze these for you."

"There's a juicer here, sobewhere."

"Don't bother, it's done."

"But your suit, hodey."

"Oh, big deal. It'll come out. Now then. I'll just pop this soup into the microwave. It's from a delicatessen. New Yorkers say kosher chicken soup has special medicinal powers. Let's put it to the test.

"And here's a very nice tea from Assam Province," he said, opening a bag. The fragrance was so pungent, Cindy could smell it right through her stuffed nose.

"Wow," she said, "Goldsbith's could barket this stuff to dab behind your ears."

"We'll put a little of this into it." Jean-Luc held up a jar of honey. "The bees make it out of the flowers in the fields of Grasse. Oh, it's heavenly there! Have you ever been to the south of France, Cindy?"

"Do. I've dever beed out of Aberica."

"Oh, good. We'll have so many fantastic places to discover together. Now, if you're up to some solid food, you can have this on crackers."

"Pâte de foie gras?"

"It's very nutritious. Builds up your immune system."

Cindy shook her head in wonder. How could anyone be so good? Her heart ached with the realization that, like everything, her time with Jean-Luc would some day end. Please, please God, make him stay a long time.

Cindy sneezed. "Please, Jean-Luc, hand be the tissues."

"Certainly not," he said, tearing open another package. "Use these."

He handed her a stack of fine linen handkerchiefs. Each one had an insert of lace. The design of the lace represented Jean-Luc's family's crest.

"Oh do, I can't use these, they bust be precious heirloobs."

"What of it? I won't let you torment your poor little nose any more with those rough tissues."

After Cindy had eaten, they lingered together over the fragrant tea.

"I went to church today," said Jean-Luc.

"Why?" said Cindy.

He leaned over the table and touched her face. Delicately, as if she were made of the thinnest glass. Thoroughly, as if he were a blind man learning her features for the first time. But he did not answer.

He came over and kissed her mouth.

"Oh, don't, sweetheart. The gerbs!"

"I don't care. I love you and I love your germs." He kissed her harder, longer.

She bucked. "Please, Jead-Luc, by dose is so stuffed. I can't breathe when you kiss be. And I don't want you to get sick . . ."

He was now kissing her all over, everywhere but her mouth. His head was burrowing into the old flannel nightgown.

When the doorbell rang.

"Oh do. Hodey, don't answer it! They're supposed to addounce all visitors. Baybe it's a robber!"

"No, my angel. I've invited a friend over tonight. You don't mind, do you?"

"Jead-Luc, look at be! How could you?"

But Jean-Luc had already opened the door and there stood a portly, disheveled man with two paper shopping bags.

"Darling, this is my friend, Jack Brighton. Jack, Cindy Prewitt, whom I told you so much about."

"Hello," said Cindy, "don't you have a jewelry store on Badison Avedue? Belissa Johd shops there."

"Melissa. Of course. A very shrewd investor."

Brighton was so friendly and easygoing that Cindy soon forgot how she looked and just sat back and giggled as he and Jean-Luc exchanged wisecracks.

"So, what's in the shopping bags, Jack?"

"Oh, a few dribs and drabs." He began taking out packages and handing them to Jean-Luc, who tore eagerly into the wrappings.

"This must be for you," said Jean-Luc, rolling something across the table to Cindy.

It was a bangle paved all around with sliverlike, rectangular-cut diamonds.

Cindy gasped as the men urged her to put it on.

"Next," said Jean-Luc, rolling another bracelet at her. This one was a twin of the first, but with hematites instead of diamonds. The faceted pieces of gray metal were not as dazzling as diamonds but the two bracelets, together on Cindy's arm, made a spectacular, unusual show.

The presents kept coming faster than Cindy could catch her breath.

Jean-Luc pitched a pair of earrings into her teacup.

"Oh!" Cindy cried as she fished them out. Was it the hot liquid that made her cry, or the incredible jewels? Each earring consisted of two triangular stones, one dangling from the other. The top stones were highest-grade diamonds, whiter than white. The dangling stones were canary diamonds, yellow as lemons.

"Catch," said Jean-Luc, tossing her a long cord of intricately worked platinum. On its end, a pearl the size of a small egg.

Finally, Brighton excused himself. Cindy was still too shocked to say good-bye.

Jean-Luc whispered, "Wish me luck."

Brighton winked and gave him a thumbs-up sign.

Jean-Luc turned back to Cindy. She was slowly shaking her head. "What is it, *petit chou*?"

"I just dow I'b going to wake up id a fevered sweat—id Arkadsas."

He kissed her cheek. "No fever. Now, let's clean up this mess." He started shoving wrappings and ribbons into the wastebasket.

"Oops, almost tossed this out. My hands are full, angel, would you see what it is?"

She took a small velvet box from amid the debris. Opening it, she found a ring.

It was a sapphire, of a blue so pure and deep it seemed from another world. In the shape of a cushion, it was bordered with diamonds, as a pillow is bordered in ruffles.

She looked at him. In her face there was astonishment, and also a question.

"I . . . I know it's customary in America to have a diamond in the ring, but Jack said this stone was super-special . . ."

"You bead this is ad . . . ad . . ."

"Will you marry me, Cindy?"

"Oh God, oh God. Yes, yes!"

"You are sure? You are sure?" he said, tears falling shamelessly from his eyes. "You know I am Catholic, and the sacrament is forever."

"Jead-Luc, I love you so buch. I want to barry you bore thad adything id the world. But, but. I have a terrible past. I dow you think I'b pure and iddocent, like the ads for the perfubes. But it's all a lie. I don't want to fool you, I don't want to shabe you, eved though I'd rather be with you thad live!"

Jean-Luc cast his eyes down. "I have heard things. My mother, I am ashamed to say, hired a private investigator when I told her my intentions. I apologize for the crudeness of what is so laughingly called the noble class. But it matters *nothing* to me.

"If it relieves you of pain, speak to me, let my ears bring you relief. But if it hurts you to remember the past, then I will forbid any word of it to be said, ever again, by anyone.

"My precious darling. I *know* you. No angel in heaven is so pure. Look at this," he said, picking up the platinum pendant. "This necklace belonged to a czarina, a bitter, superstitious woman who rejoiced in the oppression of millions. Then it came into the hands of a murderous regime that sold it to buy guns. And yet, the evil and the ignorance, the blood and the greed, they have not affected the pearl. It is as white and luminous today as the day it came out of its oyster. You are like that, you are my pearl."

"Oh Jean-Luc!" The words didn't actually come out. She was literally beyond speech.

"Let's just be happy now. Yes, Cindy?"

"Yes!"

Jean-Luc raised his teacup in a toast. "To our love."

"To our future," added Cindy.

They touched the cups and drank.

"Ulp," said Cindy and began to cough violently.

"What is it, are you okay?"

Jean-Luc got behind her, ready to apply the Heimlich maneuver.

But Cindy coughed one huge cough, then delicately spit something into her palm.

It was a four-carat yellow diamond earring, like a wedge of lemon from her tea.

Chapter Twenty-three

IT'S GOING TO BE A GREAT DAY, Erica thought, as she opened her office door. On her desk was a spreading bonfire of fresh gerberas. They'd been coming all summer, about every two weeks. But before there had been just six or eight stalks of the flowers at any one time. Always, the blossoms made an electric presence in the room. Today, they created a three-alarm fire.

Andy Fairchild sent them from his backyard nursery. He had described the gerbera as a type of daisy, but daisies were to gerberas as sno-cones were to icebergs. These daisies were jewel-bright, aristocratic as roses. These flowers were *arrogant*.

This particular bunch was red, so red that Erica hesitated for a moment before rearranging them in their vase. In their throats, yellow tongues leaped, emphasizing the heat of their fire. Erica smiled with pleasure. The flowers would keep their brilliance for more than a week, and then Andy would send more, in yet another color.

He had no doubt sent this spectacular bunch as a good luck token. Today was the day she would be presenting his proposal for an ecological agents laboratory. As a bribe, the gerberas were unnecessary; she was all for the lab, and besides, the idea was a shoo-in. Nox had bought the moth-fooler and the company's research chiefs were unanimous in their opinion that Andy's was an exceptional mind.

Erica put the vase on the sideboard. The flowers had covered most of her desk, and she had a lot of paperwork to do this morning. Even relegated to the side, the gerberas transformed the office. It had been decorated in discreet browns and beiges, tweed and leather. A silver-framed portrait of her parents was the only ornament. Not Erica's taste, but taste wasn't the issue. This office was meant to impress visitors with the conservative gravity, mature wisdom, and eminent reliability of its tenant. To a great extent, Erica held the reins of the company. People who entered it wanted to be assured that their investments were safe. And Erica knew that they were especially anxious because she was a woman, and that she had to do even more to win confidence.

Yes, indeed, she was reliable, responsible, cautious, and prudent. But there was also some gerbera in her, she thought proudly, bold and fiery.

Her first act of the day was to phone the new manager of the Nox rubber-based paint plant in Ohio. He had increased production by twenty-two percent—the second-best performance in the company (her old protegé, Quentin Shining Blue Stone, had been number one for years)—and Erica wanted to thank him, to let him know that management took note of what went on in a provincial factory. George would tell her it was a waste of time. After all, the man had already received a sizable raise. But Erica didn't think that human warmth and the profit motive were mutually exclusive.

Ruthie came in as soon as she hung up the phone. "Melissa John just called, says it's super super urgent."

Erica smiled. Ruthie did a pretty funny takeoff on Melissa's breathy, dramatic voice.

When Melissa answered her call, that voice was even more breathy and dramatic than the caricature.

"Guess what? I'm pregnant and I'm in love!"

All Erica heard was the word "pregnant." She felt as if she'd been punched in the stomach. Immediately, she censored her thoughts. It was wonderful for Melissa, and she was glad for her. But in all their years as friends, Melissa had never once mentioned wanting a baby. Of course, time was running out on that decision. Melissa was even older than she was.

"Fantastic!"

"Erica, you are the first person to know. I just did the test. You take your first morning urine and . . ."

"Good luck to you, Melissa. And send my congratulations to Sheldon." Erica was uncomfortable with the fact that she had never actually met Melissa's husband, even though they had been married for six or seven years. He was a very busy doctor. They were all very busy, but Erica and Melissa managed to get together several times a year, anyway.

"Sheldon? Sheldon has nothing to do with it."

"WHAT?"

"You know. We're like brother and sister."

The idea of any heterosexual male treating Melissa John like a sister was preposterous, thought Erica.

Melissa continued. "Didn't you hear me say I was in love?"

"No," said Erica honestly. It was the sort of thing Melissa announced periodically.

"Well, I am. Ask me who."

"Okay. With whom?"

"Sit down, Erica. With *Paul Tremain*."

"Oh."

"Aren't you excited? I'm so excited!"

"Melissa, he's married. The Tremains have one of the oldest marriages in Hollywood. It's an institution."

"Oh, please. Diana Tremain is *ancient*. Paul would give her up in a minute. And now that I'm pregnant, naturally, he will."

"Gee, Melissa, of all the messes you've ever gotten yourself into . . ."

"Erica! Don't be such a stick in the mud. If this were a business affair, you'd just sail through with complete confidence."

"If this were a movie, I'd have to rewind three times just to figure out the plot."

"Don't sweat it. Just remember 'Gentlemen Marry Brunettes.'"

Erica laughed, even though she was shaking her head disapprovingly.

"I hope so. For your sake, and the baby's, to say nothing of public morality."

"Oh, Erica, wish me good luck."

"You know I always do."

Erica kept shaking her head even after she hung up the phone. Boy, she wondered how Melissa would get out of this one. But Melissa always managed, no need to worry about her.

Now she settled in for the morning. Behind the heavy oak desk, Erica removed her pumps, tucked her feet up under her in the big leather chair, and buckled down to do what she liked best. Hours passed in silence.

At two o'clock the senior management of Nox Industries, Inc., gathered in the Sixty-third floor conference room. George Steel sat at the head of the great table. To his right sat the next-most-senior executive, Erica. The seat to Steel's left represented the number three position in the company, and several senior VPs actually jockeyed for it physically. Roy Little finally landed it with a combination of shoving and slit-eyed psyching-out.

George was his usual charismatic self, greeting men at the far end of the table.

"Good to see you, Ted. Everything going okay? You sure? You know my door's always open if you've got a problem . . . No problem? Then how about a few brews?

"Thanks for coming, Ben." As if Ben, or any other VP had the option of not attending a major policy meeting.

"Arnie, my man, I'm depending on you to point out the fact if I make a fool of myself today. Nobody else here has the balls to do it, except Erica."

They all laughed, although Arnie would never dare to do any such thing, while if Erica did, she would do so only in private. Anyway, George never made a fool of himself.

When the audience had softened, George launched into his new strategic plan for the company. He spoke in low tones, the room dead quiet. There was absolute reverence for his person, as well as for his plan.

Erica gazed at him with bright eyes. The others were no less awed. George really was brilliant. He put forth his plan in such a solid, organized, yet passionate manner. On occasion, he asked for figures or clarifications or expansion on his ideas, and the other VPs strengthened his vision with their own contributions. Deftly, he wove the wills of his management, playing competitors out in such a way that all felt victorious. At the end of the presentation a vote was taken. Management was unanimous; the plan was to be implemented as of the first day of the next quarter. It was not a matter of "yes men" bowing to the master's will. They were genuinely impressed with the plan. More than that, under George's aegis, they were *proud* to be executives of Nox.

Erica's presentation came on the heels of this triumph. She stood up, beaming congratulations at George. He beamed back with a wink that said "Good luck."

She stood straight and confident. A bright gerbera shone in the lapel of her khaki suit.

"Gentlemen, ordinarily, I wouldn't dare try to follow an act like that! In my opinion, George Steel's strategic plan heralds a new age for Nox, one for which the glorious past is a mere prelude."

There was scattered applause. George ran a hand modestly through his thick silver hair, mouthed a "thank you" to Erica, then gave her his most serious look of attention. The VPs were forced to follow suit.

"If I may say, in all modesty, the program I am about to present to you represents an important phase of this new age.

"Nox is being presented with the unique opportunity to develop the ecologically balanced products of Dr. Andy F. Fairchild. As you know, Fairchild is the inventor of the unique agent for Tussock moth control which we will be marketing next year.

"It is his hope, and my proposal to you, that a Bio-Nox Laboratory can be founded, which will discover new ways to control weeds and pests with environmentally safe agents.

"In the portfolios which Ms. Prewitt will now hand out, you will find estimated development costs for several prototypes which Dr. Fairchild wishes to tackle first. You will also see projected income from these products. As you can see, this lab will hardly be a charitable affair. In fact, we are looking at a projected major contributor to our profits in the coming decade.

"By pioneering biologically benign agricultural controls, Nox will change its image in a powerful way. And because the profits to be realized in this sector are so great, Nox will have its cake and eat it too. Not only will our company be at the forefront of public service, but its profits—from ethically 'pure' products—are going to make the stockholders merry.

"In conclusion, gentlemen, I urge you to support the establishment of the Bio-Nox Laboratory. As Bernard Shaw advised, 'Always be sure to do the right thing. It will surprise your friends and confound your enemies.'"

A smile or two greeted this conclusion. Soon, however, a pandemonium of criticism and rhetorical questions assaulted Erica. Just as the veeps were inclined to greet George's pronouncements with warm assent whether deserved or not (today it had been deserved), they were inclined to greet whatever Erica proposed with negativism. It was more than just picking on Erica; they also channeled any hostility they felt toward the CEO to his second-in-command. The criticism was laced with jealousy—that Erica was their superior at the company despite being their junior in years and experience—and fury—that she was female and had bested them on their masculine turf.

"Even the moth stuff hasn't shown it can make a profit, now you're getting us into this pie-in-the-sky laboratory," grumbled Arnie.

"But we've pre-sold six million dollars' worth of . . ."

"You expect us to bank these projected profits of yours against the billion and a half we realize from the traditional pesticides? You been sniffing Nox-Off, Erica?" taunted Roy Little.

"The figures are based on . . ."

"Who says this professor can come up with the goods, anyway?" snapped another executive.

"I've . . ."

No one was listening to Erica's responses. They didn't care if the project was the smartest thing since sliced bread. They wanted to get Erica.

"This is the most half-assed project I've heard of in *thirty-eight years* at this company," said Oscar Barnes, glaring at Erica. "I'd like to hear what George has to say about it."

All eyes turned to George Steel. Erica, too, looked toward him, expecting to be vindicated. George, after all, was the only man present who did not resent and envy her. He was the only one who had saved her from the clutches of Coby Knox when the going had gotten roughest. He was the only one who had absolute confidence in her ability to oversee and direct the company's development. He was the only one who would view her report objectively. While his support was not officially enough to pass the project through, it would undoubtedly tilt the attitudes of the majority of the executives.

George's brows were knit. He sat looking sightlessly at his steepled hands, deep in thought. At last, he broke the silence, speaking in measured tones.

"On the face of it, this laboratory is a brilliant concept. Whatever its possibilities now, it certainly seems like a comer for the future. The public is increasingly concerned about the ecology.

"My argument with this project has nothing to do with whether or not the products can succeed. My hunch is they can. Besides, with great marketing (and here he nodded to the senior vice president for marketing) any reasonable product can succeed.

"No, the problem isn't what the products are; the problem is what *we* are. What is Nox Industries seen as, ladies and gentlemen? Is it seen as an innovator? No, not usually. Is it essentially concerned with public service? We give our share to the United Fund, but let's face it, good will is not what this company is about. No, Nox is a *service* company, despite the fact that we sell tangible products. And what service do we provide? *We fulfill the expectations of our customers.* That fulfillment has always been in the form of powerful chemicals that always do the job.

"Nox-Off, Nox-Out, Chemo-Nox, these brands have become household words. To produce biologically benign new products would confuse and irritate our customers. It would show that we had no faith in our regular lines.

"We are number one in agricultural chemicals, in industrial chemicals, in building industry chemicals and paints, in consumer petroleum-based products. Any move to diversify beyond those fields had better be carefully scrutinized. I don't think this lab passes such scrutiny.

"If we were a medium-size company, I would say, sure, why not, let's take a swing at it. But we're not. We're number one. Let's not forget what butters our bread. Let's make sure our image reflects that. Let's remember that distraction kills companies, even big ones.

"I would even go so far as to say that we should chuck the moth product. True, we've already invested in development, market research, even sales. But we can write off those costs much more easily than a major assault on our image.

"Sorry, Erica. All of us back losers occasionally. This is hardly a blight on your sterling record. Get us another one of your usual winners, madam, and leave ecology to the save-the-whale people.

"Okay, what's next on the agenda? Roy, Ted . . ."

Erica was stunned. She had not expected anything like this. Maybe from the executives, but certainly never, ever from George. She felt if she stayed in the conference room another minute she would burst into tears or hurl one of the heavy glass ashtrays at George.

"Excuse me, I must go," she said, gathering her papers. There was a shocked silence. No one ever left a meeting like this before its conclusion. Erica walked out with her back ramrod-straight. The men watched, fascinated, as she left. Their satisfaction was with more than the view of her shapely rear.

Apparently George had ended the meeting early, because Erica was still clutching her portfolio in fury when he came into her office.

"George, how could you? You know that's my pet project. I feel betrayed."

"Darling, I'm sorry if you're hurt. But my first responsibility is to the company. And yours is too. I meant what I said in there. And I know you are tough enough to take the heat."

Erica just shook her head. She was mute with anger, and the area around her mouth was white.

"Erica, I can't talk now. We'll have dinner at Lutèce and . . ."

"I'm having dinner at my parents' tonight."

"Well, after, then, at your place. Please, sweetheart, let's not go to sleep tonight angry with each other."

Erica grudgingly consented. She was determined not to be placated.

The Valentas' apartment had a tiny balcony with an enormous view. It was here that they had dinner. The summer sun was still lingering on the horizon, and the air carried the bracing cologne of coming autumn. Nevertheless, Erica had little appetite. The meeting sat like ballast in her stomach, and the expected showdown with George put her on edge.

She blanched at the sight of her mother's huge pork roast, at the cabbage and noodles and potatoes. There was, however, a small green salad at which Erica nibbled.

"Getting into nouvelle cuisine, Mama?" Erica ribbed.

"Erica," her mother complained, "you are eating like a bird. What is the matter? You want better I should mash the potatoes with the cabbage?"

"No, no, Mama. It's just that I had a big lunch, and then, a . . . disagreement with George."

"Erica," her father admonished, "I hope you are not letting your temper get away with you. When George says something, you know, it is ninety-nine percentage it is right."

Erica was suddenly deeply irritated by her parents. They adored George, worshipped him. But they treated her like a baby—mashed potatoes indeed—while George's age entitled him to be treated like their peer.

Resentment welled in her, exacerbated by the fiery apricot brandy with which her father kept refilling her glass. Why were they always taking George's side, they were *her* parents. Was he really that perfect?

Well, he was a great man. As for herself: a tendency to envy was one of her worst characteristics. And perhaps, a failure to be appreciative.

"Anyway, we are going to talk about it tonight."

"Good, good, listen to what he has to say. Listen, is a woman's best skill, listening."

"Oh, he's so smart is he? Well, how do you like this one? He doesn't want me to have children. Do you like that, not ever being grandparents?"

It was cruel. She immediately regretted saying it.

Her parents looked thoughtful.

"Well, he already has grown children from the first marriage," her father said.

"You'll see, he'll change his mind when you are pregnant. Men are like that," her mother added.

"That's not the point," Erica said quietly. "He thinks it's best for me. And he's right. At this point I can't even leave the office for lunch without having someone try to ruin me. Can you imagine what would happen if I went on maternity leave?" She laughed ruefully.

"You know, we are not so old-fashioned, like you think," said her mother, raising her head proudly. "Grandchildren is nice, but your success is more important. Ya, Papa and me, we are pleased with what we have. A good daughter, American hero for son-in-law, nice life in Manhattan. Only a greedy one would ask for more."

"Good, I'm glad for you." Erica sipped some more brandy.

But what about *me*, she thought.

Her guilt at this selfish thought made her eat her mother's dessert. Czech dumplings, spheres of potato dough the size of baseballs, bursting with plum butter, rolled in cocoa and sugar; Erica had two.

Later that evening, George arrived at Erica's apartment, bearing gifts. A bouquet from Fabulous Fern, an artful arrangement of mauve orchids and gray roses, with a box of napoleons and eclairs—she loved custard—from a new French bakery.

"Got to fatten the little village maid for the wedding," he

teased. Then, sensitive to her recent anger, "Though you know I love you the way are, Skinny."

Erica had determined that she would not be appeased by either his presents or his charm.

"The attack on the laboratory, and on me, George, what the hell was that?"

He turned suddenly serious. "It's what I believe, Erica. The lab is wrong for Nox, and I won't let it pass."

"George! The worst the lab can do is launch a few duds. Nothing Nox hasn't handled before, without perceivable damage."

"I don't agree, Erica. And I'll stand by that. Do you want to fight me in persuading management? The board?"

"You know I can't do that. I can't even try," she said acidly.

"Darling," he came behind her, embracing her. "You know how great I think you are. I'd fight management, the board, every fucking moth in California, if I thought you were right. But I don't. *I'm* right on this one, no matter how pissed you are."

Erica sighed. Perhaps he had a point. Maybe the bio-products were wrong for Nox. "But how am I going to break this to Andy Fairchild? He'll be crushed. This project is his whole life."

George shrugged. "He had it coming, for putting all his eggs in one basket. Besides, what's it to you? Got the hots for him? Ruthie told Janine he's a good-looking young buck."

"George, don't be ridiculous. He's a *kid*. About thirty years old, and a complete innocent. That's why I feel for him. He has no defenses, he doesn't know what it is to play with the barracudas. He reminds me of how I was when I was young."

"Well, you can't do his growing up for him. Let him learn the ropes by himself. Everyone else does."

Erica knew that wasn't really true. But she let the comment, and the issue, pass.

Some of the tension had been relieved. Sensing that, George took off his jacket and his tie. He fixed drinks and took them into the bedroom.

"Now can we go to sleep? I'm beat." He looked at her. "But

not that beat." He swept her up in his arms and carried her to bed.

He was expert, as always, but there was a sour edge to their lovemaking. Erica couldn't understand it. She should be happy, despite the day's events; she was doing great at Nox. She was making more money than she had ever imagined possible. And the money meant a lot to a girl from the Crest Motor Lodge.

It must be just plain exhaustion. Too many things had happened today. The flowers, the meeting, her parents.

She faked an orgasm. It was easier than explaining things to George. It took less time than fantasizing herself into a real climax. George kissed her and kissed her, as if she had done him a favor.

He dozed for half an hour, as she lay wide-eyed. Then he woke.

"Hey, I'm starving, let's eat the pastries."

"Sure," said Erica, even though she didn't feel at all hungry. For some reason, she felt terribly guilty, and wanted to make up to George.

She fixed some instant coffee and they ate the cakes.

The caffeine didn't bother George. Once he was sated, he went back to bed and fell into a solid slumber.

When she was sure he was asleep, Erica went into the spare bathroom and threw up. It was disgusting. She hadn't done such a thing since she was a little kid. It was the exhaustion, the alcohol, the rich foods . . . and things.

She felt sick. Today she'd failed someone who had depended on her, she'd been mean to her parents, and she'd let George dominate her with sweet talk and seduction.

On top of all that, she was probably becoming some kind of a bulimic. Well, what did she expect? To be "America's Top Woman Executive," a titan's bride, and *happy*, too?

Chapter Twenty-four

E RICA STEELED HERSELF. She had to do it now, right now. It was 10:30 and she had already killed half the morning fidgeting. She dialed Andy Fairchild at work. It was ridiculous, he wouldn't be in yet, it was only 7:30 in California.

"Andy Fairchild, good morning!" she heard, after a single ring.

"Andy, it's Erica Eaton."

"Uh oh, I hear the 'bad telegram' voice."

"I'm afraid so. I've got some disappointing news, disappointing for both of us."

"Oh." His voice was low, like that of a boy who had been promised the circus, then denied. "I shot too high, didn't I? Sure, why would Nox grant a lab to me, with my lack of experience . . ."

"No, it isn't that at all. It isn't your fault, your idea was brilliant. It's just that . . . I can't explain, Andy, not on the phone."

"I guess it doesn't really matter."

"Of course it matters. It matters a lot. To me! Look, one of these days I'll tell you what *really* happened, but I can't talk about it on the phone." George had made her really paranoid about bugging in the office.

"Any time you're in San Jose, ma'am," he said with irony.

He sounded exactly like Quentin Shining Blue Stone, long ago.

"Hey, I'll come out to San Jose, okay? Please don't act that way. Please don't think I don't give a damn."

"I'm sorry. I shouldn't take it out on you, you did your best. The failure is mine."

"No, no, it isn't a failure. Don't think that way. We'll talk it through. It's a great idea, really. Maybe there's some way to salvage it. Let me get my calendar."

"Oh damn, I'm sorry. There isn't any time, not for six, seven weeks."

"That's okay. I've already imposed on your time. It was generous enough of you, the effort you expended on a nobody."

"Andy, *please.* I swear I have no time at all until . . . Look, how about a weekend meeting, I just can't do any better."

"Fine with me. Any time you say."

"Okay, Saturday, then. This Saturday afternoon."

"Sure, I'll see you then."

"Come on, Andy, cheer up. It's probably just the Curse of the Tussock moths."

"They got me in the end, huh?"

"Hey, buddy, you're bigger than them. Possibly smarter, too."

She could feel him smile on the other end of the line.

Saturday morning Erica hesitated in front of her closet. Would she look silly traveling in a suit? But after all, it was a business trip. What was the matter with her? She never fussed like this about her clothes. And it was just a "condolence" call. She finally settled for tailored tan pants and a matching silk blouse. Then she realized that it was a blistering end-of-summer day, there would be a lot of waiting in poorly air-conditioned airports, and San Jose was probably even hotter.

She searched through her closet for a short-sleeved cotton shirt. At last she found one, last year's impulse purchase, worn once. It was the tender chartreuse of unripe bananas. The color was why she had picked it from a sales rack, bringing it home without even trying it on. There never seemed to be any time to shop, so her erratic buying habits led to some strange acquisitions.

As it happened, the shirt fit well. Unfortunately, she realized it was much too colorful to wear to work. Unable to return it, she'd worn it—with a swinging peach skirt—to dinner at George's friends' on upper Fifth. She'd had a lovely time at the dinner, but afterwards, when George took her home, he had gently nudged her about the outfit.

"Would Ivana wear that?" he asked. "Would Blaine?" He was right. Melissa was right. They all were. She had no fashion sense. The blouse had been exiled to the back of the closet.

But no one would be comparing her with fashion leaders in laid-back San Jose. Her image didn't count today. All she really wanted to do was to fix it so that Andy Fairchild wouldn't hate her.

She had brought along some work to do on the flight, and the passenger next to her, understanding the etiquette of first-class travel, left her mercifully alone. But the flight attendant, a throwback to the old days, came around constantly to cater to the male passenger. Catering turned to flirtation, and the stewardess ended up spilling cola on Erica's blouse.

San Jose airport, despite the fact that it served the world's greatest concentration of high-tech industry, was a very pleasant, even homey place. There was a small-town feeling to it as if it were a California town in the forties or fifties, untouched by the competitiveness and aggression and economic cycles of recent decades. Erica began to feel a little less grim about the unpleasant task of bringing Andy up-to-date on the scene at Nox.

In the lobby Andy was waiting for her, tapping with his fingertips on a Lucite bell that enclosed "The Photocopier of Tomorrow." He was wearing an orange polo shirt, jeans, and sandals.

He insisted on taking her attaché, and led the way to his

car. His blue Honda was parked immediately in front of the exit, unlocked.

"You must be kidding," marveled Erica. "Can you really leave the car like that? No one will ticket it? No one will steal it?"

"That's right. Welcome to the real California."

"'The real California?' What's unreal California?"

"Los Angeles."

"I can guess your opinion of *New York*."

"It's a wildlife refuge."

"I hardly dare ask what kind of wildlife."

"Oh, you know. Lemmings. Rats, worms, and assorted parasites. Sharks and wolves. And plenty of sitting ducks."

It was hot, but Andy did not turn on the air-conditioning. They rode with the windows open. The warm, dry wind played havoc with her hair but made her feel free and adventurous. An eagle soaring over and through the Pacific foothills on a sleepy Saturday afternoon. Funny how California did that to her.

Andy's house was a modest affair, shaded by mature sycamores, run over by flowering vines the way a favorite uncle is entangled by children. Inside it was surprisingly cool, all open spaces and wooden beams. It had the slightly musty odor characteristic of bachelors' quarters.

Erica arranged her papers on the table in the dining corner while Andy fixed some lemonade, picking lemons off the tree that grew right into the kitchen window.

"Ooh, this is delicious," Erica exclaimed after a first sip.

Andy leered mischievously. "I spike it with passionfruit liquor."

Erica looked down at the papers. What she really needed was a double Scotch.

She took a deep breath, and began to explain what had happened to Andy's plans at Nox, and what his present, sorry status was.

An hour later, she was finished. Andy was silent. He had asked all his questions. Erica was silent too. She hoped that the empty space in conversation conveyed her regrets.

"So," she said at last, "what are you going to do now?"

"Do?" said Andy. "I'll do what I always do. Make new kinds of flea collars, or whatever else my boss tells me to do."

"What do you mean? You're giving up? You're going to write off your whole life's work?"

"It's not my whole life's work. I happen to do a lot of things. I work for a company that appreciates me, I teach, I hybridize flowers, I go to the movies . . ."

"But this isn't a hobby. It's a brilliant concept. It must have a future—the question is, what? Or rather, how?"

Andy shook his head and smiled. "No, it was just a dream. A pipe dream, as it turned out."

"*Andy*, don't! You can't give up. This is a big idea, an idea whose time has come. Even George Steel said so, and his instinct on these things is never wrong. Just because it won't fly at Nox, doesn't mean it won't make your fortune. Hey, Nox's rejection may even be the best thing that could have happened to you."

"But Nox is the biggest, the industry leader . . ."

"It's still not the only game in town."

"You think I should go to another company? I don't think I'll do any better elsewhere."

"No. No, you mustn't go to another chemical company. In fact it could be harmful. The more people who see your stuff, the greater the likelihood of being ripped off. And that's the chief weakness in the concept."

"But I patented the moth spray, like you told me to."

"It doesn't matter. A slightly altered parallel product can wipe out your advantage. And, off the record, you were had by Nox on the fee. It would have been okay, if they had thrown in your lab, but . . . I won't let that happen again."

"You still haven't answered my question, Erica. What do I do with my moth spray—now owned by Nox, which will bury it—and with my lab full of great ideas?"

"Where are you living, Andy, Cuba? You start your own business, of course."

"But I don't know a thing about business. I can barely balance my checkbook. I can never understand if the dollar is up or gold is down or whatever that does to the price of tea in China. Lady, I am out of my depth here."

Erica waved her hand impatiently. "That's just manage-ment. You can hire management, just like Nox hires me. You don't suffer a toothache just because you're a klutz with a drill, do you? You get yourself an expert. A dentist or a manager, professionals are for hire."

"Sure they are, but for how much. Like how much would the future owner of a Nox pay *you*, Ms. Executive Vice President?"

Erica declined to answer that most intimate of questions. "You don't need someone like me to work in your company. You can get good people on a consulting basis . . ."

"I do need you."

It was a jarring statement. Erica talked fast, trying to make it look as if she hadn't heard the words, or the way in which they were said.

"Look, I feel responsible for what happened this week to your project, and I'm going to make up for it with some business advice. But, Andy, please, please. Don't ever let on that I'm doing this. My salary is supposed to buy me lock, stock, and barrel. There are plenty of people in my company who would see this little meeting as high treason."

"I won't tell if you won't tell—or charge."

She grinned. "Okay, let's get to work."

They cleared the table, then laid out fresh pads and pencils.

"We start with a strategic plan," began Erica. "The first thing you need to make money is . . ."

"Money."

"Andy, you devil. And you pretend to know nothing about business."

"Now I'll ask you one. Where do we get it?"

"That's easy. From people who have money to spare."

"Your advice is worth every penny, Consultant."

"I happen to know some people in the spare-money busi-ness. They're called venture capitalists. In fact two of my classmates at B. School set up shop in Menlo Park. That's near here, right?"

"Just over yonder county line."

"Good. We'll deal with that later. Let's say we get the capital. What do we do with it?"

"Buy some good art for the president's office?"

"Maybe next fiscal year. Let's start with buying back the moth spray."

Andy sat up. "Will Nox let me have it? Will they charge a fortune? Would it be worth it?"

"Whoa there, one at a time. Yes, Nox might let you have it. *If* they don't suspect what you're up to. After all, it's worth nothing to them, since the decision has been made to shelve the product. What you need to do is find someone very low-level, a minion in the legal department, perhaps, who can sell it with permission from only a level or two upwards. You definitely don't want anyone from senior management to hear about it.

"Next, how much will it cost? That depends. The same rules apply here as in the Persian bazaar. You pretend you don't really need the product, you're just sentimental about it. You put it down, indicating it needs work. You underscore the obvious fact that Nox has turned thumbs down on it, so any deal is pure profit for them.

"Is it worth it? Believe it, my friend. That stuff is money in the bank. It's your company's only product right now; there's no money yet for research and development. It's cheap to produce, and easy, even with what have to be limited plant capabilities. And let's not forget this little fact: Nox pre-sold six million dollars' worth of that stuff, sight unseen.

"Of course, you won't be able to pre-sell anything near that figure. *But* even a fraction of those sales would be a nice piece of change. And, just think, the Nox sales team has already convinced those customers what a swell product this is."

"But who are the customers? Can you get the list from Nox?"

"Andy, that would be industrial espionage, totally unethical. I couldn't do that. I've already gone out far enough on the ethical limb. Anyway, it shouldn't be too hard to figure out who the targets are. There are just so many major distributors of agricultural products in California. There's probably a mailing list available . . ."

"For a price."

"Hey, you know the old saw, 'There is no free lunch.'"

"Speaking of food, I'm starved."

"Me too. What time is it, anyway?"

"Past seven. Fido needs his chow, fast."

"Fifi too. Guess I'll pack this up now. We'll have to finish this up . . . sometime."

"Let's discuss it on a full stomach. Want to go out, or are you willing to dare irradiation by my microwave?"

Erica patted her wind-tangled hair and glanced at her stained blouse. "Oh, I'll eat anything that's defrosted."

"If you'll make some salad I'll reconstitute a main dish."

Andy hummed and puttered while Erica peeled and sliced. When she looked up, the table had been covered with a pink cloth, candles and flowers set. As she finished setting the table, he uncorked some wine.

"Whatever it is, it smells delicious."

"Madame wishes to start off with some day-old bread?"

"Entrepreneurs can't be choosers."

The casserole consisted of small slithery slices of something in a rich brown sauce. "Mmm, this is great, Andy. What is it?"

"You don't want to know."

"Yes I do. I don't scare easy, about food. I've been to China, you know, one of the first trade delegations."

"All right. But it'll turn you off."

"Hey, I'm going for a second helping."

"Okay. It's artificial snails made from soybeans and Alaskan pollock. I made it in the lab."

"Hmm, I see what you mean."

"A buddy of mine from grad school is trying to sell these, but there seems to be some resistance."

"Definitely a marketing problem. You're very creative, think of a better description for it."

They sopped up the last of the gravy with the bread, then finished the wine in contented silence.

"Hey," said Andy, jumping up. "It's almost sunset and you haven't even seen my flowers."

He touched her elbow to indicate the way. They stepped out the kitchen door, past some greenhouses. And then she stopped in her tracks, awestruck by the scene before her. Rows and rows of magnificent flowers, reaching as far as the horizon.

"It's like the Brooklyn Botanical, or Huntington Gardens!"

He laughed. "Hardly. It's just two and a half acres, and I don't know beans about landscaping. Just think of this as Mother Nature's little lab."

Erica followed Andy through the field, as he pointed out the most exquisite and unusual specimens. A warm breeze ruffled the stalks, and the setting sun painted everything with gold. She saw the back of his body against the burnished field and something inside of her turned.

She'd seen handsome physiques before, of course. Whit's athletic beauty was universally admired, and George, despite his age, was in excellent shape thanks to self-disciplined exercise. But Andy had a farmer's body, his muscles honed on the ancient movements of labor. The dying sun made a halo of his yellow hair.

He turned around and explained something, but she didn't hear what it was. The blood was throbbing in her ears. It was a good thing he wore glasses. They seemed to add a note of reality, bring her back to earth. If he wasn't wearing them, she feared she might grab him by that beautiful hair and kiss him.

What an unexpected sensation! She had liked him from the beginning, of course, but as a protegé, a kid brother. She hadn't planned on this.

Erica groaned with unfulfillable desire. Those Arab tribes had a point, in circumcising their little girls so that they would never in their lives feel this agony.

That very moment Andy seized her by the shoulders. For a crazy second Erica imagined he was going to shake her, to win her attention back to his botanical lecture.

He kissed her.

Shocked, frightened, Erica wanted to pull back, as if her lips had touched poison. But she could not. Her mouth adhered to his as if she had pressed it to frozen metal.

She could feel the veins in his lips pulsing with spurts of heated blood. Or was that happening in her lips?

He finally pulled away. He pushed the glasses up on his head and rubbed his temples with his hands.

"Erica. I can't say it was love at first sight. It took a solid five minutes, that time in your office, before I began to fantasize about this moment."

"Don't talk that way, Andy. Let's just consider this a little mistake. It's so beautiful out here and . . . no one needs to know about this . . . little lapse."

"It's not a mistake. I never meant anything more in my life."

"Stop it. It's wrong. This is wrong. We have nothing in common."

"Nothing in common! How many couples do you know who are mutually fond of gerberas, fake snail gravy, and building a business empire based on ecology?"

"Don't joke, Andy. You know it won't fly. For one thing I'm older than you."

"Oh yeah, five whole years. Well, call me pervert. I prowl the geriatric wards, looking for thrills."

"Go ahead, laugh it off. But how are you going to laugh this off: I'm marrying another man! Don't you have any scruples?"

Andy put his glasses back on. "I'll speak as a biochemist. When a woman is in love—or a man for that matter—it's hard to keep it secret. Maybe it's a pheromone, maybe it's a thermal change, I don't know. All I know is any fool can see it a mile away. But you, the second I saw you I knew, no matter what *Thisweek* and *Forbes* say, your heart is free."

"No, no. I don't care if you can prove your theory mathematically, what I feel for George is real and important. Okay, I admit it isn't the moon-in-June relationship of song and story. So what? I've been through that, I've been married before. That stuff is illusion. It's only shared values and goals, mutual admiration, that can sustain a relationship."

"Thank you, Dr. Pop Psychology. That was enlightening to a bubblehead like me. And just what is it that ol' George has got that impetuous Andy has not? What are those lofty values of his? A couple of million bucks? Power?"

"That juvenile line went out with the sixties. What is wrong with money and power?"

"Not one darn thing. But they're two things for which you don't seem particularly needy. Not needy enough to marry for, anyway."

"It's none of your business!"

Andy's lips were tight. "No, it's not."

They walked in silence. Andy took a trowel and dug around the roots of occasional plants. His moves became rougher and rougher. At one point, he beheaded a delicate flower.

"You don't have to be mean," said Erica. "Do you always take your anger out on your plants?"

"I'm not usually angry."

"Well, don't kill the crop. If you must be violent, why don't you take your glasses off and challenge George Steel to meet you outside the bar?" It was an unsuccessful attempt at lightening things up.

"Because he's a head taller than I am and I'd lose," he said, not entirely joking. Erica wished she'd worn flats.

"Besides," he continued, not joking at all, "I don't have anything against George Steel. It's you I'm mad at, Erica Eaton."

Her temper suddenly flared. "Give me a break! Do you really think I'd just give up everything I've built in the past ten years for a fling with you?"

"I'm not talking about a fling."

"Well, maybe you should."

"You're saying that's all I'm worth, a quick roll in the hay?"

"I'm saying you should be honest with yourself. People have . . . needs. There's nothing wrong with that. I have them myself. It's possible to fulfill them without wreaking destruction on everything and everyone."

"Well. That's a very interesting viewpoint." Andy patted gently around a plant. He got up, brushed the dirt off his pants' knees, held the trowel like a dinner fork.

"All right. Ms. Eaton, if I promise not to be emotional, would you sleep with me?"

Erica considered the flowering bush at her feet. For some reason, she was not at all embarrassed by Andy's proposition.

"Okay," she heard herself say in a calm voice. Why not? She was a New Woman.

Andy put away his tools at an unhurried pace. He washed his hands at an outdoor tap, then courteously held the back door open for her to reenter the house.

Wordlessly, they entered the bedroom. It was an unlikely

place for romance. There was a large, overflowing bookcase. He had to remove a pile of scientific journals from the bedspread. Inexpensive prints of modern art decorated the walls, along with the framed, yellowed front page of a newspaper. It had a photo of a towheaded boy with a huge smile and heavy-rimmed glasses. The boy stood behind a table of paper cups with scraggly little seedlings rising out of them. The headline said, "Salmon River Boy Wins National Science Prize." There was also a corkboard covered with ribbons from the county fair and 4-H.

It wasn't the best sex Erica had ever had, but it was very, very good. She was rested, of course, for a change. That had something to do with it. And Andy, for all his country boy mannerisms, was either highly skilled or exceptionally intuitive.

But mostly, it was the fact that she found herself on a different planet. Today she had felt the sun and the wind. She had walked on the uncovered earth, and eaten and inhaled the things that grew from it. It was a far cry from the world she usually lived in, where the light and the ground and the temperature were controlled. In Andy's world, she too, could let Nature take control.

She sighed in satisfaction. Andy was sitting against the pillows, looking down at her. His deep brown eyes were full of things she did not want to deal with right now. Turning her back to him, she fell instantly asleep.

It was midnight when she awoke.

"Oh no! Andy, I've got to get a plane back."

"You can't. The last flight is at twelve-thirty."

"Hurry, we can still make it. There's probably no traffic out there at this hour."

"Why do you have to go?"

"Andy, remember what we agreed on. Give me one practical, unemotional reason why I shouldn't go."

"You might get hijacked. The plane might develop trouble in-flight and have to land in Las Vegas. Also, my car is low on oil."

"You're stalling, it's getting late."

"Sharp cookie, that's what you are."

"Where's my blouse?"

"I love that blouse, do you mind if I keep it?"

"*Andy.* You're driving me crazy. Please, can we get going?"

"What's your big rush to get back, anyway? Going to church tomorrow with your feller? A man who fulfills Erica Eaton's qualifications must surely be a pious soul."

"Please don't start that again."

"Where is your paragon this weekend, anyway?"

"He sees his daughters on the first weekend of the month."

"How touching. Practically *Kramer vs. Kramer.*"

"Come on, they're teenagers. He probably sees them more often than most parents of teenagers. At least he takes his adult responsibilities seriously. Believe me, I had enough emotional immaturity from my husband."

"Listen, the poor bastard is probably willing to eat anthracite if it would get you back."

"Get me back! My dear Andy, *he* dumped *me.*"

"There you have it. The poor boy was obviously not in charge of his faculties."

"Andy, you're a pretty sweet guy when you aren't a total pain in the ass."

"Permit me to show you how sweet I can be." He embraced and kissed her. Erica fantasized that she was opening up a gigantic box of soft-centered chocolates. And they were all hers. She resigned herself to the fact that there was no way she could get to the airport on time.

An hour later she realized that this time it really *was* the best sex she'd ever had.

Chapter Twenty-five

E RICA WOKE UP utterly refreshed. She stretched like a cat. Andy was not beside her. She could hear him whistling in the kitchen.

She jumped out of bed and bounded into the shower. Unable to find a bathrobe or a spare shirt, she wrapped a towel under her arms and padded into the kitchen. She kissed Andy on the back of his neck. He turned around in surprise, and barely missed hitting her with the spatula in his hand.

He adjusted his glasses and looked her up and down. "Good Lord, Erica. You're lucky. I think California is the only state where it's legal to look like that."

She giggled. "I just came to ask if you had a hair dryer I could borrow."

"Sure, first drawer of the dresser."

She found it and plugged it in. She did not hear him say "Keep it on 'low,' it's powerful." Before she knew it her hair was dry—and wild as a rock star's.

She dressed and came to the table. It had been set with linen, silver, and china. Exquisite flowers floated in a crystal bowl.

"Oh boy, I can't wait to taste the food that goes with all this elegance."

"More of the mad scientist's inventions. *Ta da.* Nonfat eggs Benedict with cottage fries."

She ate with gusto. What an appetite she had this beautiful morning.

"How is it?"

"It's okay, but it isn't greasy."

"That's the point."

"Hmm. I think you should do some more market research."

Andy sat down to eat too. He handed her part of the comics, taking the other part himself.

"Where's the rest of the paper?" asked Erica.

"I threw it out. The funnies are the only part of a Sunday paper worth reading."

"But what about what's going on in the world?"

"What about it? Life goes on, and so does ours, but never the twain shall meet, not on Sunday."

"Sometimes you surprise me, Andrew Fairchild."

"My name isn't Andrew."

"It isn't?"

"No. I rarely admit this to anyone, it's so embarrassing. My real name is Ferdinand."

"Really? How cute. I like it, I really do. It's so, unexpected, so . . . European.

"I can understand your discomfort, though, Andy. My real name is sort of a secret too."

"No kidding? Now you have to tell me. I told you mine."

"It's—don't laugh—it's America."

"Hey, I like it. I really do. It's so . . . American."

"Oh. I can't believe I actually told you. I've always felt that was such *intimate* information. And I hardly know you."

His eyes opened wide.

"Not sexually. I mean, true intimacy is so rare . . ." She stopped herself. She was so ashamed. Was she such a lowlife? Was her sexuality so devalued? Yet it was true, sharing her heart was so much harder than sharing her body.

"It's okay," said Andy gently. "Whatever you're called, your friends know who you are."

"Oh, that reminds me!" She picked up the phone and asked information for a number. It was good to be able to retreat into business, when things became this uncomfortable. She called Bob Greenspan.

Greenspan acted as if a business call at nine o'clock of a Sunday morning was the most natural thing on earth.

"We've got a meeting at eleven in Menlo Park," Erica crowed triumphantly.

"Touché," said Andy.

"Now," said Erica, sitting down again, "I could use some coffee. Got any that's not artificial?"

"Ethiopian Mocha okay with you?"

"Wow, quite an expensive brew for an altruist like you."

"But it's good."

"Is it really? I don't think I've ever tasted the stuff. All I ever have time to make at home is instant."

"You may know how to make money, Erica, but you don't know beans about spending it."

"Oooh. And we can't eat puns. What's for dessert?"

A bit later they were heading up to Menlo Park, with two bicycles strapped to the roof of the car. "Robert Greenspan–Francis X. Touhy, Investments" was located in an office complex that looked more like a spa. Low-lying wooden buildings encompassed a courtyard blazing with flowers and gurgling with fountains. Andy and Erica passed over a wooden bridge which straddled a meandering brook. All of it was man-made, but thoroughly charming. It was clear why Bob and Frank had set up shop in this little suburban byway rather than a big city.

Both Bob and Frank were in, but, of course, none of their office staff was. The interior of the office was a combination of country casual and deluxe. The waiting rooms, as well as both men's offices, were full of quirky toys, mottos, and posters. They didn't have to impress or assure anyone; they were there to hand out money.

At first, Erica felt strange about coming into a meeting with her far-from-crisp clothing and electrified hair. But Bob and Frank knew her when she had been a frightened little student adrift in a strange world, and had both been friendly. And while they had left Nox immediately after the training program, they had been present at the scene of her first corporate triumph.

Erica now felt happily confident. She knew Greenspan and Touhy could come up with the seed money for a first-rate, small venture. Andy's new company would be right up their alley: a high-tech original with a principal who was smart enough to get professional management help. Andy could make a tidy sum for Bob and Frank and they, in turn, could provide the lifeblood for his company.

Erica's pitch was low-key but assured. They carefully looked over the notes Erica had written on yellow legal paper. Although Greenspan wore shorts and Touhy was clearly about to go boating, they were the pictures of seriousness. They were considering the disbursal of hundreds of thousands of dollars and the turnover of millions.

They excused themselves to go into conference. Erica and Andy waited in silence. Erica felt good. She gave a thumbs-up sign to cheer a worried Andy. When this did not change his expression, she went and planted a long, sexy kiss on his lips. That had the desired effect.

When Bob and Frank came out of their conference, the smiles on their faces were almost as good as a contract. Plans were set up to sign the papers later that month.

"Just one thing," Erica requested. "I have no official connection with this project. None. If anyone from Nox should ask you, you haven't seen me since Nox moved its headquarters to New York."

The partners nodded in unison. It was by no means the most extraordinary request they'd had to deal with in the often-delicate business of starting new enterprises.

After the official courtesies had been offered, Bob asked Erica how she was doing.

"Hell, we haven't seen you in more than ten years. So what are you up to these days?"

"What, you don't know? Has your subscription to *The National Enquirer* run out?"

"Yeah, yeah, we've seen your PR, Ms. Famous Hot Shot. But what's going on at Nox? Are you still hanging in with them?"

"Nox? Of course! I've never been anywhere else. I'd be a real ingrate if I didn't feel thankful to Nox."

"Good to see company loyalty, for a change. But seriously, do you still see the opportunities at Nox? Most of the women in our B-school class who were really ambitious aren't with the big corps anymore. They reach this plateau where management says, 'This is it, babe, this is as far as you go.' Then they get disgusted and start their own companies."

"Well, of course I get plenty of crap from the VPs and the board. But hell, I'm no quitter."

"'I'm no quitter!' Spoken like a champ—or a boxer with permanent brain damage," said Touhy.

"Well, I'll keep you guys in mind, if I should ever change my game to table tennis."

"You do that. We'll be right here amidst the petunias."

"Yes, it is lovely here, in downtown, commercial Menlo Park."

"Hey, our city is big-time. Why there's an art festival on Santa Cruz Avenue going on right now. Don't miss it."

"Yeah, maybe we will take a look, since we're already here. Okay, thanks a lot. I really appreciate it, especially on a Sunday morning. I do apologize for disturbing your weekend."

"No hassle at all. There's no wrong day for making money. There's also no wrong day for goofing off. If God hadn't meant for us to take Thursdays and Fridays off, why would he have called it week*end*?"

They all laughed, and parted in an excellent mood.

Erica and Andy walked the few yards to Menlo Park's main thoroughfare, a shade-dappled, cobblestoned street that was all of four blocks long. The art at the fair was of the rainbows-on-glass variety, but their mood was high from the morning's victory. Breakfast had been too big to allow for lunch, so they had ice cream cones and sat at an outdoor café sipping cappuccino.

Among the sidewalk vendors were aging hippies hawking jewelry. Andy insisted on buying Erica a pair of earrings.

"But I never wear earrings," she protested. "I've got dozens of pairs already, rusting in drawers."

"How can you resist these? They're the exact shade of your blouse. Talk about kismet."

Erica put them on. The giant enameled flowers were magnificent against her wild red hair. But who was this person? She passed by a mirrored window and did not recognize herself. Erica Eaton had been left in New York (probably catching up on her paperwork) and someone brand-new had come here for the weekend.

Just for a weekend, like the cereus cactus, whose stupendous flower blooms for one or two nights a year, and then is gone forever.

"What color are your eyes?" asked Andy.

"They're hazel, according to my driver's license. Can't you tell?"

"Not really. They look very green now, with that shirt and the earrings. There are times, though, when I could swear they're the color of granite. Or shaded brown. Or no specific color at all."

"Thanks a lot!"

"I bet you can control the color, I bet you can make your eyes whatever color you want."

"You're silly."

"Keep them green. I love them green, the way they are now."

After the fair, Andy wanted to show Erica his alma mater, Stanford, which was nearby. They drove up a stately colonnade, aptly named Palm Drive, parked, and unloaded the bicycles.

"I went to school here for such a long time, undergrad, grad school, a post-doc, I feel more at home here than in Idaho."

Erica glanced around at the manicured lawns, at the self-assured students who had come to settle in before registration. It was an expensive as well as an academically elite school. The golden, laughing students seemed to know they were an aristocracy.

"This place must have been intimidating to a boy from Idaho," she said.

Andy laughed. "Intimidating? I was scared out of my wits.

The only reason I survived the first trimester was because my big sister was there to hold my hand."

"Oh, you have a sister?"

"She's chief of surgery at the county hospital and the mother of five terrific kids," he said, bursting with pride.

"Wow! How does she do it?"

"They've got a housekeeper, and my mom babysits a lot. My sister and brother-in-law always do whatever they want to and work out the details later. It doesn't always turn out the way they hope, of course. Still, they've got it all. It's a great life. I sure envy them."

They bicycled all over the beautiful campus. They sped over tiled walkways under the red eaves of the quadrangle. Inside it, quaint gardens and a richly painted church reinforced the monastery-like effect. He showed her the fancifully modern science buildings, which he knew intimately. They tossed pennies in fountains for good luck and kissed in the shadow of the founders' ornate crypt, as was the custom.

Then they pedaled hard to get up to the campus foothills, where fraternity houses loomed in Grecian splendor, professors' homes sprawled across sweet-clover meadows, and a small blue lake begged to be sailed.

"There's more, lots more," said Andy, pointing to hills sprinkled with cows and horses.

"I can't pedal another inch uphill. I haven't ridden a bicycle since I was fourteen years old. Please, let's go back now."

As they coasted down the gentle hills of Stanford, Erica felt happier than she could ever remember.

On the way back to San Jose, Andy stopped at a fancy French restaurant.

"They've got the best food south of San Francisco, we've got to have dinner here."

"But, Andy, look at how we're dressed. And you need reservations for this sort of place."

"They don't care about clothes here. And we'll take our chances about getting in."

The owner greeted Andy at the door. "Ah, Monsieur le

Docteur! What a long time it has been. You are lucky, we have only one table left."

Erica was impressed. Both George and Whit had always had to tip maître d's extravagantly to get good service in haughty restaurants.

Their table was near the kitchen, but the restaurant was so pretty and comfortable, they didn't mind. Despite its elegance and their dusty clothes, they felt at ease.

A waiter came to take their order. Andy waved the menus away. "One of everything, Luigi. We're starved."

"And to drink?"

"Champagne!"

"What brand, Monsieur André?"

"Whatever's on tap."

The waiter nodded and wrote. "I will bring the wine now, but don't spoil your appetites."

"Luigi is French?" asked Erica.

"No, Swiss."

"Oh."

The waiter really did bring one of everything on the menu, although in small portions. Everything was delicious and they both ate like gluttons. They hardly had the opportunity to exchange two words until the coffee came. Now, stuffed, they chatted lazily about Greenspan and Touhy, college experiences, and families. The restaurant emptied and the candle on their table gutted. The waiter brought the check.

"So, Erica, you picking up the check?"

"Of course not. For you, it's deductible."

"Is that really okay with the IRS? I mean, in all honesty, we only spent about a tenth of the time talking business."

"Standard operating procedure, Andy. And don't feel guilty about it. The government won't foot all those other meals we had. Even with artificial food, we talked real business."

After dinner Andy drove to a little disco where they played golden oldies.

"Oh, Andy, I can't, I really should get back to New York."

"Why? It's Labor Day tomorrow, why don't you spend it with me. Come on, I'll show you a good time. I promise."

Erica found his arguments convincing.

They danced every slow dance. They held their arms tightly around each other, like infatuated kids at a party in someone's rec room. Erica nuzzled her face into Andy's hair. This was the first time she had ever really enjoyed dancing, she realized. It was funny, she was taller than Andy, but she could lean on him, she could depend on his solid body.

He smelled of evergreen needles and earth.

Erica forced herself to forget every other time, past or future, and live for the moment. She laughed softly beneath the music, her body keeping the beat. Andy kissed her throat, again and again.

They drove back to Andy's house and made love all night. Erica fought her conscience: It was just a wild weekend after all, why shouldn't she indulge? People thought nothing of a man having one last fling before he tied the knot. Why should it be any different for a woman? And what George didn't know wouldn't hurt him. Her conscience mollified, she somehow found the energy to make hungry, uninhibited love, again and again.

They didn't wake up until noon. Erica washed her hair and dried it. When it was halfway dry, she turned the blower on high. She was beginning to like the look. Perhaps her usual hairdo, in an effort to appear appropriate, had been a little uptight.

Juice and toast sufficed, after the gormandizing of the night before. They ate quickly and went off to the Santa Cruz boardwalk. It was the first amusement park Erica had ever been to that was neither sinister nor self-consciously campy. She completely let go on the roller coaster, screaming herself hoarse, and clutching Andy for dear life. When the ride was over she insisted they go again.

They played the carny games, at which Andy proved himself invincible. He was a perfect shot, his ball went in dead center at skee-ball, he even managed to topple the bottles that, for everyone else, seem glued in place. With a handful of winners' script he ransomed a huge pink teddy bear, which he solemnly handed to Erica. She handled it awkwardly; she'd never had a stuffed animal in her life. After a while she became fiercely fond of it and carried it on her hip, like a child.

They rolled up their pants legs and went walking at the ocean's edge. Some kids came by and started a splashing battle with them. Erica had to hold her bear high to keep it dry and, thus unprotected, was thoroughly soaked. But the sun was hot until it began to sink in the water, and her clothes dried on her body.

They found a cheap diner with a million-dollar view of the setting sun. The house offered French-fried everything, and they gobbled scallops, onions, potatoes, and mushrooms. There was tartar sauce and cole slaw so thick and sweet, they were indistinguishable from each other. Everything was oily and unhealthy and delicious.

"It's hard to believe that before this weekend I needed to gain weight," Erica said, polishing off the last of the home-made pecan pie.

"It looks great on you," Andy said. His eyes were shining and his hand moved across the table to hold hers.

Erica thought, I'll have to have a size ten wedding gown now. She tore her eyes away from his gaze, and moved her hand back behind her side of the table.

They drove back to his house in silence.

Erica slowly gathered her attaché and other items, avoiding his eyes.

"Well," she said with false cheer, "it's been fun, but now it's really time to go."

Andy grasped her arms, holding them tightly against her. He said nothing, but gazed at her face as if memorizing a map.

Erica wanted to rip the heart out of her own chest and make it stop doing what it was doing.

"Just one more night," he said, with quiet force.

She wanted to speak, but she couldn't. She wanted to laugh and joke, but she couldn't. She nodded and lowered her eyes so that he could not see the tears in them.

The first plane she could get was at eight in the morning. The waiting area was full of commuting businessmen and an occasional pumped-and-suited female of the species.

The other passengers stared curiously at them. Andy was dressed casually for work in an open-necked shirt, but Erica was a spectacle. Her trousers were caked with dust and sand, her blouse was wrinkled and stained—a very bruised banana. Wild red hair and outrageous earrings framed her sunburnt face. A giant pink teddy bear completed the costume. No wonder that none of the passengers, not even those who read *Thisweek* religiously, could recognize America's Top Woman Executive.

"Don't forget. You've got to buy back the moth spray before Greenspan and Touhy will finalize their investment. I'll call you with the name of the right person to approach at Nox. No, wait, I can't call from the office, someone might over-hear."

"I'll call you at home."

"No, my home phone might be . . . It's best not to take chances. Call me at my parents' house. I have dinner there every Tuesday and Thursday."

The final boarding call. Erica's throat tightened in panic. It wasn't just the end of the weekend, it was the end of a human being. There was a woman who had to be left behind in San Jose.

"I love you," said Andy.

"Stop it. I have to go." She pulled the boarding pass out and headed for the gate.

"I love you!" he repeated loudly. Passengers turned around.

She had to face him. "Please don't make this more difficult. You promised."

He embraced her tightly and kissed her so hard that her back arched. When he released her she ran out blindly toward the plane.

Because of the time difference, it was only noon when she reached her apartment. She had to change quickly, she had not informed the office that she would be out.

No time to redo her hair. Two days without her pills and her period had begun. She threw her expensive tan trousers in the trash—they'd never be wearable again. She considered the blouse. It too would never again be wearable, but somehow she wanted to keep it. She put it into a satin lingerie roll, together with the earrings. It would be a time capsule from a different world.

The phone rang. She stiffened.

"Erica. Where the hell have you been?"

"George? Why I . . . spent the weekend away."

"That's obvious. I must have called you a thousand times since Saturday afternoon. I was about to call Nox's house dick."

"Oh how ridiculous," Erica laughed nervously. "I would have told you before I left. But I thought you were going to be with your daughters."

"They were invited to spend the weekend with friends from the Vineyard."

"And they didn't tell you?"

"That's right. I put everything on hold and drag myself to Florida, just to be with them. And I find myself stranded in Palm Beach with nothing but an apology from the gardener. I never should have trusted their education to their mother."

Erica murmured sympathetic words, buying time to make up an alibi.

"Never mind that, Erica. Where were you?"

"Why, I had the most perfect weekend at Henry Goldsmith's summer place. There were the most fascinating people there . . . what a shame you couldn't come."

"How was it?"

"The food was great. Wait till you see me, I've gained a ton."

There was a long pause. Erica froze. Had he bought the story? George was not an easy man to fool.

When, at last, he spoke, his voice was low and modulated, like a stern but gifted preacher's.

"I'm surprised at you, Erica."

Oh God, did he perceive her lie?

"Why?" croaked Erica.

"Why? Because I've never known you to act so selfishly before."

"Aren't I allowed to have some fun on a weekend? Labor Day is a national holiday."

"My dear, you are *allowed* to hang out the red flag on May Day, if your identification with the workers is so great. But you are *expected* to show some responsibility. Nox was going to be a major player in the Hefflinger Insurance offering . . ."

"Oh my God, I forgot all about it! George, I'm so sorry . . ."

"The market has been open for four hours now. Even if we were prepared, would we be able to play at an advantage? And are we prepared?"

"No," Erica admitted with shame. She had been planning to devote the weekend to studying up on it but she hadn't prepared at all. She'd let the company down, and she'd let George down by blowing a major responsibility.

"And what about your parents? Don't you feel you have any responsibility to them? They were worried sick about you. I was in their apartment all day yesterday, calling every hospital in the tri-state area, trying my best to assure them that nothing was wrong. Do you feel that one is *allowed* to put them through hell, just so that you can go munch canapés with some damn dress designers. Well, you are. At least no one can sue you for it."

Erica was destroyed. She hadn't thought *once* that her parents might miss her. She bit her bottom lip until she drew blood.

"I'm sorry, George. I really am sorry."

A pause in which Erica wallowed in guilt.

"I accept your apology," said George. "I'm afraid we can't get together today. I've got a board meeting and you'll have your hands full salvaging Hefflinger. But we'll meet tomorrow." Pause. "I love you, Erica."

"And I love you, George."

It wasn't really a lie, not like the lie about the weekend at Henry's nonexistent house. But all the whoppers slid easily to her lips, while this ambivalent little statement was like broken glass in her throat.

Erica was glad when her dinner date at her parents' house forced her to close up shop. The Hefflinger deal was a no-win where all of her hard work would result in little profit for the company and no glory for her. Trivial annoyances had filled in the rest of the day.

Ruthie's mouth had fallen open when Erica entered the office. It was amazing enough that Erica had come in at two in the afternoon without advance warning. But the hairdo took the cake!

"All *right!*" said Ruthie.

All day long various office personnel had made excuses to come by and see the hair. Erica was about ready to run out to a beauty salon and return to the old style. But a bit of rebellion remained. What right had all these strangers, these "business acquaintances," to dictate such a personal thing as the way she did her hair? She knew she would have to abide by the status quo, but for the first time she resented it.

At dinner, the Valentas carefully avoided mentioning Erica's weekend disappearance. But it ran like an uneasy current through the evening.

"You already talked with George, yes?" her father asked.

"Of course I have. And yes, he let me have it with both barrels."

"He is growling sometimes, George. Is sometimes gruff. But Erica mine, in his way he cares for you."

"Yes, Papa, I know."

The phone rang.

"That must be George now," her mother said brightly, running to take the call. She returned not smiling.

"It is another man."

"I was expecting a business call, Mama. Thanks."

As she took the phone, her parents stopped eating and looked at her.

"Hi, Erica, it's Andy."

"I know."

"Flight okay?"

"Reasonable."

"Office didn't disappear while you were away, did it?"

"No chance of that."

"You can't talk freely, can you?"

"No."

"Mr. Big present?"

"No."

"But you can't really speak with your parents around, right?"

"Right."

"If they knew about it they wouldn't exactly be thrilled about my courtship, right."

"Right."

"Is it okay to talk business?"

"Yeah, that's fine."

"Did you get a chance to dig out the information on how to get the rights to the moth spray?"

"Yes, I did. There's a guy in the legal department called Martin Parrish, that's two r's. He runs his own little fiefdom. He's the one to see. He'd have to get an okay from his boss, Mort Weinstein, but Weinstein is just about ready to retire, so he'll probably rubber stamp whatever Parrish decides on."

"Fantastic. I'll call Parrish first thing tomorrow. Maybe I'll get an appointment to see him right away. If I do, can I come see you?"

"Absolutely not!"

"I don't mean in the office. Can we meet someplace?"

"No. It's suicidal."

"Ah, you hurt me, Erica Eaton. You're everything I want, but you're just beyond my grasp. It's damn frustrating."

"I didn't think I was so frustrating at our previous meetings."

"Sex isn't everything."

Under the circumstances, it was impossible to retort that statement with any wit.

"Anyhow a meeting this week is out of the question. But I urge you to complete the purchase as soon as you possibly can."

"If I can't see you this week, when can I see you?"

"I don't know. Let's not talk about this now."

"There's a lot we have to talk about. Business and . . . and things."

"Please, please don't pressure me."

"I'm sorry. I'm sure there's a lot on your mind now."

"Yes. But, Andy . . ."

"What?"

"We *will* talk about it some other time."

"I know."

"Good-bye."

"I love you."

"Don't."

"I do. I can't help it. Even if I could, I'd still love you."

"Please . . ."

"And you love me."

"I . . ."

"You do! You do. Say it."

"I can't."

"But you love me anyway, don't you? Don't you?"

"Yes."

She slammed the phone down.

Erica returned to the table and began to stuff her mouth with food. Anything to avoid talking. Her parents stared and stared at her.

"My darling," her mother said, "I don't want to lecture you."

"Then don't, please."

"I don't want you to get hurt."

"Mama, I'm an adult. In fact I'm getting close to middle age."

"Don't exaggerate, my sweet. But don't be so headstrong. Look what happened last time."

Erica's gorge rose. It wasn't the first time they blamed her for what happened with Whit. Not that they would ever mention his name. But what could she do? She couldn't argue with them. All they wanted was what was best for her. Besides, what good would it do? How could she convince them that it was best to dump George in favor of Andy? She couldn't even convince herself.

"I'm so tired, Mama. Papa, excuse me, but I think I'll go home now and take a long, hot bath."

She made a hasty getaway, drove home quickly, and breathed a long sigh of relief as soon as she shut the door behind her.

Her eyes were grainy from lack of sleep. Her arms and face stung with sunburn. The muscles she had exercised that weekend chorused their pain and her backside hurt from the bike ride. There was the deep, helpless ache of the first day of menstruation. Her spirit was bruised from George's tongue-lashing and her soul was strafed with guilt when she thought of her parents.

And yet, and yet . . . she felt *wonderful*.

Chapter Twenty-six

From Thisweek *Magazine*, October 26, 1990

COVERSTORY: LIFE-STYLE

The New American Mother
Now Pregnant is Sexy!

Actors and celebrities are often the harbingers of new social trends and attitudes. A case in point: Megastar Melissa John. At 39, John is expecting her first baby, which is typical of the late-bearing baby boomers. Melissa John is, of course, spectacularly well established in her career. In two dozen film roles, ranging from the Virgin Mary in Brandini's classic *Pieta* to the resurrected Scarlett O'Hara in the remake of *Gone With the Wind* to a host of sexy-but-piquant contemporary heroines, Melissa John can take time out for a baby and still expect to return to the screen as a top box-office draw.

Not that she is resting on her laurels. Thoroughly modern Melissa expects to be back at work right after the baby comes, as will thousands of her less-famous expectant sisters. In fact, John's next movie, a comedy with Bette Midler and Dolly Parton, is scheduled to begin shooting just six days after the baby's due date, next April.

Melissa John and her baby are benefiting from the latest medical technology. She has undergone ultrasound testing, as well as amniocentesis, a procedure that can determine birth defects and is routinely recommended for pregnant women over 35. "Not that it matters," says the mother-to-be, "because Paul and I don't believe in abortion in any case. But it is nice to know the baby's sex beforehand."

Now that they know the baby will be a boy, the nursery and layette can be coordinated in the appropriate colors, the fetus can be addressed, *in utero*, by his proper name (Justin), and applications for nursery school, private school, and prep schools can be filled out. "We can't make up our minds about colleges," says Ms. John, not entirely in jest.

Like many of her generation, Melissa John is very health-conscious. "I was always lucky not to have to diet, but now I am eating only healthy foods. It's a drag, but I'm doing it for Justin, to give him the best possible start." John also does an hour of special exercises every day with her personal trainer.

The most trendy aspect of Melissa John's pregnancy is the nontraditional view she takes of the family unit. She is not yet married to the father of her baby, Oscar Winner Paul Tremain (in fact the divorce from husband #3, Cardiologist Sheldon Lederer, is not yet final) and is in no particular hurry to wed. "We're planning a February wedding. I want it to be big and wonderful, with all our friends present, and organizing all the details takes a lot of time. I can't see any reason for us to give up a dream wedding just because I'll be seven months pregnant. I'm having the most exquisite gown made—to look yummy on my great big tummy. Today, pregnant is *sexy.* Don't you think?"

Anyone who sees the lusciously fertile Melissa on our cover this week would have to agree.

Unlike previous generations, where most women expected to have a number of children, *au courant* expecting mothers, having delayed the event to the outer limits of the childbearing years, anticipate very small families. This colors their attitudes toward pregnancy, childbirth, and child rearing.

As Screen Goddess Melissa John says, "It's unlikely that I'll be going through this again, so I want everything to be absolutely *perfect*."[]

Chapter Twenty-seven

New York City
November 20, 1990

E RICA OPENED THE DOOR and immediately slammed it in front of her own face. Quite simply, she couldn't believe her eyes. George had called a management meeting for three, sharp, but she could swear . . .

She flung the boardroom's massive door open again.

SURPRISE!

Rainbow-colored confetti came pouring down from the chandeliers. Lights flashed on and off, party horns blasted. Erica's mouth fell open and stayed open for so long that a piece of pink confetti landed in it.

The boardroom had been transformed. Its high ceiling was completely paved with multihued balloons, and bright pink flower arrangements stood in every corner. An iridescent tablecloth covered the boardroom table, which was set for seven with precious Limoges tea things. There were dainties and dips and, in the center, a silver urn with jeroboams of champagne, and a cake. This was in the form of a large chocolate briefcase, a replica of Erica's own, overflowing not with papers but with spun-sugar flowers.

Erica looked around the room. Her mother was there, Ruthie—so that's where she'd been—Bettina, Cindy, Tangee, and Melissa.

"Which one of you scoundrels is responsible for this abomination?" asked Erica.

Ruthie spoke up. "Nominated for two Academy Awards, this actress . . ."

"Oh, Melissa! I can't believe it. Didn't you just get back from Africa yesterday?"

"Actually three days ago. But so what, it's easy to get things done in this town with a phone call or two."

Melissa looked as haggard as Erica had ever seen her, in other words, still gorgeous. Her pregnancy was barely visible, but it was already difficult, and, Erica was sure, Melissa had given the usual two hundred percent of her energy to the filming of the movie.

"You shouldn't have, Melissa. You need your rest these days. Besides, what's the big rush?"

"Erica, Erica," said Maria Valenta. "You are always saying that, but time goes more quickly than you think. I say to Melissa, I hope this reminds Erica to make a firm plan for a date."

"Hear, hear," came the calls from around the room, much to Erica's embarrassment.

The door cracked open, and a head cautiously extended into the room.

"It's safe to come in," said Tangee. "We only do the human sacrifice at night."

George Steel, looking sheepish, came in.

"Checking up on us?" asked Melissa.

George pretended to be stern. "Just want to make sure you ladies are out of here by six."

"Don't worry, George, we clean up after ourselves," said Maria.

"That's not it," said George, his arm around her small shoulders. An impish gleam warmed his light blue eyes. "I invited your husband to come help me finish off the leftovers."

Laughter and mock derision finally sent him from the room.

Erica could feel the wave of good feeling that went with him.

Melissa frowned. "Maybe we should have had a coed shower, like Cindy's."

Everyone protested vehemently. The party was perfect just as it was.

"What I really wanted to do was surprise you," said Melissa, her face animated with delight.

"Well, you sure did," said Erica. She could not believe what wonderful friends she had. She realized, once again, her special good fortune.

"Ahh," exclaimed Bettina impulsively. "It's the season for love."

"Tell us about it," said Cindy, winking.

Erica marveled at how Cindy had been transformed. You never heard a joke out of her before, much less irony. Had love really given her such confidence?

Bettina blushed and stammered. "Well, Henry and I would like to marry, but how can we? It isn't like you young folks, we have so many obligations."

"To who?" asked Melissa.

"To the business, of course. If we took time out even for a honeymoon, it would be a disaster. And there are problems with a building of that age, and the taxes . . . When things ease up a little, we'll take the time out."

Erica tried not to look ominous. There wasn't going to be a time like that. Henry and Tina were clinging to a dying economic concept. In its present state Goldsmith's could fade into genteel obscurity, or, more likely, collapse within a year or two. But Henry and Tina hadn't asked for her business advice this time, as they so often had before. And this wasn't the proper place for her to try and broach the subject.

"Presents, presents! Unwrap them, Erica," declared Melissa, happy as a child.

The shower gifts were piled on a credenza.

"Biggest first," ordered Melissa.

Erica pulled over the largest package. It was heavy, too.

"From Cindy," read Erica.

Gasps of admiration came upon the viewing of the contents. Exquisite linen sheets, with richly embroidered pillowcases, astonished the women.

Tangee fingered a drawn-thread panel carefully. "Don't bother sleeping on this stuff. Just make your veil out of it."

The next box was smaller, but also heavy. It was from Bettina, a set of five silver frames. Oohs, ahhs, and thanks, again.

"I just wish you all the luck in the world, Erica, and that those frames always be filled with the faces of those you love."

Much cheering of the sentiment, and giggles at the smallest frame, obviously meant for the picture of a baby.

Erica was getting good at gracefully bypassing the hurt.

The third box was also heavy.

"Mama!" She hugged and kissed her mother, the tears flowed.

"Come on," said Melissa, pretty misty herself, "open the present, it might be water soluble."

It was a vanity set of crystal. A covered powder box, a cologne decanter, and a perfume bottle with a silk-tasseled atomizer.

"Papa bought it. He says is the finest workmanship in the world," her mother said proudly.

The cut facets gleamed like diamonds.

The next box was much lighter.

Erica took from the tissue paper, as the others whooped it up: a sheer red chiffon-and-lace bra, matching string bikini panties, and a garter belt.

"Ruthie," Erica asked her secretary, "why so conservative?"

"Look, ever since you came into the office that day with your hair really cool, I figured, hey, she's ready for it! Besides, I love the idea of your being at some tight-assed meeting and knowing that underneath it all, you're wearing *those.*"

"If anything," said Erica with a shimmy. Everyone laughed and passed champagne around.

The package from Tangee was flat. Inside was a brass-on-wood plaque. "The America Award, in honor of Erica Valenta Eaton." Erica looked up for an explanation.

"I've established a fund at our alma mater," said Tangee. "Each year, the most deserving young woman in the senior class will receive a cash prize toward her education."

The women applauded endlessly. Erica hugged Tangee, tears were flowing freely.

"Mine, mine, mine," said Melissa.

Erica picked up the rectangular box. Something clattered gently inside.

When she opened it she found a hanger. A single, dry-cleaners' clothes hanger. Everyone looked at Melissa in expectation.

"When this party is over," she declared dramatically, "I am taking Erica to Kensington's, where the senior fashion consultant awaits us for a complete fashion makeover. We are going to have her colors done, we are going to register all sizes and preferences in a computerized file, and we are going to shop that store till it's *empty*. When I'm through with this gal we're going to plant a major story in *Thisweek*: Erica Eaton, America's Best-Dressed Executive."

After riotous cheering, they fell upon the cake.

When the party was over, Erica and Melissa walked to Kensington's. As many pedestrians paused to stare at Erica's radiant face, as tried to identify Melissa's sunglasses- and fatigue-obscured one.

"Are you sure you want to do this now?" asked Erica. "You must be completely exhausted."

"No, I'm not," insisted Melissa. "Besides, if we put it off, you know very well that you'll weasel out of it. And I've got to get back to L.A. next week. There's a script review of my post-Justin movie, I've got to see my divorce lawyer, and then, I've left Paul all alone for an awfully long time. No man can be trusted indefinitely."

Erica ached to tell someone she could trust about the weekend with Andy. Melissa would not be judgmental—but Melissa's emotional affairs were such a mess now, it seemed unfair to burden her with her own. She decided against it.

"How was Africa?"

"Horrendous. I had the choice between sleeping in a hammock, exposed to the mosquitoes, or sleeping under netting on this straw pallet."

"Didn't they put you up in a hotel?"

"Yes, but it meant driving back and forth in a jeep to location. The bumps made me vomit."

"Melissa, what a nightmare!"

"You're not kidding. Two principal players quit."

"You should have, too."

Melissa stopped dead in her tracks. "What are you talking about? Me, renege on a contract?"

"Melissa, the film is insured. And you're always telling me how they shoot around all kinds of problems."

"I never thought I'd hear those words out of your mouth, Erica Eaton. The film is my reputation, my, my everything. Even if it meant giving birth on a wildlife preserve, I'd never, ever, walk out on a movie."

"Okay, okay. Lighten up. So, how is your sex life these days, if I might ask an old question?"

"I'd rather work a jackhammer with this belly, but my heart belongs to Paul. This is it, Erica. This is really it."

"Oh, yeah?"

"Yes! I mean it. You know, I met Paul once, twenty years ago, when I first came down to the city, and I knew, I just *knew*, we were destined for one another."

"You were a kid then, Melissa," Erica said gently. "Now you're going to have a kid yourself. You've got to look at the world differently."

"What do you mean?"

"Melissa, you are still married to Sheldon, and Paul . . ."

"His divorce is almost final."

"Yes, but he was married for thirty years, raised children, has grandchildren. You can't just ignore those realities with moon-in-June gibberish."

"He cheated on Diana the whole time. And she knew it. *I'm* the only one he'd leave her for, though."

"That's such a childish triumph, Melissa. It isn't worthy of you."

"Erica, *you* lighten up. Haven't you ever heard of plain, simple, unplanned, unweighed, uninhibited love?"

"I've heard about it, but, like the Abominable Snowman, I just don't believe it."

"Come on. How about Cindy Prewitt?"

"That's different. She's young, she's innocent. It's the first time for both of them. It's got a chance at being forever. And look at you, a homebuster, a married woman carrying another man's child." It was hard to keep the disapproval out of her voice.

"Oh no, you don't understand Sheldon. He's totally understanding. The only reason the divorce is taking so long is because we both want to do the most prudent thing financially."

"How can any human being be 'totally understanding' about a mate's cheating on them, then dumping them?"

"Erica, we've always had this comfortable way of life. Sheldon's a dream. It's the reason I married him to start with."

"Oh, that's the reason. I must say I have wondered."

"Well, yes. Life with him has been very comfortable. We both got a lot out of it. But it wasn't love. Now that I've got love, I won't accept second best."

"He's a *man*, Melissa. And not just some Hollywood pretty-boy escort, either, but an important doctor, a world-renowned specialist. You can't just dismiss him like that."

"I'm not dismissing him. It's an amicable divorce. Erica, honey, I love you, but we have two very different personalities, very different needs, and very different taste in men. I could never just wait for Mr. Right and do the proper thing. I've got to live my life with passion. This is the only one I've got."

Erica sighed deeply as they entered Kensington's.

Los Angeles

Diana Tremain's bedroom was dimly shaded, an oasis in the declining day. The shadows flattered Diana. She looked as good as any woman in her mid-fifties, which is to say, not good enough to compete against Melissa at any age. The public forgave Paul Tremain his slightly softened gut, his diminished biceps, his hair, now entirely gray. But the cruel double standard could not forgive Diana a single lump in the thighs, a wrinkle as fine as a hair. Paul understood this and suddenly he felt a poignant sympathy for the woman who had shared the most important years of his life. Diana had been his beautiful bride, his graceful partner, and now, through no fault of her own, she had lost a war no woman could win.

Diana undressed quickly and awaited him. Paul did not linger long. His mind emptied of everything. No world existed except for the narrow one between the crisp cotton sheets.

They knew each other well. Their lovemaking was like that of two great cats. Like two cougars they wrestled and tore at each other.

The growls and hisses of lust rose from the bed like steam. Paul leaned into her, pawed her without consideration of her apparent delicacy. He knew there was no reason for him to hold back from anything he wanted to do. He knew she could take it—and dish it out, too.

In his whole life his cock had never been this hard, he thought.

Diana sucked on his neck as if it were a wedge of juicy orange. He bit her earlobe, harder than he had meant to, but she made no complaint. The ironed sheets grew limp with sweat.

Abruptly, Diana twisted her body. She thrust her muscular, tense buttocks on his taut penis. Suddenly he lost control, like a boy in the backseat at a drive-in. The force of his ejaculation almost propelled him across the bed.

He lay in a trance. The human body is seventy percent fluid, and it felt as if all of it had gushed out of him. There was no way to know how long he stayed in the bed, how many times they made love, or in how many positions. It felt as if he and Diana had been there since the Ice Age and would still be lying there when the sun burned itself out.

Afterwards they embraced leisurely and talked about old times and new events. It was utterly relaxing, talking to someone whom he didn't have to impress, who wouldn't mind if he was boring, who ignored thirty years of image and facade.

He even talked about Melissa, feeling that Diana understood, thinking, even, that she forgave. Her answers were spare, and soothing, and sensible.

"Want to hear something funny, Diana? I'm taking Lamaze lessons."

"You?" she hooted in her ladylike way.

"Yeah, I know. I'm not too crazy about it, but Melissa wants me to be there in the delivery room."

"You sure could have used the training when Tommy was born!"

They laughed about the old memory, the innocent joys of Diana's first pregnancy, the foibles of their firstborn.

Diana stroked his temple absently. "I suppose this baby was a bit of an accident."

"Well . . . you're psychic, Diana. But we're gonna keep him, of course. Melissa is not into abortions. Besides, I kind of like the idea of having a kid at my age. Sort of like being immortal, know what I mean?"

"Yes, I know exactly what you mean."

"I figured you would, Diana. You know, as soon as Melissa told me, my first instinct was to call you. Of course I couldn't. Melissa just wouldn't understand. She's still jealous of you, and a little scared. It's just something she'll have to work out."

"Don't worry about it. She seems like a very secure person—and quite a nonconformist."

"You can say that again. Did you know, we might not get married till after the baby's born! It's crazy, but that's what she wants. What can you do? Woodstock generation."

"Well, it really makes sense, Paul. The situation, after all, could get very messy legally."

"What do you mean, Diana?"

"Oh . . . forget about it. I'm sure nothing will come of it. The important thing is, all of you are happy about the child."

"Of course we are. What do you mean 'all' of us?"

"Well, you and Melissa, naturally. And, I assume—the father."

"What do you mean? She split with Lederer ages ago. I'm the father."

"Are you certain, darling?"

"Well, sure. Melissa and the Doc have never had much of a relationship."

"But what about the other men, honey?"

"What other men?"

"I don't want you to get hurt, dear. You know I still care

deeply about you. Besides, her past escapades don't matter. As long as you are certain the baby is yours."

"Well, of course I'm certain. Reasonably."

"That's the important thing," she said, kissing him gently on the forehead.

Dr. Lederer was just entering the mammoth parking lot of Mount Nebo Medical Center, where he was scheduled for a full afternoon of surgery, when he caught a glimpse of a rose-pink Lotus zooming out the exit.

Caustic enzymes roiled in his stomach. Melissa. The woman who, with the swing of her behind, had destroyed his life. A lifetime of labor, of brilliance, of achievement, and now what was he: a laughingstock. A toy, an idiot dangled around from her fingertips. He had been riding high, so high, before she came into his life like a vampire into a window. Now he looked at the future, and it seemed a bottomless pit of shame and disgrace. He *hated* her.

He hadn't eaten in a long time, but he felt like vomiting. His conscience was making him physically sick. For the first time in his life, he had done something against the best medical interests of another human being.

Dr. Lederer was exactly on time for the first procedure. He was, as far as his colleagues and the nurses were concerned, just about a perfect healer. The scrub nurse apologized and said the patient would not be prepped for another twenty minutes.

Lederer paced nervously. He hated empty spaces in his schedule, and thoughts of Melissa were hot and angry in his mind. The hospital had just installed a computerized filing system. Just a few buttons pushed and he could have a patient report from anywhere in the medical center within seconds. His fingers poised above the terminal keys. It angered him to see that they were shaking. After all, he was a first-rate surgeon, a man of decision.

He typed in his code number and "Mehitabel Jones," the name Melissa used when she wanted to elude the press.

The file whizzed in. Everything looked clean. No one could know that he had tampered with the record. The notes for the morning's checkup by Armbruster showed nothing amiss, other than a touch of sugar.

Lederer snorted. Armbruster, the society obstetrician. If it was his baby he would have gotten her a decent OB-man.

But it wasn't his baby. He owed the cunt nothing. Lederer wiped his sweating face with a handkerchief. It didn't really matter, anyway. The whore proclaimed her pieties everywhere, and she always believed her own press. He could even be considered to be doing her a favor.

He returned the file to the computer's maw. His green scrub suit was drenched in sweat, as if he had just performed a grueling operation.

Now it was time to clear his mind, to rid it of his own pain and concentrate solely on his patient. The afternoon's surgery would be complex and delicate. As always, he would give his patient his all, every resource of his body, mind, and soul.

His teeth were clenched so hard that his jaw ached right through the operation.

Chapter Twenty-eight

A T 11 P.M. Erica was not yet asleep, but the ringing of the phone frightened her.

It was the emergency room at Roosevelt Hospital. Could she come down right away? Her employee, Ruth Prewitt, had overdosed on a near-lethal cocktail of heroin and cocaine.

My fault, thought Erica, as she rushed to get to the hospital. I just smiled about the marijuana all this time, pretended it wasn't really a drug. I just cared about her performance on the job. I never really looked to see why she smoked so much pot. I never saw that she was in pain.

The doctor met her in front of Ruthie's room.

"She's sleeping now. The paramedics found your number at her phone. She'll be okay, but it would be a good idea to contact her nearest relative."

"Why don't I do that now? I'll call her sister. They're very close."

Cindy was there within ten minutes. She fell on her knees at Ruthie's bed.

"Please, God," she prayed. "Please don't take my baby sister from me."

"I'll wait outside." said Erica, leaving the room.

Ruthie's eyes opened slightly. Her hand reached over to Cindy's, which were clenched in prayer. Cindy started.

"Oh, baby, oh, honey. Why did you do this? Why didn't you come to me?"

"I'm sorry," said Ruthie, her voice a little girl's whisper. "I'm sorry, Earline. I have always been such a trial to you."

"Oh, no, baby, no! You've been the best thing in my life. You still are."

"No, no. And now I'm screwing things up for you and Jean-Luc. I'm so sorry."

"Oh, baby, he loves you, too. He wants you to be well."

"All the shame of your trash kin, now a drug addict, too."

"No, baby, don't talk that way. You'll get well, you'll see. You'll do us proud."

"I didn't mean to do this now. It was an accident."

"I know, angel, we'll get you well. We will. I promise. I always took care of you before, didn't I?"

"Yeah, you did. You did.

"You know, Earline, I never can close my eyes without seeing you put your body between me and Daddy. Or taking the blame for me with Ma."

"Oh no. Forget that, it's all dead and gone, the past. Think of happy things. Think of now. Your maid-of-honor dress, isn't that just the prettiest you ever . . ."

"Every time I close my eyes I see Daddy raping you. Ma hitting you."

Tuesday, December 18

The Peninsula–New York was a ravishing but largely undiscovered hotel in the heart of the city. Its beauty and obscurity made it a perfect setting for the secret meeting that was to occur at seven that morning.

George Steel had turned thumbs down on inviting Carl Connaught to his sprawling apartment in the River House. He was afraid that the rooms might be bugged, either by Connaught or by Nox people. Nor could he meet at the Plaza, the Pierre, or—much less—"21," where he was a member of the Breakfast Club.

Erica was commissioned to find the perfect, safe venue. She

felt she had done a good job of it. Indeed, she was the only one, other than George and Connaught, who even knew that the meeting was to take place.

Ever since that disconcerting Labor Day weekend, George had been going out of his way to include her in the very highest Nox negotiations. Now Erica and George would be the team to represent Nox, to determine the fate of a great American corporation and the hundreds of thousands of people who worked for it, in the secret showdown with Sir Carl Connaught.

For the occasion, they had rented the Presidential Suite, a palatial apartment. They had stayed up late the night before, discussing what might happen. First George had role-played Connaught, while Erica battled for Nox, and then they reversed roles. But the possibilities had not been exhausted.

"What if he's really not shooting for Nox," said Erica. "He hasn't filed with the Securities and Exchange Commission. I hope we aren't the ones to be giving him ideas."

"No," said George, his lips set grimly. "He wants Nox, all right. If we wait till he makes his intentions official with the SEC, it will be too late to do anything about them. He'll already have made his move, and he couldn't pull out without losing face."

Erica sighed and tugged her jacket down for the twentieth time. She was nervous about meeting the ogre Connaught. But at least she had the option of keeping her mouth shut, while George faced the music. It would be one hell of a learning experience, that was for sure.

She tugged at her jacket again, which was silly. The black wool gabardine fit perfectly, as did the cream silk blouse with the cowl collar, all gleanings from the guided shopping spree at Kensington's. She was the picture of quiet authority. Erica twisted her only ornament, the five-carat solitaire George had surprised her with the week before. The diamond was close to perfect, yet discreet in its plain platinum setting.

"Calm down," said George. "It's only a quarter to. And Connaught is not an early riser." He laughed. He was the host, so he could call the shots, calculated to unbalance his opponent at every possible turn.

She made another inspection of the premises. The dining table was magnificently laid, it promised a banquet for three. The suite's dining room was larger than the one in her own expensive co-op.

Not a blossom had wilted on any of the floral displays. An enormous one in the entry sported orchids, proteus, flowering plum, and white amaryllis. Erica fought down thoughts of Andy.

The butler announced Connaught.

Connaught strode in briskly. He could not have topped five feet five. The two towering officers of Nox were almost embarrassed by the difference between their physical stature and the Englishman's.

Yet Connaught assessed his hosts with sharp, quick, unafraid takes, like a small but agile animal that has come across some lumbering predators in a forest clearing. He was not intimidated.

"Sir Carl," said George, "may I present my fiancée, Erica Eaton."

"Ah, the very charming Miss Eaton," said Connaught, giving her hand a little squeeze.

"Please. Erica," said Erica, graciously, wondering if "fiancée" and "charming" were quite the right descriptions for someone shouldering a major part of a thirty-billion-dollar company.

So this was Carl Connaught. Of course they had seen his pictures, read endless articles about him, even seen secret videotapes and the reports of private investigators, but the man himself exuded an unmistakable presence. In the flesh he was a true—and frightening—original. Erica could tell that George, too, felt the man's unique impact.

"Would you care for a menu, Sir Carl?" said George, playing the host to the hilt.

"No, thank you. I never take breakfast."

"Clear the table, please," George said to the butler, who immediately and invisibly removed the place settings and then vanished.

Erica wondered: was this a bullshit power play? Or did

Connaught watch his waist? He probably ate conglomerates for breakfast.

She sized him up shamelessly. It didn't take a genius to conclude that Carl Connaught was greedy. But greed was an inadequate term. There wasn't enough money, enough property, enough material on the planet to sate him.

Connaught pulled a gold cigarette case out of his pocket, then a matching gold lighter. He toyed with these, then opened the case. He was in no particular rush to smoke. He had no minor compulsions to vie with his major one. At last he chose a cigarette. His initials were embossed in gold on the filter.

Erica did not smile, although even *she* knew this little conceit was pathetic and tacky.

Sir Carl Connaught. A lord by Her Majesty's decree. But few were fooled. All the barbers and tailors and speech tutors and image consultants couldn't hide what he was. A Cockney, a scrapper. One of those English who don't garden, don't sit by cozy fires, aren't related, by even the most painstaking genealogy, to the current or any other royal line. Original name, Cuthbert Gooney. Identity of father, unknown. Four wives, three children, innumerable mistresses. Intimate with none of them.

Sir Carl's greed was too great to be one man's. It was a rage that had been growing for hundreds of generations. The Saxon slave dragging paving stones for the Romans' roads, the serf herding the Norman master's swine, the fish-and-chips man burning his fingers making snacks for the German tourists who had blitzed him, their hungers collected in Carl Connaught's belly.

"Well," said George Steel, with a joyless grin. "We've a busy day ahead of us, so let's get down to business, shall we?"

There was a hint of an English accent in Steel's words, as if he was so concentrated on Carl Connaught that he had begun to identify with him.

"By all means," said the raider.

"We're aware of your inquiries in the investment community, and of your interest in a takeover of Nox," stated George.

"Oh?" said Connaught, raising an eyebrow.

He said nothing further and then Erica knew beyond any doubt that Connaught was indeed hell-bent on acquiring her company. She felt her stomach sink.

Steel had been standing, now he seated himself at the dining table and steepled his hands.

"I've asked you here today, Sir Carl, to tell you one thing about Nox Industries, Incorporated."

"And what would that be, George?"

Steel leaned across the table. His hands were splayed on the polished surface, his face was inches away from Connaught's.

"Well, Sir Carl," he said in the most measured and modulated of tones, "you can't fucking have it."

Connaught waited till his opponent straightened up, then he said, in tones just as measured and modulated, "I can have anything I can pay for. And I can *fucking well* buy Nox."

Erica swallowed. It was true. It was a documented fact that Connaught had a war chest of 6.5 *billion*. Since assuming operations in the United States he hadn't once been thwarted in his efforts to acquire a company.

"Ah, but money isn't enough, is it, Sir Carl?"

Connaught did not respond. He didn't know what Steel was driving at. Both he and Steel knew that money *was* enough. He waited.

"In this country we have certain standards, particularly for *foreigners* who seek control of our vital industries."

Connaught laughed. "Oh that. That's nothing. We ran into that objection when we bought into oil and cement interests. But nothing serious ever came of it—and I've some very good legal people to take care of these things. Besides, if your government ever put me to the wall, I could always apply for citizenship in this fair country. I'll warrant that I can prove to be a useful member of this society—or as useful as the next fellow in this line of work," he said dryly.

"Our Constitution does not permit citizens to keep their foreign titles."

"Pity. But one can live with such restrictions."

"Our laws also prohibit the naturalization of convicted felons."

"You're talking through your hat, George. My enterprises

are clean as a whistle. I even make the chauffeurs pay parking fines promptly."

"Yes, you also made your boy Swarski do time before he could talk about your role in the biggest insider trading scam Wall Street has ever known."

Connaught blanched. The mocking smile on his lips fell away and flew to George's mouth.

"What are you saying, Steel? Swarski was convicted last year, and his plea bargain revealed the whole plot, as well as all of his confederates."

"His confederates, yes. But not his boss man. Not the man with all the money to finance Swarski's schemes."

"That's nonsense! Swarski financed everything himself. He's a genius at financing . . ."

"He's a genius at *obtaining* financing, at hiding its circuitous routes. But someday someone will follow the money and keep following it—to the Caymans, and Zurich, and eventually, to *London*. And they'll find that the buck doesn't end with John Swarski."

"I don't have to sit here and listen to your insane allegations," snapped Connaught.

He picked up his smoking things and marched to the door without good-byes.

"Have a nice day," said George Steel, as the door hissed shut.

Erica waited a few seconds, until she was sure that Connaught was truly gone.

"George, I can't believe it. How did you know that Connaught was behind the Swarski scandal? I didn't see that in any of the intelligence reports. There wasn't an inkling of it anywhere."

"I *didn't* know it. I followed a hunch as far as it would go. And I struck pay dirt. That son of a bitch. Can you believe it? I wonder how much he made out of that trading? And I bet Swarski got a nice piece of change for taking the rap."

"Well, it doesn't matter. The important thing is you did the impossible. You held off Attila the Hun. He'd never dare make a bid on Nox now."

"You're wrong, Erica. All I did was scare him for a few

minutes. By the time he gets off the elevator he'll realize that all I did was guess right. I'm sure some of the boys at the SEC also guessed right. But there's no trail. Connaught covered everything up perfectly. He's too smart to pull something like this in a half-assed way. And all the good guesses in Sherlock Holmes mean shit without proof."

"What does that mean?"

"It means Connaught will be tying his napkin on again, ready to dine on Nox."

Erica looked out the great windows, down to Fifth Avenue, faintly stirring at dawn. "So. It's hopeless. The company is done for."

"No it isn't," said George, taking both her hands gently. "There's still a way out."

"I can't see how."

"By taking the company private, darling. By beating Connaught at his own game."

"An internal buyout?"

"Precisely."

"But, George, it means coming up with, what, a *billion* dollars, plus? Borrowing billions more?"

George laughed. "You know what they say in the government, 'A billion here, a billion there, and pretty soon you're talking about real money.'"

"Come *on*, George!"

His face turned deadly serious. He pulled her toward him and almost spat in her face.

"*I can do it.* But it isn't going to be easy and it isn't going to be pretty. Do you have the balls to stick it out with me, Erica?"

"You know I do, George. You know I'll do whatever has to be done to save Nox from a hostile takeover."

George smiled and patted her twice on the cheek. "That's my big, bright, beautiful baby."

He laced the fingers of his hand through hers. "I'm feeling good, honey. I'm feeling *really* good today."

They had strolled over to the main bedroom. He pulled her down to the bed, which had already been made. "I feel good; let's make love."

Erica grimaced involuntarily.

George stared at her. "What's the matter? I've been getting a lot of arctic air blowing from you lately."

"George, I'm exhausted. And Sunday night I was up till four at the hospital. Ruthie had an . . . an . . . accident."

"But it's been going on for a lot longer than that."

"I . . . I . . ."

Suddenly George stood up. "I have a feeling I know what the problem is, Erica. You're feeling insecure, aren't you? We've announced our engagement but we haven't really made plans. I know you women, you aren't really happy till you're married. There's a part of you that thinks I'm going to leave you stranded at the church. But, darling, you can depend on me. I intend to go through with it. I want you to set a date today. I want you to fix us a real extravaganza, no holds barred, okay?"

"But, George, we're going to be up to our ears in the buyout, how can I work on anything . . ."

"Shhh. Enough. We're gonna have it all. That's a promise. Now let's get our stuff together and get out of here."

"George, I'm so strung out. Let me stick around a little. We haven't even used the Jacuzzi. Did you see the gorgeous tub they have?"

"Yeah, this place is a beauty. Maybe for our wedding night, huh?"

"That would be lovely." She kissed him on the cheek.

George talked as he packed, laying plans for raising the astronomical sums to buy out Nox.

"Say, this place is really something. They don't even nail in the hair dryer." He unplugged the hair dryer and dropped it into his overnight bag.

"George!" scolded Erica.

"Baby," he said as he left, "you've got to learn to think like the rich."

Erica undressed and filled the great marble bathtub. The master bath had the best view in the entire suite. The room was almost encased in glass and it offered a panoramic view of Fifth Avenue. It was like bathing in the open, in one of the busiest places in America.

The sun had now come up in full force and it bounced upon

the Art Nouveau and mansard roofs of some of the finer old buildings of the "neighborhood."

Erica sank back with a sigh. The scented, swirling steam would soon melt away some of the terrible pressure that had been laid upon her.

The phone rang.

She moaned, but she picked up the bathroom extension on the second ring.

"There's a gentleman to see you, Mrs. Eaton," said the concierge.

Erica sat up in sheer surprise. "Who is it?"

"A Mr. Ferdinand."

Erica stood dripping and furious at the door. "Andy! How on earth did you find me here?"

"Ruthie told me."

"Ruthie!"

"Yes, I just saw her at the hospital. That was a close call. But I'm sure she'll get some therapy now."

Erica realized that Andy had been right about Ruthie all along. He had taken the drugs seriously from the beginning. She now regretted having laughed at all the medical monographs about the dangers of marijuana that he was always sending to her secretary.

Ruthie realized that about him now, she realized he was a friend. That's why she had told him about the hotel, a confidence Ruthie would never reveal to a simple business acquaintance. She hoped that Ruthie had never sensed what was between her and Andy.

"I've told you we can't meet again, never . . ."

"Oh beautiful," breathed Andy, "fabulous, mind-blowing . . ."

"These flowers are something, aren't they?" said Erica, stroking the giant arrangement.

"What flowers?"

Erica realized that her robe had opened. "Oh, come in and shut the door.

"Now, Andy, I mean it, we can't go on meeting, it's courting disaster, and . . ."

Andy ignored her words. He looked around at the living room and whistled low. "What does this place run, anyway?"

"Twenty-five hundred bucks a night."

"Whew. And Georgie sprang for it?"

"Nox paid. It's a business expense."

"Oh, sure."

"I mean it. God, Andy, you have no idea. All hell is coming down."

"Tell me about it."

"I can't. It's top secret."

"Hey, I came here to tell you my hard-luck story, you can tell me yours."

"What kind of troubles can you have? You just started the company."

"The chief executive just quit."

"Screw him. Get someone else."

"Erica, I just got here a couple of weeks ago. I don't even know where to get a decent cheeseburger."

"Ask Bob and Frank."

"Don't remind me of them. Why didn't *I* stay in the Golden State? The camellias are about to open and I'm freezing my ass off."

"Still hate New York, huh?"

"It's beginning to grow on me. Kind of like tinea pedis."

"What's that?"

"Athlete's foot."

"Oh, you're so gross."

"My beloved, you must get more in touch with living things, with the great world that hums and throbs around us."

"Stop talking dirty. What's really happening with the company?"

"I'm not happy with the way things are going."

"You've only been at it a few weeks. It'll take time."

"But I hate flying back and forth for all those meetings with lawyers and accountants . . ."

"You've got really good people, Andy. Your attitude is poor."

"I don't mind the *people*, it's those damn yellow power ties that make me puke. I belong in a lab, I want to do research. This financial stuff is pulling me apart."

"Andy, you don't know what pressure is." Erica's voice dropped to a whisper. "Do you know who Carl Connaught is?"

"Short British guy? Has a zillion dollars?"

"Yes."

"Don't know him."

"*Andy*. He's going to attempt a takeover of Nox. But you know what? George Steel and I are going to beat him to it."

"How?"

"The same way Connaught would. Beg a little, steal a little, and borrow, borrow, borrow."

"I don't get it. Why go through all the trouble? If Connaught wants it, why not let him have it?"

"Oh, Andy! If Connaught takes over the company it will be the death of Nox. To finance those immense loans he's going to have to sell off parts of the corporation. It'll be like lopping off arms and legs. Nox would never survive it."

"Well, how will *you* finance the loans?"

"By streamlining, by increasing efficiency, profitability. George and I *know* the company, and we care about it, the way you care about a baby. We'd never let it get hurt."

"It's not a baby, Erica. You can't pretend it's the same thing, you can't relate to it that way."

"You don't understand, Andy. You don't speak my language. George Steel does. That's why, in the end, he and I are going to make it; so please don't screw things up for me.

"I'm meeting a friend for lunch. I've got to get dressed."

Andy refused to leave. He followed Erica into the bedroom as she put out her clothes on the bed.

"I'm starving," he said, "I haven't had any breakfast. Mind if I have some of this stuff," he said, pointing at a towering bowl of fruit.

"You might as well. Otherwise they'll throw it out."

"You and me, buddy," said Andy, addressing a Granny Smith apple.

"Look at the color of this thing. That reminds me, whatever happened to those earrings?"

"I threw them out."

"You're lying."

"What of it?

"Oh, Andy, Andy. Please don't ruin my life. Not now. Not when I finally got it together."

"Oh yeah, together. Tell me something, Erica, since you guys spent a fortune on this suite, tell me, did you make love in it?"

"That's none of your business!"

"No, you didn't. That's clear. That's very clear."

"We were *working.*"

"All night? In a twenty-five-hundred-dollar love nest above Fifth Avenue? What happens when the honeymoon is *over?*"

Out of the blue, Erica began to cry.

"Oh, honey. I'm so sorry. I didn't mean to hurt you."

He sat down on the bed next to her and held her in his comforting farmer's arms.

"Hey, how about an apple?" he said.

She emerged from his embrace. "An apple a day keeps the doctor away."

"I'm not that kind of doctor."

He laid her gently down on the bed.

"Let me show you just what sort of treatments I offer."

He parted her robe. She didn't stop him. He parted her legs. She did not resist.

"*Andy,*" she shouted, "what the hell are you doing?"

"Shhhh . . ."

She moaned and groaned as he caressed her, back and forth, back and forth, without varying the speed, without varying the pressure of the polished green apple.

"No-o, do-ont" changed to "Please, please, harder, *harder.*

"God, Andy, you're such a pervert. Harder. Oh, oh. *Please* get undressed. This can't go on. It . . . Oh, oh!

"It, geeez . . . oh . . . can't . . . Andy, Andy, andy-andyandy . . . ANDY!"

"That was amazing," she sighed, sprawling back on the bed.

She looked at Andy with love in her eyes.

He brought the slick, glistening fruit to his face. It exuded the perfume of apples and the musk of Erica.

He bit into it, sucking the juices of it.

Chewing heartily, he stripped off his clothes. Soon he was on top of her, grounding her with his weight, warming her with his tingling vitality.

"And now," he said, "would you care to try the banana?"

Afterwards, they slept a little. When they awoke, he kissed her hair and the inside of her elbow, where the skin was so delicate, and the inside of her wrist, where the veins flowed clear as mountain streams.

And then he saw the ring, and he dropped her hand as if it were a hot coal.

"What of it?" snapped Erica, adjusting the ring on her finger.

"I always thought platinum was a cold, cruel metal without any charm."

"Really? Well, this is exactly to my taste, thank you. George took my mother along to Tiffany's to help him choose."

"Awwww."

"Stop it, Andy. It means a lot to me that George gets along with my parents."

"Why don't you introduce *me* to them? Back in Idaho I impressed the hell out of my dates' dads and moms."

"Don't be ridiculous. How could I introduce you, you're my lov—"

"Your lover? I like that."

"No. You're a mistake. A detour. And I'm never going to see you again after today. Do you hear me?"

"I hear things you aren't even saying, Erica."

"Oh, leave me alone, Andy. You ruin everything. Just look what you've done to my suit, and I've got lunch at the Four Seasons."

"Yeah? You think I'm such a lowlife? So what is it, masochism that keeps driving me back to you. Or is it something that I see in those green, green eyes."

"Look, I'd be the first to admit that you're . . ."

"Lovable, funny, smart, good-natured, well educated, dependable, from a fine family, hung like a horse . . ."

"Watch your language."

"It's true, isn't it?"

"Well . . . I'll admit you're . . . adept."

"Oh, wow. Can I put that in my advertising? Picture this: 'Erica Eaton, best lay in the Fortune 500, has called Dr. Andy Fairchild *adept!*' But enough of this merriment. Is the shower in this joint big enough for the two of us?"

"Oh, Andy, take a look at the bathroom! It's the most incredible thing."

"Jesus, this looks like something Roman emperors used for slow, painless suicides."

"Don't be morbid. What does that switch do? Ack! Stop it, stop it!"

"Hey, this is great. I always wanted to be a fireman."

"Andy! My hair is soaking. Oh my God. What am I going to do?"

"You can dry it in five minutes."

"There isn't any hair dryer."

"For twenty-five-hundred smackers a night they don't give you a hair dryer? Well, I've had it with this dive. Next time we stay at the Howard Johnson's."

"They had one, of course. But, uh, George took it."

"He *took* it. George Steel, captain of industry, the guy who's going to raise a trillion dollars like Lazarus from the dead, *took* the hair dryer. He ripped it off? He pocketed it? He lifted it? He perpetrated petty—and I mean petty—larceny? He *stole* it?

"Oh boy, Erica. Why don't you chuck this Farley and marry me? I'll take your mom to K mart and buy you the biggest, most expensive hair dryer in the store. That's a promise."

"Enough, Andy."

He whispered in her ear. "After that I'll go down on you and blow your brains out.

"It's your choice, sister. The cocksman or the thief."

Chapter Twenty-nine

T HE ORANGE SUNLIGHT that had bounced off the green copper roofs of the dowager buildings and into the Presidential Suite had made it look like a brighter day than it was. From that vantage, most days were. At ground level, however, all seemed gray. It was the municipal color of New York. Ash-gray streets, pigeon-gray buildings, gunmetal skies.

There was a thin, mean wind blowing, and it cut into Erica's wet hair. She hunkered deep into the collar of her chinchilla, and was glad she had only a few blocks to go, because at lunch hour you couldn't get a cab on Fifth Avenue for love or money.

Weather like this always reminded Erica of looking for a job. She looked at the faces around her. The harried ones were determined to finish their Christmas shopping, but the haggard ones, she imagined, were looking for work.

How many more people, she wondered, would be looking for work when the feeding frenzy at Nox was over? Would she be one of them?

"Girl, you got too much mousse in your hair," was how Tangee greeted her.

"It's not mousse, it's wet."

"I didn't know you corporate types slept this late."

Erica laughed mysteriously. "Well, it's a long story. Maybe I'll get around to it during lunch."

They ordered, they chatted, they nodded to acquaintances, they ate.

"You on drugs, Erica?"

"What? Of course not. I don't think that's funny at all."

"Well, you're acting mighty strange."

Erica leaned over the table. "I have a secret," she whispered.

Tangee leaned over the table, too, to hear better.

"I'm having an affair with another man."

"Is it anyone I know?" whispered Tangee.

"No. Nobody knows him, or of him. You're the first person I ever breathed a word to."

"I don't know if an 'affair' is technically possible if you're not married. And why are we whispering?"

"Someone could be listening."

They looked around them. Everyone was engrossed in conversation. The long, draped chiffon curtains undulated with the room's gentle air currents.

Whispering *was* silly, but Erica was determined to keep her voice very low. This information could be worth plenty to Carl Connaught, and other potential blackmailers too numerous to think of.

"I don't get it," said Tangee. "Steel is everything you always wanted in a man, you say, but you're seeing another guy on the side?"

"Hey, Tangee. The men do it all the time. They think of women in terms of madonna and whore. Why can't we think in those terms?"

"Well, most women have to think of men in terms of rent and groceries. It's a bit of a leap. Besides, you've always said *George* was a good lover, physically."

"He is. But with Andy I get to escape to another world. Someplace without obligations, without responsibilities. Someplace I can be ha . . . in a fantasy."

"You were going to say 'happy.'"

"In a manner of speaking," Erica admitted grudgingly.

"What's he look like?"

"Gorgeous. But short. And he's very young. And believe me, he's never going to make any serious money."

"But your eyes light up when you talk about him, and not for the other dude."

"It must be the naughtiness of having a lover."

"Maybe it's love."

Erica shifted uncomfortably in her chair. "Maybe it is. So what?"

"Does it happen to you so often, girl, that you can shrug it off?"

"Come on, Tangee. You're the one who was always crusading against romance, and your book calls it a trap for women, doesn't it? I happen to agree with you."

"That was romance, this is love. Isn't it?"

"You're the English professor with the fine points of semantics. I'm just a corporate gnome in a green eyeshade. All I know is the bottom line. This thing with Andy has been a lot of fun, but now it's got to stop and I'm going to stop it."

"Why? It sounds like you've got the proverbial good thing going."

"It was fun while it lasted but now it could get dangerous. I feel rotten putting one over on George. And George is not a guy you can put something over on for long. In fact, it's incredibly lucky that he hasn't caught on before this. I shouldn't push it. Besides, Tangee, I'm really getting *married*. We're setting a date and everything. Time to stop futzin' around.

"Say, that reminds me. Can I ask you something? This is something I've always wanted to do. You know, I tried to find you before my first marriage, but I couldn't. In retrospect, that was lucky. Now I can ask you to be with me at a true watershed in my life.

"Tangerine White, will you be my maid of honor?"

"Hey, Miss Erica, the honor is all mine. That is, if you really intend to go through with it."

"Oh, I do," said Erica, her chin raised in determination. "This is going to be a great wedding."

After lunch Erica stopped at a pay phone. She dialed George.

"How are things going?" she asked.

George started the loud promotional tape. From the sound of his voice she could tell that he was cupping the phone in his hand.

"Where are you calling from?" he whispered furtively.

"A pay phone."

"Good. Listen, don't come into the office today."

"Why?"

"I've called Madeline in. And Coby may be in later."

"I understand. Good luck, honey."

"I make my luck."

Although Madeline Knox Steel nursed an abiding personal resentment of her ex-husband, she didn't let it get in the way of business. George was still entrusted with the management of her financial affairs. Her brother, Cockburn, having challenged George Steel several times—and lost each time—had retired to breeding thoroughbreds on his vast farm in Kentucky. Between the two of them, Madeline and Coby owned more than a third of the stock in Nox. Controlling that stock would be a major block to Connaught's takeover bid.

Erica knew she had to stay out of their way, and she had every confidence that George would handle the matter smoothly.

She didn't know what to do with herself. It had been years since she had had the experience of killing time during a workday. She felt profoundly uneasy. Without knowing where she was going, Erica kept walking.

It was like an ancient instinct, the route she took down Fifth Avenue's east side. Many of the stores of her youth were gone, yet she stopped at their sites, the way she had, eons ago, when she went "shopping" with her mother.

Before she knew it, she had stopped in front of Goldsmith's. *Good heavens. I really am a bride. I actually need a wedding dress.*

The brass doors opened before her.

"Why, hello, Ms. Eaton. How may I help you?" said the woman at the entry. A computer winked at her side.

"Is Mrs. Marshall in?"

As they were speaking, Bettina herself burst through the salon doors.

"Erica, what brings you in in the middle of the work day?"

"Well, I need a wedding gown. And everything else."

"All right! And about time, too. So," said Bettina, labeling a new portfolio "Eaton-Steel," "when is the wedding planned for?"

"Ahhhh . . . June!"

"When in June?"

"I don't know."

"Where will it be held?"

"I don't know."

"Daytime or evening?"

"Hmmm. Day, I guess."

"Will it be in a church, or a hotel, or a restaurant? A garden?"

"Gee, I really haven't thought about that."

"It's very important to make arrangements for the venue. For one thing, many of the choicest places are booked as much as a year in advance. Especially for June. And the location has a great deal to do with the formality of the event—which largely determines the type of dress you will want."

"Oh, I already know *exactly* what dress I want."

"Really?"

"Yes. It was in the left window in, oh, spring of 1971."

Bettina laughed. "So many people have those memories, and I've got records of the windows. But I'm sure you'd be very disappointed if you saw the dress today."

"All right, then. I'll tell you how I remember it, and perhaps we can have something made up like the *dream* of that gown."

"Go ahead, I'm taking notes."

"Okay, Bettina, it's like this. Made of this very light, very shiny silk."

"Charmeuse."

"Whatever. Anyway, the skirt is full, with swags caught up in big ribbon bows, with silk roses in the middle of each."

"I hear you."

"The top is cut low . . ."

"Not too low."

"No, no décolletage. But off the shoulder. And there are ribbons and roses on the sleeves, too."

"Got it. I know just the designer for you. I'll have her do some sketches."

"And the headdress."

"Keep it simple."

"The hell I will. Have you ever seen those Russian peasant crowns? That's what I want, with pearls and stuff. And a veil that goes from here to Piscataway."

"Erica, I have to advise you. There isn't any stigma to a second wedding anymore. The white dress and everything else are entirely in order. But the one exception is the veil. It really isn't done. Not when both bride and groom have been married before."

"Bettina, we have a very large legal department at Nox. There must be dozens of lawyers in it. Some of the best eagles in the business."

"I don't understand."

"The veil. In case someone wants to sue me."

"Piscataway veil," Mrs. Marshall said, as she wrote.

"And nice, medium-low heels. Ten and a half A."

"Check. How about the colors?"

"Something hot. Red, orange."

"Persimmon?"

"Sure. Persimmon satin tablecloths, with gold lace on top."

"Attendants?"

"One. Something sophisticated. Tangee's not a kid anymore, either."

"Maybe, apricot chiffon?"

"Maybe. And my mother in ice blue, please. I don't care if it clashes with the whole scheme, she looks good in ice blue."

"No problem."

The phone rang. Bettina jumped at it, catching it before the end of the first ring.

She listened, saying nothing. Her lips tightened, she nodded. "I see," she said, and put the receiver back on the hook.

She apologized for the interruption, then shook herself back into work mode.

"Any thoughts about flowers?"

"I don't know . . . roses, I suppose."

"Yes, there are nice roses in that color range, 'Tropicana,' 'Mojave,' 'Sundowner.' There are marvelous lilies, too, all up and down the yellow-orange spectrum. And gerberas . . . "

"What?"

"Gerberas. They're daisylike, very clean . . ."

"I know what they are. I don't want any at my wedding."

"All right. I think I have a general idea about what you'd like, Erica. I'm going to get to work with the designer, and I'd like you to set an exact time and place for the wedding."

"I'll get cracking. And thank you, Bettina."

"My pleasure, dear."

"It sure is different from last time."

Even with Erica introducing the subject, Bettina refused to rehash the mistakes of the past. "This time it will be perfect, Erica."

There was a sudden rapping on the door.

"Sorry to interrupt you, Mrs. Marshall, but this is urgent."

"What is it?"

"Svetlana Ivanova, the ballerina?, has just announced her engagement to Konstantin Skorpios, the shipping heir. When can she come in for a consultation?"

"She can't."

"But Mrs. Marshall, Svetlana Ivanova . . ."

"It doesn't matter. No new clients as of last Friday. You are to make no exceptions."

With tears in her eyes, the assistant closed the door.

"Do you want to talk about this?" Erica asked.

Bettina shook her head, not trusting herself to speak for a while.

"I can't . . . Henry . . ."

"I understand," said Erica. She had known this was coming. The end of Goldsmith's. Thank God Bettina would still be taking care of her wedding.

"Well, I've got to get going," said Erica, saying good-bye.

"By the way, Bettina? Those gerberas?"

"Yes?"

"Maybe just one or two in my bouquet."

Chapter Thirty

January 6, 1991

MELISSA TRAVELED as she always did, in the entire first row of the coach section of the plane. This way she had plenty of room to stretch out—far more than in first class— and it almost eliminated the gawkers. Most of the budget travelers did not pass by the first row, and the few who did just couldn't believe that a celebrity like Melissa John would travel in steerage. At most she would be bothered by one or two passengers who would comment on her remarkable resemblance to the movie star.

When going coast to coast, Melissa would wrap herself up in a blanket and take a nap the minute the seat belt sign dimmed. But there was no sleep for her today.

Men. The dirty bastards.

First and foremost, Paul Tremain. She could just kill him. She could just kill *herself* for ever starting a stupid affair with that lowlife. It was unbelievable that she had ever consented to marry him. And the darkest secret within her was her regret in having conceived a child by him. The worm!

She shivered with fury when she thought of the way Paul had sashayed in that day, innocent as some of his fifties' romantic comedies, and said to her, with that fucking *lilt* to his voice: "Say, honey, is Justin, you know, really *my* baby?"

She had been so stunned, she didn't quite realize what he

was asking, and had casually answered, "Darling! The two of us will always be your babykinses."

He hadn't said anything to that, but later that day, as she dragged him to yet another of those shops, adding to her hoard of Porthault crib sheets and cashmere booties, he'd asked it again, with a bit less of his professional insouciance and a bit more insistence. "Am I the baby's father, or what?"

Well of course the Archbitch Diana had set him up to it; Paul didn't have either the imagination or the balls to ask it all by himself.

It was then she recognized just how infantile he was. She began to realize all his faults, and they started adding up like figures on a calculator.

Item: He was childish and irresponsible. You wouldn't believe that he had three grown children. They must have grown up all by themselves. The whole time she was pregnant Paul hadn't once asked her how she was feeling. When she pointed that out, he just said, well, he assumed she was seeing doctors and nutritionists and everything so they must be taking good care of her. He had dropped out of Lamaze classes after one lesson.

Denying his own fatherhood was just the last straw. He was too selfish to let anyone into his life. Including *her*, obviously.

Item: He was untrustworthy. They weren't even married yet and already his eyes were wandering. Twice she'd seen that twat in the spandex jumpsuit in his dressing room. Well, nobody screwed around on Melissa John, nobody. There were still a couple of hundred million men out there who would be only too happy to devote themselves to her exclusively.

Not, of course, that he actually preferred Miss Herpes to her. It was a symptom of his fear of aging. Which brought up . . .

Item: He was not as young as he used to be. Still clinging to the PR image of himself as America's eternal golden-haired boy. Not to be cruel, but he did have a gut that felt like a plucked chicken. And those darling curls that had turned gray on his chest weren't nearly so cute in the real-life close-up.

But the worst item of all was that he was goddamn boring.

The man was so *conventional*. Why didn't he and Diana do a remake of the "Ozzie and Harriet Show"?

It was all over with Paul Tremain.

Not that she was rushing into any other relationship. Hell, she'd had it up to here with men. What did they ever bring you but suffering.

Even the good ones, the dependable ones. Sheldon Lederer. He'd called her up and asked to see her one evening at his house. She had assumed it was about the divorce.

When she arrived, no one answered the bell. But the door was open and she walked in. There, in the entrance hall, hanging from the chandelier by a sturdy Mark Cross belt . . . She should stop this. She should try to erase that scene from her brain.

Why did he do it? A doctor can easily get drugs, do himself in neatly and painlessly, if all he wants is to die.

Later the cops handed her the note he'd left.

"Dear Melissa,

"The revenge wasn't sweet at all. I'm sorry. I know it's too late but I am sorry."

Now what on earth could *that* be about? Since he couldn't get her attention in life, was it one desperate last cry from the grave?

Melissa briefly considered, what if she were to claim that Justin was Sheldon's child. It would have meant a lot to Sheldon, to leave a child on earth. But no, it was a lie, and it would be a torment to Justin to think his father was a suicide. Not that Paul was such a bargain, but he was the real father, and, no matter how indifferent a parent, at least he was alive. There might be some hope for the future.

She could just see Justin as a teenager. An obnoxious know-it-all, like they all were. "At least I provided you with gorgeous genes," she'd yell back at him, after one of his wise-ass criticisms. Melissa smiled at the thought. Justin the teen might have a pimple or two, but he'd be sensational looking. And difficult as he might be, her son would be nobody's fool.

Melissa smiled to herself. Having a kid would be fun. On the other hand, let's face it, a baby is an awesome responsibility. It was probably none too early to start looking for a nanny. Someone thoroughly professional. Firm but loving. One of those British spinsters who didn't mind staying weekends. A fiercely devoted type who would gladly postpone her vacation so that Melissa could continue shooting on location somewhere. Yes, a fanatically dedicated woman. That would show Paul, with his boring yammering about how servants were so loyal to Diana.

Melissa shifted uncomfortably on her makeshift bed. She was getting to be a tub! She should have brought her trainer along with her, it would take ages to find the right kind of exercise person in New York. If she didn't find someone perfect this week, she'd just have her L.A. guy fly in. After all, she had to hit the ground running for that comedy the second the baby was born.

Had she done the right thing, going to New York? There were so many inconveniences. New York was not a place to coddle you. Even in a Rolls you got stuck in gridlock. She sure appreciated California, its cult of comfort, anyway.

But she had to get away from L.A., away from Paul, from Sheldon's ghost.

Besides, New York could be fun. Cold, true, but after all, she was from Akela. Upstate girls knew what *cold* was, and it wasn't this namby-pamby thing where even the worst snow melted in a week.

Akela. Maybe she should go home for Christmas. Nah. It wasn't exactly Norman Rockwell country, and even if it were, she no longer fit into it. Her relatives were like strangers now. No matter how much of her wealth she spread around, they acted as if she were a visitor from Planet X.

The city had always been good luck for her, maybe she'd stay awhile. She didn't have a home in Los Angeles; she'd sold all her property there. Even if she were awarded Sheldon's house, she didn't want to enter it ever again.

She could buy some luxey co-op on Fifth or Park, or even live permanently in a hotel suite, there were plenty of people who did that. Justin could be kind of like Eloise, the little terror of the Plaza. He'd be practically the mascot of whatever hotel they would live in. It would be nice for him to get all that attention from the staff, especially since he wouldn't have a real father to speak of.

But would she be able to tend her career in New York the way she did on the Coast? Well, for heaven's sake, she had certainly reached the point where the projects came to *her*. Melissa John didn't need to sit around on her hind legs begging for parts. And she had earned the right to be choosy, after so many years of giving her all to the industry.

Now that she was in New York, maybe she'd take a shot at Broadway. True, the money was shit, but she could afford to do something just for the learning experience. Shakespeare, maybe. That would show the Tremains! To hell with the moldy reputation of Diana, the Princess of the Great White Way—when the thunder lizards walked the earth! She, Melissa John, uncontested Queen of the Screen, could do the Bard today, as we live and breathe. She'd be great *and* gorgeous.

With that comforting thought, Melissa fell asleep.

The next morning, instead of shopping or starting the search for an exercise trainer, Melissa was driven to Goldsmith's by the hotel's limousine. No sooner did her shoe touch the sidewalk, than a little group of fans gathered around the cloud of her pale fur coat.

Smiling and gracious, she gave everyone who asked an autograph. It took ages, and she was so tired, but she didn't show it. She just pretended charmingly that her pen had run out of ink and dashed into the store. She'd never insult her fans, never. They were precious to her, they were her *family*.

She rapped on Mrs. Marshall's office door, then let herself in.

"Tina," she shouted in glee.

Despite the disturbance, Bettina beamed.

"How's my steadiest customer?" Her ribbing did not obscure the fact that she was still besotted, after all these years, by the young woman's magnetism, enthusiasm, and total joy in life. As with a naughty but utterly charming child, you could recognize all Melissa's faults without holding them against her.

"But what are you doing here? You can't run around zigzagging coast to coast at your stage of pregnancy. Has Paul come with you?"

"Oh, screw him. He's history."

"Melissa, cut that out. You can't just drop Paul Tremain because you've had a little quarrel. Things are different now, honey. You've got to have more patience, more commitment. You've got to work harder at this marriage. You're a family now."

"We're a family, all right. Me and Justin. Paul doesn't want us. And we don't need him."

"Now, dear. What's all this about?"

"Oh, Bettina," wailed Melissa. She hadn't intended to come here and act ridiculous, just to cancel her wedding gown. But her emotions were so screwy these days, and Bettina's shoulders, so capable and soft, were suddenly irresistible.

"I've been so miserable. It's all been such a nightmare. Paul is such a horrid, horrid man; he hates the baby. And Sheldon is dead. I wish I were just back the way I was before, making movies, hanging out at spas, going to Hollywood parties. I wish I'd had an abortion, instead of shooting my mouth off to the press."

"You don't mean that, Melissa."

"Oh yes I do," said Melissa, helping herself to a wad of tissues from Bettina's desk. "But now it's too late. Isn't it?"

"Yes, it is."

"Well," said Melissa, patting her belly and feeling somewhat better for the cry, "at least the two of us are in this together. What a shame, though, about the beautiful wedding dress. It's the prettiest one I ever had, don't you think?"

Bettina couldn't help but smile.

"Oh course I'll pay for it, anyway." Her brows knitted. Melissa hated to throw away money.

"But hey. Why should I junk that gorgeous thing just because of that beast, Paul? Let's go ahead with the next fitting, Tina."

Mrs. Marshall's mouth opened. It wasn't beyond Melissa John to order up a groom to go with her wedding dress.

"Wha . . . what would you do with it, Melissa?"

"Wear it to the Oscars. It would be fine, don't you think?"

Bettina released a sigh of relief. "Yes, it would. It's dramatic and sexy. And it will photograph and film beautifully." In recognition of Melissa's previous marriages, the dress was not white but a pastel aqua. Who would guess?

"Oh, goody," said Melissa, her blues chased away like a summer shower. "Maybe I'll get lucky, even though my performances weren't really that great this year."

She rubbed her belly. "Maybe I'll get lucky," she repeated. "Shucks, I should have called the kid Oscar. But it's too late now."

"Melissa, the baby isn't born yet. You can name him whatever you like."

"No, I know everything there is to be known about this little guy, and believe me, a cute, smart little heartbreaker like this is no 'Oscar.' Justin it is and Justin it will be."

Bettina laughed, sharing Melissa's joy.

This was not lost on Melissa. She looked at the older woman and her face got serious.

"Bettina. Could I ask a favor of you?"

"Sure."

"No, this is really serious. You can think it over if you want to. And I won't be offended if you refuse. It's really a lot of nerve on my part to ask."

"Well, what is it?"

"I've decided to stay in New York, at least to have the baby here. Paul is out, and besides, he was a washout at Lamaze. My mom and I don't relate at all. She still wishes I'd get back together with my first husband. And Erica travels a lot.

"What I'm trying to say is, well, would you be with me when I have the baby? Could you coach me?"

"Oh, Melissa. I don't know what to say. No one's ever flattered me so before. I can't imagine anything that would be more wonderful! But, honey, I've never had a baby. I wouldn't know how to help you out in there. I'm afraid I'd be more of a hindrance than a help."

"Oh no. How much experience does the average dad have, after all. And I'm sure you're more reliable than any man I've ever met. You can come to take the course with me. Then you'll know as much as any of us."

"Well, if you're absolutely sure you want me," said Bettina, her eyes dancing with excitement.

"I do, I do!"

"Then I'd love to."

The phone rang.

"Excuse me," said Bettina, "I've been waiting for a very important call."

She mumbled monosyllables, then hung up without saying good-bye. Her face was ashen.

"What's going on?" Melissa asked.

Tina swallowed. To Melissa's horror, Bettina, that rock of fortitude, began to cry.

"For God's sake, Tina, what's going on?"

"We're trying to keep this out of the press as long as possible, but Goldsmith's is going to close."

"Impossible! What if I should want to get married again?"

Bettina Marshall smiled wryly. "I think there's a couturier or two who wouldn't mind dressing you."

"That's not the point. This place is an institution. Practically a national monument."

"Monuments are sometimes dismantled."

"I don't get it. Why?"

Bettina shrugged. "We're no longer a 'viable economic entity.'"

"*What?* You charge a zillion bucks for a couple of yards of silk. And the place is packed. Don't tell me you're not making money."

"I won't tell you that. Goldsmith's is making a profit. But that, apparently, is not enough in this day and age. The property, the land the building stands on, is worth a fortune. Developers are clamoring to put up office towers, linear shopping malls, pricey apartment complexes here. Any profit we make from the bridal business is minuscule compared to the money that would be paid for the real estate."

"That's been true for years, why the crisis now?"

"Henry's getting on in years, and he's not in the best of health. It's time he retires, while he still has some control of the business.

"Henry's boys are professionals with careers of their own.

When they inherit, they're likely to sell the property to the highest bidder. Chances are a buyer will make Goldsmith's into a tacky franchise operation. That would just kill Henry. He's better off terminating the business himself. That way, at least Goldsmith's honor and memory will be preserved."

"Can't you get someone decent to buy the company?"

"The bridal industry is not what it once was. No one I can think of has this kind of money to spend."

"Look, there must be some way out. You can't just let Goldsmith's *die*. What does Erica say?"

Bettina looked sheepish. "We haven't told her about it."

"Are you crazy? One of the top business brains in the country, practically family, and you haven't told her?"

Bettina spoke quietly. "Here's something you should know about. We decided some months ago to sell the cosmetics business. It was doing well, in fact it had outstripped our ability to oversee its operations. We hired all sorts of people, nice people, but, you know, not Goldsmith's people, really.

"One day Henry and I looked around and we said, 'What have we got to do with this place? We don't even know the people, except for Cindy, who ended up full-time on the other side of the building.' We were strapped for cash for the bridal salon—we're taxed on what the building is supposedly worth, not the reality, the potential—and we knew the cosmetics wing would bring in good money.

"It was a complicated affair, not the sort of thing we would have asked Erica to do for nothing, and she would never accept money from us, so we hired an independent consultant to look around for a buyer.

"What does he come up with? A chemical company! We explained to him about our relationship with Erica. If we're selling to a chemical company, it might as well be Nox. But the consultant asked us to think about it. Nox, he emphasized, has no experience with cosmetics. Neither does this firm, we pointed out. True, he answered, but at least they're edging over with soap, shaving cream, shampoo, while Nox has nothing in personal care.

"We didn't want to go for it. Erica will see to it that Nox gives us a good deal, we told the consultant. It will hurt her with the company, he said. She'll resent it, Nox will resent it. In the end it will destroy our relationship, and no one will benefit.

"Henry and I considered it and we decided the consultant was right. We signed a deal, but what with the lawyers and everything, it'll be summer before it's official. Then Erica will find out, but it will already be a done deal, and I hope she won't be too angry."

"Bettina, you are making a big mistake. You better tell Erica everything, now. If the cosmetics deal is a good one, she'll wish you the best. I know she won't take the competition's win personally. What she *will* take personally is reading about it for the first time in the *Wall Street Journal* some morning."

"Maybe you're right, Melissa. Anyway, the situation with the bridal salon just couldn't get any worse."

The next day Bettina, Melissa, Erica, Cindy, and Henry met in Henry's office.

Erica couldn't get over how Melissa, dressed in a gabardine maternity outfit, looked as slinky and beguiling as a mermaid. "It's disgusting, how glamorous you are."

"Look up *glamour* in the dictionary, sometime. The last entry says: 'often illusory.'"

"Nothing illusory about these, I'm afraid," said Henry Goldsmith, passing a sheaf of financial papers to Erica.

The others pondered the store's fate, while Erica read.

"I'm afraid this isn't good news," said Erica. She was sorry, but business blows were something she had learned to both dish out and swallow without a lot of emotional involvement.

"From what I can see, Henry, if you and Bettina are ready to retire, Goldsmith, Inc., would best liquidate its assets.

"A 'Goldsmith's' franchise operation featuring moderately priced bridal apparel may or may not make financial sense— depending on factors beyond our consideration here. But since such a business offends your sensibilities, it's a moot point anyway.

"My advice to you is, take the money and run."

Bettina looked resignedly at her shoes. But Melissa leaped

up from her seat, as if she weren't carrying a medicine ball under her heart.

"Wait a minute. I don't get it. It's a great business, they make oodles of money, and the clothes are the prettiest anywhere."

"And there's something more," said Cindy, "something special. Everyone has a personal tie to this place, staff, customers—even window shoppers!"

"You don't have to convince me," said Erica. "I've got a silk charmeuse number on order—for about twenty years."

"Okay, so why can't they hand the business over to someone, or sell it, and have it continue as it is?" said Melissa.

"Because the people who make this business, Bettina and Henry, are retiring. And without them, the company will die. All of you know very well that this is an intensely personal business. It works because two people give it their all. Without them, things will collapse quickly. It doesn't matter how well ordered the company is or how well trained the staff. The fact is that without Bettina and Henry, Goldsmith's would either fail or become a completely different entity, probably one that is even more upsetting to you than the franchise concept.

"It's a classic personal service business. Unless it's a family business—with the members sharing the basic concept, it isn't likely to make it. Look, this is hardly a tragedy. The real estate value is enormous. No one lives forever, and no company lives forever, why not take this nest egg, I must say, a Fabergé nest egg, and enjoy it.

"I just want to check on one thing. First of all, I'm thrilled that you got a good price on the cosmetics company, and, off the record, Nox is not acquiring very much right now, particularly in unfamiliar fields."

"Whew," said Bettina.

"Whew for me, too," said Erica. "I'd hate to be in a position where you needed me and I couldn't do anything to help. But anyway, while we never had the emotional attachment to the cosmetics salon that we had for the dresses, it has been crucial for someone." She turned to Cindy. "It's been practically your entire career, and it certainly pulled you into the top ranks of models. If your interests aren't protected with the new owners, a lot of harm can be done to your future. Henry, has she got a decent contract written into the terms of the sale?"

Henry shook his head. "The buyers would love it if she did."

Cindy smiled shyly but her voice was firm. "As soon as my current obligations are over, I'm going to retire from modeling."

"What! Be realistic, Cindy. I don't care how rich Jean-Luc is, a woman needs an occupation today. You've been such a success at modeling, it would be criminal to give it up to get married."

"That's not why I'm doing it. Next September I'm going back to school."

Erica and Melissa, fierce workers both, greeted this announcement with looks of cynical disbelief.

"It's what I've always dreamed of," she said. And there was nothing dreamy about the way she said it.

"You're kidding," said Melissa. "Boy, Cindy, you sure had me fooled. But it's just great, it really takes guts to make a decision like that."

"Well, a lot of things have changed in my life. Ruthie and I have been in therapy, and . . . well, there are other things that can change you, change you from the inside out."

"Like what?" asked Melissa. She was really curious.

"Like, it's hard to explain, but I've been studying with a priest."

"Of course it would be easier for Jean-Luc if you were a Catholic," observed Erica.

"There's a lot more to it than that." Cindy paused. One of the things she'd discovered was her own deep need for privacy. "But, Erica, let's get back to the future of Goldsmith's. So you are certain that nothing can be done?"

Erica said nothing.

"I still can't help feeling that we're betraying the Goldsmith's legacy by cashing out," said Bettina sadly.

"Well, yes, there is something you could do. But it would take more money, work, energy, and initiative than are at our disposal."

Melissa jumped up. "Just a minute. There's plenty of initiative here. Plenty!"

Bettina joined in. "Work and energy, that's Goldsmith's middle name."

"And money you can borrow," said Henry.

"Well, here's one possibility. It's wild, but if you're interested . . ."

They spent the next three hours sequestered.

Henry shook her hand. "You've given us a lot to think about, Erica. Thank you."

"Hear, hear," said Bettina.

"You're a really good person, Erica," said Cindy, looking deeply into her eyes. Erica knew she had in mind not Goldsmith's but her sister. Ruthie had been hospitalized for a while, would need to take it easy for a long time, but Erica had assured her that her job was safe.

"You lost me about an hour ago," said Melissa, "but geez, Erica, you're even more of a genius than I thought."

"And you're a doll for giving your time," added Henry.

"The pleasure, let me assure you, was mine."

It was, too. Having a nice, neat little company to think about, instead of Nox, multiplying eternally like some exploding nova. Talking dollars and cents, instead of thinking about Andy.

Later that afternoon, a reporter from one of the big women's magazines came to interview Melissa at her hotel. He was a sweet young thing, and the interview was a breeze. Mrs. Middle America would tut-tut Melissa's "immorality," but would simultaneously worship her. Melissa John was beautiful, famous, glamorous. Lucky. Every reader hoped some of it would rub off the pages onto her.

As the reporter clumsily packed up his tape recorder and notes, she decided to seduce him.

It turned out that he wasn't quite adequate. Too nervous.

Why am I doing this, thought Melissa. Why am I torturing myself? I hate men, I hate them, and every goddamn one is a disappointment. They fall apart on you, they fall short. They deceive you. They die on you.

But, as an article in the health column of the same magazine said, sex *was* very good for the baby.

Chapter Thirty-one

E RICA PUT HER CLOTHES OUT and surveyed them critically. Dressing up wasn't nearly as awful a chore as it used to be. An olive-green suit, her best color according to the analysis, exactly what she would wear to the office, except that this suit was in discreetly shimmering silk-and-wool. A deep-red satin blouse. Should she wear the cashmere vest? Those big churches could be awfully chilly. No, a vest wouldn't be dressy enough for what the papers were calling the wedding of the decade.

She considered jewelry. She had a pin that matched perfectly and would look wonderful on the jacket lapel. It was a bunch of cherries, each cherry paved in rubies. She had bought if herself years ago, to celebrate a promotion. But it would look pretty anemic, she was certain, compared to the rocks that would be in evidence at the chic-Manhattan/baronial-Belgian nuptials.

Oh well, she couldn't compete with the Eurocrats in terms of cash available for baubles. And she didn't have the time that the American chichi set devoted to style and flair, so there just wasn't any point in competing. It was enough, as the lady from Kensington's had said, to be "dressed for yourself."

She smiled wickedly as she looked at the underwear she had arranged neatly. Her friends from the shower might guess, but anyone else wouldn't dream what would be under that sober olive suit! Ruthie's gift: the plunging bra in brilliant red lace, the panties, no bigger than a G-string, and the licentious red-and-black garter belt to hold up sheer olive stockings that primly matched the sedate suit and high-heeled pumps. She had, after all, more than one affair to attend today.

The phone rang.

Who on earth?

"So!" said a jaunty voice, a happy voice, the primal voice of her life.

"Mama! I was just about to call." A lie, a dismal lie. She had thought about the wedding, she had thought about after, and of course she thought constantly about the buyout, but she hadn't given a single thought to her parents, and here they were, about to go off on vacation for a whole month. "You're all packed up?"

"Oh sure. I even buy a second bathing suit."

"Well, you'll need it. Are you sure you don't want me to take you to the airport?"

"No, no, no, no. You go to the fancy wedding and pay attention. Take notes. We will want nice things. Not like those royal people, but the same idea."

"Mama, we can have anything we want at our wedding. I've told you, when you get back from your trip you can go to the caterers with a blank check."

"Yes, yes, we hurry back. But pay attention to the details, Erica."

"Okay. About the airport, though . . ."

"Absolutely not. We are going with high style you can't match, darling. Rolls-Royce and chauffeur! He has packages to pick up from the airport, anyway."

"Well . . ." George was once again one-upping her as the family foundation. *She* would have arranged for a limousine to take her parents; George was outdoing her with the Rolls.

It wasn't that she resented his caring for her parents. On the contrary, he was the only man she'd ever met who was truly concerned about them, and that was hardly the least of his virtues as a husband-to-be. What bugged her was that Mama and Papa treated him as the son they never had. As if he, just by being male, was more dependable than she.

For example: every year since their retirement she had been urging them to go south for the winter, and every year they pooh-poohed her suggestion. "We've survived cold winters since long before you were born, Erica."

It didn't matter what medical reports she showed them, it didn't matter what luxury she promised them in the sun, they remained stubbornly opposed to leaving the city.

But one little suggestion from George, and off they flew. Nassau, he had suggested casually, and, naturally, of all the tropical islands in the world, it was to Nassau they were going.

Erica gritted her teeth. *She* would have preferred to have them go to Florida. There they would be in easy access and within the familiar and manageable surroundings of the mainland, in case something went wrong. After all, her father was almost eighty, and her mother, too, was old by any standards.

It was funny how their age no longer frightened her. She had spent so much of her girlhood terrified of their imminent death, but, as things turned out, they had survived to old age in relatively good health, and, she hoped, had more healthy years ahead of them. As for her classmates and acquaintances with youthful parents, she had seen them orphaned in early adulthood, and her envy of them had vanished.

Gone, also, was the terrible fear and worse pity that she had felt back when her parents had begun to age significantly. Mama, wrinkled and wizened by sixty, simply refused to decline any further. In both looks and spirit she had dug in, so that now she seemed entirely youthful and energetic compared to her peers.

Erica had no illusions that Papa had become anything but an old man. His vibrant color had drained completely and he had shrunk, dried up and shriveled so that now he was close to his wife in height and weight, and barely reached Erica's shoulders. Whatever anger he had harbored before, whatever cantankerousness, had disappeared, so that his sweetness shone through without lens. Each of his many years showed frankly on his face and in his posture. But the hardness of those years showed little; their dignity, much.

"You've got the number to call, right?"

"Yes, dear. Every day."

"And the number of the cardiologist on the island?"

"Right here, in the waterproof purse, and a copy of the book."

"You have Dramamine? Laxative?"

"Plenty. Kaopectate, too."

"What about the arthritis medicine?"

"Doctor says Papa won't need it."

"Take it along, anyway."

"We will."

"Don't forget. Have a great time, Mama."

"We will."

"And call every day."

"We will."

"And buy what you need. Don't worry about what things cost, buy them if you need them. The islands might be expensive."

"We will."

"I'll try to get some time to come down, if only for a few days."

"No! Don't do that. It's only a month. Besides, you are too busy now. The wedding, and the business . . . No. You *promise* me that you don't come."

"Well, I won't make any promises, either way."

"Erica!"

"Have a fabulous trip. I love you and Papa *so* much."

Erica put the receiver back on its hook slowly. She was surprised to see her face wet with tears. It was a good thing she hadn't put her makeup on yet.

St. Patrick's Cathedral was an astonishment. Its spires of faith reached for the heavens—though not nearly as high as the towers of ambition around it. From far away the great flags could be seen snapping in the morning wind. Today, the flag of Belgium was hoisted between Old Glory and the papal flag.

The guests showed their invitations to the ushers and were seated on either side of the central aisle of the main sanctuary. The outer pews were left open to the public, but they were already filled since early morning with members of the press and with legions of worshippers more dedicated to the celebrities in the center than to any of the saints whose shrines lined the walls.

The great pillars of the church were decked in roses, special roses that the new owner of the former Goldsmith cosmetic company had found after an exhaustive search in experimental nurseries. Each flower had a heart of blush pink, which deepened gradually to true, rich rose, and then, at the edge of each petal, to fuchsia. The roses and their special colors were to be the motifs for next autumn's ad campaign: The Last Rose of Summer.

The great altar, the ends of the pews, and every saint in sight, had also been decked with blankets of roses, which were, mercifully, unscented.

Erica was seated on the bride's side, next to Melissa.

"You look more beautiful with every passing month, Melissa. You have such a *glow*."

"Thanks, Erica." She searched her friend's face carefully. "You're kind of glowing yourself."

Erica quickly turned toward the aisle.

Jean-Luc's mother was now being seated. Genuflecting on entry, she moved with hauteur and ease. The Americans might have taken her for Queen Elizabeth. Indeed, the smiling features and the sapphire-blue, ever-so-slightly-dowdy dress, coat, and hat were much like the British monarch's. To say nothing of the confidence that emanated from knowing one had dozens of titled forebears.

Melissa detected that she had touched on something sensitive. She was curious, yes, and a little hurt by Erica's lack of candor, but she also respected Erica's need for privacy.

"I wonder where Cindy's mother is," she whispered.

"Ruthie says their parents are both ailing. An older sister stays home to care for them."

"God, isn't that touching? You don't hear about that kind of closeness any more."

"No, but it figures. Cindy is such a sweet, old-fashioned kind of girl, you expect her to have a family like that. The mystery is Ruthie!"

Jean-Luc's best man was the Belgian ambassador. The two men looked as comfortable in full-blown formal morning wear—striped trousers, pearl-gray waistcoats, military decorations and all—as other men would in jeans and a flannel shirt.

Jean-Luc radiated his joy. You could see it from *behind* him. Once again Erica felt an overwhelming envy of him, of what she imagined to be his pure, simple, uncomplicated love.

The sounds of the organ swelled the church. The choir belted out its song, Bach's "In Thee Is Joy," to the great vaulted ceilings.

Ruthie, the maid of honor, came down the aisle with the grace of a professional model and the formality of an aristocrat. She looked so healthy! Erica and Melissa gave each other surprised, delighted smiles at the sight.

The transformed sister wore a simple dress of a material that resembled Gobelin tapestry. Rich swirls of rose, fuchsia, blue, and green covered Ruthie from the batteau neckline to her embroidered shoes. Although the dress looked stiff and heavy, Ruthie carried it with noble aplomb. Gone was the punk coiffure. In its place sleek hair was coiled in a chignon at the nape of her neck, from which radiated a rose-red sunburst of stiff horsehair.

Next came half a dozen little girls in pale pink, mincing and tripping down the long aisle, distributing rose petals diligently with every step. With their serious European faces, bottle-blond curls and tulip-shaped organdy skirts, they looked like six Velázquez infantas.

At last it was time for the bride to come. With a mighty rustle that was amplified through the cathedral, the congregation turned.

Escorting the bride was Henry Goldsmith, and no father could have looked more proud.

And the bride. Oh, the bride. The bride was a vision, a dream conceived by a little girl drunk on the tales of Hans Christian Andersen.

The gown was of silk taffeta, scooped at the neck, gently

padded at the shoulders, fitting close against Cindy's slender arms and coming to a point below her waist. The bodice ended in a low basque waist, which added curves to her adolescent figure. A simple A-line skirt of taffeta broke as she walked, so that panels of lace could be seen. Her train, also, was made of this lace, which was the finest in all the world.

Lace emblazoned with her bridegroom's coat-of-arms ornamented the front of each of her silk slippers. Their curved louis heels were decorated with real pearls.

The bridal veil was held by a diamond tiara. The stones had been cut and set centuries before the invention of modern techniques which give diamonds their flash and fire, so the jewels burned with a subtle heat.

The tiara was massive, and the velvet band on which it was mounted had long ago worn thin, so that Cindy's head was heavily weighed down and her scalp was chafed. But she bore herself with the same fortitude that generations of de Gramont brides, each with the same burden, had mustered.

The curtain of time, however, did not obscure the brilliance of her necklace, Jean-Luc's bridal gift. One hundred diamonds, each weighing a carat, and one hundred pearls, each the size of its sister diamond, were set in a lacy net of white gold. The necklace extended up her long throat and formed a bib that filled the décolletage of her dress. Each time Cindy breathed, or stepped, or swallowed, or moved her head, the necklace would ripple on her collarbones and undulate on her bosom as if it were made of liquid. And each time the diamonds would blaze electrically, the pearls would shimmer with soft light.

The bridal bouquet was an overflowing cascade whose source, at Cindy's bent arm, was two feet wide. On a glossy dark frame of myrtle leaves, a bed of pure white flowers rippled down to her hem. Easter lilies, white hyacinths, and giant gardenias protruded from among languid white lilacs and wisteria. As the bride proceeded down the aisle, she cut the cathedral in half with the powerful fragrance of her flowers.

As the necklace was to sight and the bouquet was to scent, so was the face of the bride to the spirit. The thin film of her sheer veil hid nothing of the luminescence, a glow that welled from her very soul.

With the zeal of the convert, Cindy had insisted on fasting before mass, so that, in addition to her natural pallor, there was an ascetic sheen to her complexion. As she looked up to her beloved, her eyes shone, so bright, so pure, that the rumors of her past that had been heard by some of the guests were immediately entombed.

There wasn't a man or woman present who did not believe her a virgin.

At last Cindy reached the altar, although her train extended so far back, that, in their pew, Erica and Melissa could not see the end of it without turning their heads. And they had no intention of turning their heads.

The mass was celebrated by Bishop Cedric Carnoy, second cousin to the bridegroom. His gorgeous raiment completed the spectacular tableau.

As the mass proceeded, Erica sighed wistfully. While religious rites of any sort made her uncomfortable, the scene before her was of such perfection that she yearned to be part of it, ached to duplicate it exactly. Oh, if only George were here, he would understand what she really wanted in a wedding.

Of course that was impossible. He was away, not on his own advice but on hers. It was she who had suggested his trip to Switzerland. Reviewing the major holdings of Nox, with an eye toward pruning the deadwood and spinning off subsidiaries after the buyout, Erica had hit upon a large and hugely profitable pharmaceutical plant outside Zurich. It would hurt to sell it, but *something* had to be sold, and it might as well be a company that wouldn't ax any American workers. Besides, the sale of the subsidiary would bring in a handsome price.

George had agreed immediately. Within hours of the conversation he was packing his bags. She would have felt herself a sentimental fool to have argued with him, to insist that he stay for the wedding.

Still she was disappointed. Why was her fiancé leaving her alone on this supremely romantic occasion? Why did he assume that every business detail was always, always her top priority? Why did he leave her so open to the temptation of her lover?

George, George. Why was she always picking on him?

The mass was drawing to its conclusion. The Catholics among the guests lined up before five priests to receive communion.

At last the wedding drew to a close. In contrast to the solemn processional, the recessional was joyous, almost abandoned. Cindy and Jean-Luc beamed and laughed on the way back from the altar, breaking time with the music, grasping both hands on their way out of the cathedral. For the first time, the great front doors of St. Patrick's were opened wide, and the couple ran down the stairs to the cheers of hundreds of strangers, held off by police cordons.

Erica waited inside for the church to empty. She had to offer polite regrets to Bettina, who was filling in for the mother of the bride. Erica was not going to the reception, enticing as it seemed.

A man with a note pad and tape recorder jumped over a pew and landed right in front of Erica's nose.

Instinctively, she tried to shield Melissa from the paparazzi, only to find that Melissa wasn't there.

The newsman was coming for *her*.

"Chris Chaplin, *Thisweek* magazine. Ms. Eaton, what is your opinion of the latest rash of major corporate takeovers?"

Erica was about to sputter that he had some nerve attacking her in a church, when she changed her mind. Connaught had a clipping service; let him see that she, and not just George Steel, would stand up to any raid at Nox.

"Generally speaking, I believe it's a pernicious trend. There is not now, nor will there ever be, a substitute for the true generation of profit: producing and marketing excellent products efficiently. In the end, that's where the gold is, for management, labor, *and* the stockholders."

Erica's comments seemed to satisfy the reporter, and he bounded away in the same direction from which he had appeared.

She waited to make sure that neither he nor anyone else followed her out of the church.

Chapter Thirty-two

ERICA LOPED DOWN THE STEPS of the cathedral in greater haste than was seemly. She had mumbled her excuses to Bettina—about having to see her parents off at the airport, about not wanting to go to the reception if George couldn't be with her—and they had been jarring to her own ears. She didn't know if that was because the excuses were lies or because too many good reasons always ring false. When she hopped into a cab and the driver asked, "Where to?" she blushed as if he had made an obscene remark.

"Lower East Side," directed Erica. The driver's mood picked up. It was a long ride, and Erica looked generous. "Shopping for bargains, huh?" he asked, making friendly conversation.

"Yes," mumbled Erica, "something cheap."

In fact, she always felt cheap, like a whore or an embezzler, stealing down to Andy's tiny apartment. And she hadn't gotten used to it. Every time he came to New York she *had* to be with him. And the more she saw of Andy, the more she wanted him. The need for him grew geometrically, like an addiction.

How was she going to stop? How would she ever get off the roller coaster of this affair?

She shook her head as the taxi neared his neighborhood. How could he live here, even temporarily, on the edge of Chinatown? No one lived here. Why couldn't he live in a *fashionably* shabby area—Soho or TriBeCa? Of course Andy's sole criterion was a location where the *food* was good.

Andy and his appetites! Always ready to eat, and eat enormously. Yet he remained muscular and compact because of the energy that never let him sit still.

The truth was that the weird neighborhood suited her just fine. No one she knew ever came here. No one in the real world could ever connect her with her lover.

She trudged up the ancient tiled stairway to Andy's place. The apartment was small and he opened the door before her finger had lifted from the bell. His greeting was predictable.

"Hi, Erica. I'm starved."

"I'm reasonably hungry too. But I don't want to go to that little Cantonese place again."

"I thought you loved the food."

"I do. But every time we go there we order something different, and each time the ideograms are translated as 'braised sea-things.' My life's a cyclone already, I'd like to at least be able to pin down my meals. Maybe we can order in a pizza."

"Pizza? Pizza is the solution when the problem is in Idaho. In Chinatown you can have fresh food, even on weekends. There's a place around the corner with fresh, fresh fish."

"Oh, I passed it. You mean the place with those catfish swimming in the window?"

"Not catfish, carp, you urban yahoo. You go choose a fat victim and I'll buy some fresh bok choy . . ."

"Uh, uh. No way will I preside over the fish slaughter."

"I'll steam it just right and . . ."

"No, let's eat out."

"Well. There's a change. Madame usually prefers the safety of her dark little love nest, does she not?"

Erica shrugged.

"Georgie out of town?"

"Yes, as a matter of fact. And can we talk about something else?"

"Sure. Semiotics? Integrated circuits? Race relations? Baseball?"

"I thought we were talking about food."

"Ah yes."

"Let's go eat. No Cantonese and no ichthyocides. And nothing more than five blocks north of here."

"I know just the spot. A huge Art Deco place with a lot of heart. The heart is completely clogged with cholesterol, but never mind. The portions are a lot more generous than Lutèce's."

"How would you know about Lutèce?"

"Bob and Frank were in town last week and they took me to dinner."

"They took you to Lutèce?"

"Indeed they did. The *chausson* had a *sauce choron* with far too much tarragon in it, but I forced myself to finish it anyway."

"Wait a minute. You guys are on a start-up budget. I can understand blowing big money on entertaining a client but you all should have more sense than to party frivolously on your own. I mean, even if a few hundred dollars doesn't make much actual difference, it's bad for your morale."

"Sweetie, don't the industrial heavies go there for important commercial tête-à-têtes?"

"Lutèce is nobody's substitute for a company dining room."

"No, but what better place is there for us heavy rollers to discuss bankruptcy?"

"What the hell are you talking about? There is no way that you can be going Chapter Eleven."

"No, not formally. Not yet. But I better liquidate soon, before innocent people, people who put their cash—read trust—in me get hurt."

"Andy, that's insane! Non-invasive pest control is a great idea. If you'd only change your attitude, you could have a wonderful little company. You *can* make a go of it."

"No, *you* could make a go of it," shouted Andy, throwing his glasses onto his bed.

"I'm not your alter ego. I'm not some kind of male Erica Eaton. I do what I do, and I do it damn well. But I can't fly with the Walendas and I can't play for the NFL and I can't stick it to Steel or Carl Connaught or Darth Vader or whoever runs your show, Ms. Executive Vice President.

"I've been a fool to try, a fool to stop myself in the middle of a perfectly satisfying life to live out *your* dream. I've lost track of who I am, trying to make myself into someone Erica Eaton could love."

Erica had never seen him so angry. She turned away from him, clasping her hands behind her. They were both quiet for a long time.

At last Erica broke the silence. "Let's go eat," she said quietly.

The icy silence continued between them as they walked to the restaurant. The most malicious gossip could have seen them and never suspected that they were lovers.

They lunched at Ratner's.

"Order the potato soup," said Andy, unable to maintain a perfect state of umbrage in the presence of a menu.

"Oh, my mother makes that. It can't be as good as my mother's," she said, desperately trying to keep the conversation rolling.

It didn't work. The soup, and the little mountain of fresh rolls and rye, were the only warm things present.

"What are you going to do?" she ventured in a tiny voice. It was all so hopeless. Always had been. And the soup was better than her mother's.

"I've applied at some major companies. I've got a few interviews lined up."

"With who?" Heaping, sizzling dishes were piling up on the table, like sacrifices to ravenous gods.

"Du Pont, Dow, Ortho."

"None of those are in New York."

"Sorry to inconvenience you."

"Why are you so cruel to me?"

"I guess I'm just fed up with being your zipless fuck."

She covered her face with her napkin, for shame, and for the starting tears.

"Andy, Andy. I always said it was impossible. I always said what's between us is impossible."

"Why can't you at least call it love?"

"I'm afraid to. Even the word, I think, has the power to destroy me."

"God, Erica. Can you really make me out as the heavy?

When have I ever hurt you? What are my sins against you, other than being short, nearsighted, and a few years too young? Why can't you accept me for what I am? Is it that awful, a future with a guy who turns his cartwheels in a lab instead of a boardroom? Why are you so insecure? I mean, it's not as if I plan to live off you. It's not as if I'm going to plunge you into poverty."

Erica shook her head. "How can I say this without sounding like some spoiled brat? I know that I'm doing what I'm doing for good reasons, but out loud I know they'll sound selfish. As far back as I can remember there's been only one constant in my life: As long as I lead from the head, things turn out okay. The second I let the heart have its way, everything starts falling apart. I've told you about my marriage, what a disaster that was."

"Look, Erica, you remember Whit, every detail about him, because you were in love with _him_. That he was a jerk is not the point. That you were young is not the point."

"The fact remains, I'm in control of my life now, and I'm making my decision and it's a good decision, the right decision."

"Selling out isn't control."

"What do you mean, selling out?"

"Selling yourself to that invertebrate, Steel, just for a false sense of security in the corporation. You could be the wife of a guy who loves you, the mother of the children you want, and _still_ be the Empress of Household Chemicals and Industrial Paints. Who would hold it against you?"

"Wife-and-mother, wife-and-mother. Nice work, unfortunately, it isn't equal opportunity employment. Hiring is often based on such criteria as how big one's breasts are, and the most qualified people often find themselves populating the bottom of this nation's poverty line."

"Thank you for that lecture. I apologize on behalf of all my Neanderthal brethren for Adam's sins.

"Speaking only for myself, I intend to be one of the sixty percent of American men who remain married for life. I hope to count myself among the forty percent who never cheat on their wives.

"As you know, I already cook and launder for myself, as well as remove all household wastes. If you don't tell me, I'll never find out that these are tasks best done with a vagina.

"Thanks to the doctoral program at Stanford University, I am able to load a dishwasher all by myself and figure out how much the cleaning lady gets if she charges nine and a half dollars per hour.

"And finally, in the event that we have daughters, I feel confident in assuring you that I will never, ever abuse them sexually. Now, any other points on which I can put your mind to rest?"

Erica shook her head again. "You would be perfect for a million really wonderful and really worthy women. But you'd be all wrong for me, for the kind of life I lead. If we tried to make a go of it you'd get as hurt as I would, probably more. Face it, George is the right guy for me. He may not be as young and flexible as you are, but he has a realistic idea of my future and will do his all—which is a lot—to help me get there. And he's a wonderful person, really, capable of great feeling and caring and decency. The fact that I have cheated on him is to my shame, not his."

"Erica Eaton," Andy shouted, banging the table with a closed fist so that the dishes, which had mysteriously emptied, jumped. "You are so damn insecure it drives me crazy."

A shadow came over the table. They both looked up. How long had the waiter been standing there?

"So, you're having cheesecake," the waiter stated.

"No. We've both had enough," Andy said.

"Believe me, you need my cheesecake. A plain for you, a strawberry for the lady."

"Look," said Erica, her voice rising, "he said we don't. Want. Cheesecake."

"Believe me, miss, forty years I'm a waiter. I see kids like you come in, I hear their problems, I know what the solution is."

"You mean to say," said Erica, who couldn't believe she was actually witnessing this scene, much less part of it, "that the cheesecake here will solve our problems?"

"I'm not just saying it, lady, I guarantee it. What is it now,

March? You come back with this young fella in September. If you're not married, I will personally reimburse the cost of your cheesecakes. Cash on the barrelhead."

Andy held up his index finger. "Two slices of cheesecake, my man. And make it snappy."

"I don't think I can make it back to your apartment, Andy. I can't believe I finished that cheesecake."

"Well, if you can hold out for two blocks, my car is parked in what is supposed to be a community vegetable garden."

"You're out of your mind to keep a car in this part of Manhattan."

"Hey, I'm a westerner. Mah transportation is mah freedom, ma'am."

"A beat-up Mazda is your freedom?"

"It's a Honda. And don't you scoff at freedom."

"Are you really going to drive me three blocks to your apartment? Where will you park then?"

"Let's make it worth our while. Why don't we go someplace else for a change?"

"You don't mean my place. It would be insane . . ."

"What I meant was a date."

"A date?"

"You know. Not a meeting. Not an appointment. Not a liaison. A date."

"Where?"

"How about the Met?"

"The opera?"

"No, the museum."

"Oh."

"I was there last week, but I figure you can't have too much of the Met, right?"

"Sure."

"You *have* been there, haven't you?"

"Don't be such a culture snob, Andy. Of course I've been there. We were there just a month ago or so. Benefit dinner. For the Costume Institute, I think."

"Uh huh. And when was the last time you looked at the pictures, my little philistine?"

"Oh. That would be our class field trip. Seventh grade."

"Oh boy. Well, let's get going, then."

"But, Andy, my heels. And you'll never get parking."

He ignored her protests and drove. Too many excuses again, she thought. Her real fear was that they would be spotted. But then again, who would be at a museum on a crowded weekend? Not George's crowd, they owned their own great art or pretended they did. Senior execs at Nox? She giggled to think that Bert Hickey or Roy Little would voluntarily view art in their free time. They probably couldn't spell it.

Andy found a parking spot right across the street from the museum.

"That's not a spot," said Erica. "You couldn't get in there with a can opener."

He got in. There was a full inch, too, between his car and the Mercedes in front. No such comfort zone, however, with the Cadillac behind.

They crossed over to the museum. How odd I must look, thought Erica, with my cocktail suit and ruby pin. Andy was wearing sweats and ancient running shoes. She towered over him.

But when they entered and became part of the milling scene of thousands, Erica didn't feel so weird.

There was a couple in black leather, he in stovepipe pants, she in a microskirt. They sported matching Mohawk haircuts in lime green. Then there was the woman, very pregnant, lustfully biting the ear of her companion—also pregnant.

So they wandered happily among the plenty. Rembrandt made them hold hands, and Degas made them put their arms around each other's waist, and Fragonard made them nuzzle.

They were beginning to wend their way back when she saw it.

"Oh my God," she breathed, as if they were having sex.

Andy looked in the direction she was staring at. "Erica! I can't believe it. That's my favorite piece in the whole museum. And you love it. Of course you love it!"

He hugged her, as if they had just won a lottery.

"White Irises." She had seen it before. Frame-store reproductions. Photos in books. But they hadn't hinted at this. She could never have guessed how the real thing would affect her.

Fire and ice chased each other up her spine. She could not swallow for the emotion. She was terrified that she might do something horribly embarrassing, laugh hysterically, choke and faint, wet herself.

"If I had a hundred million dollars to spend," said Andy, and Erica tore her eyes away from the painting to look upon her lover, "I'd send grain and seed to Africa. And I'd leave 'White Irises' just exactly where it is."

Erica knew several men who had a hundred million dollars to spend. Not one would choose as Andy did.

Across the street from the museum, a man in an expensive warm-up suit was cursing and swearing like an old-time sailor. His Mercedes had been towed away. The owner of the Cadillac had not yet returned. So much the better—its hood was deeply scarred and dented, one of its doors was hanging by a hinge. Someone with a need for the crack a radio would buy had taken a crowbar to the dash.

The little Honda slipped out of its parking space. Erica considered: Andy would never have to make the choice between the painting and the grain; he would never have that kind of money. Men like him never did. That's why Africa withered and Van Goghs gathered dust in old men's vaults.

On the other hand, he seemed to be blessed with blind luck, that uncanny ability to ride home free. It had to count for something, luck.

When they got back to his place they made love immediately. It was very quiet love, a little somber. It was the first time they'd had sex without jokes, Erica realized.

Love was lazy and leisurely. The heavy meal lingered in her stomach, and the paintings they had seen remained fixed to the back of her eyes. Erica took a more passive role than usual.

Despite Andy's strenuous efforts, Erica did not reach orgasm.

"I'm sorry I lost my temper today," he said.

"That's not it. Look, it's okay for me just as it is. Right now it's good. I mean that. Look, if I wanted to lie to you I would have faked it."

"I know you never lie to me. If there's one thing you have, it's honor."

It was the most beautiful compliment she had ever received. She looked at his blond head, dark at the hairline from sweat, and she loved him intensely, more intensely, even, than when he sent her to the farthest reaches of ecstasy.

He shifted in the bed. His body slipped out of hers. She missed him, the way an amputee misses a limb.

"Your respect is too fine a gift, Andy. I don't deserve it."

"How can you say that?"

"You know how it will all end."

"No, I don't. See, I only play God when it comes to gene transplants. With prophesy, I'm in the same boat as the average Joe."

"You know that with us, there will be no happy ending."

"I don't know any such thing. Like every red-blooded American, I play to win."

Erica shook her head. "Andy, Andy. Why do you persist?"

He sighed. "I don't rightly know. I think it's like a problem in pure mathematics, you work on it because it's *hard*. But you know in your heart that there's a solution. Since the problem was posed by humans, humans must be able to find the solution. You just have to apply yourself to it, till it cracks."

"And then what do you have?"

"Then you have the prize. A little nugget of truth."

"And what would you have if I left George and married you?"

He crushed her hand in his sinewy one. "Like the truth, I would have you forever."

It was a little while until she forced herself to speak again. "If you truly love me, Andy, give up. Let me go. Let me do what I must do."

"And what is that?"

"Protect all those who depend on me. My parents, Nox."

"You're really prepared to do that at the cost of your own happiness?"

"Yes."

"That isn't right. I'll keep going until I convince you that your sacrifice isn't right, and can't possibly work."

"You'll never change my mind about my commitments."

"I'll try."

"For how long?"

"As long as it takes."

"I'm going to set a date for the wedding."

He frowned deeply. "You'll never keep that date."

"You're wrong, Andy. You don't know the strength of my loyalty."

"Sure I do. And I mean to get it for myself."

"No, Andy. Resign yourself to reality. What we have now is all we will ever have. I am going to marry George Steel, and then things won't be the same."

Andy got up from the bed, put on some pants, buckled the belt. He turned to her and spoke in a voice of barely suppressed rage.

"You marry him, and you'll never see me again."

"I see. So your passion ends at convention's door."

"Yeah. I come from *conventional* stock. There are some things we Fairchilds never do. We don't piss in swimming pools. We don't make angel dust in the lab. And we don't fuck married women!"

"But perhaps you would make an exception for me," said Erica, with the cruelty of a woman who knows she is loved too much.

He said nothing, and she burrowed between the sheets. They reeked of semen and sebum and salt. The odors of maleness. The fetid but irresistible perfume of the Crest Motor Lodge, ever whispering of the secret lives of grown-ups.

Andy ripped the sheets from her. She raised herself on her elbows. She gasped at the animal look on his face.

He was going to hit her. He was going to rape her.

He jerked her up by the shoulders, as if she were a rag doll.

Then he seemed to change his mind and a different and even uglier look came on his face. He let her drop back on the pillows.

"There are times, Erica Eaton," the words were like gobs of spit from his mouth, "when I wish I had never seen your face."

Chapter Thirty-three

From Thisweek *Magazine, March 22, 1991*

COMMERCE

Metamorphosis of a Glamorous Tradition

IT WAS FITTING indeed that groundbreaking for Manhattan's new Goldsmith Tower should be marked by the ringing of wedding bells. Last week the builder of the skyscraping mall and president of the venerable Fifth Avenue bridal shop, Henry Goldsmith, 79, was united in matrimony with his long-time chief bridal consultant, Bettina Marshall, 65.

Occupying a close-to-priceless plot of New York real estate, the old-fashioned bridal emporium, with its genteel brand of personal service, was fated to fall, as did its stately neighbors, to the juggernaut of Manhattan mega-development.

But Goldsmith's was not about to hang up the old veil. With some fast and fancy financial footwork, Henry Goldsmith pulled together a real estate consortium to tear down the old building and construct a vertical commercial mall with a distinct identity.

The bridal salon will be at the heart of the building, facing an open atrium, lined in marble and spouting a three-story waterfall, that may be more romantic than many a honeymoon site.

During the year-long construction of its monumental new building, Goldsmith's will continue its sacred—and profitable—service from a homey Seventh Avenue showroom. But a Goldsmith wedding will still be the choice of the upper crust. A typical bash: the posh union, earlier this month, between the scion of the aristocratic de Gramont clan (early European railroads) with Top Model Cindy Prewitt. The nuptial mass saw St. Patrick's Cathedral bursting at the seams, and the luckier guests were whisked away to a reception at a Pennsylvania estate.

The laundry bill alone (ivory lace tablecloths over gold lamé) must have been higher than the cost of many weddings. Quail, grouse, and plover—freshly shot in England—were accompanied by the year's harvest of Carolina Gold rice. There was nothing but champagne to drink, until dessert, when you could also quench your thirst with Château d'Yquem.

The full-service Goldsmith's makes it easy as pie to get wedding cakes like this couple's—including a five-foot white cake with raspberry cream filling, covered with lilacs and moiré ribbons, and its twin, covered with Last Rose of Summer "designer" roses and velvet ribbons, all decorations ingeniously contrived of sugar paste. The $200,000 reputedly spent on cake also bought a chocolate-on-chocolate Art Deco torte, shaped like a Busby Berkeley musical set, and, for the health-conscious, a carrot cake scaled with 24-*karat* gold leaf. Get it?

Goldsmith's bread-and-butter has been more modest affairs, of course. At Mr. and Mrs. Goldsmith's tasteful ceremony, held at the Plaza Hotel, there were fewer than a hundred guests. The bride looked lovely in a short dress of apricot chiffon, beaded with crystals, as did her honor attendant, Old Friend Melissa John, in a flower-print maternity smock.

Besides the bridal salon, the complex will house the first Fifth Avenue branch of the Kensington High Street department store; a midtown outpost of Jack Brighton, the Madison Avenue jewel box; and the new flagship store of the carriage-trade florists, Fabulous Fern. Dozens of other ritzy tenants, most catering to the demands of today's marrying couples, who are spending record sums on ceremony, reception, and "ever after," are expected to follow.

Because the building is near the seriously overcrowded diamond district, it is expected that gem traders will be clamoring for office space, particularly in the upper stories of the building with unobstructed views to the north. Northern light is best for the close inspection of precious stones.

The inventory will be ranging from lace veils to diamond engagement rings, the services will cover the gamut between prime rib for 500 and two weeks for two in Tahiti. On this intensely profitable stretch of Fifth Avenue, the theme song remains, "Here Comes the Bride."[]

Chapter Thirty-four

At 1:07 A.M. ON THE FIRST OF APRIL, Melissa John woke with a sharp, pushing pain in her lower abdomen. She immediately set the Olympic-quality precision quartz stopwatch that had been kept on her nightstand.

The pain slowly subsided. It returned at 1:12 A.M. At this point she went to the bathroom, slipped on an orange jersey tent dress by Isaac Mizrahi and waited nervously for 1:17, at which time the third pain came, as expected.

Now she went into action. Calls started going through automatically. To the obstetrician, to the hospital, to the reporter on the *Post* who had been promised a scoop. And to the Goldsmiths' apartment.

Henry answered the phone.

"Tina's getting dressed right now. She'll meet you at the maternity ward. Good luck, sweetie!"

What a doll the old guy was. He was as enthusiastic about the baby as Bettina was. He had delayed their honeymoon—a cruise around the world—until after the baby came. A quality human being, which was exactly what Tina deserved. And cute for an old geezer.

The nanny, already settled into the adjoining but separate suite that would serve as the nursery, helped her on with a light coat. A bellman was already at the door, bringing down the four suitcases and labor-room "goody bag."

The hotel chauffeur was not at all put out by having to get out in the middle of the night. He considered it an exciting privilege to take Melissa John, the hotel's most famous guest, to the hospital.

Service like this, Melissa assured herself, was why she stayed at a hotel. It had been tempting to take George Steel up on his offer to stay at his New Jersey house (amazingly, Erica didn't even set him up to it!) but that would mean a trip over the bridge to the hospital. And having to do without the terrific staff.

At the emergency room, Melissa was transferred to a wheelchair and whisked up to maternity.

It was a quiet night—in birth as in life, humans tend to cluster—and the nurses gathered curiously at the station.

"Good evening," said a woman in a lab coat bearing the tag "Janet Tierney, R.N." Nurse Tierney did not look like any of the girls in high school who had announced that they would be nurses. She looked like Margaret Thatcher, and was about as likely to wear a fluted cupcake on her head.

The nurse started wheeling Melissa down the hall. Melissa slapped the wheels still.

"You're supposed to take me to the Princess Jamilla Center."

Tierney shrugged and changed directions.

The Princess Jamilla bint Abdul Azziz Birthing Experience Center was a labor room redesigned to meet the demands of contemporary, informed, urban parenting partners. Its bed had flowered sheets instead of white ones and in lieu of the view from the other labor rooms—a deli and the entrance to the hospital's methadone clinic—was a stereoscopic mural featuring an aerial view of Mecca. The eponymous Saudi princess had here been delivered of a male child, the first after five female misses, and her husband, in a burst of Western sentimentality (he had attended USC) had endowed the hospital.

"Let's get those panties off," the nurse directed.

"Certainly not!" said Melissa. "Dr. Richards should be here any minute. *He* can examine me."

"Mrs. John," the nurse sighed patiently. Every woman in a maternity ward is a "Mrs.," including illiterate twelve-year-olds and the woman who harangues "Nightline" viewers about the inevitability of armed revolution.

"The doctor won't get here until you are quite ready to deliver. Now, I'd like to take a look and see how dilated you are," she gave Melissa's abdomen a skeptical look, "if at all."

"What are you talking about?" shouted Melissa, complying anyway. "I timed those contractions and they're really regular. Five minutes apart. I'm about ready to pop."

"Hm," said the nurse, putting a hand on Melissa's obscenely naked belly and an eye on a high-tech watch. "When was this?"

"When I woke up, 1:07."

It was now 1:53. Bettina Marshall Goldsmith burst into the room, catching her breath.

"I'm the birthing coach. Sorry I'm so late . . ."

"No big rush," said Janet Tierney.

"What!" cried Melissa.

"I still haven't felt a contraction. Have you?"

"Why of course I . . ." It occurred to Melissa that she hadn't timed any sensations since the third long pain in the hotel. Had she felt anything since then? She had been too busy to notice.

She looked at her abdomen for an answer. It was still and hard. And ugly. Very ugly. Melissa John with what might be the most envied body in the world, had a foreign object between her luscious breasts and her silky vulva. It wasn't the smooth round cushion of the stretch-mark cream ads. It looked like a gourd snaked with blue veins, and was not round but ovoid, with a sharp little ridge running down the middle. It looked like the back of a stegosaurus. It looked like a pod in the kind of science fiction movie she would never have made, even early in her career.

The condition of labor was now in such doubt that an internal exam had to be done. Melissa's feet went into the stirrups. A sheet was draped over her, making the situation even more humiliating as it spotlighted her vagina and her rump.

Melissa pushed herself down and open. No slave on a block ever had to reveal himself so utterly. The act of sex, for her, was an open door to an invited guest. But getting a pelvic exam was like having your house ravaged by looters. When a doctor examines a man's scrotum, he bends with respect to Its Majesty, the maleness. But a woman must satisfy her examiner's curiosity at any cost to her person. And the satisfaction would be complete only if the woman could turn herself completely inside out.

"False labor," declared the nurse. "It's a good thing we didn't wake up Dr. Richards, isn't it?"

"God damn Richards," Melissa swore, pulling on her clothes. She was as angry as she was shamed, and she was deeply, deeply shamed.

Why was that? What had she done that was so awful? The pains had been real, and regular—exactly according to the book. Why did she feel like some cheap liar? This business of birth, it was beginning to look shockingly unfair.

Bettina had to run to keep up with Melissa, as the pregnant woman dashed fiercely to the exit.

"The books say it happens all the time, false labor. Don't run, Melissa, you'll strain yourself."

But Melissa ran anyway. She had to get out of that damn place. She ran stomach first into an orderly. He recognized her and did a double take.

"April fools!" he said.

Two weeks later Melissa awoke near midnight. The sheet under her was soaking and her underpants were sloshing with fluid. She knew she had not urinated, she knew it was the bag of waters which had broken, but it still felt as if she had done something bad, as if she should apologize.

The jolt of pain that followed sent her smashing into the headboard. Her back arched viciously until the pain began to subside. She was so tired she sank back into the puddle, hoping to sleep.

Another shock of pain jackhammered her. It hurt too much to reach for the stopwatch. She waited for the ebbing, and then, before the precious down-time was gone, called the Goldsmiths.

The nanny and other personnel must have gotten her downstairs. She couldn't be sure. Her concentration was completely hogged by the pain. She had never felt such longing as for the hotel limousine. But the driver could not be summoned. Another guest was using the car. She sat down on one of her suitcases, like a homeless person, and began to cry in bitter disappointment.

"Don't cry, Miss John," the doorman begged. He immediately hailed a cab. The taxi crawled. Each time the pain relaxed enough to let her look up, she saw that the taxi was standing still.

"Listen," she groaned hoarsely, "here's fifty bucks. Just get me to the friggin hospital NOW."

"I'm trying, lady, believe me. But I can't move cross town. Every year it's the same damn thing. These jerks waiting till the last minute to pay their taxes. They all got to get to the main post office, so's they can file by midnight. I bet it's the same people every year."

Bettina was already waiting in the emergency room and helped whisk her up to maternity. Janet Tierney was on duty once again, and despite the heavy action on the ward, a bumper crop of next year's deductions, was in a sympathetic mood. Parliament must have passed all her bills, thought Melissa between gut-wrenching stabs.

A new mother had just been evacuated from the Princess Jamilla Center and the room was being cleaned.

"Please hurry," sobbed Melissa at the door, bending over so sharply she almost fell out of the wheelchair.

"They're laundering the Ralph Lauren sheets, it'll take a little while. Unless you don't mind their making the bed with plain sheets," said the nurse.

"*Arggggggggg* . . ." said Melissa.

Once they were settled in, Ms. Tierney did another internal exam. Any activity, anything that felt like an advance in the birthing, was avidly agreed to by Melissa.

"Well, you're definitely in labor this time," the nurse said cheerily.

"Thanks," grunted Melissa.

"Two centimeters."

Melissa and Bettina groaned in unison. That was *it*? All this and there were still eight more centimeters to go?

"Sometimes it goes quickly," said the nurse.

They finished the thought silently. Usually, it does not.

"We have to let Nature take its course," said the nurse.

Fuck nature to hell, thought Melissa. Nature! No polysorbate ever did her like this.

The nurse left. Bettina took out the goody bag. She massaged, powdered, creamed, iced, wiped, soothed, kneaded.

"Let's do breathing," she urged.

When the contraction came they did huffing and panting to the beat of "The Battle Hymn of the Republic." They fixed tightly on a spot on the wall—the holy Kaaba of Islam, as it was. They concentrated on going in with the pain, going out with the pain, going through with the pain, going over, around, and in figure eights—but always with the pain.

The enlightened tactics of prepared childbirth worked like peashooters against a Sherman tank.

"Oh, God," cried Melissa weakly, "I'll do anything, screw anyone, pay everything, to get *out* of here."

"There, there, darling. You're doing so well! Go the distance, you've got the courage!"

"Courage, shit! I'm a *victim*. What difference does it make if I've got courage or not? Did anybody ever get out of this by being a coward? Then, hey, I'm ready to join 'em."

"Let's see if there's anything on TV," suggested Tina.

A M*A*S*H rerun irritated her.

The news roundup irritated her.

An old Star Trek irritated her.

The Royal Ballet in "Giselle" irritated her.

Bettina finally turned off the set when a Marx Brothers movie had the expected effect.

"Where the hell is my doctor? He gets to double his practice with the publicity from being my obstetrician. So where is he? Where is my *deliverer*?"

"When you're a bit more dilated . . ."

"It's got to be there now. It's *got* to be at least nine centimeters. Where's the nurse? Where's that Tierney bitch?"

They waited and waited. Still no nurse. Melissa's agony was really disturbing Bettina now. She decided to take charge and marched out of the room. Fifteen minutes later she was back.

"I've hired a private nurse."

Within the hour Paulette Temple, R.N., came in. Her lilting Jamaican accent, broad bosom, and sensible shoes seemed promising. She rapidly assessed the case.

"Everything seems to be very well in hand," she sang, "now there's nothing to do but wait." And she sat down and took out her knitting.

Melissa stared longingly at the knitting needles.

They used to use those for abortions . . . She should have had one . . . Women die in those abortions . . . But lots more women die in childbirth . . . You don't hear about them, but lots of women die that way . . . It's kept quiet; it's a schmucky way to die . . . Old-fashioned, ridiculously passé, like getting themselves bled by a barber . . . And their own fault . . . like AIDS . . .

Why doesn't someone do a realistic picture about childbirth . . . A TVM . . . Condom people could advertise . . . They'd make billions . . .

The sun rose. It burned red over Mecca. Dr. Richards came in. He had already delivered one baby that morning, and fielded questions from the fellow from the *Post*, but his face was bright pink and he looked rested.

"Good morning, ladies," he said.

"Fuck your goddamn lazy ass to hell," said Melissa.

The smile didn't leave his face. He heard worse most days. Melissa John herself could probably come up with richer curses, but she'd been through eight hours of labor already. Geez, she was exhausted. Some of them forgot all about it as soon as the baby was born. But a lot of them had long memories these days. Soon as the stitches healed, they sued. And they used to call obstetrics "the happy profession."

He examined her. Her limbs felt like putty.

"Well, everything's fine, everything looks normal."

"When is the baby gonna come out?"

"Well, probably a little while yet."

"How many centimeters am I?"

"Oh, not so many."

"How many?"

"This is no time to worry your head about math!"

"How many centimeters, you son of a whore?"

"Uh, about three." It was a lie. It was really still two.

"Three centimeters? *Three* centimeters. A whole night in hell for one shitty centimeter?" She started to cry, contorting her face in a grimace, letting the snot run down into her mouth.

Melissa had a good idea of what she looked like. This is the truth about beauty: it's nothing but a tool of that wicked stepmother, nature. Oh the flower's very pretty, smells so sweet, attracting the bee. But once it's pollinated, it can stink like a pig and fall to the ground like a turd. Who cares?

"Doctor," said Bettina, in her well-honed, everything-will-be-perfect-darling-or-I'll-kill-the-caterer tone of voice. "Isn't there something that can be done?"

"Well, we can administer Pitocin. It'll speed up the process, but it does intensify the contractions."

Tina Goldsmith did not like the way the doctor switched into the plural pronoun. "We" always does something more sinister than "I." And "intensified contractions" sounded suspiciously like "more pain," something Melissa could not use right now, thank you.

But Melissa didn't wait for discussion. "Do it!" she croaked.

They stuck it in and pretty soon, sure enough, the pain got worse.

"You know that Iranian secret police under the Shah?" said Paulette.

"SAVAK?" said Bettina. Melissa was beyond conversation, or other human intercourse.

"Yeah. Well, I heard that one time they commissioned this study on pregnant women. Seems that women in labor can handle four times as much pain as anyone else. See, people being tortured just faint after a while, but women having babies almost never do. They were trying to figure out how to keep prisoners conscious through higher levels of pain."

"So what did they find out?" asked Bettina, fascinated despite herself.

"Nothing much. The Ayatollah took over and they just went back to regular, nonscientific torture."

Melissa went huff-huff-pant, huff-huff-pant, like a character in a children's story. If Bettina dwelt on it too long, she too hyperventilated.

After a while Melissa discovered that she could also go huff-huff-scream, without any change in effect. Then she discovered huff-scream-scream, and finally, just plain scream. Hey, wait till the Lamaze people find out about this! It didn't actually make the pain any better, but then, it couldn't get any worse.

Melissa John's dramatically trained voice eventually pierced the pretty wallpaper of the Princess Jamilla Center. Dr. Richards was summoned. He thought about his malpractice insurance, and how they'd weasel out of a claim for damages to Melissa's vocal chords.

"I'm calling up an anesthesiologist. He'll discuss additional analgesic alternatives with you, Melissa."

Additional to what, Bettina and Paulette thought simultaneously.

"Get the asshole up here," said Melissa.

He arrived an hour later. It can take a long time to get an anesthesiologist up, apparently.

"I'm Dr. Bailey," said the anesthesiologist.

"Hello, Dr. Bay leaf," she slurred.

"I'd like to discuss some ways we can take the edge off your pain, Mrs. John."

"My pain is *all* edge, Doc."

"Naturally, we want to interfere as little as possible with the course of the birth. Allow you the maximum flexibility in controlling the events of labor."

"Put me out."

"Use the means least likely to affect the baby . . ."

"Give me heroin."

"An epidural would give you considerable relief."

"Whatever. Where do I sign?"

"But there are serious risks, of which you must be apprised before making your decision.

"An epidural, should you choose to go with this modality, would be injected into the base of your spine."

"Why? Couldn't you guys find a more painful place to inject it?"

"Should you, in the course of the injection, flinch, or move even a fraction of a centimeter, you could be paralyzed for life, and/or your child may suffer irreversible brain damage."

"HURRY UP! STICK IT IN, ALREADY."

"Very well. If you are absolutely certain you want to go through with it, I'll go down and get the necessary release forms."

The anesthesiologist had to go so very far down, and then come up again, just as far, that before he got back Melissa went into the final stage of labor.

She was wheeled speedily into the delivery room, as Bettina, Dr. Richards, and three nurses got masked and gowned.

Melissa gave a little shriek. How different it was from the other sounds she had made. This was a cry of joy. Here was a real operating room in a real hospital. It had sparkling white tiles and big reflecting lamps and the throat-tickling odor of antiseptics. This was a place where they cured illness and relieved pain. A hospital, not Gestapo headquarters done up in chintz.

"Don't push yet," said the doctor.

"Don't push yet," said the nurse.

"Hold back, dear," said Bettina, standing at her head.

But Melissa felt like pushing. She felt instantly strong. She felt like giving a great big push, as if she would deliver a grand piano.

"You'll want to view the birth," said a nurse, adjusting an overhead mirror.

"No, I don't," snapped Melissa, "but if I ever have my gallbladder out you can have the video rights."

So the nurse readjusted the mirror, which, unfortunately, gave Tina Goldsmith a perfect view. At first it was interesting, the crown of the black, hairy head pumping against Melissa's purple tissues.

Then it erupted in blood and feces.

"You can pu—" said the doctor, as Melissa heaved.

Twice more. With the third push the baby came out.

Bettina put her hands on Melissa's shoulders, as if to congratulate the new mother. But she was really steadying herself.

"It's a boy, it's a boy," came the calls from around the room.

Melissa was not surprised. Nor was she particularly interested in the infant. She was feeling great! Wide awake, happier, fresher, than she had felt in months.

The afterbirth was being delivered with powerful kneading of Melissa's abdomen.

Tina, who had had nothing but a handful of dried fruit to eat, struggled mightily to keep it down.

Melissa chuckled. Sure it hurt. So did the sutures Dr. Richards was sewing. But so what? She felt great! She passed a hand over her own wobbly, flattened tummy. It had never felt so deliciously empty.

One of the nurses was cleaning the baby and swaddling him. She brought him over to Dr. Richards. She put a thumb into his clenched little fist, opening it. It had a deep crease across the palm.

Richards wiped his gloved hand on a towel and opened the baby's other closed fist. It too had the crease. The eyes of the doctor and the nurse held each other for a moment, then lowered to their masks.

The baby was placed on Melissa's chest.

"Hiya, Justin," she said groggily. "Let's you and me take a nap."

Bettina beamed. Then, when Melissa was taken to a private room, she realized how tired she was, too. With a mental note to make a few calls and check on a wedding that took place the night before, she went home.

Melissa slept the rest of the day and through the night. She woke bright and early the next morning in a room full of flowers. There was a huge teddy bear made of pompoms. The card said "Happiness is being a grandpa again, Love, Henry." A charming country basket of wildflowers had come from Erica; a blue-foil heart of Belgian chocolates was sent by Cindy and Jean-Luc, still honeymooning in Europe, and a crystal vase overflowing with sky-blue lilacs had been delivered from George Steel.

Justin was brought in to her. She was going to get a shot to stop the milk—you couldn't start filming a major picture with leaking breasts—but just once she thought she'd try nursing him. He didn't suck very well, and she didn't have any milk yet, but his warm tongue tickled her nipples. She laughed and, Justin, somehow sensing her laughter, twisted his lips for an instant in what may have been a smile.

Melissa stroked his head. The hair was black and silky, her hair. He was lucky, good hair was a blessing in a world of baldies. There was a deep cleft in his chin. No doubt *now* as to whose son he was.

Dr. Richards came in to check up on her.

"Well, everything seems to be A-okay with you," he said heartily.

"Ahhh," he said, "I see Mother went home to rest."

"She's not my mother, she's a friend."

The doctor's face fell a bit.

"But she's just like a mother to me."

His face picked up some. "Will she be back this morning?"

"Yes. She should be coming in about ten-thirty. She has a business to check up on."

"Good, good. I'll be in the hospital all morning. Have me paged when she comes in."

"Fine. Why? Is there something wrong?"

"Well . . . Your baby has a congenital abnormality of the heart."

Melissa sat bolt upright, right on her stitches. She ignored the pain that shot through her vagina.

"Is it serious?"

"It's not life-threatening. But the neonatologist recommends that surgery be done soon."

Melissa relaxed against her pillows.

Dr. Richards rose. "Well, I'll be back later. Ah, do you have any more questions?"

"Yes. When can I have sex again?"

Bettina came in, bearing regards from the Goldsmith staff, a bottle of champagne, and breakfast from a fancy caterer. She helped Melissa do her hair and makeup, and eased her into a slinky turquoise negligee. Then a photographer from the *Post* took pictures of Melissa with Justin. The reporter read aloud the article that would accompany the photos. It was full of cloying "quotes" from Melissa.

"Isn't that a bit, ah, *gushing*?" said Tina.

"Well," said Melissa, "people don't expect new mothers to say anything smart."

Finally, they were gone, and Justin was settled comfortably in his transparent bassinet.

Dr. Richards came in. He sat down at bedside. He had done this before, of course, but there are things in medicine that do not get easier with experience.

"Melissa, Mrs. Goldsmith," he began, in an unusually soft voice. "I'm sorry that I must inform you that Justin suffers from a marked congenital condition."

"Yeah, the heart condition," said Melissa.

"I'm afraid that's only one symptom. Melissa, your baby has Down's syndrome."

The silence was like the silence after a beheading.

"Are you sure?" said Bettina.

"Yes. Genetic testing shows he has an aberrant chromosome. The condition is also known as trisomy 21."

"What does this mean?" asked Bettina.

"The range of intelligence varies widely, but the average retarded person has an IQ of about fifty. Depending on the resolution of the heart defect, the child can live to adulthood, although life expectancy is generally shortened in Down's syndrome. Many adults with this condition, however, lead happy and productive lives. There continue to be strides in treatment, particularly in education."

"You're crazy!" Melissa burst out. "That kid isn't retarded. *All* babies look like drooling idiots."

"I'm afraid the physical and laboratory evidence is conclusive," the doctor said quietly.

"But I had amniocentesis. It showed the baby was normal."

"Yes, I can't quite understand how that happened. I'll be calling Dr. Armbruster later today. But, I'm afraid that no test is a hundred percent accurate."

"But I would have aborted it, if I knew!"

Richards and Tina said nothing.

"Now what am I going to do? What am I going to *do with it*?" she screamed.

The doctor kept talking very quietly. "Thank heaven you have the means to give him every medical and therapeutic advantage."

"It's your fault," Melissa snarled. "You screwed up the delivery, didn't you?"

Richards bristled. "But you had a perfectly normal delivery, Melissa."

"Well, I won't keep it. I won't! I don't want it. Maybe somebody wants to adopt it."

"Handicapped children are difficult to place."

"Well, let it stay in an institution somewhere. I'll pay. I'll pay whatever they want. Just get it out of here."

"I have patients waiting in the office. We'll speak later."

"Stick it up your ass."

Bettina sat with her in silence.

Melissa pulled at the phone. She dialed long distance.

"Tremain residence." It was the butler.

"Mr. Tremain, please. This is Melissa John."

"One moment, if you please." A long hold.

"I'm afraid Mr. Tremain isn't in, Miss John."

The hell he wasn't. It was nine, California time. Paul was probably shaving about now.

"I'll speak to Mrs. Tremain, then."

Another wait, but not so long.

"Well, good morning, Melissa. How *are* you?"

The voice was excessively modulated. Somebody tell the old hoofer this was real life, not Shakespeare.

"Just splen-did, Diana. Listen, I have some news. I thought I should tell Paul."

"I *am* sorry, Paul isn't in right now."

"Oh yeah? I can hear him breathing on the extension."

The breathing immediately stopped. The dolt had belatedly covered the mouthpiece.

"Is there any way *I* can help you, Melissa dear?" said Diana.

"Sure. You can pass along the message that Justin has been born."

"Well. How very nice for you."

"No. Not very. You see he has Down's syndrome."

"Oh. How very unpleasant."

"Yes. I'm sure that thought will penetrate even Paul's consciousness."

"Now, darling, we all know that this Mongoloid idiot is not his. Why, our three children, who happen to be home just now, for the remarriage, are all normal. In fact they have exceptionally high IQs."

"Really? Then Paul isn't their dad, either?"

"Melissa," Paul had finally broken into the conversation. "I . . . I'm really sorry . . ."

"Paul!" warned Diana.

He ignored her for the moment. "Is there anything I can do? I can send some money . . ."

"PAUL!" Diana was horrified.

"This isn't to say that I admit to paternity, but I'd be happy to contribute something, as a friend."

"I don't want your money," spat Melissa. "We both know I get more for my pictures than you do. And I put my dough into IBM and Nox, not abalone on the half-shell for Greater Los Angeles County." The Tremains had resumed giving their famous parties the minute Melissa had left town.

"Well, what can I do, then? What do you want?"

"I want . . . I want someone to . . ." She didn't finish the sentence. In fact, she had severed the connection. The last thing she wanted was to have Paul and Diana hear her cry.

How she cried. For the first time since Melissa had been an infant herself, she felt completely helpless.

Bettina could bear it for only a few minutes.

"I'm going to ask the nurse to give you something to help you sleep. You need to rest, darling. I'll be back later."

A nurse Melissa hadn't seen before entered. She was the first one Melissa had seen with a cap. But the cap was wilted and gray curls slipped from beneath it. The nurse's face was homely, competent, and kind. *She* looked like Golda Meir.

"Take it away," ordered Melissa, pointing at the bassinet.

"It's our policy to keep baby in the room with mother, except for medical reasons."

"What's the matter, don't want the *geek* in the nursery?"

"Mrs. John! How can you speak that way? This baby is a sweetheart. Why there are half a dozen babies on this floor who haven't stopped crying ten minutes since they were born. And this little doll doesn't make a peep."

"Yeah, it doesn't even have the brains to cry."

"Aw, Mrs. John, all any of us can do is the best we can."

"Us. But not retards."

"I've worked with plenty of retarded babies in my day. And I've seen a lot of them grow up, too. You know something, every Down's kid I know is the family favorite."

"Sure, because they break the parents' hearts. It's pity."

"I don't think so. Even little kids take to them, and kids don't learn to pity till they're, oh, pretty old. About when they learn to hate and lust, I'd say. I think folks just love them, that's all. You don't love someone for their intelligence, after all. People don't love *you* for your IQ, do they?"

Melissa hooted. "Not likely. It's my bod they go for."

The nurse joined in the laughter. "Well look at me. I've got no looks. Never did. But I've got a man who loves me, and four kids, and six grandkids.

"Love makes its own beauty. And its own brains."

"I don't care," said Melissa, gritting her teeth. "As soon as it recovers from heart surgery it goes into an institution as far away as I can find."

"Oh, please, Mrs. John. Don't do that! Even healthy kids wither in institutions. He needs you. He needs family more than anything money can buy!"

"I don't care! I've got to think about myself, my career, my reputation. Who's going to take care of *me*?"

"You seem to do a real fine job of that, Mrs. John. But don't you have anything left over to give this little fellow?"

"No! And get out of here. Get out!"

The second the nurse left, Melissa began to cry. Unaccustomed to grief, she soon fell asleep.

A few hours later she woke to a tiny sound. It was coming

from the bassinet. Not a cry, just a little snuffle, yet it somehow managed to pierce her like an ice pick.

Disturbed, she reached for the bell. She heard the sounds of bustling outside. The nurses would be busy. She dropped the bell.

The snuffling continued. She sighed and got up to see. It was damned unhappy, that was clear. Geez, it hadn't had a diaper change in hours. She thought of calling a nurse now.

Oh hell, she could change a silly little diaper. Come on, even *men* could do that, these days. If there was one thing she couldn't stand it was those Hollywood princesses who became incapable of wiping their own noses the minute they got a speaking role.

There was a stack of disposables on the bottom rack of the bassinet. She took the baby out, laid him on the bed, changed his diaper. There, it was ridiculously easy.

His undershirt was wet, where it had been tucked into the diaper. She scouted around and found a stack of clean ones. This was a little more difficult. There were all these snaps that didn't seem to fit anywhere reasonable. She tried again. And again.

"Hey," she said, not about to lose her temper, "between the two of us we should be able to figure this out."

At last she had him neatly changed.

"There. Clothes make the man, right, kid?"

The baby continued to snuffle sadly.

"Hey, I bet you haven't had any chow in ages. What is this, California? No purifying fasts for you, bro'."

She climbed back into the bed. She pulled the cover up, pulled the baby with it. She settled him in her arm.

The sexy negligee barely covered her nipples, as it was, so it was easy to pull her breast out to nurse the baby.

But the baby had a hard time sucking. His mouth had a hard time holding on. And then, he had an unusually long tongue that kept getting in his way.

Again and again the breast slipped out. Again and again Melissa and the baby tried. Finally, Melissa figured out a workable configuration. The baby sucked.

She felt something flowing out of her breast. It wouldn't be milk, not yet. The childbirth people said there was something else that came out the first few days. Meconium? No, that was baby shit. Speaking of which, she should get that diaper off her bed. Later.

Right now it was very nice, the stuff flowing out of her, into Justin. A lot of women had trouble nursing. But of course, her breasts were perfect. Always had been. This gig was good, as satisfying as work.

"Hey, guy. It's a print."

Justin made a snuffling noise. Someone else might have thought it was identical to the noise he had made minutes before, but Melissa knew for a fact that it was the exact opposite signal; he was happy.

She looked down at the soft, silky black strands of Justin's—her—hair curling on her tit. A lot of males (hundreds? thousands?) had been at that breast.

It was just that Justin was the first one to fall asleep on it.

Chapter Thirty-five

May 14

E RICA TOOK HER SEAT at the head of the corporate table. Behind her was a glowing, blown-up version of a poster that had won advertising prizes: a rainbow of Pigmento paints aflutter with iridescent butterflies. Well, that would be the last great ad for a long time. There would be no room in the budget of the new, reorganized Nox for any but bare-bones advertising.

She hoped she didn't look as weary as she felt. The Chanel suit she wore was zippy. Real Chanel, with gold buttons, chains, fringes, and fake pearls galore. The New Chanel on the New Erica. The kind of too-fashionable outfit she would not have dreamed of wearing a year ago. Dear fashion adviser: What's new and different to wear while purchasing a thirty-billion-dollar company?

When she had entered the room, Ron Davis was cracking bigoted jokes, but now his demeanor changed. He introduced her to some people she hadn't met, referring to her, deferentially, as Mrs. Eaton. The men—and one woman lawyer—looked up expectantly. There was an undertow of exhilaration in the room. And why not? Whichever way today's agenda was resolved, the investment bankers, commercial banks, and legal experts stood to make well over a billion in fees.

Erica cleared her throat. She was a little nervous. George

should be here, presiding over this meeting. But he was out of town again, buttering up the major shareholders, ensuring that they would go along with his plans of an inside buyout of the company.

She, in turn, was left to raise the astronomical sums, to build a giant structure of debt. No woman had ever done this before. And very few men, as a matter of fact. Not even George Steel. It was a tremendous show of confidence in her on George's part. His entire future was staked in her performance now.

But why did she have to do it all alone? *I'm just a little girl,* cried a tiny voice inside. Jeered another: *If you can't stand the heat, go back to Brooklyn.*

Davis saw her hesitate and launched into a joke. Everyone who knew him stiffened: What element of taste would he breach? Which ethnic group would he offend?

But Ron Davis was no fool.

"Seems lahk the Devil went after an investment banker."

They tittered. No joke like a joke on the teller.

"Old Lucifer offers him riches, fame, youth, and good looks in exchange for his soul. The banker thinks it over for a while, and finally, he asks the Devil, 'So what's the hitch?'"

Everyone, including Erica, roared.

Relaxed, the meeting began in earnest. It was all rather simple. Currently, Nox was selling for $95 a share. There were 251 million shares outstanding. Connaught's bid would probably be in the neighborhood of $125 a share. Therefore, Erica, George, and Ron's investment house, Wellington, Parks, would have to do better. They would have to offer some arrangement totaling $140 per share. This came to thirty-five billion dollars, more or less, to be borrowed from the commercial banks.

It is a fact of life that thirty-five billion dollars can be borrowed more easily than thirty-five hundred. That's where the commercial banks came in.

Arranging the loan was Erica's task. George's was to convince the largest shareholders—notably his ex-wife and his former brother-in-law—to agree to the offer, rather than to hold out for a while to see if Connaught would up the ante. A three-and-a-half-billion-dollar profit in the hand, most people *would* agree, beats who-knows-what in the bush.

Once Steel, Ron's bank, and Erica had bought out the company, it would be a privately owned concern, and they could resist any further onslaughts by Carl Connaught. It would be their option to refuse to sell at any price.

The Princess Nox was thus saved from Connaught, the fire-breathing dragon. But the good guys were not going to live happily ever after. The good guys would have a stupendous debt to pay off. To service it, Nox would have to trim itself to the bone. It had always been a well-managed company, hence its handsome profits, and there were few glaring instances of waste. But the cuts would have to be substantial, and muscle would inevitably go with the fat.

Still, the cuts would be made by George and Erica, not Connaught, and that made a world of difference. For one thing, senior management would stay put. The top layer of executives was the first thing to go in a hostile takeover, so Erica knew that whatever resentments were harbored against her by various vice presidents, she had their full support in this venture. Everyone wanted to keep his job.

After the dust settled, jobs and salaries would be the most painful issue. Just before George had left for Coby Knox's farm in bluegrass country, she had begged him to detour to Pellsville, Kansas, where Nox had a large synthetic-fibers plant. The town had recently been hit by a major tornado and while the factory itself had been spared, many of its employees were left homeless.

It would be a long time until insurance and government funds began to come in. Erica had urged George to make short-term loans to the employees so that they could begin rebuilding their homes immediately. George had hesitated. They could hardly afford to *lend* money now, he pointed out.

"Please," she'd begged, "those people are going to have to take big cuts in their paychecks when we take over. This way they're bound to see that we're in this with them, that we help them when we can, and they in turn must do their bit for us when push comes to shove."

George shook his head. "Nox is the only major employer in the town. They'll take the pay cut or they'll go jobless."

That was true. They would all have to make that painful adjustment. Erica thought about the ramifications. She and George, as husband and wife, would make a great deal of money. But they would each have to take at least a symbolic cut in salary, it was only fair. It wouldn't make any difference to their life-style, of course—which was more than the citizens of Pellsville could say, unfortunately—but it still hurt. It had been a long way up from Brooklyn; who wanted to slide down, even a little bit?

And then the executives would take their cuts, but at the same time would keep an eye out for positions elsewhere. Nox would probably end up losing some of its best people.

Erica shrugged and got on with the business at hand. You didn't spend any time looking back, you didn't waste your energy mourning the inevitable. Those were some of the cardinal rules you learned in the Graduate School of Hard Knocks.

And then it was all over. The hordes of bankers, lawyers, accountants, and secretaries went their way, she was left all alone in the conference room, and it was only eleven-thirty in the morning.

So, what sort of act can follow a corporate buyout? Planning a wedding, of course. A quick appointment was arranged with the banquet manager at Windows on the World, the restaurant at the top of the World Trade Center.

Within the hour she was looking down from the 107th floor. It was a surrealistic scene. New York seemed like a very expensive toy railroad set. Lady Liberty on her own little island stood no bigger than a Cracker Jack prize.

Erica had often lunched at the private club here, and she'd attended meetings in several of the dining rooms. This seemed like the perfect place for the wedding. Not for them the sentimental traditions—and definitely not for their guests, most of whom would be business acquaintances. Windows was sharp, sophisticated, and uncompromisingly modern. Spectacular without being ostentatious.

The banquet manager arrived promptly.

"Has anything opened up in June?" asked Erica. "It's our last chance to send out invitations."

"Wow, you really lucked out. The couple that had the Governor's Suite for the last Sunday in June broke up."

"I want a Saturday. Saturdays are for weddings."

"No, ma'am. Not for your people. By June they're week-ending at their summer homes. You've got to marry on a Thursday night or a Sunday."

"Thursday? No way. Everyone's exhausted by the work week. Especially me. But Sunday?"

"Definitely. They'll get back to town early for a wedding."

"Okay. We're on."

"Great. The Governor's is my favorite. It faces west and you'll have the sun setting right at the ceremony. It's breath-taking. Schedule eight o'clock for the ceremony. We'll have cocktails, say, at six-thirty. You'll have to keep the guest list under two hundred, though. But there will be room to dance. Oh, it'll be great!"

"Yes, I like that room too. It's so airy and angular. And those beveled mirrors! I was at a meeting here once. You could hardly keep your mind on the speakers."

"Okay, let's talk colors."

"I like red. Orangy red. Persimmon, I think it's called."

The banquet manager shook her head. Her disapproval was clear without being patronizing.

What the hell, thought Erica. She didn't have the time or desire to be a wedding expert. She was going to entrust details to professionals—this woman and Bettina—the way she did in business. "What would you suggest?"

The banquet manager took out a shopping bag full of swatches. She pulled out a square of pewter-gray satin.

"Gray!" cried Erica in dismay. "That's supposed to be a redhead's worst color."

"*You* will be wearing white. This is what the tables will be wearing." And she placed a small piece of white grosgrain on the square, and a thin curl of crimson ribbon on the white. The effect was smashing.

"Perfect," said Erica. "You were absolutely right."

"You're a pleasure to work with, you know, Ms. Eaton."

In short order they disposed of decor, table settings, food, and wine.

"Now what would you like in music?"

"Gee, I have no idea. Nothing syrupy, that's for sure. And no rock, George hates it. I like good jazz, myself. Would that be appropriate?"

"Anything you like—it's your wedding. You go ahead and look for a group you like, nobody can really do that for you. But may I suggest that for the cocktail party and the ceremony you get a classical guitarist?"

"I'm sure that would be delightful. And oh, before I forget, we must have Hruska's Polka-Magic Accordions for my relatives."

"Oh, are you Polish?"

"No," said Erica, a bit on the defensive about this. "The Bohemians invented the polka, you know."

They were done with their business in record time. Erica thanked the banquet manager. "This wedding must seem very unromantic to you, but you see, it's a second marriage for both of us."

"Oh, I *prefer* doing second marriages. I'd rather exercise my creative skills than my psychiatric ones. See, first-time brides come with their mothers. Or is it the other way around?"

Erica laughed uneasily. Since coming back from vacation her own mother had had scant interest in helping to plan the wedding. There seemed to be a subtle change in their relationship.

Erica descended to the ground floor just as the last of the lunch crowd was swarming in the sprawling lobby. Getting a taxi would be hell at this hour. She really should get used to using the Rolls. There was a subway station just steps away. Well, why not; it would save time.

As she stood on line to buy a token, she heard the most beautiful music, strands of silk in the air. There they were, right beyond the turnstiles: the best jazz band she had ever heard, playing for change.

"Do you gentlemen ever do private gigs?"

"You bet!"

"Believe it, sister!"

"Want us now?"

"Actually, I need a trio for the last Sunday in June, the thirtieth. Right here. That is, up in Windows on the World. Can you do it?"

"Sure."

"You bet."

"Believe it."

"Great. Where can I reach you?"

The three musicians looked forlorn.

"Sometimes we stay at Gates' woman."

"Sometimes she throws us out."

"Anyway, she got no phone."

"Well, where do you live otherwise?"

"The men's shelter in the armory."

"Unless the weather's nice."

"It's getting nice now."

"How will I get in touch with you? How can we decide what you'll be playing?"

"We play anything you want, sister."

"We'll be right here. Right here till the last Sunday in June."

"Come any time."

"Will you play some dance music? Maybe some Fats Waller? Nothing too blue till later."

They went into a version of "Ain't Misbehavin'" that sent waiting passengers dipping on the platform.

The three sang in harmony, "Anything you want, la-a-dy."

"Look, I'm really serious. This is all the cash I have on me now, but show up at six on that Sunday evening and I'll give you triple union. Have we got a deal?"

"Deal!" they sang.

"Terrific. And I'll have some tuxes for you, too."

"Nice. Maybe you can get us a place to shower?"

"I'll arrange it. Okay, thanks a lot. By the way, any of you guys know which subway I take up to the West Side?"

A silver nova of sound burst in the tunnel, as the band broke into "Take the 'A' Train."

She dropped in at the office to check with Ruthie. Then she headed off to Goldsmith's temporary quarters. If her luck held, she'd be able to dispose of all wedding details today. There was so much occupying her mind, it would be a relief not to have to think about the wedding for a month.

"How is Melissa doing these days, Bettina?" They'd had nothing but the briefest phone conversations since Justin's birth, they were both so busy.

"I have never seen her as happy as she is now. She's been loved before—maybe too well loved, if there is such a thing—but this is the first time she has ever been *needed*. It has changed her."

"Good for her! The filming schedule must be hard for her, though."

"She pulled out of the movie she was supposed to start this month. She's still testing out the nanny, and she's looking for a house. She doesn't want to raise Justin in a hotel."

"It must be hard for her, being all alone with the responsibility."

"Oddly enough, she's had a rapprochement with her mother, whom she hadn't seen in years. Her mother is living with them now. Not a traditional family, maybe, but it seems to be working."

"That's what counts, right?"

"Speaking of working, what have you got for me, Erica? More excuses for procrastinating?"

"Nope. You're going to be proud of me! I've just been with the banquet manager at Windows on the World, and we've decided on every last detail. If the dress is finished, we're all set."

"Well, the dress should need only slight adjustments—you keep putting on and taking off weight so radically—and the young woman at Windows is extremely capable, but the walk down the aisle is always longer than you expect. Anyway, let's see what you've got."

As they sat down with the swatches, the door opened and George Steel walked in.

Both women rose. He always had that effect.

"George!" said Erica. "I wasn't expecting you back till Saturday."

"I changed my mind, and came back early."

Then why the hell couldn't you get here for this morning's meeting, instead of letting me sweat it on my own?

"Bettina, how are you?" he said, kissing her on the cheek.

"You ladies don't mind my being here, do you? We modern bridegrooms don't want to be left out of all the important decisions. Henry will back me on this one."

He came over to Erica and squeezed her shoulder in greeting. Erica flinched. She looked up quickly to see if Bettina had seen, but the older woman's gaze was fixed on something across the room.

Had his gesture been loving or possessive?

"Erica was just showing me the wedding colors she chose," said Bettina.

"Superb!" declared George.

Erica was relieved, then instantly angry that she had been relieved. Why couldn't she have confidence in her choice, whether he approved or not?

"We'll be starting off with a cocktail reception at six-thirty. There will be a premium bar, of course, with the waiters taking orders."

"No champagne?" asked George.

"No. This party's too cool for that."

"There will be three cold food tables: an oyster bar, with Belons, crab legs, whatever, shucked right there; a beef tartare station, with all the fixings; and, of course, the caviar display. Malossol Beluga in a carved ice block."

"Not swans, I hope," said George.

"Of course not," said Erica. *Don't patronize me.* "Something geodesic. With onions, chopped egg, sour cream, lemon, toast points. And Absolut vodka in an ice block, too. And frozen shot glasses.

"We're keeping the butlered hors d'oeuvres down to five, all hot. Baby lamb chops, bureks stuffed with Roquefort and spinach, grilled swordfish brochettes, tempura scallops, and negima, which are Japanese beef rolls," explained Erica, with a bit of condescension herself.

"And a classical guitar for music."

"Lovely," said George.

Erica stared at him. "Lovely" wasn't his type of word, but he did look sincere.

"The guitar at the ceremony, too."

"Who will be officiating at the ceremony?" asked Bettina.

"Someone from St. James or Heavenly Rest," said George.

"Since when are you a churchgoer?" asked Erica.

"Never. But one marries Episcopalian," he laughed.

"I don't care what 'one' does," said Erica, her color rising. "I don't want any society ministers here." *The Reverend Quimby was one too many, thank you.* "Why don't we get a judge?"

"Oh, is marriage a crime these days?" said George.

"I think a dignified justice would be just my speed," said Erica.

"Oh, Erica. Everyone will think we're Jews."

Bettina interrupted quickly. "There are a number of Unitarian and other liberal clergymen who do very moving nondenominational ceremonies."

The couple accepted this compromise.

"The dining tables are oval, sort of intimate. There will be gray satin tablecloths, with red edging. Matching napkins, satin on one side, cotton on the other. They change the napkins after the cheese to red with gray edges. The china is pure white—think how pretty it will look. We'll have tall smoked-glass vases with white flowers, peonies, lilies, cymbidium orchids, freesia, and just a touch of red—curly willow painted scarlet. Later, when the sun sets, they'll light white votive candles."

"I love it," said Tina. "Tell about the food."

"First the music. I found the most fabulous jazz trio."

"Do they play any place significant?" asked George.

"Absolutely!" said Erica with relish. "They've played at the World Trade Center longer than anyone else in history."

"Please tell them to avoid anything syrupy," he said.

Although Erica had done that very thing in the exact same words, she still felt annoyed. Why was she so irritable? It was unfair. George was really doing his best.

She went on with the menu. "The first course will be fish. No soup."

"Your guests will be thankful," said Bettina. "Just try and get a tomato-bisque stain out of a starched shirt front, or pastel chiffon."

"We'll have hot poached salmon with two-caviar sauce, and a fish fleuron. Okay, now the main dish."

"Prime rib, of course," said George.

Erica shook her head vehemently. "No one eats red meat in public any more. But your point is well taken. We don't want wimpy food. Grilled veal chops is what I had in mind, with fresh wild mushrooms, princess potatoes with ginger, and a fan of baby vegetables: eggplant, carrot, sugar pea, squash.

"After that, a salad of endive, radicchio, and bib, with balsamic vinegar dressing. For the cheese course . . ."

"Easy does it, Erica. I've never seen Americans make a dent on a classic cheese board," said Tina.

"No big selection. Just individual warm goat cheese terrines. All right, this is my favorite part: the desserts."

"Not those groaning board buffets, please!"

"*Au contraire!* Look at this drawing." Erica pulled a sheet from her briefcase. It showed a diagram, a circle with a pinwheel in it.

"Each plate has the following: a warm apple tart, a Calvados mousse, and a dollop of apple sorbet. On the bottom is a glazed apple star, and in the middle, a pool of apple-vanilla sauce.

"Of course, there will be truffles with the coffee, for people who need their chocolate fix. All in all, much more elegant than wedding cake, don't you think?"

"Yes," said Bettina. "Of course, a lot of my couples are compromising. They have the most darling little cake, just for the cutting ceremony, and then they take it home for themselves."

George smiled. "Sweet. What do you think, Erica?"

Erica agreed to it, although she didn't care one way or another. She went on to the next item.

"Wines. Mostly California, of course."

"Erica, Erica. Would it be so terrible to splurge just this once? Get the French wines, for God's sake."

Erica could not suppress a smile.

"People who really know their wine, people for whom wine is a living adventure, not a dead art, much prefer the best

Californians. Which is not to put down the great French. But if you're going to spend, say, a hundred fifty dollars a bottle for a '76 Chambertin, it's insulting to serve it at a table groaning with all sorts of competing and obfuscating flavors. This is a meal, for heaven's sake, not an *homage.*"

George Steel's piercing blue eyes opened wide. Were he a different man, his mouth would have fallen open.

"Darling, you never cease to surprise me."

Amazing what you could pick up, thought Erica, at the *école* Andy.

"We'll start with a Sonoma-Cutrere, Russian River, then, with the veal, Jordan Cabernet Sauvignon, 1984. With the cheese, I think, an Italian, Barolo Riserva. And, of course, we do want champagne with dessert. The house champagne, Veuve Clicquot Brut, is very nice. If you like, darling, we *can* treat ourselves to Krug Clos de Mesnil, '66. I'll have them put it on ice in our honeymoon suite."

"Well," said Bettina, "you *have* been industrious, Erica. I guess that wraps it up for now. Oh, will you have favors for the lady guests?"

Erica sighed. "Oh, right, that is done today, isn't it?"

"Definitely. Speaking of champagne, how about sets of crystal champagne flutes from Tiffany?" suggested Bettina.

"Yes! But not Tiffany. Ceska. And my father can pick them out."

"That's the best idea you've had all day," praised George. "Your father and mother should be brought in for the wedding preparations as much as possible. This is one of the most joyful experiences of their lives. And after all, at their age, how many more will they have?"

Erica's heart melted. She beamed at George. What a thoughtful, kind man he could be. What a shit she was to have picked on him. Of course he had his faults, major ones. But, as his last remark proved, he had some beautiful qualities, qualities that made him wonderful husband material. She should really spend more of her energy cultivating those qualities, instead of wasting the energy on that sordid affair. Well, that was all over now.

George got up to go. "I have a meeting at dinner, Erica. I'll be over at ten or so."

Over at her place, of course. Erica wondered what would happen to their residences after they were married. Should she sell her apartment? Would she be mistress of the much-painted Englewood mansion? Would they live at his too-expensive-to-touch decorator showcase at the River House? George hadn't discussed any of this with her. Perhaps it would be best to maintain separate residences, the way they did now. Wasteful, but chic.

After George was gone, she said good-bye to Bettina.

"Oh, Erica," said Tina, giving her arm a little squeeze. "Don't worry about . . . things. There is always a lot of tension around weddings. Always."

Back at her own apartment, Erica turned on the computer and reviewed the day's stock market activities. The trading in Nox was very active but with no significant trends. That was understandable, the waters were frothing with rumors of takeovers, buyouts, and even mergers, although who Nox could merge with and still not defy the antitrust laws was anybody's guess.

Not particularly satisfied, but not concerned, either, she hung up the Chanel and got into jeans. She roamed from room to room. Erica realized she hadn't eaten all day and pulled a dinner out of the freezer. When the microwave rang she jumped, then promptly forgot all about it.

She sat down with the telephone on the kitchen table. Her hand paused above it, wavered, and finally picked up the receiver. She was an addict giving in to the compulsion.

He picked it up at the first ring. A very disconcerting habit of Andy's.

"Hi!"

"This is Erica."

"I know."

She giggled nervously. "How have you been? It's been such a long time." *Four days, thirteen hours.*

"Why are you calling, Erica?"

"Well. It's like this. This is hard to say. I . . . The wedding plans have been finalized. June thirtieth. Eight o'clock."

Long pause.

"I see. Well, good luck."

"Good luck to you, too!"

Another pause. An eon.

"Uh, Andy?"

"Yes."

"I was wondering if you were free for dinner tonight?"

"Yes, I'm free. But I don't think it would be a very good idea."

Of course he was right. Things between them had just gotten colder and colder since the day of Cindy's wedding. The meals were full of bile and contention. And sex had gotten meaner and more desperate.

"No. I guess not."

"It's best not to see each other any more."

"Yes." *Not to touch you any more? Not to smell your skin? Not to crush you against my breasts with all my strength? Not to lick the tiny indentation at the bottom of your spine?* "Maybe we should meet, though. Just to say good-bye."

"You already said it."

"You haven't." *Don't say it! Don't let me go! Fight for me, damn it. What kind of man are you, anyway? Don't let me go!*

"Good-bye, Erica."

She sat there listening to the dial tone until the shrill off-the-hook alarm blasted in her ear.

What was going on? What was going on today? First they gave you the right to vote. Then they gave you the right to run a company. Now they were giving you the right to choose your love. So what did that mean? Did it mean you were supposed to do all these things *entirely by yourself?*

The men had gotten so resentful of sharing power, she was convinced, that they were out to get revenge by throwing over all responsibility.

"Get back here, you wimp!" she screamed at the telephone. "Come back here and get me!"

The phone rang.

"Yes!" she breathed.

"I didn't mean to be rude, Erica. You did what you had to do, and I respect that.

"Actually, your decisiveness is good for me. I finally got moving on a lot of odds and ends that I should have tied up long ago.

"Six weeks is about right for packing up in New York. I thought it would be a good idea for me to get out of town by the time you tied the knot. I'll just make it, too. I managed to book a seat on the seven-thirty United out of Newark."

"You're going back to San Jose?"

"Just to sell the house. Du Pont is paying my moving expenses to Delaware."

"Du Pont! That's terrible."

"Oh, no. They're giving me a lab, freedom—even a decent salary. It's everything I wanted."

"But they're our competition!"

"No, they aren't, Erica. Nox has no intention of funding this type of research."

"No, they don't. R&D is going to hell in a handbasket with the company's financial restructuring."

"Sorry to hear that. Well, good-bye again."

"Yes, good-bye. And Andy?"

"Yes?"

"I . . ."

"Yes?"

"I . . . wish you a lot of success."

George was back shortly after nine. It was a lucky thing she had not gone out to dinner. He recounted to her the events of his evening, a petty bout of jockeying for power among Roy Little, Oscar Barnes, and Gerry Crosby.

"I'm sick and tired of this," Erica exploded. "The company is in a desperate situation, and all these bozos can think of is their own small-time politics. Why can't they buckle down and get their jobs done for a change."

"Grow up, Erica," said George, coolly. "Getting Nox-Off to

kill more roaches than Raid, selling Rust-Nox to paint the Eiffel Tower—these aren't going to make or break them.

"Get real. Business is politics."

"Uh-uh." She shook her head savagely. "Don't forget the bottom line. Sales, productivity, innovation. Without them, a company's sunk."

"So what? A company sinks, the managers look out for number one. They'll jump off a loser like fleas off a carcass."

"I can't believe this is you speaking, George. You've spent your entire working life at Nox. I'm not going to accuse you of being sentimental if you express some loyalty."

"Look, Erica. You've got to make up your mind. You want to follow the textbook? Fine. You can teach in business school or work for a nonprofit, like all the other nice girls with MBAs. But if you're going to go all the way—if you're coming with me—you're going to have to take all the blinders off. You're going to have to think with absolute clarity.

"I know this is tough for you to grasp, emotionally. But I want you to think about it."

She did think about it. She thought about it until her mind boiled.

When she came up for air, she found herself in bed, being made love to. She must have been there for a while; her vagina hurt from the frequency of his thrusting.

Erica quickly faked an orgasm. She ground her face in the pillow, thinking of Andy's praise for her sexual integrity. George's breathing soon grew deep and even. She, however, twisted in the sheets as if they were full of chiggers.

After a while she got up, got into the shower, adjusted it to a cruel needle spray, scalding hot. For a long time Erica watched the water sheet down her body as if she were a disinterested observer.

Old Lucifer offered America's Top Woman Executive wealth, fame, power, the love and guidance of a brilliant man, and a wedding in the heavens of Manhattan.

So what was the hitch?

The hitch was, there was the Devil to pay.

Chapter Thirty-six

T HE WEDDING DAY DAWNED CLEAR and stayed clear. It would probably be the last day of the season completely free of haze, the World Trade Center employees told each other. How auspicious, thought Erica, that it was George's kind of weather. The breathtaking scene below her glittered hard and bright as a crystal.

The Tulip Room had been transformed into a bridal dressing chamber. It was cluttered with full-length mirrors, portable dress racks, and carts of cosmetics and hairdressing equipment.

Bettina, a slew of Goldsmith assistants (whom she was now seriously training), and a hairdresser were gathered to beautify the bride. The hairdresser began by putting electric rollers in Erica's hair. The assistants conferred with Bettina about the logistics of the outfit.

"Oh my God," said Erica, jumping up. "I completely forgot about the musicians!" She dashed down in the elevator, crossed over to the hotel that was in another wing of the complex, and ran to the room she had reserved for the band. What if they had forgotten? What if they were drunk or stoned?

Her frantic knocks were answered, fortunately. As she entered the room, the band broke into the theme from "The Twilight Zone." She reached a hand up to the electric rollers.

"Hey, you guys look terrific. The groom should look this good."

The three took the compliment in stride. Some men are born to the tuxedo. They were perfecting the placement of their boutonnieres.

"You gonna feed us tonight, lady? Or do we get us some burgers?"

"Dinner is waiting for you now. There'll be a lot of food left over after the party too. Come to think of it, why don't you take the leftovers up to the men's shelter."

As she walked to the door, and all the way down the hall, she could hear the sound of a muted trumpet doing "Three Times a Lady."

Back in the Tulip Room Erica undressed. Bettina helped her on with a strapless merry widow bra.

"Pull it tighter, Mammy," Erica joked. "Get it down to seventeen inches."

"No laces on this thing, Scarlett," said Tina. "But a twenty-four-inch waistline is nothing to sneeze at. Unless you lost more weight since Friday. I'm about to retire," she grumbled, "and I still can't figure out why you girls starve yourselves for your weddings."

Bettina stood on a chair to drop a wide petticoat over Erica's head.

"How do you get the flounces so stiff?" asked an assistant.

"Trade secret. You soak it in water in which a cup of sugar is dissolved. Then press with a medium iron."

Erica sat in her glamorous underwear as makeup was applied. When that was done, Bettina got up on the chair again, and the assistants gave her a hand with lifting the dress. There was silence. It was an ancient and magical ritual, the dressing of the bride.

Next, the hairdresser draped a cloth over Erica's shoulders and brushed out her hair. It was combed back simply from her forehead, soft and smooth, and caught in a loose chignon with a flowered clip.

Bettina brought over the headpiece, a white velvet Russian diadem. The pointed arch was delicately embroidered with wheat sheaves and fruit. It carried a long veil of silk illusion.

Erica sat stiffly. "I'm terrified that this thing will fall right down on my face in the middle of the ceremony."

"Don't you worry," said Bettina, her mouth full of pins. "When *I* attach a hairpiece it stays on until it is deliberately removed. Sometimes, even then."

The makeup artist searched her trays for just the right shade of lipstick. "Ah, here it is, one of the best colors in the Last Rose of Summer collection."

"No, no! It's purple," Erica cried. Having had her "colors" done at Kensington's, Erica was quite dogmatic about being faithful to them.

"Magenta, honey. 'Magenta Miracle,' to be exact."

"But I'm a redhead. That's the worst possible shade . . ."

Of course Erica submitted. Any expert's fashion sense had to be better than her own.

Erica grabbed the hand mirror. She could not believe what she saw. The lipstick had turned her skin to porcelain, her hair to fire, and her eyes to spring grass. She nodded silently.

"Here come your dear parents," Bettina announced. "Let's go, ladies. We deserve a drink."

"Hi, Mama. Hi, Papa!"

"Is okay for man to come in now?"

"Sure. All I've got left is the shoes." Erica bent to tie them. They were simple silk shoes with small curved heels. For ornament they had two silk bows tied over the arch. They were very, very comfortable.

"Ah, Erica. Remember those white shoes you bought in Bergdorf Goodman?"

Erica paused in her tying. "Of course."

"Your first beautiful things. And now look at you!"

Erica rose, smoothed her dress, fluffed back the veil. She went to consider herself in the three-way mirror.

Good heavens! She was *beautiful.* Really, really beautiful for the first time in her life. Now, now when it didn't matter that much to her anymore, now that she had a successful career, money in the bank, self-confidence, and a man, now, *now* she was beautiful. It would have been ironic if it weren't so perfect. But it *was* perfect; nothing tainted the glorious creature in the mirror.

The dress had been a compromise with Bettina, a compromise between Erica's girlhood dreams and the true realization of who she was. Not billowing charmeuse but substantial, intriguingly flawed shantung. Not sexy but elegantly bare, shawled with a stiff Grace Kelly collar that dipped gracefully between her breasts. Not an eighteenth-century skirt swagged with roses but an authoritative expanse of fabric trimmed with big crisp bows. Not a train to sweep a cathedral but a sheer veil floating a foot behind her.

This was not the princess of fantasy. This was a real, live queen.

"Oh, Erica," her mother sighed. "This is the happiest day of my life."

"Stop it, Mama. You'll make me cry—and I have three different kinds of mascara on. Tell me seriously, does everything look all right?"

"You are the most beautiful girl in the whole world. And you always were, and you always will be," her father said.

"Oh, Papa. I better be. I'll be led down the aisle by the handsomest father in the world, won't I?

"And you, Mama. You must never buy a dress again unless it's that color. Isn't it stunning, Papa?"

Her mother did look lovely in ice blue, a lace tunic over Fortuny pleats.

"Hello-o."

It was Tangee. "I don't want to bug anybody, but I just know I'll forget my bouquet if I don't carry it around all evening."

"Come on in, Tangee. Let's check you out."

Tangee shimmered like an elegant snake. She had lost so much weight there was teasing that her own wedding was imminent. She wore an empire-waisted dress of silver-gray moiré. Her hair was done in a complex corn-row pattern, with hundreds of silver beads that clinked against each other.

The oohs and ahs disconcerted Tangee. Like many women who had struggled to realize their worth through achievement, Tangee couldn't handle a compliment on her looks.

"Shit, these bridesmaid's dresses. You never get any use out of them again."

"Sure you will. It's perfect for Sweden."

"What say?"

"Nobel ceremony. They don't let you have the prize unless you dress formal."

"Give me those flowers, you nut. I need some caviar, it's a good source of protein."

Tangee took her bouquet, three long-stemmed Casablanca lilies, red silk ribbons braided with the stalks.

Erica left her own bouquet on the table. It was similar, but with five lilies and white ribbons. At their center was a single red gerbera.

"Let's go check out the cocktail party, everybody."

"But the custom . . ."

"What is this, a harem? Why shouldn't I enjoy my own wedding? Let's go, Mama."

The party was already in full swing. Everything's perfect, thought Erica, appraising the beautiful view, the stylish guests, the bountiful arrays of food and drink. Ficus trees rustled to the guitar music, their pots wrapped in gray satin and red velvet bows.

"Brian Mulligan!"

"Well, doesn't the bride look extraordinary tonight."

She surveyed him closely, as one did gay friends, nowadays. Had he lost weight? Were there telltale splotches on his skin? But Brian was as handsome as ever, and, if anything, gone portly with prosperity. He'd gotten out of clubs, while the going was good, made a killing in downtown real estate, then gotten out of that at the last minute.

"Tell me, Erica," he whispered discreetly, "is this guy Goldsmith trustworthy?"

"Absolutely. Why do you ask?"

"He's looking to get rid of a prewar treasure on Fifty-seventh . . ."

It was by no means the only business deal hatching in the room.

"Hello, Erica. Congratulations." It was Bert Hickey with a smile as fake as a painted mustache. Erica winced at the white rose in his lapel. George had gone and made Hickey his best man. It was a consolation prize for having lost an office face-off with Roy Little.

She passed by Melissa, a knockout in ultramarine sequins, arguing with an arbitrageur's wife about the right time to start infants on solid foods. A dozen men stood panting around the actress.

"Oh my Lord," shrieked Melissa. "I have never seen anything so gorgeous in my life."

"Why, don't you look in the mirror in the morning?"

"Don't be silly. You look out of this world."

Erica left the goddess to her worshippers.

A gaggle of Valenta kin, already pink with drink, surrounded Erica and toasted her happiness in Czech.

She moved on. There was Cindy, professionally scrutinizing the complexion of Tangee's daughter, Ricky. "The thing now is to use only your first name in modeling. Besides, America White sounds like a group of right-wing fanatics."

The de Gramonts had just come back from three months' honeymoon. They had tans like a caramel glaze, and both seemed to have gained weight. In Cindy's eyes something empty had filled up.

"The south of France was heavenly," said Cindy. "Are you going on a honeymoon, Erica?"

"George is crazy about Nassau, but I think we'll be too busy to get away for a while."

Erica saw Ron Davis approaching. *Uh, oh, here comes the ethnic "humor." And wait till he sees Tangee and K.O.*

"Erica, Erica, Erica. You look better than an annual report with a hundred percent profit increase."

"Why, thank you, Ron."

"Boy oh boy oh boy. That son of a gun Steel don't know how lucky he is."

"Thanks, Ron. You tell him when I'm up for a compensation review."

Davis lifted his glass. "To the big, beautiful, brainy Bohunk. The best of everything."

She was touched. Despite his crudities, on Wall Street and elsewhere, Ron Davis's high opinion was not a small thing.

And it was a bit embarrassing. She cleared her throat. "So, are you having a good time?"

"Hell, yes. You do great party, Erica. Nice crowd. And hey! It's real good to see your dad again.'"

"My father? You know my father?"

"Sure do. Fine old gentleman of the old school."

"You've met him before?" It was too absurd. Of all the unlikely people . . . and Papa would surely have told her.

"Sure have. Last month, in Zurich."

"Oh, no. You're mistaking him for someone else. My father's never been to Switzerland."

"Oh, it's him, all right. I just had no idea, before, that he was your dad."

"Ron, it's impossible!"

"Erica, I'm telling you I met him right there at the Algemeiner Bank. See, the fucking Swiss wouldn't let him use the men's room. I couldn't stand it, them treating an old fella like that. I went right up to that wimpy little Vice Manager, told him I'd piss right there on the marble floor if they didn't give him the key. Whoa, they sure moved fast after that! Afterwards, we met again in a hotel breakfast room. Told me his name was Valenta, but I had no idea that was *your* name."

Erica swallowed dryly. "Thanks for taking care of him."

"Hey, we Americans have to look out for each other, specially in foreign parts."

Erica looked about for her father. She saw him right away, he was staring at her. She took his arm gently and walked with him to the Tulip Room. In the silence between them she could hear her heart thunder.

"Papa, were you in Switzerland last month?" Her voice was very low, a whisper, but she knew he could hear her.

Jaroslav said nothing. His eyes rested on her bridal bouquet, which was lying on the coffee table like a floral tribute on a coffin.

"Were you handling financial transactions for George in Zurich? Did you make stock purchases on the New York Exchange from Nassau?"

He didn't answer these questions either. Erica's father took a handkerchief from his pocket and wiped his sad face.

"Who tell you all this, Erica? Mama, she keep her mouth closed."

"Oh, Papa, Papa. What you've done, insider trading, is illegal. Did you know that?"

He hung his head. Suddenly, he was an old, old man whom the sun couldn't warm.

"Why, Papa? Why did you do it?"

"In the old country, a man gave his daughter a dowry. I had nothing to give you, my daughter. But, George, he showed me how I could help you. Now you will have so much money, and such a big company like no one else has, my Erica. You will be happy with your husband. For that I would do anything, even much worse than this."

Erica embraced him, fighting back her tears. He seemed so small and fragile in her arms.

"Oh, God, Papa."

Then she pulled herself back. "Look, this is an outrage. I can't believe George could be so underhanded. I'm going to . . ."

"No, Erica. Wait till after the wedding. This is not a time to . . ."

"Okay, okay. I'm calming down. Maybe there's an explanation. We'll talk this over together. I'd like to hear what he has to say. Because I just can't believe this, I can't."

"But, Erica, he will be angry! And soon is ceremony . . ."

She charged out into the hallway, looking around until she found one of the Goldsmith's assistants.

"Please get George Steel. Tell him to come to the Tulip Room right away."

"But it's unlucky to have the groom see the bride before the cere—"

"This is no time for superstition. Find him!"

She returned to the room, but Papa wasn't there. A minute later, George came in. He looked imposing in his evening clothes. There was one perfect narcissus in his lapel, but it was ordorless.

"Darling, you look like a goddess."

"George, there is something you need to tell me, and it is absolutely vital that you tell me the whole truth."

"Of course." He looked as if he were swallowing an insult to his honor.

"Why are you using my father to trade illegally offshore?"

"Well, partly because I genuinely like Jaroslav. For once in his life he can walk around with a little change in his pocket that isn't a handout from you. For another, I feel we should maximize our advantage in the coming chaos."

"What are you talking about?"

"As of tomorrow morning, darling, Carl Connaught is the owner of Nox. You can imagine what that will do to the market."

"Oh my God! What's his offer?"

"One hundred and ten."

"*What?* But we offer a package up to one hundred forty."

"We aren't going to offer one forty. We aren't going to offer any counterbid."

"You're just going to let him take over? Just like that? Why?"

George smiled. "For the very best reason. He paid me to."

"Wait a minute, wait a minute. The Knoxes are not going to sell for less when they know they can get more. At most, they'll just sit on the stock till things cool down."

"But they've already agreed to sell. You know Madeline and Coby do whatever I tell them to."

"George, that's your daughters' inheritance. How much could Connaught have paid you to do such a thing?"

George shrugged. "A rather large amount of money. Five hundred million dollars. In assorted strong currencies through Swiss accounts. That's half a billion dollars—and not a red cent to the tax man."

"You'll never get away with it. What's more, Connaught's a rotten bastard. You know it. You know if he's in on Monday, we're out of work by Tuesday. By next Sunday he'll have screwed us seven ways."

"Erica, Erica." He shook his head in pity. "I'm hardly the man to take an overly rosy view of human nature. Naturally, he'll try to screw me. But it'll be too late. By the time the market closes next Friday, I should have, oh, a billion two to a billion seven. Maybe more. You see, that five hundred million is just seed money. First thing tomorrow, the phone rings in two dozen different brokerage houses with some very unusual orders. Lots of people will be playing Nox, but only I know which way the cookie is going to crumble."

"Get off it, George. Why don't you just go into a bank with a sawed-off shotgun? The SEC doesn't jerk around with insider trading anymore. Forget the easy billions; you'll be getting fifty cents an hour painting license plates."

George said nothing.

"Oh, I get it. *You* aren't going to jail. *You* haven't been doing any trading at all. My father will take the rap, right?"

"Of course not. He won't go to prison for something he doesn't even understand. I told you, I really like him and I'll make sure he doesn't get hurt."

"Oh, really?" Erica snarled.

"Darling, we're going to have enough money to buy off the Supreme Court, if necessary."

"Sure. If you can corrupt Jaroslav Valenta, you can corrupt anybody."

He gently squeezed her bare upper arms. "Your idealism is endearing, but Erica, this isn't the eighties any more. The golden years of business have passed and we've got to look after our own interests in new and creative ways."

"But why this, George? Why? We could have had Nox for ourselves, we could have pulled off the buyout. It would take a lot of hard work, a lot of sacrifice. But neither of us has ever been afraid of that."

"The era of the big leveraged buyout is over. We'd end up killing ourselves for nothing, servicing debt for the remainder of our careers.

"Erica, my love. Let's not look at what might have been. There is so much that remains for us, the future is so bright.

"Look, after we've milked this cash cow for all she's got, we can take over our own company. All right, not as big as Nox, not at first. But big. I'll put you in as CEO. What do you think of that? The first woman to be CEO of a Fortune 500 company!"

Erica fell into a chair and the weight of her gown pulled her off the side. She picked herself up slowly, balancing herself against the table. "That's what I've always wanted, and I thought I wanted it at any price. But you know something, I don't.

"Know what? I've got sticker shock. I see the product, I like it, but it costs too damn much. It's like these shoes I saw the other day. They were beautiful, they fit comfortably, they went with a lot of clothes I have. But they cost seven hundred dollars. I've *got* seven hundred dollars. I could have bought ten pairs and felt no fiscal pain. But seven hundred dollars is too much for a pair of shoes. It's too fucking much for any pair of shoes. Do you understand what I'm saying? Do you understand, George?"

George's penetrating eyes, the color of permafrost, softened suddenly.

"You don't have to go back to work at all. This money will give you the freedom to do anything, to do all those things you've always wanted to. Why, you could have a baby, Erica. You could have anything."

"You unspeakable manipulator. You're so good at this. You got my father, didn't you, luring him into the sewer after a whole lifetime lived in decency. And me? You figure you'll hit a few nerves and *something* will respond.

"Well, let me tell you, George, you aren't God. You don't get to tell any woman if and when she can have a child."

When he spoke, George's voice held only the thinnest edge of anger. "So moral, so liberated, so self-righteous. Tell me, dear, where did you pick up these exalted values, your gigolo, perhaps? What else did you pick up from him? I hope not the clap."

Erica reeled from shock. He knew, of course he knew. He had known all along. She wanted to vomit. She wanted to die.

George's voice dropped down to a softer register. "I'm sorry. I don't want a contest of recrimination. Please, let's stop hurting each other. Let's not judge. Let's forgive and forget.

"Please, darling, please, please believe me. I just want us to be happy together. I just want both of us to have the life we want, the life we're in a unique position to *take*.

"Oh, Erica, you've come so far. The world you've made for yourself and your family—and that I hope you will make for me—a world of work and excitement and friendship with fabulous people, you can't blow it all on some lower-middle-class pieties, can you?"

Erica cringed, hunkered back down in the chair. He really did know which of her buttons to push. He did.

George turned to leave. "I'm going to send in a double cognac for you, darling. You need to collect yourself before the ceremony. But I know you, you'll do the right thing. See, I know how smart you are. Knew it from the first."

He put his arm around her. "Did I tell you how beautiful you look tonight? I can't say it often enough. You're the most beautiful, the best. All the other women I know, they're bimbos, doormats, scheming little hustlers. But you're different, Erica. Nobody's got a woman like you. Nobody else is that lucky.

"Okay, now. You stay here and relax. There's an hour till the ceremony, you can take a nap. You won't miss anything. Who needs shucked oysters? The *world* is our oyster."

It was a while after he left before Erica stirred. She looked at the sun slanting through the window. She could break through it with a chair. She could follow it, go all the way down. With her dress and her veil, she'd make a pretty kite, wouldn't she?

Hell no. Suicide was *weak. Women* attempted suicide. She ought to do as the men do. She ought to murder him!

Fantasies of revenge, more of the dumb-cluck thinking of the powerless.

She *wasn't* powerless. But if she really had the power, she would *act on it.*

She flung open the door. Lurched a little on her feet, but finally, got to the caviar station.

"Ladies and gentlemen," she called at the top of her voice. The room buzzed for a second, then quieted completely.

"I have an announcement to make. There's been a terrible mistake. I . . . there isn't going to be a wedding tonight. I'm sorry to have imposed on your time. Look, there's a lot of food, you might as well . . . Please stay for dinner.

"What time is it?"

Cindy de Gramont was the only one to take this as a reasonable question. She looked at her watch, a wide diamond cuff with a face made of half a gigantic fire opal. "It's seven o'clock."

"Seven o'clock. I've got half an hour. Half an hour to run after the man I really love. Please, I've got to get to Newark airport. Does anyone have a driver waiting? No? Do you know, could I get a cab now? Somebody?"

"Yo, Erica!" Melissa John held up a set of keys and a parking validation sticker. "Violet Lamborghini. You can't miss it."

She threw the keys. Erica caught them, already running toward the elevator.

George Steel, ashen, followed after, quick as an eel. But, in the middle of his pursuit, he ran into a wall. The wall wore a custom dinner jacket and a formal shirt with a twenty-three-inch neck. The wall was K.O. Tolliver.

Erica was now on the elevator, heading down. She smashed the keys on the brass fittings.

"Hurry, damn it! What is the matter with you? I could have *walked* down faster!"

The elevator descended 107 floors in well under a minute.

Melissa's car *was* easy to spot. Erica buckled up and faced a dashboard like a cockpit.

What did they expect her to do? She was a New Yorker, she barely remembered when she last drove. In frustration she punched every button. The wipers swished, the lights flashed, the top of the convertible came down.

She roared out to the West Side Highway. On a Sunday evening, traffic was light. The sun was still high over New Jersey. It would be okay. She would make it.

Slip into the Holland Tunnel. Once she was over in Jersey, it would be a piece of cake. They had real highways on the American mainland.

"Hey, what is this?"

"Tunnel's closed, lady."

"What do you mean, closed?"

"Closed. *Cerrado. Capisce?*"

"No. NO, I DO NOT UNDERSTAND. I do not understand why this tunnel is always closed. ALWAYS! Why do they have it? Why does it exist? So they can say they're repairing something? Your tax dollar is going into repairing the Holland Tunnel. ALL THE TIME!"

"You still can't go in there."

Great.

Somewhere, she lost sight of the West Side Highway. It's okay. Weave through lower Manhattan and get up to the Lincoln Tunnel. Can't miss it if you try.

Greenwich Village. Cobblestoned streets. Charming, unless you're planning to get somewhere.

What was this? Who were all these people? What was going on?

A parade.

The annual Gay Pride parade.

"Ooh, that dress. To die for!"

The speaker knew fashion, all right. Gold lamé, curls frothing from a banana clip, exquisite red nails. Only the oversized Adam's apple and the stevedore forearms spoiled the effect.

"Let me ride with you. My dress matches perfectly."

A bruiser in purple Mylar was trying to get into her car.

"Idiot!" she yelled at him. "Don't you know the difference between purple and violet?"

He stopped to be incensed, just long enough for her to swerve around a lesbian marching band.

She spotted two cops, their arms folded on their chests.

"Excuse me. How do I get to the Lincoln Tunnel?"

One of the policemen gave her directions. The other watched the parade through bored, half-mast eyes.

"Thanks a lot, officer," said Erica.

"You're welcome, mister."

Okay. Okay, okay, okay. It was fine now, she was moving. She was shooting through the Lincoln Tunnel. She was going to make it, for sure.

And then what?

She hadn't spoken to Andy in six weeks. He didn't try to contact her in all that time; he was reconciled to living without her.

What if he'd found someone else? A guy like Andy, smart, great-looking, young, could have any of a million women.

What if he wasn't on the plane? Why should he be? He had all kinds of plans, he had a future, he had his freedom. Any of a million things could have changed in his life.

What if he didn't love her anymore?

She saw light. It was the end of the tunnel. She looped into a highway.

She was not going to think now. Just drive.

Allowed to strut its stuff, the Lamborghini was fast. To the press of her foot, it responded like an aroused lover. Her veil streamed behind her, parallel to the car. Hadn't Isadora Duncan died this way? *Stop that.* Just drive.

She heard the siren. She hadn't adjusted the rearview mirror and she did not see what it was. If you don't see it, it isn't there. *Go faster.* Must look pretty, a violet blur. You don't get that a lot in New Jersey.

Then there was no ignoring it. A cop car to her left, one getting in ahead of her, forcing her to slow down or rear-end it.

The trooper came up to her, real slow. He had reflective sunglasses and a paunch. Why did all troopers look alike? Why did they all talk the same way? Had all state troopers been trained in the same state? It was Alabama, wasn't it?

"Any idea how fast you were going, ma'am?"

"No, sir. I don't even know which one of these things is the speedometer."

"Let's see your license and registration."

"I don't have either on me."

"Do you want to explain what's going on, miss? Keep your hands where I can see them."

"Well, to make a long story short, I've got to get to the airport before seven-thirty or the man I love is lost forever. Tell you what, if you let me go for it and I catch him in time, I can produce all the documentation and pay any fines. If I can't, you can just execute me."

The trooper gave her a lo-ong look from behind his sunglasses. No fashion expert, he took in the formal white gown, the headpiece, and the veil.

"What airline?"

"United."

"All right, follow me."

Erica got to the airport with a police escort such as many foreign dictators might envy.

"You go," said the trooper. "I'm going to impound this vehicle. And I'm also going to check on who's taking care of the kid. If there's no one responsible at home, you're dead meat."

"Excuse me?"

He pointed. There was a violet leather infant seat in the passenger bucket of the Lamborghini.

Erica ran. She ran as hard as she could. The pain in her side soon began, and grew. Breathe in, breathe out. Rhythm, the secret was rhythm. Remember, consistency rather than speed. Endurance.

What else? What had they taught her in phys ed class? What was it those enthusiastic joggers were always saying? Why, oh why did she always tune those people out?

Don't stop, don't stop, don't stop.

No pain, no gain.

Run.

A flight from St. Louis was deplaning.

"Look, Mom, look!" said a boy, pointing at the flash of shantung and veiling.

His mother slapped his hand down. "Don't stare. They let the loonies out of the institutions over here. Kill you soon as spit."

Security check. No problem, she had no hand baggage. Through the metal detector, and . . .

The alarm went off.

"You got keys on you, lady?"

"No. I don't have anything on me."

"You'll have to step aside."

"No, I won't. Hey, I know what it is, it's the wires in my bra."

"I'm sorry, I can't . . ."

"Unzip me! I'm taking it off."

"Lady!"

"Hey, it's all right, bro'."

One of the state troopers! *Somebody up there likes me.*

The gate. The gate was right there.

The blond next to it had a uniform, and a voice like metallic tape. "I'm sorry, but all boarding for Flight . . ."

"Get me on it."

"You don't even have a boarding pass. Besides, the . . ."

"GET ME ON THIS MINUTE. There's a cop coming right behind me, he'll explain everything."

"I'm *terribly* sorry, but at the present time all boarding embarkations have been finalized."

"What are you talking about, it's only 7:29. Look!" Erica pointed at the digital clock in the passenger area. The two and the nine rolled up like the eyeballs of a fainting woman.

"Departure time for this flight is 19:30 hours, Daylight Savings Time."

"What is this? The first time in the history of manned flight that a plane left before schedule?"

"We at United are proud of our on-time record. Federal statistics show that . . ."

Erica rushed from one window to the next. The plane was rolling out of the gate.

"No, damn it!"

The sign above the steel door said "Exit."

She rammed through it. Clang, clang, clang, went her heels, down the iron stairs. *Sturdy bridal slippers, an investment in your future.*

Out in the field. The stink and roar of jet exhaust. The cyclonic wind of revving engines.

Erica ran around like a madwoman. The wind whipped her skirts so hard that the clothes transported her for yards, shantung and starched petticoats acting like sails. Erica screamed with all her strength, again and again, until she herself could no longer tell if there was sound coming out of her throat.

The sun sank, a giant persimmon dissolving into jelly. Sickly sweet and biting tart at the same time.

But what was this coming out of the left? A *deus ex machina* in real life! A wheeled ladder, the gangplank. In slow motion it coupled with the airplane. Two workers helped Erica onto the first stairs. For their troubles they were lashed by her veil.

One hand steadying herself on the rail, one hand seizing her skirts, she crawled up to the forward entrance of the plane.

A matched pair of flight attendants helped her in.

Erica scraped her eyes through the cabin.

Andy was not there.

Despite everything that had happened today, she hadn't cried once. But now she felt the tears begging irresistibly.

But wait. Of course he isn't here! There are still some people in the world who don't travel first class.

Faster than she'd run all day, Erica ran through the cabin.

And there he was. You couldn't miss him. Wearing a polo shirt the color of her own eyes. His fingers on the headrest before him, practically crushing it.

The passengers whistled, stomped, cheered.

Erica approached him.

"Women," said Andy to the man sitting next to him. "Always late."

"Don't you believe him," said the man, vacating his seat. "He near to broke the window when he saw you coming."

She sat down in his seat, using the third one for the excess of her skirts.

The tears were coming down seriously now, stinging her cheeks where they fell on windburn.

"Do you think, Andy, that you could give our relationship another chance?"

"To hell with relationships. I thought we were in love."

"Yes, but it's been six weeks . . ."

"Six weeks? You figure love can die in a month and a half? I've got broccoli in the refrigerator that's lasted longer."

"Oh, Andy. You're the most wonderful man on earth."

"There's a cue out of Shakespeare."

They kissed.

"Ladies and gentlemen, this is your captain speaking. Let's see. Dearly beloved, by the powers entrusted in me, I do *not* have the right to perform marriages. However, I *do* have the right to order champagne for all."

A mighty cheer went up. The plane was in a party mood.

"Well," said Andy, "since you're already dressed, maybe we should just rent a car in San Francisco and drive to Nevada."

"Don't you want a wedding with the family? We could go to Idaho. I've always loved Idaho."

"It certainly has plenty of parking."

"We'll think it out, Andy. There's time. Right now we've got to get back to New York."

"What for?"

"I've got to get a lawyer for my father, the best lawyer in town."

"Your father?"

So she told him everything that had happened right down to the desserts.

"Oh God, Erica. I wish there was something I could do to help you."

"Your love is all I want."

"But your work, it means so much to you. What's going to happen?"

Erica sank back in her seat. Then she straightened, and spoke with control.

"I'm going ahead with the buyout."

"By yourself?"

"No, of course not. With Wellington, Parks. Maybe with the Knox family. Possibly with the support of senior management. It's hard to tell how things will fall out after all of George's dead bodies surface.

"I don't know if this country is ready for a woman as the head of one of its largest industrial concerns. But maybe the time *has* come.

"If not, well, I'm still one of the best managers in this country. I know it, and others do too.

"So you see, Andy, you won't be getting a dependent wife around your neck."

"Hell, no. But what about me?"

"Well Du Pont's out, of course. Too bad it's not in New York."

"So the girl comes with New York attached?"

"Let's put it this way, New York comes with girls like me attached."

"I've got to walk away from the Du Pont deal, huh? No wonder men can't get decent jobs. They offer a position in good faith and what do we do, we up and quit to get married."

"Hey, I'm not asking you to put your career on hold for me. There are tons of opportunities for you in New York."

"Yes. For example, at Nox."

"Oh, no. I couldn't do that."

"Why not? You said yourself you were convinced the lab was viable for the company."

"I am, but don't you see, if I'm number one at Nox and I assign the lab to you, everyone will say I did it because you're my fiancé or husband or whatever."

"That's what they said when Steel promoted *you*, isn't it?"

"But that was different."

"Why, because he's a man and it's understood men can jolly their girlfriends with business favors?"

"No! I was fully qualified, and more, for every position he put me in."

"*And I'm not?*"

"Okay. Your point is well taken."

"Sorry to put you on the spot, Erica. But there are a lot of things to consider when you're blazing trail. And my feelings are by no means the hardest of them."

"I know, and a lot of things, maybe even your feelings, will get hurt. But, Andy, you understand, I've got to forge ahead anyway."

"I do, I really do. Erica, do you have regrets about us?"

"Regrets! Whatever for? Doesn't making a total fool of myself in public indicate my true choice in husbands?"

"I know we're good together, the way a man and a woman should be. But I can't do for you what Steel could. Not in the business world. And that's really important to you. Maybe the most important."

"Maybe making it in business is the most important thing to me. Maybe. But I don't need Steel, or anyone like him. saviors. No mentors. No gray eminences. I've got to stand fall on my own—or what's the point?

"You know, Andy, I think I can make it. I *know* I can. But first things first. I've got to take care of my father before the shame of what he did kills him. Is there a phone on this plane? I'm going to wake up some lawyers."

"I understand. I'm looking forward to meeting your father. I'd like to tell him that what he did was exactly what my dad would have done for me.

"Also, he's the guy who made you 'arrogant,' isn't he? 'Arrogant.' It's what I like best about you. I'll tell him over breakfast."

"How can we do that? There won't be a flight out of San Francisco till morning."

"This is a stopover flight. We should be in St. Louis in about an hour. Unless the captain's poured himself some of that champagne."

"An hour? That's great. Gosh, St. Louis?"

"I can't think of anywhere I'd rather be. With the possible exception of the men's shelter in the armory."

"It's gonna be some job, feeding my husband. Thank God, I can always escape to the office.

"What do you think? Is there a place near the St. Louis airport where I could buy some clothes on a Sunday night?"

"Probably not. But I've got some sweats in my luggage that you can borrow. Although I do like you in this outfit. Talk about dress for success!"

"Oh, please! Help me get this headpiece off, will you? I think Bettina soldered it into my skull."

"There you go. You must be completely zonked, honey. Put your head on my lap and close your eyes."

"Oh, I couldn't sleep now," said Erica, snuggling her face into the warm place between Andy's chest and his embracing arm.

"Rest, then. And tell me more about that Calvados mousse."